## "You think I'm completely crazy, don't you?"

"No, actually, I think you're in perfect mental health, and I'd be willing to testify to that at your trial," Marcus replied.

The sheriff laughed. "I wish we would have met under different circumstances, but you can't change the hand that you've been dealt."

"How about I develop a case of amnesia, let you get on with your business, and go along my way like nothing happened?" Marcus said, having no intention of doing so and no expectations that the sheriff would agree.

"You know in your heart that what I'm doing is right. Take this animal we have here." The sheriff gestured toward Ackerman. "I can't let another person suffer at his hands. These aren't men we're dealing with here. They're monsters, and they don't deserve to live."

"And who are you to decide who has a right to live and who should die? You're playing God here, Sheriff, and I don't think the good Lord looks too kindly upon impersonators."

Their gazes locked, and the sheriff said, "I'm sorry, son." With those words, the gun in the sheriff's hand began to rise....

## *ETHAN CROSS*

When a fireman or a policeman would visit his school, most of his classmates' heads would swim with aspirations of growing up and catching bad guys or saving someone from a blazing inferno. When these moments came for Ethan Cross, however, his dreams weren't to someday be a cop or put out fires; he just wanted to write about it.

In addition to writing and working in the publishing industry, Ethan has also served as the chief technology officer for a national franchise, recorded albums and opened for national recording artists as lead singer and guitar player in a musical group, and been an active and highly involved member of the International Thriller Writers organization.

Ethan Cross is the pen name of an author who lives and writes in Illinois with his wife, three kids and two Shih Tzus.

# THE SHEPHERD

# ETHAN CROSS

**WORLDWIDE**®

TORONTO • NEW YORK • LONDON
AMSTERDAM • PARIS • SYDNEY • HAMBURG
STOCKHOLM • ATHENS • TOKYO • MILAN
MADRID • WARSAW • BUDAPEST • AUCKLAND

For my beautiful wife, Gina…

Recycling programs
for this product may
not exist in your area.

ISBN-13: 978-0-373-18965-6

THE SHEPHERD

Copyright © 2011 by Aaron Brown

A Worldwide Library Suspense/July 2014

First published by The Story Plant

This edition published by arrangement with Harlequin Books S.A.

® and TM are trademarks of the publisher. Trademarks indicated with ® are registered in the United States Patent and Trademark Office, the Canadian Intellectual Property Office and in other countries.

www.Harlequin.com

**Printed in U.S.A.**

# THE
# SHEPHERD

I want to start off by saying that an enormous number of people have helped and supported me with this project and in my life in general—way too many to list here. The most notable of these is my wonderful wife, Gina, who put up with all my eccentricities and supported me as I reached for this dream. I also want to thank the rest of my family for all of their support and encouragement, especially those who served as my early readers and copy editors. (Yes, Teresa, I'm listing you by name, as I promised).

But there is also a large group within the publishing industry without whom this project would not have been possible. If I have any success with this novel, it will be due largely to the efforts of my editor, publisher and friend, Lou Aronica, who helped take my work to the next level. Thank you, Lou, for your patience and wisdom. Overwhelming gratitude is also due to my agents, Danny Baror and Heather Baror—for taking a chance on an unknown writer—and to my friend and business partner, Stan Tremblay—for helping to bring the world of *The Shepherd* to the masses. Big thanks to my copy editor, Steven Manchester, who helped to give that extra layer of polish to the book. I also want to thank my fellow authors who have helped and encouraged me on my writer's journey: Jeremy Robinson, Andrew Gross, AJ Hartley, James Scott Bell, Karen Dionne, James Rollins, Travis Thrasher, Andrew Peterson, Steven James, DB Henson, Jeremy Burns, Brian Wheeler, and many more. Also, many thanks to the International Thriller Writers. Without the ITW and their collective instruction and wisdom, I would not be anywhere close to accomplishing my dream right now.

# Part One:

*The Flock*

# ONE

JIM MORGAN WATCHED as reflections of the patrol car's flashing lights danced across the front window of the remote gas station. He strained to see beyond the strange and ominous shadows into the building's interior. Although the call from dispatch warranted only a routine robbery report, for some reason, an irrational yet overwhelming feeling of dread crept over the edges of his consciousness. He couldn't explain the sensation—cop instincts, intuition, or premonition—but he knew something wasn't right. He took a deep breath and released a prolonged and deliberate exhalation. As he exited the vehicle, he forced away the feeling that something dark awaited him.

He noted the absence of the moon. The darkness seemed solid and eternal beyond the pool of radiance cast by the lights of the cruiser and gas station. He felt as if he sat on the edge of the world, and nothing else existed in the universe. Turning his gaze back toward the station, the feeling took root again.

He couldn't pinpoint the source of his fear, which frightened him even more. For Jim, the worst kind of fear had always been one without a name. Out of trepidation, he considered calling to check on his wife, Emily, and their daughter. He consulted his watch and decided against it. He didn't want to wake them.

His partner, Tom Delaine, said, "You okay? You look like somebody pissed in your cornflakes."

"I'm fine. Let's get this over with. It's past my bedtime, and I just want to go home."

The look of concern was still evident on Tom's face, but he nodded and walked toward the front door of the station. Neither man had drawn his weapon, since they knew from dispatch that the assailant had already fled the premises. Nevertheless, a proper report needed to be filed, and the station's attendant had seemed adamant that someone should come right away.

As they entered the building, Jim caught the hint of a strangely familiar smell, but he was unable to identify it. He pushed the thought away and focused his mind on the task at hand.

Once inside, he scanned the room. The station's counter rested along the back wall, parallel to the door. A man with dark hair and haunting gray eyes sat behind it. The attendant's midnight black T-shirt stretched tight across his chest, firm muscles bunched underneath. The man didn't say a word; he simply stared without expression at the two policemen.

As their gazes locked, Jim instinctively moved his hand closer to the pistol holstered at his side.

"Nice night, huh?" the attendant said. "The darkness tonight is…oppressive. It has weight."

He couldn't comprehend the logic that associated an oppressive darkness with a nice night, and he distrusted the man possessing a mind in which the two were linked. The significance of such a statement was apparently lost on his partner. Tom just raised his eyebrows and replied with a drawn-out, "Okay." After a pause, he said, "Were you the one who reported the robbery?"

"No," the man said. "I reported a murder."

Upon hearing the statement, Jim's breath caught in his

throat. He moved his hand over his gun but didn't draw the 9mm Glock semiautomatic from its holster.

"Who was murdered?" Tom said.

The attendant didn't answer, and although Jim couldn't be sure, he thought a suppressed grin had passed over the man's face. Instead of a reply, the attendant leaned forward and shifted his gaze down one of the station's aisles.

Jim followed the man's stare to where a gruesome image caught him unprepared, bombarding his senses.

The dead man at the end of the aisle had been stripped naked. Blood was everywhere. Numerous lacerations ran along the length of his body, but the frenzied slashes were most prevalent around the heart, lungs, and sexual organs. His eyes had been gouged out.

Without hesitation, both troopers drew their weapons and pointed them at the strange man behind the counter. Tom took a step forward and said, "Get your hands where I can see them!"

The suspect made no attempt to bring his hands up from beneath the counter. In fact, the formation of a smile constituted his only movement as a malicious grin spread across his face. The smile held no joy, nor love, nor warmth. It was cold, making Jim feel like a fly trapped in a spider's web.

Tom took another step forward and repeated himself with no better results. He had now advanced to no more than three feet from the counter. Jim, on the other hand, had taken a step back and wanted to scream at Tom that he had moved too close. The thought dissipated when the man behind the counter spoke in a calm, yet commanding voice. "Do you like it? It's my version of a killing by Andrei Chikatilo, Russia's Rostov Ripper. You're probably not familiar with him. While you were learning about Lincoln and Washington, I was learning about Jack the Ripper,

Albert Fish, Ed Gein, the Zodiac. Those were just a few of my founding fathers." The killer's eyes darted between them. "You boys don't recognize me, do you?"

Tom screamed at the man with even greater ferocity. "I don't care who you are…just put your hands on your head. NOW!"

The killer shot Tom an uninterested glance and said, "You should show me a little more respect. After all, I am a bit of a celebrity. My name is Ackerman."

Jim felt his breath stripped away once again. When he had first laid eyes upon the man, he had noticed a vague familiarity. Now, his synapses fired, and he made the connection. He had seen the man's face on television, a two-hour special presented by one of those network news shows. He tried to remember the name of the special. It was something along the lines of *An Experiment in Madness*, but he couldn't remember the exact title. He did, however, remember the description of the man and his hideous crimes. The program had described the kind of monster that was only supposed to exist in the minds of Hollywood's most creative—not a person of flesh and blood who found substance in the real world.

Tom repeated his ultimatum, but this time he spoke the words in a soft voice, as if beseeching the madman to submit and end the confrontation without a fight. "Put your hands where I can see them. I'm going to count to three, and then—"

"I wouldn't do anything rash, officer. If you're not careful, my pretty little hostage might get her pretty little face blown off."

"What hostage?"

Ackerman redirected his gaze from Tom to Jim. "The one under this counter with the sawed-off shotgun strapped against her right temple. It'll make a real mess of her, believe me on that. I've seen it before. It's not pretty. And I know exactly what you're thinking. You think I'm bluffing." He turned back to Tom. "And you're thinking that even if I am telling the truth, you can probably put one between my eyes before I could get my shot off. You'd be wrong, though. My finger's resting right on that trigger and, as soon as your bullet struck, my muscles would clench and her head would be blown out the other side of this counter. So, gentlemen, it appears that what we have here is a Mexican stand-off."

Ackerman took a deep breath and continued in his honeyed tone. "Isn't this fun? You both began your day like any other. You kissed your loved ones good-bye, enjoyed a cup of coffee, maybe read the morning paper, but little did you know that this would be the most significant day of your lives. Today is a day that makes or breaks everything you've ever said or done, everything you've stood for or believed in. At some point, we all come to a place where we have to choose whether to be the hero, the villain, or to walk away and remain one of the sheep. This is one of those moments, gentlemen.

"I'm going to give you both a choice. You can walk away now and continue on with your lives. Maybe I have a hostage under this counter that I'm going to carve up the second you walk out that door, and maybe I don't. Maybe you can catch me and make a name for yourselves, or maybe you'll die trying. There's no way you can know for sure, but that's the beauty of it, isn't it? There's no meaning. Good doesn't triumph over evil. There's just random chance and death. You were the unlucky ones who got the call tonight. The gentleman down the aisle was the unlucky one who was working the station tonight. We like to walk around and think of ourselves as being so damn evolved, so much better and more intelligent than all of the other wildlife. But you know what?"

Ackerman looked at the two men as if he was a hungry animal and they were his next meal. He lowered his voice. "In the end, no matter how many delusions of grandeur we blind ourselves with, we are all either hunters or the hunted, predators or prey. Life is just one big game, gentlemen. The winners survive and the losers rot. The choices we make determine our fate. So…make your choice."

Jim stood at rigid attention, entranced by the madman behind the counter. Ackerman had recited the speech with passion, as if the killer were a politician rallying the constituency behind some noble cause. He had never seen a man with two guns pointed at his face remain so impassive. There was no fear in him. Fear to Ackerman seemed as alien a concept as an airplane to a Neanderthal. More than that, it appeared as if the man felt in complete control of the situation.

Despite the gun in his hand, the realization of that fact made Jim feel defenseless.

Tom's voice cracked and contained a noticeable tremor. "There is no hostage," he said. "There were no other cars out front. Now, you put your hands where I can see them, or I swear to God in heaven, I will put a bullet right between your eyes."

Jim wasn't convinced by Tom's statement, and neither did it seem to influence Ackerman. He knew that Ackerman would have most likely stashed his own car in back, in order to keep up the appearance of being the attendant. If some woman had stopped and come across the killer, he would have moved her car to the back with his own. The possibility that Ackerman had brought the hostage with him in his own car also occurred to him.

He wasn't sure whether his partner had overlooked

those scenarios, or if Tom's actions merely represented a desperate attempt to end the situation. Either way, he knew it wouldn't work. Ackerman wouldn't allow this to end without things getting messy. He could see that much in the killer's eyes.

Ackerman sighed. "Well, darling, they apparently don't believe you're real. Why don't you scream for them?"

With Ackerman's last word, the front of the counter exploded outward, sending pieces of wooden shrapnel in all directions. The shotgun blast tore into Tom's left side, sending a spray of blood into Jim's face and dropping Tom onto the linoleum.

Jim dove into the closest aisle. An instant after he was clear, the end cap display of Doritos chips erupted from a second blast.

He regained his feet and fired two shots in quick succession around the corner. He barely had time to see his shots strike the counter when the shotgun answered, sending him back to cover.

He could hear Tom crying and cursing. *His gun must have been lost in the confusion*, he thought. And Tom must have been half delirious with pain since he wasn't even attempting to find cover. Jim knew that his partner wouldn't survive if he didn't immediately end the confrontation and get help.

"Trooper down. Send medical," he said into his portable packset radio. He didn't bother to announce his name or location. The radio carried a unique code that dispatch would identify while the GPS in the patrol car would alert backup units of their position.

But, unless he acted now, he also knew that he and Tom would be dead by the time backup arrived.

He tried to stay focused, but he couldn't keep his thoughts from wandering onto his wife and daughter.

*Will I see them again? Will I get to watch my daughter grow up?* He thought of brushing the golden, curly locks of hair away from her face and kissing her on the forehead. He thought of the way her eyes lit up with awe and wonder as she sat on his lap and listened to him read.

He thought of his wife kissing him good-bye and telling him to be careful. He thought of holding her, skin against skin, and running his fingers through her raven black hair.

*I have to be strong. I have to make it home to them.* He tried to tell himself that he would see them again, but somehow he knew better. At that moment, he would have given anything for one more chance to hold them.

The smell of gunpowder mixed with the aromas of scented cleaning fluids attacked his senses and made him feel lightheaded. It was that or the adrenaline. Either way, he felt as if he was in a washing machine on spin cycle. He tried to get himself under control, but he was terrified beyond reason. He had no idea of what to do next.

He knew that he wouldn't survive a frontal assault against the shotgun, so he decided his best option would be to move around to the back of the aisles and perhaps catch Ackerman off guard. Plus, the greater the distance, the more advantage his 9mm would have over the less accurate shotgun.

Moving as quietly as possible, he made his way down the aisle. Reaching the opposite end cap, he peered around the corner into the next row.

*All clear.*

He dashed to the next end cap.

*So far, so good.*

There were only four rows of food in the small station, which meant that if he made it to the next end cap without Ackerman seeing him, he would have an unobstructed view of his opponent's hiding place.

He checked the next aisle for danger and was about to make a dash for the next end cap when he heard a small but strange noise coming from the front of the store. It took him a moment to associate the sound with anything tangible, but then he made the connection of a liquid being pressed from a squeeze bottle. Following the sound, Tom's wailing increased in intensity, and the injured officer screamed an almost unintelligible call for help.

"Your friend is having a very bad day, officer. He made his choice to stay and fight, but I guess that I didn't really give you much of a choice, so here it is. Your partner was right. There was no hostage before. But there is one now, and he's not going to leave here alive. I will, however, let you walk right out that door, get in your car, and leave this place behind like it was nothing more than a nightmare. If you stay, maybe you can stop me and save your friend, but let's be honest. I'm better at this game than you are. If you stay, odds are you'll both die. The choice is yours, officer."

He gritted his teeth. Ackerman most likely knew his position, so the chance to sneak around behind the madman was gone. He knew that Ackerman was right. He had never been in a situation like this. He had never seen any real action other than a few rowdy traffic stops and a hostage situation at a diner a few years back, where he had been one of about twenty policemen on the scene. He had been involved in some murder investigations after the fact, but he had never been in a shootout with the killer.

His adversary, however, had taken countless victims, several of which were law enforcement. The killer outgunned and outmatched him; yet, he knew that he could never abandon his friend.

Tom Delaine was a hotheaded, irrational jerk, but he had also been his partner and best friend for nine years. Tom had been there the day that Emily had given birth, handing out the cigars and grinning like a proud uncle. Tom had been the only person who could comfort him on the day they placed his father in the ground. His partner had counseled him through every tough moment of his life and had never asked for anything in return.

"You come on back here where I can get a good look at you, and I'll give you my answer," he said, without the slightest tremble in his voice.

"All right, officer, but don't say I didn't warn you."

He didn't respond. He was already on the move.

He made his way down the middle aisle, staying low and trying to zero in on Ackerman's location from the sound of his voice. If his instincts proved correct, Ackerman awaited him at the end cap of the third row.

When he reached the end of the aisle, he peeked one eye around the corner, but couldn't see the killer. Tom lay only a few feet away.

He edged farther out of the aisle, but still no Ackerman. He was about to reach for Tom, when he heard a match being struck. In that split second, he noticed the line of liquid running from around the side of the station's counter to where Tom lay. He sniffed the air and realized that the sound he had heard earlier was the spraying of lighter fluid. Before he could react, a hand appeared from around the corner of the counter and dropped a match into the trail of liquid.

The stream of lighter fluid ignited, a blue spark questing out and morphing into hues of red and yellow. Within the blink of an eye, the fire shot back to Tom and engulfed him in flames.

Tom's tortured screams of agony filled the gas station and reverberated off the walls and glass. The echoes compounded on each other, giving the effect of a chorus of the damned.

In that moment, Jim lost the capacity for rational thought and acted on pure instinct. He dropped his pistol, ripped off his coat, and slapped at the flames in a last-ditch effort to save his friend. After a few swings, his coat glowed with reds and yellows, as well. He dropped it to the linoleum next to Tom.

A part of his rational mind, which had now been thrown to the back of his consciousness, realized that his friend and partner of many years was gone, but terror had usurped coherent thought. His own screams added to the cacophony of suffering.

After what felt like an eternity, his partner's thrashing ceased, and only the flames remained. The smell of charred flesh filled the space all around him, adding to the whirlwind of emotions swirling in his mind.

A mixture of terror, grief, and anger consumed his consciousness. He sat on his knees, weeping for his friend and knowing that he would be next. For some time, he had been aware of the man with the shotgun standing behind him in the aisle. Ackerman had used Tom as a distraction, and the ploy had succeeded.

His voice trembled and tears ran down his cheeks. "Why did you do this? You called us here just so you could kill us? Why?"

"Why?" Ackerman said. "That is the eternal question, isn't it? From the beginning of human existence, we have sought frantically for the answer to one question: *Why?* Well, I'm afraid that I don't really have an answer for you, other than to say that it is simply who I am. Some people paint beautiful works of art. Some people are doctors, lawyers, butchers and bakers and candlestick makers. I am a predator, a killer. Life's a game, and I like to play. But I'm not quite through playing with you yet. Give me your wallet."

"My wallet?"

A kick to the back of the head answered his question. "Your wallet, now. Please."

He complied, and Ackerman took the proffered item. The killer sifted through the wallet's contents, pausing to study the driver's license and a tattered family photo. "You've got a beautiful family here, Jim Morgan. I'd love to meet them."

"Don't even look at them!" he said as he charged at his best friend's murderer.

Ackerman used the shotgun as a club to knock him to the floor. Then, the killer pummeled him until blood flowed from several large gashes on his face. He could feel his flesh tearing with every blow, but he could do nothing to stop the barrage.

After a moment, the blows ceased. Ackerman stood over him, aiming the shotgun. "I was just going to toy with you a bit before ending your life, but now…I think I've got a better idea."

Ackerman walked behind the counter and retrieved a bottle and a cloth, his eyes never leaving Jim.

He writhed in agony on the floor as he watched Ackerman dump some of the contents of the bottle onto the piece of torn cloth. His vision blurred as his eyes filled with tears. He could taste his own blood in his mouth and still smell the acrid smoke from Tom's charred remains. His brain couldn't process the onslaught of information transmitted by his senses, and his mind threatened to shut down.

Ackerman knelt and placed the cloth over his mouth. He tried to fight back, but his efforts were futile. Within a moment, he succumbed to the chemicals and darkness overtook him.

JIM AWOKE AND scanned his surroundings. He noticed that he was home. His first thought was that the entire ordeal at the gas station had been nothing more than a nightmare.

When he saw his wife and daughter, his relief dissipated like a warm breath on a winter's day.

His wife, Emily, and their young daughter, Ashley, sat across from him in their living room. The chairs from the dining room had been arranged, as if for an intervention, with Emily and Ashley facing him. They were bound, and duct tape covered their mouths. Their disheveled hair matted together and clung to their foreheads, sticking in a mixture of sweat and tears.

"Ashley!" He tried to run to her, but his own restraints held him at bay. He fought with the ropes, and the fibers dug into his skin.

He turned to his wife. Her raven-black hair hung in her face, and fear contorted her features. Her light complexion, one of the traits she had inherited from an odd pairing of an Irish-American grandmother and a Japanese grandfather, had flushed with red. He thought of the countless moments in which he had run his fingers over her smooth, delicate skin. She had always hated her pale pigmentation and complained of how easily she burned in the sun, but he adored her milky complexion. It reminded him of fine porcelain. He had always felt undeserving of her. Although he had never seemed to find the words to tell her, he felt like the luckiest man in the world to have her as his wife.

Tears cascaded down his cheeks, and his heart broke. He wanted to tear the heart from the monster who had done this to his family. He wanted to light the monster on fire, like the killer had done to Tom, and give the psychopath a glimpse of the hell that clearly awaited him.

As he fumed with impotent rage, Emily caught his attention, and with her eyes, she indicated for him to look to his right.

He followed her gaze, and the cold gray eyes of a madman greeted him.

The sawed-off shotgun in one hand, Ackerman stood and walked to Jim's side. "It's about time you woke up," Ackerman said, patting him on the shoulder. "We've been having a great sleepover so far, Dad, but we're ready to start the night's entertainment."

Ackerman moved behind him and leaned in close to his ear. "You've got a real nice family here, Jim. You've built a good life for yourself. Nice house, cutest little girl I've ever seen, and your wife...man, she's gorgeous. And I don't mean that in a vulgar or crude way, Jim. I'm just telling you, honestly, she is a beautiful woman. She reminds me of one of those old-time movie stars, with her dark hair and pale skin. You know, from the thirties or forties. Back when the world was black and white. Anyway, I'm just saying that you're a very lucky man."

Jim gritted his teeth and shook with rage. He wanted to scream at Ackerman. He wanted to tell him to shut up and go to hell, but he didn't want to do anything to play into the madman's fantasies. So he just sat there, praying that his girls would make it through this alive. He didn't care what happened to himself. If he had to die to save them, then so be it, but he begged God to save his wife and daughter.

"What are your thoughts on death, Jim? Do you believe that our lives flash before our eyes...that we relive it all in that final moment? What about the whole light at the end of the tunnel thing, do you buy that? Or what about the spiritual aspects? Do you believe, when I kill your family, that they'll go to a better place?"

Jim couldn't contain his fury for another second. He couldn't listen to another moment of the killer's musings.

He convulsed and tried to wrench his limbs free from his bonds. He screamed at the top of his lungs, but without any words. The English language lacked the ability to convey the emotions that coursed through him. His scream was something more ancient than words, more primal.

After a long moment, the screaming stopped. He took in each breath with fury, his nostrils flaring on every inhalation.

Ackerman patted him on the shoulder. "It's okay, Jim. I understand your pain."

He felt defeated and helpless, but he needed to be strong and think. He couldn't see any means of escape or rescue. They lived in the woods, so no one would hear his screaming. But then, he remembered that he would be missed. *A backup unit will travel to the gas station. They'll find Tom's body and realize that I'm missing. Eventually, they'll check my home. But how long will that take? How much time has already passed?* He needed to stall the killer. He needed to keep him talking. "Why are you doing this?"

Ackerman's eyes narrowed. "Why? We've been over that. The why doesn't matter. Have you ever heard that old adage about the 10/90 rule? It says that life is ten percent what happens to us, and ninety percent how we react. That's what's important. It's not imperative to think of why this has happened to you and your family. Everyone is always whining. 'Why me?' 'Why did this happen to me?' They think it's the end of the world when their forty-thousand-dollar car won't start, and they can't make it to that cushy desk job to pay off that family vacation to Hawaii. But they don't even know the meaning of the word pain. Don't whine to me, Jim. Why is not important. You need to concentrate on what you're going to do about it. How are you going to save them? How are you going to stop me?"

Ackerman leaned in close. He could feel the killer's hot

breath on his neck. "I'll let you in on a little secret. I've been looking for someone to play with…a worthy opponent. I *want* you to beat me."

Ackerman retrieved Jim's gun from the waistband of his pants and placed it in Jim's lap. "Here's the game. Let's call this one… *Two Is the Price for One*. Two of you are going to die here tonight. I don't care which two. If you kill yourself first, then I'll finish your daughter. If you break the rules or refuse to play, then I'll make you watch as I kill your wife and child. I will take my time with them. They will pray for death, and you will wish that you had given it to them. You could choose to shoot both of them and save yourself, but I don't see that happening. If you kill your wife, you can finish yourself or let me do it. Either way, in that scenario, your daughter lives. I'll call 911 after I leave here and tell them to come get her. She might have some emotional issues, but otherwise she'll be fine.

"But before we begin, I want you to come to the realization that no matter what you choose to do or not to do, two of you don't leave here alive. And you do not want me to have to finish this for you. Trust me on that. I know you're thinking that eventually they'll find the mess at the station and come looking for you. Rest assured that I've taken that into consideration, so we'll have ample time to finish our little game. Now, let's play."

Ackerman cut Jim's hands free. He knew what to do. He saw an opportunity, and he took it. He scooped up the gun from his lap and turned it on his captor.

But the killer was ready.

Ackerman wrenched the gun from his hand and slammed the shotgun into the bridge of his nose. Then, the killer swung the shotgun toward Ashley.

JIM HAD TIME to scream, "NO!" before the shotgun blast thundered through the house.

He didn't want to look. He clenched his eyes shut, but he knew that he couldn't shut out the monster that had stepped from his nightmares into the real world.

When he opened his eyes, his heart leapt when he saw that the blast had discharged into the floor, and his daughter still lived.

"Are you ready to play nice?"

Tears flowed from his eyes. "I'll do whatever you want. I'll play your game…just don't hurt them."

"Good. I'll give you one more chance. But if you try anything this time, I'll get tired of this game and move on to another. You'll like that game even less than you like this one. Let's continue."

Ackerman slammed the pistol back onto his lap.

This time, he didn't pick it up. His mind reeled. *There has to be a way out of this. I'm a good cop. I have to find a way to save my family. But what can I do? The madman has a shotgun pointed at my head, and if I fail again, we're all as good as dead.* From the corner of his mind, the only available path began to take form, but he pushed the thought away. It was too horrible. He couldn't bring himself to consider the possibility. And yet, he did.

When he looked into his wife's eyes, he knew that she had followed the same train of thought to the only possible conclusion. If only one of them could survive, it had to be Ashley.

The look in Emily's eyes conveyed what she was thinking. *I love you. I understand. And it's okay.* His wife, the love of his life, the woman with whom he planned to grow old, nodded her head and closed her eyes.

He picked up the gun and raised his shaking hand. He

placed his finger over the trigger, but he couldn't bring himself to squeeze. He lowered the gun.

*How can I kill the woman I love?* He searched his mind again for an alternative. The only way to save his daughter was to kill her mother. An idea began to take form, but it was such a long shot.

He raised the gun again. He knew that he couldn't move forward without his wife's consent, but she had made her feelings clear. Her courage and resolve gave him the strength to do what had to be done.

He took aim and squeezed the trigger.

JIM SOBBED INTO his hands. He prayed and begged for God's forgiveness. He wanted the pain to end, but his beliefs told him that suicide might keep him from seeing his wife again in the next world. He couldn't bear the thought of eternity without her.

The gun fell from his hand and struck the hardwood floor with a metallic thud.

Ackerman spoke as he reached down and sliced the rope that restrained Jim's feet. "Well done. Let's move onto another game. We'll call this one…*The Easy Way or the Hard Way.* I'm going to give you a choice about how you die. Option number one is a shotgun blast to the back of the head. It would be quick and painless, but you would be very, very dead. Option number two is that I let you run out the backdoor. Of course, this means that you would have to leave your daughter behind, but don't think about that. You don't have a choice in the matter. If you stay, I'll blow your head off, and she'll be left alone with me anyway. Besides, I don't care about your daughter. You're much more fun to play with.

"I'll give you a head start, and then I'll come and find you. I won't use the shotgun. I'll use a knife. It will not be quick. It will be the most agonizing death that I can give you, but there is always the possibility that I won't find you or that you could overpower me. That's the decision that you have to make. Do you give up now and put an end to all your suffering, or do you hold on to the hope of salvation and face the possibility of a gruesome end? You have thirty seconds…"

With one last, long look at his baby girl, he stood and bounded toward the back door. He didn't want to leave her behind, but he didn't want her to watch him die either. Ackerman was right. He didn't have any other choice.

His mind screamed one singular thought: *revenge*. He no longer cared about his own life or how he died, but the killer had given him a chance to avenge his wife's death, and he would take it.

He exited the back of the house and ran headlong into the awaiting arms of the dark forest.

BEHIND JIM, IN the kitchen of the trooper's once-peaceful home, Francis Ackerman Jr. picked up the phone and dialed. The man on the other end of the line answered on the fifth ring.

"Hello, this is Father Joseph. How may I help you?"

"Forgive me, Father, for I have sinned."

Silence answered.

"Are you there, Padre?"

The man on the end of the line exhaled slowly. "I'm here, Francis."

"I've killed three tonight, and I'm about to do another… a cop."

"Why do you call me? Is it just another of your games?"

"No. I just…I just needed someone to talk to. And you're all I've got." He clenched his eyes shut and fought back the tears. "I'm so tired, Father."

"Through the Lord, you can find peace, but you have to want it."

"I don't believe in your God. I don't want your heaven or your hell. I just want to sleep. I want darkness. Oblivion. I want it to be as if I never was."

"It doesn't work that way. One day, you will face judgment, whether you believe in God or not. But it's not too late, Francis. Turn yourself in. I can help you. I can—"

"No one can help me. I'm far beyond your redemption."

"No one is beyond redemption." After a hesitation, Father Joseph said, "You can't blame your father for all that you've become."

Ackerman unconsciously rubbed at the scars on his hands and forearms as he thought about his father. He could still hear the man's voice in his head; whispers in the dark. *We're going to play a game, Francis… Kill her… Kill her and the pain will stop…*

"At some point, you have to take responsibility for your own actions," the priest said. "He might have set you on this path, but you've chosen to walk down it. You have to want to stop."

"I can't stop. It's all that I am. I'm a monster."

"I don't believe that. You wouldn't keep reaching out to me if there wasn't a part of you that wanted to be better than this."

"Don't presume to understand me, Padre. It doesn't matter what I want. I wish that I was a real person, but I'm not. And I never will be. I'm broken, and no one can put me back together again. Besides, I'm just giving the people what they want."

"No one wants this."

"Sure they do. Do you know how many letters I received when I was in the institution? They want a villain. They're fascinated by me. I'm their god. To some, anyway.

Others just need to see people like me out there to make them feel better about the darkness inside themselves. To make them feel normal. And if some cop gets lucky and kills me, it doesn't even matter. I'll live on forever. They'll study me in psychology classes. Others will duplicate my work. They'll write books and produce documentaries. The longer I evade capture, the more victims I take, the more shocking my crimes…the more my legend grows."

"You know what would really make you a legend? Turning your life around. Think about it. People would be truly fascinated by a man who could do the things that you've done and still find his way to the light. You could be the villain and the hero. The Bible says, 'Joy shall be nine just persons, which need no repentance.' There is a way to have everlasting life, Frank. I can show you. I can help you. You just need to turn yourself in."

"Good night, Padre."

"Wait. Don't—"

Ackerman hung up the phone. He dried the tears from his eyes and checked the time. He knew the possibility existed that the officer might escape from his grasp, but they never did. He was too skilled at his job.

He would find his new friend, and he would make good on his promise. Jim would die a slow death. The cop would scream until his lungs filled with blood and he drowned on the same liquid that once pumped the life through his veins. In the end, however, the taking of Jim's life paled in comparison to devouring his spirit, and he knew that he had broken the man. He had made Jim realize and appreciate all that he had taken for granted, and then, he had stripped it all away.

He placed the shotgun on the counter and removed a hunting knife from a sheath at his back. He slowly turned it in his hand, admiring the blade. He pondered the glorious suffering that he would soon administer. He would savor and prolong every moment of Jim's agony and of his own ecstasy. Then, in the end, when every exquisite scream had been extracted and every avenue of torture had been exhausted, he would take Jim's life.

FRANCIS ACKERMAN STROLLED into the diner and took a seat at the counter.

After a moment, the waitress said, "What'll it be, mister?"

He looked deep into her eyes. "Coffee and steak."

She scribbled on her notepad. "How would you like that cooked?"

"Bloody."

"Baked potato, salad?"

"Just steak and caffeine, thanks."

He turned his attention toward the television set mounted on the wall. Something caught his eye, and he asked the waitress to turn up the volume.

"In an incident that has shocked the entire state of Colorado, three men, including two State Troopers, were brutally slain last night. A fourth victim is currently being treated for a gunshot wound to the head but is expected to make a full recovery."

He leaned forward in his seat. *Full recovery?*

An image of a State Trooper at a podium replaced that of the anchorman. The subtitle read, *Major Christian Steinhoff, Colorado State Patrol.* He committed the name to memory. The perspiring policeman said, "Emily Morgan is expected to make a full recovery and has now regained consciousness. We will issue more details later, but according to Mrs. Morgan, an assailant matching the description of Francis Ackerman Jr. forced her husband to choose between her life and that of their daughter. Based on the findings of the preliminary investigation, we believe that the quick thinking of Trooper Jim Morgan saved his wife."

The cop on the screen drank from a glass of water and continued. "Trooper Morgan and his partner, Trooper Tom Delaine, responded to a call a few weeks ago in which a young woman had been shot in the head. They had entered the residence in response to a domestic disturbance and found the woman lying in a pool of her own blood. They had thought she was dead, but upon further examination, she was found to be alive. The young woman had been shot in the head at an angle with a .22-caliber pistol, and the bullet had deflected off her skull. The impact knocked her unconscious but left her with a survivable wound.

"The wound to Emily Morgan's head is almost identical to the wound sustained by the woman in the previous case. Although the previous incident involved a lower-caliber weapon, Trooper Morgan had gone to the shooting range on the day of the incident and still had his weapon loaded with a cheaper brand of ammo containing a lower grade of gunpowder. Although we can't know for sure, we believe that Trooper Morgan successfully attempted to recreate the previous incident in order to save both his wife and daughter. Although Mrs. Morgan did lose pieces of her skull and ear and is being treated for swelling around the brain, she is expected to make a full recovery and is currently under our protection."

He reclined back. *I'll be damned.*

"Congratulations, Jim," he said aloud. "Guess we'll have to call that one a tie."

He noticed that the older man sitting next to him at the counter held a spoonful of mashed potatoes halfway between his mouth and plate. He turned to find the man staring at him. A half-read newspaper rested on the counter in front of the older man, which undoubtedly contained a picture of the killer named Francis Ackerman Jr. The man trembled, and small chunks of mashed potatoes fell into his lap. The man didn't seem to notice.

Ackerman sighed and shook his head. *My work is never done.* "Do you want to play a game?" he said.

# TWO

MARCUS WILLIAMS COCKED his head to the side, cracking his neck and getting into fight mode. "Listen," he said. "I'm sorry if she prefers the company of someone who can speak to her with actual words instead of a series of grunts."

"Don't get smart with me, boy," the cowboy said, nostrils flaring like a bull about to charge.

"You're right. I should get dumb with you. That way, we're on the same wavelength."

He watched two men join the cowboy, Glenn, at one end of the alley, and he heard footsteps approaching from behind. He reached out and pulled Maggie behind him. *Morons always travel in packs.* The alley was long and narrow with no windows or doors to provide a means of escape.

He heard one of the men behind them rhythmically slapping what sounded like a baseball bat into an open hand. Another man standing to the right of Glenn held a tire iron at his side. He counted two others with Glenn, for a total of five. He knew that at least two of the group carried weapons, and the others could possess knives, fistpacks, brass knuckles, or worse.

"You big-city boys think you're so damn smart. I'm sick to death of people like you comin' here and thinking that we're all just a bunch of stupid hicks who can't read or write or tie our damn shoes. Well, I've got some news for ya. We've got a few things we'd like to teach you, and class is now in session."

Marcus had to think fast. He only had a few seconds before the men were upon him. He knew that, even if their intention was only to rough him up, the confrontation could easily escalate from assault to manslaughter. He also realized that, once they were finished with him, they wouldn't just let Maggie walk away unscathed. The angry mob mentality could be a powerful force.

Adrenaline surged through his veins, the same kind of adrenaline that allowed a mother to lift a car off her trapped child. He grabbed a corner of a nearby dumpster and threw all of his weight into it. The Dumpster was almost empty, and the wheels were unobstructed. This allowed him to spin it into the path of the two men coming at him from one end of the alley, blocking their approach.

He gently pushed Maggie toward one wall and moved to the opposite side. He wanted to draw the attackers away and shield her from the fight as much as possible.

He turned back to face the two men coming from the other direction. He figured Glenn for a coward and had theorized that the big talker would let his friends do his dirty work. He saw that he had been right.

The first man landed flat on the pavement as Marcus's foot struck him in the chest, knocking him off his feet and sending him plummeting toward the earth, dazed but not unconscious. The second man attacked and landed a hard blow with the tire iron into Marcus's side.

He stumbled and almost fell to his knees. The pain shot up his spine, but he willed it away. He didn't have time to feel pain.

He swung back around on the second attacker and threw the entire weight of his body into a massive, locomotive punch aimed dead center of the man's pudgy face. The heavyset man also landed on his back, but he wouldn't be getting up without the aid of smelling salts.

The first man attempted to pull himself off the ground, but hopes of rejoining the battle crumbled away as a foot hammered into the side of his head.

Glenn hung back, shuffling from one side of the alleyway to the other. Marcus wondered whether the big talker was waiting for him to lie down on the ground and take his beating with quiet dignity.

By now, the thugs from the other side of the alley had bypassed their obstacle. He grabbed the tire iron lying beside the unconscious attacker. Knowing that its reach wouldn't compare to that of the baseball bat, he hurled it at the man holding the wooden weapon.

The iron found its mark but didn't deal a crushing blow. The momentary distraction served its purpose, however, and allowed him to overtake the bat-wielding aggressor before the man could swing. He grabbed the fat end of the bat with his left hand and sent his right cutting through the air and into the man's face.

The dazed attacker released the bat but still landed a blow into Marcus's side.

He tensed, and the man quickly landed another punch into the side of his head. He stumbled back but retaliated with a hard jab of his newly acquired Kirby Puckett—signed Louisville Slugger.

The blow knocked the man cold.

In his mind, since Glenn seemed to be more of a spectator than an attacker, only one opponent remained. The last man eyed him warily, looking for an opening.

He tightened his grip on the bat. "Better be sure."

The man hesitated for a moment. Then, the final aggressor ran toward the end of the alley with a speed that he wouldn't have thought possible for a man of that size. But then again, he had learned that a person never knew how fast they could run until they were being chased.

He, however, had no intentions of chasing the man. Instead, he decided that it was time to deal with the instigator of the brawl, a certain beer-gutted gorilla. He turned and walked to where Glenn shuffled. He threw down the bat, knowing that he wouldn't need it.

Glenn stared at him for a few long seconds. He wondered if Glenn was psyching himself up for an attack, or if the tough-looking cowboy was about to piss his pants and run away. With a trembling voice, Glenn said, "I guess I'm going to have to teach you a lesson myself."

The cowboy reached into a pocket and revealed a switchblade knife.

*This is going to be fun.*

Glenn charged with the knife. The cowboy made a quick stab but sliced only air as he moved clear. Glenn countered with an arcing slash that nearly sliced him across the abdomen, but he was able to jump backward and arch his back enough to avoid the blade.

Glenn attempted two more quick stabs, both unsuccessful. On the third thrust, he grabbed Glenn by the wrist and pulled as hard as he could. Propelled by his own weight, Glenn rocketed forward.

He caught Glenn with an outstretched arm, clotheslining the burly cowboy and slamming him to the ground. Glenn lost his grip on the knife, and it clattered down the alley. Glenn's head thudded against the pavement, and he wheezed as the impact expelled all the air from his lungs.

Marcus looked down on his opponent. He had always been a huge fan of action movies and great one-liners. Although this wasn't a movie and it would never go down in history with the catch phrases of *Dirty Harry* or *The Terminator*, he filled with great pride as he said, "Class dismissed."

"ARE YOU OKAY?" Maggie said, taking a cell phone from her purse and placing it against her ear. "You're bleeding."

Marcus reached up and wiped a trail of blood from his lip. He rubbed it between his fingers. "I'm—"

Maggie held up a finger to him, and he guessed that her call had connected. He had always found that you could tell a lot about a person by the way they reacted to a stressful or dangerous situation. As she spoke into the cell phone, he watched her mannerisms, cadence, pitch, tone, breathing, eyes. The words she spoke could have just as easily been issued from the mouth of a valley girl, but he looked beyond the words at the person underneath. Her voice was calm. Her tone was insistent yet professional. Her breathing was steady, and her body language exuded confidence. Her eyes scanned their unconscious attackers. At the edge of his perception, he detected a slight tremble, but that was to be expected. She reminded him of a cop calling in for backup.

"Glenn and some of his buddies just tried to jump me and a friend… We're fine… My friend took care of them… Yes, Father, it's a guy friend… No, you don't know him. Now's not the time. Just get over here. We're in an alley next to the bar… Okay. Hurry."

She closed the phone and placed it back in her purse.

Marcus watched as Glenn tried to get up but then fell back down and lay still. "Don't you think we should call the cops?"

Maggie smiled. "My dad is the cops. He's the Sheriff."

"Oh, great."

"That's not a problem, is it? Lotta guys head for the hills when they hear my father's the Sheriff. Guess they're a little intimidated."

"Not me. I've got a lot of respect for anyone who carries a badge. I'm a third-generation cop myself. Or…I was anyway."

"But not anymore?"

"Not anymore."

For the first time, it occurred to him that maybe he could be a cop again. *Maybe I can get a job as one of the Sheriff's deputies, sitting next to the highway, issuing the occasional citation?* It would be a far cry from the world he had left behind. But calling his previous employer for a reference would pose a problem.

Not pressing the issue, Maggie sighed and brushed a strand of blonde hair from her face. A dark, bronze tan made her hair seem lighter than it actually was. She wasn't wearing any makeup and didn't need any. Her pink T-shirt bore the name of *The Asherton Tap*, the bar where she worked as a waitress and where they had met earlier in the evening. He had offered to walk her home.

"Sorry about all this," she said. "I knew Glenn had a thing for me, but I never thought that he would take it this far."

He smiled. He couldn't believe that he had met someone like her on his first day in town. Although in his experience, things that seemed too good to be true usually were. "Don't worry about it. I can take care of myself."

"Kinda noticed."

He shrugged. "Chuck Norris movies."

Maggie chuckled. "Don't get me wrong, you look like a man who can take care of himself, but that usually doesn't mean anything."

"I had some martial arts training and did some boxing when I was on the force. Plus, I was a pretty tough kid growing up. But to be honest, what happened here was one part ability and three parts luck."

He had been lucky. Then again, he had always been

lucky in similar situations. He always seemed to come out on top in a fight. When did luck become skill? When did a skill become a talent? In the end, he knew that he had a gift for hurting people, and it scared him. He wished it was only luck, but deep down, he knew better. He knew what he was capable of.

He saw flashing lights coming from around the corner. A moment later, a patrol car stopped in front of them. A middle-aged man with silver hair and goatee stepped out of the vehicle. Maggie relayed the situation to the man who Marcus assumed to be her father.

A crowd from the bar had gathered at one end of the alley. The sounds of a top-forty cover band echoed out of the Asherton Tap as more patrons walked from the bar to see what was happening. Many of the spectators looked disappointed that they had missed the action.

People always seemed to be in awe of the infliction of pain. *Why do we find it so interesting to see people beat each other's brains in?* He wasn't judging. He liked to watch a fight as much as anyone, but he wondered what it was in the nature of human beings that caused a fascination with violence and suffering.

After hearing the story, the Sheriff walked over to Glenn and hauled him up from the pavement while one of his deputies rounded up the cowboy's friends. "Do you have anything to say for yourself?"

Still dazed, Glenn said, "Sheriff, I didn't do nothin'. We were just trying to welcome the new guy, and he got all smart with me. Next thing you know, he's kickin' and punchin' people. It was craziness."

The Sheriff nodded. "Right. I've always thought that you should be head of the welcoming committee. Plus, it was real nice of you and your boys to bring that base-ball bat and tire iron as housewarming gifts." The Sheriff shoved Glenn in the direction of his deputy. "Get him out of here."

Her father pulled Maggie aside.

After a moment, they returned, and turning in Marcus's direction, the Sheriff said, "Sorry about Glenn, son. Sharp like a spoon, that one. Anyway, it's against my better judgment, but Maggie has convinced me to let you walk her home. That doesn't mean you're off the hook. I want you to come into my office tomorrow and give a formal statement. I'll be gone in the morning, but you stop by in the afternoon. That'll give us a chance to sit down and have a nice visit."

Marcus didn't like the sound of a "nice visit." The conversation would probably revolve around Maggie and the removal of certain parts of his anatomy if she weren't shown respect. "I'll be there, sir."

"See that you are."

Maggie gave her father an awkward hug before she and Marcus continued on. After a moment of silence, Maggie spoke. "So why aren't you a cop anymore?"

*A dark alleyway, a scream, the blood, the tears*—the memories came rushing back and swirled through his mind like a tornado that leaves a house standing but uninhabitable. *What business is it of hers? Why don't you ask about how my parents died, or maybe if I had a dog that was run over when I was a kid?*

*But she doesn't know it's a painful memory. She's just trying to get to know you better, idiot. Maybe because she likes you, but now she probably thinks you're some kind of burned-out psycho, since you're taking an hour to respond to a simple question.*

"Well…"

*What do I tell her?*

"I think that's a question we should save for at least our second or third date."

"How do you know there'll even be a second or third date?"

"Because you want to learn all my secrets."

She smiled. As he looked into her eyes, his painful memories slipped to the back of his mind and away from his immediate thoughts. For now, the pain had subsided. For now, his demons were sleeping.

"Thanks for walking with me," she said. "You're really a nice guy."

He grimaced. "The kiss of death."

She gave him a confused look.

"Nice guys get calls for advice on how to handle bad-boy boyfriends. They drive you to the airport and help you move. Nice guys finish last. And…I'm not all that nice."

"I disagree. I think that you are a nice guy, and I also think that you haven't been hanging around with the right kind of women. I happen to like nice guys."

Their eyes met, and he felt a warmth in her gaze that made his heart race and his mind reel with possibilities. They held the connection for a few seconds. When her cheeks began to turn red, she looked away.

The warm smell of cinnamon rolls straight from the oven made his stomach rumble. The lights were on in the bakery. Maggie was so caught up in the moment that she almost passed by the entrance to her apartment, a small place above The Magnolia Bakery. He remembered a place with the same name on Bleecker Street back in New York. He had loved their red velvet cupcakes.

She stopped and removed a key from her purse. She hesitated, giving him the impression that she was waiting for him to make a move.

It had been a long time since he had done anything like this. "Dinner...tomorrow night?"

Maggie reached into her purse and produced a small pad of paper and pen. She jotted down her number and handed it to him. "Give me a call tomorrow."

He took the piece of paper, folded it with care, and placed it in his pocket.

They stared at each other for a moment.

He leaned in.

She closed her eyes and appeared to be awaiting his lips.

He touched her on the shoulder, but instead of kissing her, he whispered in her ear. "I don't kiss on the first date."

Her eyes opened and narrowed at him. "You're an odd man."

He smiled. "I'll take that as a compliment."

"ARE YOU SURE that we're doing the right thing?" the big man said as he thrummed his fingers upon the antique desk.

The smaller man chuckled. He stepped away from the window that overlooked the estate's lush veranda and took a seat behind his ornate walnut desk. "I find that the older I get, the less I'm sure about anything."

The big man smiled at his long-time friend, a man known as the Director. "I know what you mean, but I'm starting to have my doubts about this plan. There are a million things that could go wrong."

"There are a million things that could go right as well. Such is the way of life."

"I know that, but I can't shake the feeling that we're taking unnecessary risks. We're putting a lot of good people in danger, and this thing could get very messy. Do the ends really justify the means?"

"Do they ever?"

The big man ran a hand through his gray-white hair. His compatriot broke the silence first. "I think I'm going to fix myself a drink and get some fresh air. Would you like to join me?"

"Make mine a double."

They exited the Director's office and strolled the walk that encompassed the massive white house. After a moment, the big man said, "Does it have to be Ackerman?"

"We've been over this. You and I both know from past experience that it will take someone of his…his caliber to accomplish our goal. Plus, you know his connection to all of this. We need him. Hell, we've set the whole thing up around him. Besides, we've done things similar in the past."

"Not with someone like Ackerman." The big man shook his head. "He scares me."

"I know. I feel the same way, but events were set in motion years ago that have led us to this day. It's fate. Well, fate with a little help from us anyway. We both know that it sometimes takes extreme actions in order to radically change a person's way of thinking. We've planned everything as best we can, and our people know their jobs. They're the best. You trained most of them. We can pull this off."

The big man tilted back his head and let the contents of the entire glass slide down his throat. "God help us if you're wrong."

The Director shrugged. "God help us, either way."

# THREE

MAUREEN HILL SAT alone at her kitchen table and stared at the chair that had once belonged to her husband. Jack had sat across from her every morning for forty-two years as they drank coffee and ate breakfast. The realization that he would never sit in that chair again still shocked her even after nearly two years of being without him.

She and Jack had hoarded their money for years, never indulging themselves, never spending or enjoying it. They had planned to travel and see the world. She had wanted to see Paris and Venice before she died, and her husband had always dreamed of Australia. The couple had nurtured hopes of one day growing old in style while they indulged in the simple pleasures that they had denied themselves for so many years. Their children were grown, and they had been good providers and protectors. Their golden years were supposed to be their own, a time for them to enjoy life and each other.

Now, all the years of saving and sacrificing seemed a terrible waste to her. She searched her memory for one instance where they had gone out to eat at a nice restaurant or had splurged on a night of simple enjoyment. There were none to remember.

The diagnosis of cancer had changed all of their well-laid plans. She wished that she could turn back the hands of time and do things differently. She wished that they had lived in the present rather than always looking toward the future. As the tears ran down her cheeks, she wished that they had enjoyed the time they were given rather than assuming that their time would never run out. She dried her tears and attempted to distract herself from old memories and regrets.

With kind eyes and a warm smile, she glanced over at a family photo. Twenty-two grandchildren, whom she adored, filled a modest portion of her time, but they could never truly fill the space left by her husband's passing—nothing could.

She let out an audible sigh and picked up the paperback David Morrell novel from the table. She read a few pages but had been up late the previous night enjoying a good movie on TV, and her eyelids felt heavy and eventually closed. The book fell to the floor as her head lolled to one side and she fell fast asleep.

A MAN WITH cold, gray eyes watched the silver-haired woman through the kitchen window. The dark soul behind the eyes contemplated the manner in which she would die.

Ackerman watched her stare at the chair opposite her. He reasoned from the woman's actions that she had recently lost her spouse and was now feeling depressed and alone. Although she was unaware of the fact, she wasn't alone anymore. She had company.

He felt sorry for her. He knew that it would only be a matter of time before she joined her husband and passed on into obscurity. Only a handful of family and friends would mourn her passing. After a few years, she would only be thought of when family members examined old photo albums. No one beyond her small circle would ever know her name, and she would fade away as if she never existed—forgotten and forsaken.

He would change all that.

His presence at her home ensured that everyone in the

surrounding area would remember the kind grandmother who had been murdered by the sadistic killer. Someday, he was certain that countless books would be written about his exploits. He would be psychoanalyzed and dissected as America's fascination with the sinister propelled the works of his followers to the bestseller lists.

He would be hated by most, revered by some like him, but remembered by all. He would live on forever in infamy. Through association with him, the silver-haired woman would be remembered as well. She may even warrant her own chapter in some yet-to-be-written account of his deeds. Although the woman—like the countless victims that came before her—would never appreciate the gift, through death, he would give her immortality.

PART OF MAUREEN's sleeping mind registered a noise in the room, and she awoke from her slumber. She blinked the cobwebs from her vision, but her heart was unprepared for what her eyes found.

A man with haunting, gray eyes sat in her husband's chair.

She trembled with fear and was at a loss for words. One of her hands lay quivering on top of the table and shook with such force that it rattled the decorative centerpiece, a vase filled with lilies and orchids. She was about to speak when, without warning, the man produced a knife and drove the blade into the table, directly through the center of her shaking hand.

She screamed in agony. She tried to pull her hand free, but it was pinned to the table's top. The more she worked to free it, the more intense the pain became. She searched the area within her reach for some kind of weapon to use against the intruder. Ironically, the only thing within arm's length was a paperback novel that dealt with the hunt for a serial killer.

"Shhhh. Quiet, please. We have much to discuss."

She convulsed with terror and brought her shrieking under control. But she could not halt her short, raspy breaths or the tears that flowed from her eyes. Between intakes of air that bordered on hyperventilation, she managed to ask, "Who are you? What do you want?"

"My name is Francis Ackerman Jr., and I want to play a game."

Between sobs, she said, "Why are you doing this?"

Ackerman seemed perplexed by the question. "Do you ask a lion why he eats meat? Why is the grass green and the sky blue? Some things just are the way that they are, and this is who I am."

Ackerman stood and walked over to the kitchen counter. He picked up a baking timer. The small plastic device was white with a round dial. Black, ornate script, located in the bottom right corner of the tool's face, spelled out the brand name, *Lux*.

The killer sat back down at the table. He held up the timer in front of her and rotated it in his hand, as if examining such a device for the first time. "I love these things," he said, looking deep into her eyes, as though she was his oldest friend. "I have to admit that I am completely fascinated by any device that measures the concept of time. Strange, isn't it? I mean, time is such an elusive and fluid thing. And yet, we design devices to put this grand concept into a nice, neat little box that we can understand, measure, and assign value to. Time is ever flowing and changing around us. It's the fabric of the universe, and we are nothing—only single drops in the grand ocean of time.

"I also love that time, in regards to personal perception, is completely relative. For example, as you sit there in terror with a knife stuck in your hand, time feels as if it has slowed to a crawl. But as I sit here in great enjoyment of the moment, it feels as if time is slipping away at an amazing pace. It's all relative, but that's what is so interesting about this device."

He held up the baking timer. "No matter how the passage of time may feel to a person whose perception is altered by their situation, this device is constant. In all actuality, the seconds count down on this device no faster or slower based upon who you are, and that's something else I love about time. It's fair. No matter who you are, what you've done, or how much money is in your bank account, time passes the same for us all. And sooner or later, it will catch up to every living thing on this planet. Time is the greatest killer of all."

He placed the timer on the tabletop in front of her. "So, in honor of this most interesting device, the little game we're going to play is a fight against the clock for the both of us. We'll call this game…*The Theory of Relativity*. First of all, I'll set this timer to six minutes. Then, I'm going to let you go hide somewhere in the house. While you're hiding, I'm going to sit here at the table and watch as three minutes' worth of time counts off the timer. After the three minutes have passed, I'll have three minutes remaining to find you. If I find you within that time, you will die a death more horrible than anything you've ever imagined. If you manage to elude me and the timer reaches six minutes, then I'll leave you unharmed, and you'll never see me again."

Ackerman stood and picked up a dishtowel from the counter. He moved to one of the kitchen cabinets and removed two glass cups. Her eyes followed the madman as he put the cups in the dishtowel, closed the towel tight, and smashed the glasses within, leaving a towel full of broken glass.

He turned back to her and continued. "But before we play, we need to establish some rules for the game. Number one, you must remain inside the house." Ackerman walked to the back door and sprinkled some of the glass shards in front of the exit. Once finished, he moved down the hall toward the front door.

While her attacker was out of the room, she stiffened her resolve and grabbed the knife that pinned her in place. She wiggled it back and forth slowly, but each movement caused her great pain and forced her closer to the brink of unconsciousness.

She could hear the killer approaching, his footsteps growing in volume as he grew nearer.

With her heart thudding violently in her chest, she intensified her efforts. *If only I can free the knife, I can stab the killer before he knows that I'm free.*

She rocked the knife back and forth, desperately trying to release it from the grasp of the table's thick wooden top. She was not a weakling, but she was not a strong woman either. Her wounds, both physical and emotional, had sapped any strength that she did possess.

Each movement of the blade severed skin and cut nerve endings, sending sharp, shooting pains up her arm and down her spine.

The killer was now in the hallway just outside the kitchen.

She steeled herself for one final effort, and with every ounce of strength that she had left, she yanked up on the knife. She felt sweat running down her forehead from the exertion of her efforts. The streams of sweat and tears coalesced into one. The knife moved up slightly.

She continued her efforts, but it would not budge a millimeter farther. It was of no use. The knife was secure, and her traumatized muscles could not remove it.

Ackerman reemerged from the hallway and eyed her like a parent who had found their child with a hand in the cookie jar. He walked over to the table and stood over her. "You see, darling, a knife is kind of like a Band-Aid. You just have to rip it off."

With a quick movement, he grasped the knife and pulled it from the table and out of her hand.

The trauma almost overwhelmed her. Cold tendrils of pain shot up her arm. She could feel her vision tunneling down into unconsciousness, but she fought to remain awake. She shuddered to think what the psychopath might do to her while she slept.

"Okay, back to the rules," Ackerman said. "As I was saying, you must remain inside the house. That's why I sprinkled the broken glass in front of the exits, so you won't be able to slip out without me hearing you. Rule number two, no trying to call for help. I'm not going to cut the phone lines, but I think we both know that no one will arrive in time to make a bit of difference. Your only real chance of survival is me not finding you within the allotted time. If you break the rules, it'll just give me more time to find you. All right, now that we've established the ground rules, let's begin."

Ackerman sat down, twisted the timer to six minutes, and placed it back on the table's mahogany top. She stared at him in confusion. She couldn't comprehend that this was actually happening.

Ackerman raised his eyebrows. "You better get going," he said. "Time's running out."

MAUREEN LEAPT UP and ran from the kitchen. She fell over a small table in the hallway and crashed to the floor. She popped up, caught her breath, and willed herself to be calm. *I have to think clearly if I'm going to make it out alive.* She grabbed a cloth from the small table and wrapped it around her bleeding hand. With her wound contained, she collected her thoughts and contemplated where to hide.

As she moved from room to room, the spaces of her own home looked as dark and alien to her as the surface of a distant planet. She racked her brain for a spot where the madman would never find her, but she could think of none. And, as the killer had stated, time was running out.

Then, an idea for the perfect hiding place burst into her mind—a spot where she would be concealed and the killer would never notice her.

Trying to be as quiet as possible, she moved up the front stairs. With each step, the stairs issued loud creaks in protest to the placement of her weight. She had never noticed how badly they squeaked before that moment, but she had also never felt the need to sneak through her own house. Every time that her foot fell upon one of the stairs, it issued a moan and pop that sounded like nails being driven into her own coffin. After moving a quarter of the way up, she dropped all attempts at stealth and bounded forward.

Once on the second floor, she resumed her attempt at discretion and tried to mute each footfall. The boards of the hallway creaked, as well, but not nearly as bad as the stairs. She moved down the hall to her bedroom with at least some feeling that the killer may not have been alerted to her exact location.

She turned the knob, entered, and shut the door behind her. Once inside, she stood on her bed and reached up to the ceiling where a concealed panel could be pulled down. A foldout ladder used for easy access to the attic sat atop the panel.

She climbed up the ladder and pulled the panel shut behind her. In order to conceal the attic entrance, for aesthetic purposes, her late husband had covered the panel with drywall in such a way that only a tiny seam and a thin pull chain would alert anyone to the panel's presence. She prayed that the killer wouldn't notice.

She had no real reason to think that he would leave after the time had elapsed—*but what choice do I have other than to believe that he will?* If the madman didn't play by the rules of his own game, then only a miracle could save her.

MAUREEN LAY MOTIONLESS on the attic rafters. She searched her mind for something that she could use as a weapon if the killer discovered her hiding place, but the attic was almost empty. The only item contained in the small space was a large trunk in which she had placed many of her husband's belongings after he had passed on. It mostly contained old clothes, photo albums, picture frames, home movies, and other assorted keepsakes. She thought about breaking the glass on one of the picture frames, but that would alert the killer to her position. And she wouldn't know how to use a makeshift knife, even if she had one.

She wondered how much time had passed. It felt like an eternity. She quieted her breathing and waited.

A few seconds later, she heard a sound that conjured images of a freight train tearing through the house. She knew the source of the sound, however, and it wasn't a train. The sound was that of a man running at full speed up the stairs and down the hallway.

She heard the door to the bedroom, only a few feet below her current position on the other side of the ceiling, slam open with a loud crash.

Her heart thundered. She couldn't breathe. *How has he found me so soon?*

She bit down upon her knuckle with crushing force in

order to keep from issuing a sob or a scream. She trembled all over and felt colder than she had ever been in her entire life.

She prayed for God to save her, or at least make her death quick, but then she reconsidered her prayer when she remembered that God doesn't make life easy for his followers. He merely gives them hope that through faith, a greater plane of existence can be attained. Upon consideration, she changed her prayer and prayed instead for strength, something that with God's help she had found at many difficult points in her life.

She tasted a strange, coppery liquid in her mouth and realized that she had drawn blood from her knuckle. At this point, it hardly mattered. She bit down harder and tried to lose herself within the pain.

With a creak, the killer pulled down the panel and said, "Come out, come out, wherever you are."

She heard him unfold the ladder and begin his ascent toward her.

Tears flowed like rain down her cheeks, and she realized that she didn't want to die. There were many times after her husband was taken that she had wished to join him, but now, all she wanted was another chance to live.

In that moment, the realization that once again she had wasted the time she had been given engulfed her mind. When her husband had been alive, they had squandered their present on the hope of a better tomorrow. But after his death, she had not found a greater appreciation for life. Instead of devoting herself to some pursuit or enjoying all the time she could with her children and grandchildren, she had spent most days moping around the house.

In that moment, she cried out to God for one last chance. Then, like a lightning strike on a clear, blue day, a thought struck her with great force. A possible hope for salvation sprang into her mind, and she leapt into action.

She grabbed hold of the large trunk containing her old memories, and using all of the might she could will into her muscles, she hurled it down the stairs and onto the ascending killer.

MAUREEN PEERED DOWN into her bedroom and saw the madman sprawled out on the floor, his eyes closed. Nearby, the trunk lay on its side, its contents scattered. She could see a small rivulet of blood on the man's forehead, and she hoped that he was dead.

Her only thought was of escape. If the killer was merely unconscious, then he could awaken at any moment and finish what he had started. She needed to get as far away from the house as possible.

With cautious steps, she descended. The killer's limp body lay at the foot of the ladder. She would have to move over him in order to reach the doorway and freedom. She reached the bottom rung, took a deep intake of breath, and without exhaling, stepped over the killer. She took great pains in her movements, so as not to touch the man or even disturb the air around him. She didn't want to take any chances of awakening the sleeping monster.

As the killer had stated, time was relative, so it felt to her as if the climb down the ladder had taken minutes. In reality, she knew that only a few seconds had elapsed.

As she cleared the madman's body, she released her held breath. She reached out for the door and began to turn the knob. Before she could do so, a hard blow slammed her from behind and stole the air from her lungs.

A silent scream came from her mouth, but only God could hear it, since she had no air to propel it beyond her mind. In her head, however, the shriek was deafening.

The killer spun her around and smashed her against the wall. The blade of his knife pressed against her throat with enough force that she could feel it slicing slowly into her skin. Terror overwhelmed her beyond the point of rational thought, and she couldn't even comprehend the need to fight back.

She felt Ackerman's hot breath on her face as he said, "Found you."

Behind the serial killer, a buzzing sound filled the bedroom. The baking timer lay on the floor where the killer had dropped it, and the device was going off.

Ackerman turned to look at the small device but kept the knife firmly in place. He turned back to her and stared deep into her eyes, as if trying to invade the soul that dwelt within. "Time's up."

# FOUR

THE DREAM ALWAYS started the same. With the darkness, came memories and pain. Every night, Marcus Williams found himself trapped in a prison without walls. His recollections painted a dark portrait that didn't simply reside somewhere deep within his subconscious. He had seen it with his own eyes. The world of his memories and the setting of his nightmares had left a stain on his soul and blood on his hands—neither of which could ever truly be washed away.

Like countless others before him, he had begun his career as a young police officer with a head filled by ideals like *justice will prevail* and *good always triumphs over evil.* It didn't take him long to discover that the old cliché of justice being blind was fairly accurate, and more often than not, evil was better funded than good. He had sat on the outside, looking in on a world fueled more by money and power than by the long-forgotten concepts of honor and virtue.

During his time as a protector of the peace, he witnessed many atrocities. He beheld injustices that consisted not only of the acts that men committed, but also of the punishment, or lack thereof, that they received. He had seen good people, who had committed crimes out of desperation and necessity, sentenced to the harshest degree of the law. By the same token, he witnessed justice turn a blind eye to certain individuals because of the size of their bank account or the amount of power that they wielded.

His time as a caretaker of chaos had left him not only haunted by painful memories, but also plagued by soul-shaking visions that tormented him upon entering the deepest recesses of sleep.

His heart raced as the events of a fateful night from his past played out deep inside his mind. He knew that he was dreaming and that nothing could erase the events recorded forever upon the pages of his memory. The fact that it wasn't real didn't make the experience seem any less authentic. He could feel the same chill in the air. He could smell the same scent of the river nearby. And he could hear the same scream that called to him on that night; a scream that his dreams would never allow him to forget.

Through the endurance of countless nights of restless sleep, he had learned that if he focused hard enough and screamed with enough ferocity inside his mind, the echoes from his subconscious triggered a reaction in the conscious side of his brain. Through the act of silently screaming, he could break the chains of sleep and save himself from reliving the painful events of his past.

He awoke alone, drenched in sweat from forehead to rib cage. The clock read *5:15*.

He stumbled down the hallway to a room containing the device that would transport him from semiconsciousness to alert coherence. Entering the kitchen, he headed to his trusty coffeepot. *Caiffeine…every aspiring insomniac's best friend.*

Moving to the living room, he flipped on the television and cycled through the channels. He sat on a folding chair. Unpacked boxes surrounded him. The television and the coffeepot had been the first items to be unboxed.

Only five channels came in clearly, and he found himself forced to choose between a multitude of infomercials or a local news program. Since he had yet to come to the place in his life where he felt the need for knives that could cut through a tin can as easily as a tomato, a boxed set of the greatest country songs from the 60s, or a can of spray-on hair replacement, he switched to Channel Four News.

As he sipped his coffee and watched, an image flashed onto the screen that drew his attention. He was certain that he had never seen the face that stared back at him, but he sensed a vague familiarity in the man's features that he couldn't pinpoint. He also recognized something in the man's eyes that he knew all too well. The man's gray eyes reflected a hunger that dwelled in the darkest regions of a tainted soul. He saw a raging fire inside the man and knew that neither food nor drink could quench his thirst or appease his never-ceasing appetite. He had seen a similar hunger on a night from his past that he could never remember to forget. He turned up the volume.

"Most recently, Ackerman is believed to be responsible for the brutal murders of three men, including two Colorado State Troopers. But there was an unexpected twist to the story. Ackerman allegedly took one of the men's family hostage and forced them to play a sadistic game. This is what a representative from the Colorado State Patrol, Major Christian Steinhoff, had to say at a recent press conference."

The image cut to a man at a podium who expounded upon the details of the incident with the family, describing the miraculous survival of one of the victims, a woman named Emily Morgan. A picture of the woman flashed onto the screen. Her pale features seemed luminescent.

"Francis Ackerman Jr. is considered armed and highly dangerous. He is believed to be responsible for the brutal slayings of an undetermined number of men and women since his recent escape from a mental institution in Michigan and is wanted for questioning in several other ongoing criminal investigations. In an interview yesterday afternoon, a representative from the Dimmit County Sheriff's Department told one of our reporters, Julian Harms, that this man will likely be remembered as one of the most prolific serial killers in U.S. history... In other news, presidential candidate and front runner, Paul Phillips, will be speaking in San Antonio..."

In the last moment before politics replaced the killer's image, Marcus felt frightened and yet curious in regard to the killer from the TV. *What could drive a man to commit such terrible acts?* He realized that the world was a vast sea of infinite possibilities. Any number of circumstances could account for an ordinary man's departure from the world of the mentally stable and socially acceptable into the realm of the criminally insane.

He considered that—sometime in the not too distant future—a scientist might discover that the root of all serial killers and violent offenders did not stem from a connection with an abused childhood or dark suggestion from the realm below. Perhaps, the root of insanity was actually yellow dye number five or red dye number forty, either of which could be found in the common Twinkie.

The concept of *Insanity by Reason of Twinkie* brought a smile to his face and allowed him to stop thinking about the killer from the TV and, if only for a few precious seconds, the dark deeds of his own past.

AFTER SHUTTING OFF the TV and moving to the porch, Marcus decided to explore the large farm he had inherited from his aunt, Ellen, who to the best of his knowledge had never even seen a farm, let alone owned one. Ellen had raised him after the murder of his parents. According to a note left with her last will and testament, the ranch had been her dream.

Now, it was his dream—a new beginning.

As he sat on his new front porch, he stared awe-struck at the early morning sky. He wondered if anyone else ever looked at the sky with a similar sense of wonder. Was it a miracle of divine creation to them, or was it more like a priceless work of art that had been locked away, forgotten, and never looked upon with curious eyes? For the first time in a long time, he felt at peace.

But his peace was short-lived. As a sense of awareness crept up his spine, it faded away like a mirage. *I'm not alone. I'm being watched.*

Fear extended its cold fingers throughout his body, but he pushed the feeling away as best he could. A man like him wasn't supposed to be frightened. He was supposed to be strong. He was supposed to be the protector, not the victim. He was supposed to be the shepherd, not the lamb. It was the worst kind of fear, a menace without a name. He had never been afraid of a danger that he could see and fight. The only thing that scared him was the unknown. When his time did come, he planned to go down swinging.

He couldn't help but remember the eyes of the predator from the television. *Francis Ackerman Jr.*

He tried to convince himself that his dread was merely the product of an overactive imagination, but a former cop's intuition told him differently.

Out of the corner of his eye, he thought he caught a glimpse of movement. With a quick look in that direction, he could find no trace of the beast that stalked him.

A thousand questions raced through his mind. *What are the killer's methods? Does he carry a gun?*

In his experience, men like Ackerman didn't attain the same satisfaction from killing with a gun as they did with knives or bare hands. That could work in his favor, but it didn't always hold true.

He reasoned that remaining watchful and waiting for the killer to make a mistake might be the best plan, the best offense being a good defense. But he hated defense. He favored action over reaction, but only if the action was properly calculated.

He thought that he heard a noise to his right, but his heart beat with such force that he wondered if the sound had really come from within his own chest.

He watched.

He waited.

A few minutes passed, but nothing happened.

He felt foolish. *Maybe the only real threat is the impending danger of cabin fever?* After all, he had grown up in a place where another person was seldom a stone's throw away. Now, he was truly alone for perhaps the first time in his life.

He pushed away the still-lingering sensation of dread and decided to continue with his planned exploration. He looked toward the horizon and spotted a small hill in the distance that would give him a better vantage point to see at least a partial layout of his new property.

Upon arrival at the hill, he sat down and leaned against a lone tree, converting dry ground and tree trunk into a makeshift recliner. He gazed across the South Texas plain and realized for the first time why they called it God's country. It wasn't simply because only God could have made such beauty, but also because if he were to scream as loudly as his lungs would allow, God would be the only one to hear him.

The memory of his aunt's death crept into his mind and cast a shadow on his newfound peace. She was gone, but not forgotten. She could no longer laugh or cry or feel joy or pain, all of which were true tests of one's verifiable existence. Yet, somehow, he couldn't seem to wrap his mind around the thought that he would never see her again. Never again would he tell her how much she meant to him. Never again would he wake up to the smell of pancakes and bacon—at least not ones that would taste as sweet as the ones she had made for him. Never again would he be able to ask for her advice and counsel and receive the small tidbits of wisdom that lightened the burdens of his past and gave his tired soul a few moments of serenity.

*Or will I get to see her again?*

He had no real answers. He believed in heaven and hell and felt confident that his aunt was making her famous pancakes for the divine creator of the heavens and Earth at that very moment.

He just wasn't sure whether he would get to see her wonderful new home. He suspected that his destination would be different.

He dug into the dry ground and pulled up a handful of loose soil. He let it slip from his grasp and be scattered by the wind. As the handful of earth was taken by the breeze, he could almost feel the fragility of his own life and of all life that existed on the planet. He knew that this was the way of the world: to be held by the hands of creation, live for only a second in the eyes of Father Time, be scattered to the wind, and then be returned to the ground.

THE MAN IN the dark shirt watched Marcus from a distance. He lowered his binoculars. Earlier, the observation of his quarry had almost elevated into interaction when he was sure that Marcus had sensed his presence.

A disturbing look had passed over the younger man's face. He was sure that he had made little sound, if any, but somehow Marcus had known he was there. He had ceased his movements and remained still and invisible.

As he watched, he saw the same look in the young

man's eyes that he saw when he looked in the mirror at his own gaze. He saw the soul of a predator and the instincts of a killer.

He consulted his watch. It was time to go. He had a feeling that the games would begin soon. And he would need to be ready.

# FIVE

MARCUS GLANCED AT his watch, and the hour shocked him. He had spent the biggest part of the day in quiet contemplation, yet it had felt like only a few minutes. In all his life, he had never stopped to smell the roses, never taken the time to relax. He had the time to do so now, and the sensation was liberating.

He stood, dusted off his jeans, and continued his exploration. He crossed a large meadow filled with tall, brown grass and topped another hill. From the hill's apex, he could see a farmhouse in the distance and felt relieved to learn that his neighbor was a lot closer than he had previously imagined. He had learned from Maggie that his only neighbor was a kind woman whose husband had died.

He tried to think of her name. *Marsha...Marjorie... Maureen. Maureen Hill...that's it.*

The distance to the house blurred its details in his vision. It was white and two stories, but he could see little else. He checked his watch again. With prior engagements, he didn't have time for a visit.

He retraced his steps back home, cleaned himself up, and drove into his new hometown of Asherton.

THE DEPUTY KNOCKED on the ornate oak door to the Sheriff's office. "Come in," a voice said from the other side.

The elegance of the Sheriff's department shocked Marcus. The intricate woodwork, plush leather chairs, and soothing natural tones of the walls and decor seemed to be stolen from a New York law firm. It was not the kind of ambience he had expected to find at a local sheriff's office. Then again, he'd never been in a local sheriff's office, and television was his only frame of reference. He knew better than to believe everything he saw on TV.

He stepped into the office, and the deputy closed the door behind him. The Sheriff sat behind a beautiful mahogany desk, watching a film of some kind on a computer screen. The Sheriff didn't turn to greet him. The older man seemed hypnotized. His interest piqued, he moved around the desk enough to see the screen.

As he rounded its corner, he scanned the top of the desk. The papers and files formed neat, tidy stacks. He noticed a file under one of the stacks with his name on it.

*Great. Second day in town and they've already put together a file on me.*

His eyes darted over the other papers. Nothing of importance. Files labeled with the name *Francis Ackerman Jr.* A flyer for an auction, a two-story white house displayed prominently on its face. Several of the typical bureaucratic forms that filled the tedium of most cops' lives. He thought back on the hours he had spent filling out reports, hours that should have been spent on the street protecting and serving. *But it's all part of the job.*

His eyes moved to the computer screen. A slight man with glasses filled the display and spoke in a calm, quiet voice. A feeling of déjà vu washed over him at the sight of the man. The man's face and eyes seemed to prompt a recollection that swirled at the edge of his consciousness, but the grainy image and camera angle lacked the detail necessary to make a connection. The video looked like some type of clinical trial.

"Today, we're going to be performing a recreation of a traumatic event that occurred in the life of Albert DeSalvo,

better known as the Boston Strangler. I have documented
the exact procedure in my journals and will be videotaping
the entire process. I plan to observe the boy's reactions to
the event over the next week and conduct a few behavioral
tests before moving on to the next experiment."

The man, who Marcus assumed was some type of doctor or psychiatrist, reached up and stopped the camera.
The display flashed, and a bare white room containing a
cot and a toilet replaced the image of the doctor. A young
boy sat on the cot and stared vacantly at the wall. In a moment, the door to the room opened, and the doctor entered.

"Hello, Francis," the doctor said. "We're going to play
a game."

The Sheriff reached up and pressed a key on the keyboard. The image on the screen froze, and the look on the
boy's face gave Marcus chills. The expression of pure terror etched across the child's features reminded him of an
illustration he had once seen of Dante's Inferno. In that
image, a demon tortured a soul that possessed an expression similar to the boy's. He wondered if the scene before
him now was all that different.

"I think I'm going to be sick," the Sheriff said under
his breath.

"What are you watching?"

The Sheriff seemed to register that he had entered for
the first time and said, "Marcus. Hello. Where are my
manners? Go ahead and have a seat." The Sheriff gestured toward one of the leather chairs in front of the desk.

Marcus sat down and repeated his question. "What was
that?"

The Sheriff shook his head, and a look of disgust contorted his features. "That was a recording that a friend of
mine at the FBI's Behavioral Analysis Unit just sent me.
They have hours upon hours of this. The bureau refers to

them as the Ackerman tapes. I don't know if you've heard anything about it, but Francis Ackerman is suspected to be traveling through this area. We, of course, don't know that for sure, but I contacted an old friend at the bureau and asked him to send me some more info. I want to be prepared, just in case. It's a fascinating story really. Anyway, I wanted you to stop by so we could—"

"What's a fascinating story?"

"Ackerman. I'm sure you've seen something about it on TV?"

"I don't watch much TV. I'm more of a book and movie kinda guy. If I am watching TV and a news story about murder comes on, I usually change the channel."

"Really. Well, the long and short of it is that Francis Ackerman Sr. was a twisted individual. He was a second-rate psychology professor. His theories and papers were pretty much ignored by the medical community. Basically, he had a theory that killers were made and not born— pure products of their environment. He blamed society for creating these monsters. I'm not a psychologist or a psychiatrist or whatever you're supposed to be, but from what I gather, most experts agree that the root of violent crime and abhorrent behavior stems from a combination of both. Certain environmental factors causing a reaction in people with certain genetically inherited characteristics. After all, most people who suffer a traumatic event during childhood don't grow up to be serial killers. And not all killers had traumatic childhoods."

"Didn't the FBI release a study a while back that stated that something like three quarters of killers suffered some type of abuse during childhood?"

The Sheriff nodded. "Apparently, you don't always change the channel. You're right. Nature versus nurture is a huge debate in the behavior and personality camp. Both sides seem to have compelling evidence. That's probably why most experts believe it to be a combination of many factors. Ackerman Sr. wanted so desperately to make a name for himself that he decided that the only way to prove his theories would be to conduct real-life experiments upon a child—his own son."

"What? He wanted to prove that he could make his own son go crazy?"

"That's exactly what he set out to do. He wanted to prove that he could take a normal child and create a psychopath. Close your eyes for a moment. Imagine that you're a very young boy. Then, think of every bad thing that has ever happened in the life of every bad person. The tragic events that molded them into monsters. Abuse, physical and psychological. Torture. Death. Anything you can think of that no child should ever see or experience. Now imagine that all of those things happened to you."

Marcus slowly opened his eyes. "My God," he whispered. "But that would make anyone lose their mind. It doesn't prove anything."

"That's the worst part. Ackerman Sr. thought that his experiments would provide insight into the minds of killers and ultimately save lives. He thought that his work would light the way to finding a cure for abhorrent behavior. He expected to be a hero. Of course, he understood that everyone would be shocked and outraged at what he had done, but he planned to move overseas and continue his work after his findings were revealed. He planned to create a vicious killer and then cure him. But when his work was discovered, as you said, it didn't prove anything. The bottom line was that he was a poor psychologist."

"I'd say he was a lot worse than that. Anyone who could do that to their own son has to have more than a few loose screws."

"Precisely. He set out to prove the nurture theory, but ultimately he gave credence to the nature theory as well. Many psychologists surmised that Ackerman Sr. was broken to begin with and simply passed his psychosis along to his son. Either way, this kid went through hell for no good reason."

"Is there ever a good reason?"

"I suppose not."

"What happened to the father?"

"Same thing that happens to every mad scientist. His creation turned on him."

Silence hung in the air for a moment.

"That's one heck of a story," Marcus said.

"Yes, it is, but that's just the beginning. Now, we're left to deal with the monster that he created. The good doctor wanted to prove that he could construct a murderer, and he succeeded. His son will go down in history as one of the most notorious."

The Sheriff seemed to stare off at something that only he could see. "He's extremely intelligent and plays these elaborate games, but he's also reckless. He kills at random, at least on the surface. Doesn't care about being caught. He definitely falls into the mixed category of killers, those displaying traits of both the organized and disorganized offender. Of course, that's the FBI's investigative classification system for an UNSUB. But even if we think in terms of the Holmes and DeBurger method, which focuses more on classifying the killer by motive, he's still a mix. A cross between a hedonist thrill killer, who derives a sadistic pleasure from the process of killing, and a power/control killer, whose primary motive is controlling and dominating the victim.

"He's a mystery from a psychiatric standpoint as well. Before he escaped, the doctors pored over him. Is he a narcissist? A true sociopath? Does he have emotions, or is he devoid? Does he feel remorse? Hell, some even believed that Ackerman was schizophrenic. During their sessions, one doctor would come to a conclusion, and the next would come in only to have Ackerman's reactions lead him down another path."

"Sounds to me like he was screwing with them."

"That could be, but one of the shrinks had a different theory. This doctor, I forget his name, watched all of the tapes Ackerman Sr. made. He noticed that eventually the boy would become whatever his father wanted. If he wanted him to kill, he killed. If he wanted him to lack emotion, then the boy suppressed his feelings and became stone. This doctor felt that Ackerman had merely been programmed to unconsciously and intuitively become whoever the shrinks wanted him to be. If the nature of the questions seemed to be trying to prove that he felt no remorse, then he showed no remorse—on the outside, at least. And vice versa. That's why he's such an interesting case. He's really not his own man. He often imitates other killers and not just those from real life, but also those found in pop culture. It's almost as if he doesn't kill for himself. It's like he's trying to give the world what they expect a crazed killer to be. He's playing the role that he feels was assigned to him."

Marcus considered this for a moment and then, wanting to change the subject, said, "No offense, but you seem to know a lot about serial killers for a local sheriff."

The Sheriff laughed. "In another life, I was a special agent with the FBI. I worked out of the Behavioral Analysis Unit. Loved the work, but I didn't get to see much of my daughter. It was as much a calling as it was a job. Shortly after my wife…passed away, this position came open, and

I took it. With this job, I was home almost every night. Things worked out for the best. I don't regret it one bit."

He registered that the Sheriff volunteered his lack of regret without being prompted. He wondered who the Sheriff was trying to convince, his guest or himself?

The Sheriff continued. "That's my story. Why don't you give me yours?"

"Not much to tell. Born and raised in New York. Used to be a homicide detective there. The work didn't agree with me. My aunt passed away, and I inherited a small ranch outside of town."

"A bit young to have been a detective, aren't you?"

He shrugged. "There were a lot of cops that agreed with you."

"Hmm, apparently not all of them."

"Meaning?"

"I made a few phone calls and talked to one of your former commanding officers."

His chest tightened. *That can't be good.*

The Sheriff hesitated a moment, as if gauging his reaction. "The gentleman I talked to said that you were a fine officer and a brilliant detective."

"Really?" He tried to hide his shock but realized that he had failed miserably.

"He seemed to like you, and so does my daughter. That's good enough for me. Don't worry. I'm not going to give you the *don't break my little girl's heart* speech. She's a big girl. She can take care of herself. I just wanted to take a moment to get to know you a little better and welcome you to Asherton. You seem like a good kid, and the fight at the bar didn't appear to be your fault. But this isn't New York. I'm the law here. Keep your nose clean, and we'll get along just fine. Did you fill out a statement about the incident from last night?"

"Yes, sir, your deputy took care of it."

The Sheriff stood. "Good. If you need anything, just let me know. Maybe we can talk more later, but I really need to get back to work." The Sheriff extended a hand, and Marcus took it. "Thanks for coming in."

Marcus stood and moved to the door. As he was about to walk though the entryway, the Sheriff said, "And Marcus…don't break my little girl's heart."

# SIX

MAGGIE SCRUBBED HER hands with soap and water. She had done so five times within the span of thirty minutes, which exceeded her average.

She wasn't afraid of germs or dirt. She didn't necessarily feel unclean. She just had a compulsion to wash her hands and make sure that things were in their proper places. She imagined that her psychology professors would attribute her behaviors to a minor imbalance of serotonin in her brain, but she had never sought treatment. Her compulsions didn't affect her everyday life, and she could overcome them, if necessary. But she had always noted that the small urges—especially the hand washing—increased in ferocity when she was nervous.

She dried her hands and stared at her reflection in the mirror. She took a deep breath and washed her hands for a sixth time.

She exited the bathroom of The Magnolia Bakery and walked into the kitchen. She found Alexei, the bakery's owner, straining noodles in preparation for her and Marcus's dinner. Two young children, a boy and a girl, skittered around his legs and banged utensils on pots and pans.

"My little matryoshkas, please, settle down. Did your mother give you the Mountain Dew before she dropped you off?" Alexei grumbled something more in Russian under his breath.

She smiled. "Do you want me to get them out of your hair?"

"What hair?" He rubbed the bald spot on the crown of

his head. "I've already pulled it all out. Don't you need to get ready?"

"I'm as ready as I'm going to be," she said, with a slight tremble in her voice.

He set down the strainer and raised his eyebrows. "Nervous?"

"Not too bad."

"Let me see your hands."

She rolled her eyes but thrust out her arms. He ran his hands over her skin and sniffed her palms. "How many times have you washed your hands in the past hour?"

"I'm fine. I'm really not that nervous."

"Maggie, you're trembling. If you are not nervous, then I am President of United States. Settle down. Just be yourself. This boy can't help but fall madly in love with you."

The date wasn't the only thing that she was nervous about, but she couldn't share that with Alexei. "Thank you, Mr. President. But I'm fine…really." She looked down at the kids as they scurried around Alexci's legs. "I'll take the kids upstairs with me. I think they might be able to help me with a little experiment. You just focus on dinner."

"As you wish, my dear Magd—"

She pressed a finger over his lips. "I shoulda never told you. Come on, kids." She took the children by the hands and led them toward the door.

He chuckled. "I think it's a beautiful name."

She didn't acknowledge him.

MARCUS ASCENDED THE stairs with slow, deliberate steps. It had been a long time since he'd been on a real date, or at least one where he cared about the outcome. He had forgotten about the butterflies. He knew that most people felt the winged creatures swirl in their guts during moments of anxious anticipation, but his butterflies seemed to have razorblade wings.

He heard footsteps and looked up, but the face that greeted him was not the one he expected. Andrew Garrison, the local Realtor, smiled as he approached. "Hello. Marcus, right?"

He had met Garrison when he picked up the keys to the ranch. They had been cordial, but there was something in the man's eyes that didn't sit well with him; an intensity that shouldn't have been there. Sandy blonde hair topped Garrison's head, and he possessed a trim athletic build.

*Good-looking guy.* He felt a twinge of jealousy and a hint of suspicion to find Garrison coming down Maggie's stairs, but he dismissed the emotions. He had neither the right nor the reason to feel either one.

"That's right."

"I heard about what happened last night. Don't worry about them. When I first moved here, Glenn gave me a hard time too. But most of the people around here aren't like him."

"You're not from here?"

"No, I've only been here a couple months. It's a nice place to live. My commission checks aren't quite what they were in the city, but the cost of living is so much lower that it evens out."

As they met on the stairs, Marcus fought the urge to take up more than his fair share of the stairwell. He recognized the feeling as the instinct to establish dominancy, an impulse left over from man's more primitive days. He always tried to overcome such urges and gave Garrison three quarters of the path.

"Excuse me. Have a nice night," Garrison said, squeezing past.

He nodded and continued to ascend. He knocked on

Maggie's door, and she called for him to come in. He entered, and her voice greeted him from down the hall. "Have a seat. I'll be out in a sec."

He moved toward the couch but examined the apartment as he did so. As he gazed around the room, he tried not to focus his analytical spotlight upon her, but he couldn't help it. His cop instincts were too strong, and he recognized that there was something off. It took him a moment to put his finger on it, but then he realized. It wasn't what was there, but what was absent.

He peered into the kitchen and down the hallway and found more of the same. There wasn't an actual photo in sight. No family portraits. No captured memories of cookouts or sunny days at the beach. Tasteful decor filled the space, but there was something cold and distant about it.

He also noted the absence of dust. Upon a cursory examination, he reasoned that every corner of Maggie's dwelling would stand up to the white glove test. More than that, every picture and grouping was in precise symmetric arrangement. Not a single picture hung askew. Everything seemed in perfect balance.

It didn't tell him much. He hadn't even seen the whole apartment, but it was still a piece to the puzzle that he filed away in his memory banks. Every investigation had its pieces.

He closed his eyes and chastised himself. *This isn't an investigation. You're not a cop. Switch off.*

When he opened his eyes, he jumped back in surprise. Two young children stood a foot in front of him. They gazed up with wide, curious eyes. *Maggie's kids?*

"Have you seen the Mama Load?" the little boy said.

He blinked in rapid succession. "I...I don't think so."

"Me neither, but I really want to go. My grandpa said that he would take me."

With apprehension, Marcus said, "What's the Mama Load?"

"You know, where Davy Crockett killed the bear when he was only three."

He laughed, but the little boy didn't seem to find it humorous. "You mean The Alamo."

"That's what I said. The Mama Load."

He knelt down and stuck out his hand. "I'm Marcus. What're your names?"

The little boy shook his hand as if they had just concluded a business deal. "I'm Alex, and that's my little sister, Abigail. Do you know why sharks can't sleep?"

"Well...I..."

MAGGIE WASHED HER hands again.

She had been ready for the date for quite some time, but she wanted to conduct a little experiment with Marcus. Kids always seemed to be a great judge of character, and a man's reactions to them could provide substantial insight into his personality.

She checked the time. Five minutes had passed since she'd sent in the troops, so she reasoned that Marcus should have been sufficiently flustered.

As she approached the living room, she didn't hear the patter of rambunctious feet or the howling of the two hyperactive kids. All was quiet. She peered around the corner and found Marcus on the couch with the two children on his lap.

The kids listened with rapt attention while Marcus spoke in a strange, throaty voice. His impression reminded her more of Yoda than a *Sesame Street* character, but she gave him an A+ for effort.

"I, lovable, furry old Grover, am the monster at the end of this book. And you were so SCARED! I told you and told you there was nothing to be afraid of... Oh, I am so embarrassed. The End."

"Again!"

"Okay, one more time."

"All right, kids," Maggie said. "It's time to head back downstairs."

"But we want to stay with you and Marcus."

She cocked a sideways grin at him. "Sorry, kids. Marcus is all mine tonight."

As they stood and exited, he said, "Yours?"

"Goodness, no. Our chef for the evening is babysitting his grandkids, so I offered to watch them while he worked."

"Oh."

"Relieved or disappointed?"

He seemed to ponder her question. "A little of both, I guess."

As THEY ATE, Maggie stared into Marcus's eyes and noticed an anomaly. "Your eyes are different colors."

"Yeah, most people don't notice. My eyes are kinda gray-green, but the right one is half brown. It's called sectoral heterochromia."

"Is that some kind of disorder? Nothing contagious, I hope?"

He laughed. "It can be related to certain syndromes, but I don't think I have any of them. It can also be a sign that you had a twin you absorbed in the womb. They call it chimerism. In that case, I could actually have multiple sets of DNA in different body parts. I don't think I have that either. I also read once that some believe it to be a sign that you're descended from Swedish royalty, or something like that. I think I'm just a dude with a funny-colored eye."

"I told you that you were an odd man."

"I didn't dispute it. What about you? You have any oddities?"

She straightened her silverware and folded her napkin into a perfectly symmetrical square. "No, I'm completely normal."

He grinned. "Nobody's completely normal."

"I am."

"Really. You're not mildly obsessive compulsive?"

She started to open her mouth but stopped. After a moment, she said, "What makes you say that?"

"I pay attention. Your apartment is impeccably clean— not a single picture or decoration is out of place. Every grouping is perfectly balanced. When you eat, you cut every bite into the same size. You make sure that the silverware you're not using is in perfect alignment. You folded your napkin into a square. And when you put the sweetener into your tea, you made sure that the markings on the two packets lined up before you opened them. You even put one back because it was longer than the other packet."

She felt naked before him. She started to say something, decided against it, and stared down at the table.

He reached across and laid a hand over hers. "There's nothing wrong with wanting the world to be in order and make sense."

"But my compulsions don't make any sense. They're irrational. I don't have a good reason for doing them. I just feel like that's the way things should be done. Most people don't notice, so I try to hide it. It makes me feel like a freak."

"Does it make sense to you?"

"What do you mean?"

"Do all the things that you do make sense to you? We each see the world through different eyes. We all have our nuances…our little tics. I'll give you an example. I always sit facing any points of ingress. I always know what's behind me. When I walk into a room, the first thing I do is scan it to find the entrances and exits. I consider what could be used as a weapon in this space. I play out in my mind what I would do if someone walked in the door with a gun. Where's the best place to take cover? What's the best route to flank an armed assailant who just entered? And other things. Who in the room could pose a threat? Who's potentially armed? What's here that's out of place? What's missing? All that runs through my head every time I enter a room. Some people call that cop instincts or training. I call it paranoia."

Marcus squeezed her hand, and she met his gaze. "I don't have a good reason to do all that," he said. "Nobody's after me. I don't have any enemies. Even back in New York, I was never in a restaurant that somebody shot up. Maybe one day it'll save my life, but probably not. Odds are that I'll never be in that situation. But I can't help but run through it. It's just my nature."

Her face brightened. "Thank you."

"For what?"

"For being stranger than me."

They laughed together, and the butterflies in her stomach finally found a perch. After they finished, she cleaned up and offered to take him on a tour of Asherton. The town was small, and the tour didn't last long. She tried to live in the moment and stay focused on enjoying the evening, but her mind kept wandering. She couldn't help but play out the events that would soon take place. "How about I introduce you to your neighbor? She's a wonderful lady."

"Sounds good to me."

She drove out of town in the direction of Maureen Hill's home. After a moment on the road, Marcus said, "Where do you work at, Maggie? Obviously, you help out at the bar where we met, but do you have a day job? And what's Maggie short for, by the way?"

She ignored the second question. "I work at Garrison Realty."

"Oh, okay."

She noticed something in his voice. *Realization? Relief?* She wondered about the reaction for a second but continued, "I'm just doing that until I finish my psychology degree. Believe it or not, I used to be one of my father's deputies, but…that didn't work out. I've considered staying within law enforcement, though. Maybe even applying to the FBI."

"I don't want to overstep the second-date rules here, but you and your father seem to have a bit of a strained relationship."

"You could say that. My father is a good man, but he… well, like you said, he has his nuances. What about your parents?"

A pained look fell over him, and she immediately regretted the question. "They died when I was young. Lots of great memories, though. You haven't answered my question about your name."

"And I'm not going to."

"Oh, come on. Now I have to know. What is it? Marjorie? Margaret? Marigold?"

"I'd rather not."

"I tell you what, I'll tell you my middle name. Believe me, yours can't be any worse than mine. And I've never told anyone other than the IRS."

She bit her lip and thought for a moment. "My name is Magdalania."

He laughed, and she shot him a withering glance.

"I've never heard that one before."

"Shut up."

"It's very pretty."

"Shut up."

"All right, you listen to my middle name and see if you can keep from laughing. My given name is Marcus Aurelius Williams."

She tried to keep a straight face. She clenched her lips shut and forced the corners of her mouth from rising, but she couldn't contain it. The laughter burst from her.

"What'd I tell you? It's hard to top that one."

"That is pretty bad," she said, between chuckles. She looked over at his smiling face and gazed into his strangely colored eyes. She had never felt quite the same way around anyone, even though they couldn't have met under worse circumstances.

She pulled into Maureen Hill's driveway and shut off the car. "Ready to meet your neighbor?"

# SEVEN

SEEING IT UP close for the first time, Maureen Hill's two-story white house seemed vaguely familiar to Marcus, but he couldn't pinpoint the origins of the memory. He reasoned that he had probably seen a hundred homes just like it over the course of his lifetime. He looked over at Maggie. The waning sunlight shone through her blonde hair, framing her in radiance and painting her as an ethereal being descending from a realm of light.

"Hold on a sec," he said, as she was about to exit the vehicle.

"What is it?"

"Come closer. You've got something in your hair."

He reached out and brushed away a strand of golden hair. He let his fingertips continue down the side of her face and travel along her jawline to the bottom of her chin. He gently guided her mouth toward his.

Their lips touched. He restrained the kiss at first, but it increased in intensity with every second of contact.

His hand moved to the back of her head. He felt her hands slide across his chest.

He couldn't decide whether the sudden warmth in the vehicle originated from the summer sun pouring in through the windows, or if her touch was melting him from the inside out.

After a moment, they separated, and she said, "There really wasn't anything in my hair, was there?"

"Afraid not," he said in a whisper.

"You use that little maneuver on all the ladies?"

"Not for a long time."

She smiled. "I'm glad you broke it out of retirement." After a moment, she cleared her throat and said, "Maureen's probably watching us through the window—like the characters from one of her romance books just stepped off the page."

He chuckled. "Guess you better introduce me. Although I don't think I could live up to the hero in a romance novel."

She patted him on the shoulder. "With a little tutelage, we'll get you there."

They exited the car and walked up Maureen's front steps. He knew that the woman had lived alone since her husband's passing but received occasional visits from her children and grandchildren. Maggie had described her as the kind of person who, if you were sick or having a bad day, would concoct some sweet confection to bring a smile to your face and make you forget your troubles.

Maggie pressed the doorbell. They waited a moment, but no one came to greet them. She pressed the doorbell again. Nothing.

"That's strange."

"What?"

"She just doesn't leave very often. Even when she sees her kids, they usually come to her."

"Maybe she had to get groceries?"

Maggie shook her head. "She pays a kid from town to deliver them to her. I even told her that we might stop by today, and she never mentioned anything about being gone."

He could see the onset of fear in her eyes. He knew that it was probably his own paranoia, but his thoughts turned to Ackerman. He knocked, but with no better results. He reached out and grasped the doorknob. He twisted, and the door swung inward on its own inertia.

"HELLO?" Maggie called out but received no response.

"Okay, here's what we're gonna do. You get back in the car and drive halfway down the lane. You should be able to see anyone coming from all directions. Lock the doors and keep a sharp eye out. I'll check the house. She's probably upstairs taking a nap or something, but better safe than sorry. If I'm not back out in five minutes or you see anything strange, you get out of here. Call your father on the way."

"Why don't we just call him now?"

"Listen. Maybe it's just a stupid macho guy thing, but I'm not going to call in the cops because someone didn't answer their door. I'll check things out, and if anything's out of place, we'll go from there."

"But what if—"

"I can take care of myself."

"If something's wrong, you'll need backup."

"You're right, I will. That's why you need to be ready to call your father."

She let out a deep sigh. "Be careful."

He walked her back to the car, returned to the front door, and stepped through the entryway. He scanned his surroundings and couldn't help but notice the spotless condition of the hardwood floors, even in front of the main entrance. The floor was clear of debris and dust of any kind. He checked his shoes. A layer of dirt caked the soles.

He listened for a moment. Like a black hole waiting to consume the universe, the house exuded an eerie calm. The two-story farmhouse—which only a few moments earlier seemed to be a place of happiness, a place where grandchildren played in the backyard and freshly baked apple pies cooled on open window sills—now seemed to be a place of darkness; an ominous vortex pregnant with malignant secrets.

A voice in the back of his mind told him that something horrible awaited him, but a louder and more compelling voice told him to move forward. At that moment, he wished that he could let someone else reveal the house's secrets, but that was something he couldn't do. There could be someone in trouble here, and he had to do everything in his power to help. He wondered how much simpler his life would be if he could just walk away. "Hello?"

There was no sound.

He called out again, louder this time. "HELLO, IS ANYONE HOME?"

Nothing.

The two-story house was white with black shutters, and a wrap-around porch encompassed half its diameter. The front door opened into a spacious living room with a large picture window. Curio cabinets lined the walls with shelves populated by antique pottery and glassware. A partially open staircase was on his left and an open dining room, attached to the living room in an L-shape, sat to his right. He moved into the dining room and noticed a stack of mail on the table. Part of the stack had been opened, and part sat unread.

He looked back toward the flight of steps and decided to investigate the second story. He moved up the hardwood stairs without making a sound.

At the top, a bathroom door stood open on his left. He peered inside. The shower curtain had been pulled back, so he wouldn't have to jerk it open and pray that no one stood on the other side. A closed door waited at the far end of the hallway with two additional doors along the way. As his eyes adjusted to the dimly lit corridor, the dark wood grain of the closed door seemed to swirl and pulse like worms in an open grave.

He crept forward, hugging the right wall. He balled his fists into weapons. If his own mother had stepped out of one of the rooms, she would have found herself lying flat on her back.

A door on his left was closed, but the room on his right was open. Light beamed through the doorway, casting strange shadows upon the wall. He peeked around the corner and, seeing no immediate danger, stepped into the room.

The space contained an exercise bike, a rowing machine, a small television, and some other baffling contraptions. A layer of dust covered them all. He saw that the source of the shadows in the hallway was a tree swaying just outside the window. He checked the closet and then turned his attention to the first of the other closed doors.

He twisted the knob and pushed the door inward. He stepped to the side and scanned what portions of the room he could see from the hallway. The bed had been made with care, and decorative pillows covered its surface. A huge pile of stuffed animals, ranging from pink elephants to curious monkeys, rested in one corner. A shelf full of collectable dolls sat above the stuffed animal zoo. He checked the room but found no trace of wrongdoing.

*One more bedroom...*

*Maybe my imagination is getting the better of me? This morning, I feel a presence that turns out to be nothing, and here I am chasing shadows. Maybe I'm losing my—*

He stopped dead in his tracks.

Doubt and wishful thinking were now beyond the realm of possibility.

Blood covered the doorknob of the next room.

MARCUS'S HEART POUNDED, and his pulse throbbed. He reached out, grasped the knob, but then hesitated. Once again, he had blood on his hands. He turned the knob and gave the door a gentle push.

Blood was everywhere. The smell of rotting meat and decay filled the small space. Clumps of flies swarmed the room. Their buzzing stabbed at his consciousness like needles into his brain. He felt light-headed. The room spun. Bile rose to the back of his throat. *A man couldn't have done this…this was a monster…a demon…the devil himself.*

The newscaster had used the word "brutal" to describe the acts of random violence committed by the man named Ackerman. Now, it seemed to him that "brutal" lacked the proper depth. He searched for a more fitting word but found none. He wondered whether human language contained a word to describe such acts of lunacy. Perhaps only the language of the damned and the devil could describe the horror contained within the bedroom's four walls.

One question remained. *Where's the body?*

He surveyed the rest of the room. Within the reflection on the dresser mirror, he noticed something out of place. The image on the mirror showed a pair of bloody hands jutting out over the door that he had just opened.

He turned around. Although he knew the image would be etched into his memory until the day he died, he pushed the door closed to reveal the bloody body of a kind and innocent woman.

Two large spikes pierced her hands, nailing her to the wall. She had been stripped naked. Long cuts defiled the flesh. They were not quick slashes or stabs. The killer had stuck the knife in just far enough to break the skin and then ran the blade down the entire length of the body.

He prayed to God that she had lost consciousness from

the trauma of her wounds, but he knew that a killer like Ackerman would possess the knowledge necessary to prevent shock and prolong agony. At some point, he guessed that she had bled to death.

He tried to turn away but was unable to keep himself from thinking like a cop. He noticed that signs of decay had taken hold. The body showed evidence of hypostasis, and a milky film covered the eyes. Flies swarmed the remains.

He noted that things were wrong somehow. There was something about the hands and the blood, but he couldn't concentrate. Emotion eclipsed deduction.

He imagined the last moments of her life. He could see her screaming with a pain that no one should ever have to endure. He saw her executioner smiling with the same sense of pride that a painter or sculptor receives after completing a beautiful and soulful masterpiece.

The victim's cold, dead eyes were wide with unimaginable terror. They screamed out to him. They begged for help. *I could've helped her... I could have saved her.*

He knew the look in her eyes. He saw it almost every night in his dreams. *If I had gotten here sooner, she might still be alive.*

He stood transfixed. His entire body shook. Fury built up within him and boiled toward the point of eruption. It was a righteous rage, the kind that a person with a good soul feels when staring into the face of pure evil. It was the kind of rage that a father wields when confronting his child's killer, or that a mother feels after discovering that her husband has been molesting their child. He could not allow another person to endure such pain. She deserved justice, and he would see to it that justice was done.

His thoughts turned to Maggie. He ran down the hallway to the front of the house and peered through the window. The car was gone.

He checked his watch. Seven minutes had passed. *Good girl.*

*The Sheriff should be on his way, but I can't count on that.* He suspected that cellular coverage might not be comprehensive in such an isolated and unpopulated area.

He turned away from the window and moved back to the bedroom. There was only one thing that he could do for Maureen now. He scanned the room. It took only a few seconds to find a trail of blood leading toward a door on his left.

He moved with a purpose. He opened the door and discovered a set of stairs. He wasn't paying attention to the blood trail any longer. The volcano had erupted inside him, and a blanket of red had fallen over his eyes like a shroud. The flower of his righteous rage was in full bloom.

Once in the kitchen, he ran to a door leading into a small office. He opened the door with such force that it nearly came off its hinges. He moved to the closet, opened the door, and searched inside. No killer.

He exited the office and headed for another door that led into a bathroom. The shower curtain was closed. Unlike earlier, when he would have thrown it open and prayed not to find anyone, he now hoped to find a killer hiding behind the curtain. He found nothing but an empty shower stall.

He returned to the kitchen and noticed that the blood trail led to the porch. He followed the droplets of crimson liquid to the back door. He noticed the spotless condition of the mudroom and entertained the ludicrous thought of how angry the grandmother would have been that the killer had tracked her blood across the immaculate floors.

He twisted the knob, but a deadbolt secured the back door. He undid the lock and left the house of pain behind.

As he exited, he felt as if a pressure lifted. Once again, he was surrounded by blue skies and open spaces. He wondered if the house would always carry the stain of blood and the smell of death, a taint that no amount of cleaning or coats of paint could conceal.

Once again, he stood surrounded on all sides by the beauty of nature, but the world didn't seem as bright to him as it had before entering the grandmother's house. He had felt that his new home was immune to the evil that plagued the rest of the world, but now he knew that darkness and ugliness could thrive and grow even in the center of the brightest light and the most breathtaking beauty. Somehow, such knowledge made the light seem dimmer and the beauty less magnificent.

The trail of blood had stopped, and he knew that the killer could have gone in any direction. As the adrenaline faded, he realized that his prey was long gone, and the hunt was over. He saw a few buildings scattered behind the house but decided not to bother searching them.

Although he would have preferred to never set foot in the house again, it contained the closest phone. He decided that it couldn't hurt to call the authorities, in case Maggie couldn't obtain a cellular signal.

He re-entered the tainted house and dialed nine-one-one. The operator asked about the nature of the emergency. "Send the police to…" He stopped and realized that he didn't know the address.

He remembered the stack of mail on the dining room table. "Hold on." He rushed to the table and returned with one of the unopened letters. "Send the police to 91244 Foxbrook Road in Asherton, the home of Maureen Hill."

He heard the rhythmic click of a computer keyboard. "I'm not showing that address anywhere in the county, sir. Are you at the location where the police are needed now?"

"Yes." He looked back down at the envelope and noticed something strange.

"Okay, I have your location. Do you need an ambulance, sir?"

He considered the request and said, "No, but tell them to bring the coroner."

# EIGHT

THE SHERIFF STARED at the body of Maureen Hill and gazed into her milky, dead eyes. He clenched his own eyelids shut, but the tears found their way free, nonetheless. The look of pain in the lifeless orbs was familiar to him. He had seen the same fear the last time he looked into the eyes of his wife, Kathleen.

The memories flashed through his mind. Coming home. Finding her mutilated body in their living room.

She had been dead for two days. Two days, and he hadn't even noticed that her calls had ceased.

He had been in Kansas City at the time of her death, consulting on a missing persons case. But most of his time there was spent contemplating another active investigation, a serial rapist and murderer in the Virginia and Washington D.C. area. He had put a profile together for the investigators. The police used his analysis to isolate a suspect, but the man avoided capture and was on the run.

He was proud of his work on the case. The lead investigator had even thanked him personally during a press conference, stating that his profile played an integral role in identifying the possible killer. He remembered the feeling of pride he felt at the mention of his name on television. *Human nature*, he supposed. Everyone wanted his or her fifteen minutes of fame. More than that, everyone wanted to be recognized for his or her hard work and diligence.

And he was most definitely recognized for his role in the case, not by his superiors, but by the rapist and murderer he had helped to identify. With nothing to lose, the killer had decided to go after the families of his pursuers. The man raped and murdered Kathleen and then the lead investigator's wife and stepdaughter.

For him, losing Kathleen wasn't the worst part. He had dealt with death every day and knew that losing a loved one didn't require the intervention of a serial killer. Disease, a fall down the stairs, a car accident; all were constant possibilities.

But the hardest thing to stomach was the fact that *he* had killed her, that his work had been the catalyst to her demise. Even worse than that was the realization that he hadn't appreciated her while she was still alive.

He stumbled into the stairwell that led down to the kitchen and slumped against the sidewall. He thought of Kathleen. He thought of Ackerman. Then, he thought of Marcus. He straightened, wiped away the tears, and collected himself. He had a job to do.

MARCUS LAID OUT the story in detail. The Sheriff listened, letting it unfold in its entirety. Now and again, the Sheriff would ask a question, in order to clarify some small detail, but then ask him to continue. The Sheriff's chief deputy, Lewis Foster, also listened, taking notes on a small pad of paper.

Foster was a young man, late twenties or early thirties. The deputy wore a snug-fitting, tan uniform, and Marcus could see that the man spent too much time in the weight room. Foster watched with accusing eyes. He could tell that the deputy's preferred method of questioning was a thick phone book and a locked room. He knew the type—the scrawny kid who got bullied before discovering steroids. Then, Foster became the bully.

Unlike Foster, the Sheriff exuded confidence and competence, and the man's face showed no accusatory expressions or doubt.

"Quite a story," Foster said with an edge to his voice.

"Yes, a senseless tragedy," the Sheriff said. "Before I forget, Marcus, we're going to need to borrow your shoes."

"My shoes?"

"Yes, we'll need to get a casting and a sample to compare with any footprints that we may find."

He nodded and removed his shoes. The Sheriff walked them over to a young man who disappeared with them.

The Sheriff returned and said, "So you didn't actually see anyone in the house or on the property?"

"No, whoever did this was long gone by the time I got here."

"Or they never left," Foster said.

The statement caught him off guard, and his eyes narrowed at the deputy. "What's that supposed to mean?"

"I don't know. Just seems a little funny to me that a new guy moves in, and within two days, he's put a couple guys in the hospital and conveniently stumbled upon a homicide. Guess you're just unlucky, right?"

"I'm sitting here talking to an inbred moron, so things could be better."

"If it was up to me, we'd be doin' more than just talking."

"Sorry. I don't kiss on the first date."

"You cocky little—"

"Lewis, that's enough," the Sheriff said.

"It's all right, Sheriff. Let him keep talking. Someday, he's bound to say something intelligent. Kinda like the deal where they theorize that a bunch of monkeys in a room full of typewriters will eventually write Shakespeare."

Foster moved closer. "Next time, you're going to find

yourself all alone with me in a dark room. You won't be so funny then."

He cocked his head to the side, cracking his neck. When he spoke, his voice was calm and modulated. "You try that with me, and they'll take you out of that room on a stretcher."

"You threatening me?"

"No. I don't make threats. Just stating facts."

Foster made a move toward him, but the Sheriff put an arm out and stopped his advance. "Why don't you go help the boys upstairs, Lewis?"

Foster stared with fire in his eyes for a few seconds before turning and walking away.

Turning back to Marcus, the Sheriff said, "Not very good at making friends, are you?"

"I'm an acquired taste."

"You used to be a cop, so I would think that you would be able to see things from Lewis's point of view."

"I could try, sir. But, honestly, I don't think that I could get my head that far up my ass."

The Sheriff stared at him with a blank expression and scratched his goatee. "Listen, kid, I don't think that you had anything to do with this, but you're not making very good first impressions around here. And the circumstances do seem pretty suspicious, so you better watch yourself. If you're going to stick around, you need to learn a little self-control when it comes to that mouth of yours."

He nodded. "I'll try, sir."

"Good. Now, I want you to go home, get some rest, and put this whole thing out of your mind. I know that it's easier for me to say that than it is for you to do it, but I think you need to try anyway. This is our responsibility now. The best thing for you to do is to forget this house and everything in it. If you don't, it'll eat you up inside. Trust me, son, I know."

There was truth in the Sheriff's words, and he knew it. He also knew that he hated sitting on the sidelines, and it wasn't in his nature to forget. "Do I get my shoes back?"

The Sheriff shook his head. "Yes, you get your damn shoes back. If you think of anything else, here's my card. My cell number's on there."

Marcus stuck the card in his pocket. "There is one other thing that you should keep in mind when you look at this case."

"And that is?"

He glanced around the room and lowered his voice. "You have a notorious serial killer traveling through the area. It would be a terribly convenient time for anyone who had been planning a murder to execute his or her plans. Think about it. The first thing I thought of when I saw that body was Ackerman. Someone wanting to commit a murder has the perfect opportunity to do so and a completely believable fall guy. Our minds are already tainted with the knowledge that Ackerman might be in the area. I'm just saying that you need to base your investigation on the facts alone—no assumptions."

The Sheriff seemed to consider his words a moment. "Thanks, kid, but we know how to do our jobs. Put the case out of your mind. We don't need your help." The Sheriff started to turn away but looked back. "And Marcus, until this thing is cleared up, stay away from my daughter."

MARCUS SAT IN the dark and relived his experience in the grandmother's house. He wished he could forget. He prayed for the ability to put the past behind him and start a new life. He prayed to sleep and be carried off to a dream world filled with happy memories. Instead, he knew that he would be transported to a dark world of pain and suffering. A place with gray skies where the sun never graced the world. A place whose only inhabitants were monsters and their victims. A place where every surface seemed to possess teeth and a ravenous longing to consume his soul. He wondered if his dreams held a glimpse of his own personal hell.

Unlike in his dreams, he was now wide awake and reliving the day's events on his own volition. He studied every detail of the experience, searching for clues or small details that in the heat of the moment he may have overlooked. He had been blessed with the gift of a powerful photographic memory, and with this ability, he could transform himself into a reasonable facsimile of a human computer. He could store the data gathered in the house and re-access it later from his mental databanks. It wasn't quite as easy as using a computer terminal, but he often discovered something that he had missed on first glance.

And he knew he had missed something. He could feel it.

His eyes shifted back and forth, as his mind traveled over every minute detail. An observer would have seen a man staring at a wall. In reality, he didn't even notice the wall. He looked through it, into the past, into his memories.

As he had thought, there was much that he had overlooked, but he still couldn't make sense of any of it. He needed time, but a killer was on the loose. And he owed it to Maureen Hill to stop him before another suffered as she had.

He thought about Maggie. After taking her statement, her father had sent her home with one of the deputies. He decided to give her a call and see how she was holding up.

He sifted through a few papers lying on his kitchen table. Two items drew his attention. One was Maggie's number scrawled on a small sheet of paper. The other was a tattered business card that her father had given him after the questioning.

Both Maggie and her father had given him their numbers within the past day. Each number represented a different path, one of love and life and fond memories and one of pain and death. One path offered great happiness, but if he could stop the killer, the other offered great meaning. He knew which path any normal, sane person would choose. He hated to admit it, even to himself, but the path of happiness wasn't the one that called to him.

Since he had yet to purchase a cell phone that worked in the area, he picked up the handset of an old rotary phone that had come with the house and dialed Maggie's number. He didn't need to read it from the sheet of paper. He'd only seen it once, but he had it memorized. Each subsequent ring made his heart sink. For some reason, he had expected her to be sitting by the phone awaiting his call.

"Hello," she said.

"Hi, it's Marcus. I was beginning to think you weren't home."

"I was in the shower. I've been in there since I got back to the apartment. I didn't even go into that house, but somehow I still feel dirty."

He searched for words that could comfort her. He found none. "I know what you mean."

"My God, Marcus, that poor woman. She was a wonderful person and definitely didn't deserve…not that anyone…" Her unfinished words hung in the air, and only silence transmitted over the telephone lines.

Once again, Maggie broke the silence with a question that made him cringe. "Did you ever see anything like that when you were a cop?"

*Now I remember. This is why I don't get into relationships.*

"I saw some things that I wish I could forget," he said.

Silence. She changed the subject. "We didn't really get a chance to talk at the scene, but I was wondering about what you did after you found the body. Were you in shock?"

He didn't want to talk about it anymore, but he did anyway. "I stood there, looking into her eyes. It was like she was calling out to me, screaming for help…a silent scream." Tears rolled down his face. "I felt completely powerless. It was the same feeling as when… Maybe we all have a monster inside. Maybe we all have the same capacity for evil as we do for good. I don't know. But I do know that my monster lives a little bit closer to the surface, and sometimes I can't control it." He forced a laugh. "If that doesn't scare you off, then I don't know what will."

"I'm not scared of you. Go on."

"When I looked into her eyes, I lost control. I ran through that house, and then I ran to that back door, and I…unlocked it."

His eyes grew large as his mind fixed upon the one important factor that he had missed. When he had used his memory trick earlier, he had focused on the body and the bedroom. He had yet to think of the rest of the house.

*I had to unlock the deadbolt on the back door, and it could only have been locked from the inside or with a key. The killer was gone, and unless he cleaned the blood from his feet and came back in for some reason… Someone else was in that house before me…someone other than the killer.*

"I'm going to have to let you go."

"Wait. What's going on? What did—"

He hung up the phone and ran to grab the Sheriff's business card.

A flood of urgency washed over him. He knew that the first forty-eight hours were the most important in any investigation. He wanted to look at the whole scene with this new information in mind. Maybe there was something else that he had missed, something that could only be seen once you knew that someone else had been in the house?

He spun each digit on the rotary phone, and his annoyance grew with every rotation of the antique device. After a few rings, the Sheriff said, "Hello?"

"This is Marcus, Sheriff. Where are you now?"

"I just left the crime scene. Packed everything up for the night. Why? What's happened?"

"I need you to meet me back there, as soon as possible."

"Wait a minute, I—"

"You told me to call if I thought of anything. Well, I thought of something. And it can't wait."

# NINE

MARCUS WAITED IN the driveway of Maureen Hill's beautiful home. Earlier in the day, he had wished to never set foot inside the grandmother's house again. It was a dark place that he wished he could forget.

Now, however, he needed to get back inside. The urgency to discover the truth overwhelmed him, a feeling that had once been a daily part of his life. He felt like a cop again.

In the distance, he saw headlights approaching. The car pulled into the driveway, and the Sheriff stepped out of the vehicle onto the dusty ground. "What was important enough to drag me away from my supper?"

"I've been doing a lot of thinking about what happened here. When I got home today, I kept replaying everything in my mind, searching for something I had missed, something that I overlooked. Finally, it hit me."

"What hit you?"

"Let me show you."

He led the Sheriff through the house to the kitchen.

"When I saw her upstairs, her body desecrated like that, I was so angry that I ran through the house like a madman. That's why, when I went to the back door, I didn't notice that it was locked from the inside. Which could mean that—"

"Someone else was in the house before you and locked the door behind them," the Sheriff said. The older man's face took on a dark, somber expression. "Or it could mean absolutely nothing."

The Sheriff turned to Marcus and voiced his concerns. "Say that it does mean what you think it means. Who, other than the killer, would have come in this house and not immediately reported the murder? Accomplice of some kind? And whoever it was must have taken great care not to step in any of the blood that the killer left behind. We didn't find any other sets of footprints, other than the killer's and yours. Any ideas?"

Marcus shook his head. "I was hoping that maybe this new information might shed light on some other clue. Lead us in the right direction. I don't know, I just…" He looked out the back window and noticed something strange. He walked to the back door, unlocked it, and stepped outside. The Sheriff followed.

The skyline had morphed into a glistening spectrum of reds and purples as the last fingers of the sun spread out across the darkening sky and began to lose their grip on the world. It was a sight of deep and majestic beauty. Under any other circumstance, he would have stood in awe of its magnificence. Now, however, something else had caught his eye.

A light shone in the window of one of the farm buildings behind the house.

"We checked all of the buildings and found nothing. None of them had any lights on," the Sheriff said.

"You know that old cliché about the killer returning to the scene of the crime? This time, that may hold true."

"You may be right." The Sheriff pulled up his right pant leg to reveal a holster containing a backup weapon. The elder cop pulled back the slide, checked the gun, and then handed it to Marcus. "I suppose you know how to use one of these?"

The compact nine-millimeter resembled a backup weapon that he had carried himself in another life. It had been a long time since he had held a gun. He hated guns, even though he had always been talented in their use. He loathed the fact that his only real skills seemed to be the ability to cause damage and inflict pain.

*Why couldn't I have been born a painter?*

AWARE OF THEIR presence, a dark figure moved like a shadow among the buildings behind Maureen Hill's home. He moved in the direction opposite the house. He floated unseen among the outbuildings. Then, he doubled back and swung around the far corner of the property. He circled behind Marcus and the Sheriff, preparing to spring the trap.

MARCUS AND THE Sheriff crept up to the building, trying to stay out of sight. The small toolshed had doors on both ends, and the Sheriff motioned for Marcus to enter the east door.

*Well, at least I'm getting a chance to bond with Maggie's dad.*

Marcus moved to the door and mentally prepared himself. His heart raced with adrenaline-inducing anticipation. He could feel that on the other side of the door lurked a wolf in the henhouse. It fell on him to play the part of the good shepherd and drive the wolf back into the darkness from whence it came.

Steeling himself, he entered the small shed. He scanned the room, paying special attention to the corners, but found no one on first glance.

The shed contained all manner of tools and equipment. Woodworking implements and devices that he guessed would be used in the butchering of animals littered the shelves. The shed was larger than the impression given by its exterior. The inside consisted of one open room lined with several rows of tall shelves.

He had expected the shed to provide little cover to someone trying to avoid detection, but he had been mistaken. It offered several places to hide.

With cautious movements, he checked every row of the shelving.

A cold and foreboding silence filled the space. The only audible sound that he registered was a slight rustling of dirt that he reasoned to be the footfalls of the Sheriff. The smell of oil and dirt clung to everything.

A main workbench surrounded by open space stood in the middle of the room. He glanced around the corner of a shelf and could see a few other tables and tools littering the open space.

Weapon at the ready, he stepped around the corner, and his heart jumped as he realized that he had been right. The killer had returned to the scene of the crime.

A man with cold, gray eyes sat next to one of the tables. They were eyes that had stared down upon countless victims. They were the dead eyes of a predator that killed without remorse or mercy and held no capacity for either emotion.

Marcus knew that no good would come of this. Good things never came from days when the devil climbed up to play.

# Part Two:

*The Wolf and the Shepherd*

# TEN

IN A SHED behind the home of a murdered woman, Marcus Williams stared into the eyes of a madman. He stood frozen, entranced by the killer's hypnotic gaze. It took a moment for him to look beyond the eyes and notice the rest of the man.

Handcuffs and ankle chains bound Ackerman's hands and legs to the chair. An old cloth with duct tape placed over it covered his mouth and ensured that the killer would issue no screams for help. Dried blood encrusted his face. The term *Southern Justice* was the first thing that came to mind, and after seeing the psychopath's handiwork, Marcus couldn't pose much of an argument against the concept.

The man in the chair deserved whatever he had coming to him. But then again, where was the line drawn? When does a person cross the boundary between punishing a murderer and becoming one? What's the real difference between justice and vengeance? It wasn't his job to ask those questions anymore. That was the Sheriff's concern now.

He expected the Sheriff to join him in his astonishment, but as the older man came around the corner, he seemed no more surprised to see the bound man than he would be surprised to see stars in the heavens.

The Sheriff stood with his gun dangling in his left hand. His posture wasn't indicative of a man entering a room containing even a murder suspect, let alone a serial killer. *Unless, the Sheriff already knew what to expect...*

*This is going to be a really long day.*

He turned the aim of his weapon away from the killer and toward the Sheriff. "It looks like you've caught a big one this time. Are you going to keep him or throw him back?"

"I think he's a keeper," the Sheriff said, his gun still pointed at the floor. The Sheriff seemed almost as worried about the gun pointed at him as he would be about rain on a Sunday afternoon.

"You want to tell me what's going on here?"

Their eyes met. In that moment, he realized from whom he had received the gun. He chastised himself for not checking the ammo. Now that he thought about it, the gun did seem light. He should have known that it wasn't loaded. *I'm getting rusty—no doubt about it.*

Since the Sheriff was still going along with the charade, he figured that he might as well keep up the act as well. He continued to point the nine-millimeter paperweight at its target.

"I bet you were a good cop, Marcus," the Sheriff said. "I think being a law-enforcement officer is one of the hardest jobs in the world. People count on you to make the world safe. And the fact of the matter is that sometimes the world is a dark place filled with evil. There are monsters under the bed. There are wolves out in the darkness, waiting for one of us to stray from the herd. And to whom do we turn to keep the darkness at bay? We look to the police, a group of regular men and women who have taken a supreme oath to protect and serve."

The Sheriff walked forward as he spoke. "We're not like knights in shining armor. We can't just ride out and slay the beasts of this world. But sometimes, we're expected to rise to that challenge anyway. We operate within a system where an innocent man can be put to death, and a man who's without a doubt a cold-blooded murderer can go free on a technicality. Where are the people who will stand up for what's right, even when it's not popular; the ones who sacrifice themselves for the good of others? You know, I don't think of myself as an enforcer of the law. I think a cop is more like a shepherd, protecting the flock. We keep the wolves away."

"Is that what you're doing here? You keeping the wolves away?"

"I don't expect you to understand. But in a sense, that's precisely what I'm doing. I've caught up to a lot of people who thought they could run from justice. But contrary to popular belief, true justice isn't blind. She'll find you, no matter where you go. No juries, no trials. We skipped all the formalities and went straight to the punishment."

"That's not your decision to—"

The Sheriff moved closer and interrupted. "I found a car that he had stolen and abandoned. Knew he was on foot, so I set the dogs on him and tracked him here. If only I would have gotten here sooner...Well, anyway, thoughts like that'll drive you crazy. I followed the trail out here and caught this psychopath sharpening one of the knives he had used on Maureen. Apparently, he wanted to make sure it was nice and sharp for the next kind grandmother he planned to mutilate. So I caught him, chained him up, and beat him unconscious. Then, when I went back into the house, I must have locked the back door behind me. Force of habit, I guess."

While the Sheriff spoke, Marcus considered the older man's words. In many ways, he agreed with what the Sheriff was doing, but he also knew that the more you kill, the easier it becomes. The more you rationalize your actions, the more excuses you tell yourself. The farther you go down that path, the more the lines between good and evil begin to blur until you don't know which side you're standing on anymore.

He didn't know what to think about the moral ramifications of what the Sheriff was doing, but it didn't really matter. Whether he agreed with him or not, he did know one thing for sure. The Sheriff had no intentions of letting him leave there alive.

"Don't come any closer," he said.

The Sheriff ignored him. "My plan was to cover up Maureen's death and somehow make it look like an accident. And then...I had some bigger plans for our friend, Ackerman. Your theory from earlier was accurate."

"What theory?"

"The one about it being the perfect time to kill someone. Like you said, we've got the perfect scapegoat right here. Completely believable. And, you see, I have someone that I need to kill." The Sheriff sighed and shook his head. "But damn it, kid, you stumbled into this mess and changed those plans. I guess I didn't act soon enough. I'm telling you this because I just want to say that I'm sorry, son, but sometimes the wolves aren't the only danger to the flock. Sometimes, one of the flock becomes sick and is a danger to the whole group. For the greater good, you have to sacrifice the one for the many. Sometimes, people need to be protected from themselves, and I'm truly sorry for that."

"How about I develop a case of amnesia, let you get on with your business, and go along my way like nothing happened?" Marcus said, having no intentions of doing so and no expectations that the Sheriff would agree.

"You think I'm completely crazy, don't you?"

"No, actually, I think you're in perfect mental health, and I'd be willing to testify to that at your trial."

The Sheriff laughed. "I wish we would have met under different circumstances, but you can't change the hand that you've been dealt. You know in your heart that what I'm doing is right. Take this animal we have here." He gestured toward Ackerman. "He's probably sitting there thinking of all the different ways he could make us suffer. I feel for the little boy in that video, but that little boy is dead. I can't let another person suffer at his hands. I won't allow it. These aren't men we're dealing with here. They're monsters, and they don't deserve to live."

"And who are you to decide who has a right to live and who should die? You're playing God here, Sheriff, and I don't think the good Lord looks too kindly upon impersonators."

Their gazes locked, and the Sheriff said, "I'm sorry, son." With those words, the gun in the Sheriff's hand began to rise.

Without thinking and acting on pure instinct, Marcus hurled the useless handgun at the Sheriff.

The world slowed.

As soon as the gun left his hand, he grabbed the end of the table on his right. With all his strength, he flipped up the table and heaved it onto the Sheriff.

It struck the older man on the left side. A shot—likely intended for Marcus's chest—ricocheted off the grimy part-filled shelves.

With blazing speed, he navigated the maze of shelving. He heard the Sheriff's footfalls behind him, and as he reached the door, he turned and gave a hard kick to the last set of shelves. Like dominoes, the shelves fell into each other and cascaded toward the center of the shed.

He didn't take the time to watch. As he slipped through the door, he heard the Sheriff cry out in pain behind him.

As he stepped out of the shed, the darkness engulfed

him. Night had fallen, the only light being cast by a couple of scattered pole lights. He ran into the cover of darkness and started moving back to where he had parked his truck.

He knew that he had to move fast. It wouldn't take long for the Sheriff to climb out of the mess and exit the door on the other side of the shed.

*But where will I go even if I make it to my truck? I can't go to the local police, for obvious reasons, which only leaves the state police. But even if I make it to the state cops, what proof do I have? How do I convince them that a local Sheriff, whom they probably all know, has gone rogue and tried to kill me?*

He pushed the thoughts from his mind. Such questions weren't important now. He had to focus on one thing at a time, and right now, escaping with his life took the highest precedence.

# ELEVEN

MARCUS MADE HIS way around the western side of the farm-house. He ran in a full sprint, having no intentions of giving the Sheriff a chance to catch up.

As he reached the edge of the house and was about to turn the corner into the front yard, he heard a noise that seemed out of place. His instincts cried out and told him to stop. Momentum carried him around the corner, but he was able to put the brakes on just in time to pull back.

As he did so, a gunshot cut the night air, the bullet slicing a path right where his head would have been. He peeked around the corner and caught a glimpse of the perpetrator just before another shot rang out. He saw Lewis Foster dressed all in black and crouching near the Sheriff's cruiser.

He pounded the bottom of his fist on the side of the house. There were no new cars out front, so Foster must have already been there, waiting. The Sheriff had this planned, and he had fallen right into their trap.

He heard footfalls approaching the house from the direction of the shed. It had taken the Sheriff even less time than he had estimated to recover and engage in pursuit.

*Great…caught between a rock and a hard-ass.* He looked around for anything that he could use against them. A multitude of thoughts rushed through his mind, but not one of them did him any good.

He scanned the area, searching. Then, he spotted a potential weapon, probably the oldest weapon known to man.

Ever since man had been given the capacity for love and compassion, the door had also been opened for hatred and envy. Such emotions led men and women to kill for what was not rightfully their own. And whenever man discovered the urge to kill, there always seemed to be a rock close at hand.

"Just surrender, son. You've got nowhere left to go," the Sheriff said from around the corner of the house.

They were almost upon him. The trap was almost sprung. He could feel the noose tightening, and he didn't have the first clue as to how he was going to escape.

*Think, think, think. NO! Don't think. React.*

He knew that if he poked his head around the corner of the house, he would get it blown off. *But what if I can distract Foster, even for a second?* He found the answer coiled near him on the side of the house: a garden hose with a spray end.

He didn't think. He reacted. If he would have taken the time to think it through, he probably wouldn't have even tried it, but the time for thinking had long passed.

He grabbed the sprayer in his left hand and cranked the valve all the way open. He snatched up the rock with his right hand and headed toward the front of the house. As he started around the corner, he sprayed Foster in the face with the hose. The sudden spray of water caught the man by surprise and gave just enough of a distraction.

Foster squeezed off a shot, but missed.

Marcus hurled the rock at Foster like Nolan Ryan possessed by the spirit of an angry caveman. He had been a pitcher on his high-school baseball team. He hadn't been the greatest, but he hadn't been terrible either. Regardless, on this particular night, his aim was dead-on, and the rock struck Foster in the middle of his forehead.

Foster screamed in agony and squeezed off another blind shot, hitting nothing but the cold black of the night.

He covered the distance between them, and just as Foster regained his bearings, he struck the deputy again. Foster staggered back. He landed another hard blow to the dead center of Foster's face, and the deputy went down.

*Strike three, you're out. Next batter.*

He scooped up the deputy's gun and headed for his truck, but another obstacle confronted him. Foster had slashed his tires.

A shot cut through the air. He dove behind the truck and fired a quick succession of bullets in the Sheriff's direction, keeping him pinned on the side of the house. His hands were steady as he fired the weapon at his pursuer, but on the inside, he trembled with fear. He felt overwhelmed and wasn't sure if he still retained the necessary fortitude to take another man's life.

He had no reservations regarding the fight at the bar and any injuries that he had inflicted upon his attackers. After all, their wounds would heal. Taking a man's life was an entirely different matter. He had been there. He had done that. Up close and personal, he had taken what only God could give.

Now, he found himself in the wrong place at the wrong time once again, engaging in a life-or-death, kill-or-be-killed struggle. He knew that his opponent would have no reservations or hesitations at the prospect of taking his life, but he wasn't sure if he could live with more blood on his hands.

He tried to make a move for the patrol car, but the Sheriff released his own barrage of pinning fire. Marcus fired two shots aimed at the side of the house, but the weapon's slide-lock caught after the second shot. He was out of ammo. With no other options, he tossed the gun away and took the only door left open to him.

He ran as fast as he could into the darkness, trying to put as much distance as possible between himself and the men who wanted to kill him.

THE SHERIFF PEERED in the direction of his opponent's position. Marcus was gone. He heard someone running off into the darkness and realized that he wasn't going to catch the younger man on foot.

The Sheriff came around the corner just as Lewis Foster pulled himself up from the ground. Foster stood and wiped the blood from his face while he scanned the area for the man who had inflicted his injuries. The Sheriff could see that Lewis burned with a deep desire to tear Marcus's head off.

"Where is he?" Foster said, his voice shaking.

"He ran off, probably heading for the highway," the Sheriff replied in a calm, matter-of-fact tone.

"Well, are we going after him?" Foster said, as he stood hunched over with his hands on his knees.

"Not on foot. Don't worry. I know where he's going. He won't make it far."

WHILE THE HUNT distracted the Sheriff and his deputy, the taker of life and eater of souls broke his way free of bondage.

When the man that the Sheriff had called "Marcus" kicked over the shelves, the one nearest to Ackerman had fallen on the table to which he was anchored and cracked the chair to which he was tied. This knocked him and the chair on their sides. Breaking free of the sturdy table and chair would have been almost impossible, but once the table had been smashed and the chair cracked, he exploited the chair's weakened joints and freed himself.

*I'll have to remember to thank Marcus for his help...*

He was now mobile but still chained at the wrists and ankles. His hands had been chained behind his back, but with a little maneuvering, he brought them under his feet and to the front of his body.

He scoured his surroundings for something that would help him break free of the chains. Alongside the shop's far wall, he spotted his ticket to freedom. Fate truly smiled upon him.

He made his way over to the acetylene cutting torch that seemed as if it had been placed there just for such a momentous occasion.

He adjusted the mixture and lit the torch, using a striker left hanging on one of the tank's valves. He fine-tuned the fire into a pure blue flame and began cutting himself free of his shackles. He realized that he would burn himself during the process, but he gave such facts little consideration. After all, he was no stranger to pain. And his flesh was already scarred.

He had decided to stick around the little town of Asherton for a while longer. He had faked unconsciousness and overheard most of what the Sheriff was planning. His interest had been piqued. He was starting to enjoy the Sheriff's little game—*but maybe it's time to change the rules?*

He enjoyed a good game. He just never played well with others.

# TWELVE

Marcus ran like the devil was on his heels. He moved through a cold blackness that seemed to permeate osmotically through his skin and into his heart. The dim luminescence of the moon served as his only light.

He had hated the darkness all of his life, and although he would never admit it to another living soul, he actually feared it. He felt childish even thinking the thought, but it was one childhood fear that he had never outgrown.

The thought of some evil creature lurking in the shadows didn't make the hairs on the back of his neck stand on end. It was the fact that he knew there were real monsters in the world. Maybe there were creatures like in the horror flicks and maybe not, but he knew for certain that there were monsters that lived inside human skin. He had seen them. He had seen what they were capable of.

And in the dark, he was vulnerable. In the darkness, he couldn't see the monsters when they came for him. If he could see what was coming, he knew he could fight it. After all, that was his gift: to fight, to kill.

He wondered who he could trust. *The state police? The Texas Rangers? Can I trust anyone?* He realized that he couldn't go to Maggie. Telling someone that their father was trying to kill you didn't strike him as second-date material.

He had to make it to the state police or FBI. He didn't like it, but they seemed to be his only options.

He knew that he couldn't return to his new home. They

might be waiting for him. Besides, he couldn't think of anything there that would do him any good—except for maybe an ice-cold beer or a shot of whiskey.

His only option was to make it to the highway. From there, he could catch a ride to the next town or find a state cop along the way. Even if he had to hitchhike all the way into one of the major cities to find a state cop, he could report what he had seen, and the worst-case scenario would be the Sheriff killing Ackerman before the cops arrived. The world would be a better place without the psychopath, and he could walk away with a clean conscience, knowing that he had done his best to do the right thing.

After what seemed like an eternity wandering in darkness, he reached the highway. The two parallel lanes of asphalt curving off into the black horizon seemed like an oasis in the desert to his tired eyes. He wiped the sweat from his brow, and a renewed determination filled him as he began the long walk down a lonely stretch of South Texas highway.

# THIRTEEN

ACKERMAN WANDERED IN darkness for a couple of hours. He loved the dark. It made him feel at peace.

Eventually, he came upon a quaint, little house at the end of a long dirt lane. The dwelling wasn't nearly as beautiful and inviting as the home of Maureen Hill, but he was certain that the inhabitants would prove to be just as accommodating. He hoped that his visit would be as significant an event in their lives as it had been in Maureen's.

Old aluminum siding, yellowed and cracking, covered the ranch-style home. The wooden soffitting and fascia sagged in several spots, leaving open fissures. A dusty green El Camino that appeared to be on its last legs sat in the driveway, and a swing set rested in the sparse vegetation of the yard.

He could tell that this family didn't have a lot of money, but such things didn't matter to him. Black or white, rich or poor—he was an equal-opportunity killer.

Moving with purpose, he stalked through the front yard and past the inviting front porch like a lion creeping through the tall grass. The hunger was upon him now. He felt that, if he didn't appease it soon, it would devour him from the inside out.

He often felt like a man trapped in a well but dying of thirst. He felt cursed by the fates to wander the world, trying to propitiate a thirst that could never be quenched and satisfy a hunger that would never diminish. He sometimes compared his own situation to the fates that the Greek gods bestowed upon the likes of Tantalus and Prometheus, destined to spend eternity in torment. He felt trapped in a world in which he would never belong, surrounded by people whom he hated with a voracity that he could not truly explain. Maybe some part of him sought an end to all of the death and madness, but the unrelenting urge to kill eclipsed any misgivings.

He crept around the house and into the backyard, where he could see a light shining from one of the home's windows. Despite his unrelenting urges, he continued with calculated and silent movements.

He had honed his capabilities for stealth, learning to control his hunger—at least enough to facilitate the necessary caution.

He peered into the window and saw a beautiful, young woman in her late twenties, washing dishes in her kitchen sink. Her dark brown hair was tousled, and although it was tied in a ponytail, untamed strands flowed down her cheeks. She reminded him of someone, but he couldn't place the vague familiarity. She wore a light-blue tank top and a pair of dirty blue jeans. She looked exhausted as she toiled over the menial chore. Her eyes were a lovely shade of green, but the dark circles that had taken up residence beneath them overshadowed their brilliance.

He wondered what poor job choice or unfortunate circumstance had cultivated the dark patches under her lovely eyes. Was she a waitress? A factory worker? A single mom, or was there a man in the house? Was an unfaithful husband the source of her stress, or did her worry stem from guilt over her own infidelities? Maybe the dark areas could be attributed to a simple lack of sleep? There were a million different possibilities, but he would never learn the real cause. And that disturbed him.

He watched and soaked her in. He found himself in-

toxicated by her. An urge to hold her, to love her, overwhelmed him. He wanted to pull her close and whisper
that everything was going to be all right. He was strong.
He could protect her. He could give her all that she lacked.

Ackerman had always dreamed of loving someone.
Other than the distant memory of his mother, he had never
truly experienced love. He had never loved and had never
been loved in return. He wondered whether it would be
possible to walk away from his life and start over as a
normal person.

*I wonder if she would come if I asked her to run away
with me?*

*You're not worthy of love.*

*Shut up. I can be better than this.*

*You're a monster. You can't deny what you are.*

He clenched his eyes shut and pressed his hands into
his temples, but he couldn't shut out his father's voice.

*We're going to play a little game, Francis.*

*No, I don't want to play anymore. I want the game to
be over.*

*Kill her, and the pain will stop.*

But he knew the pain wouldn't stop. It never did.

He thought back on the first time he had killed. His father had started him small. Ackerman Sr. had captured an
alley cat for use in his little experiment. He ordered his
son to murder the animal, but the boy didn't want to kill
it. When he refused…

Ackerman unconsciously ran his hands over the scar
tissue on his arms.

*Kill her, and the pain will stop.*

But no matter what he did, no matter what he killed,
his father never let the pain stop.

He lowered his hands and wiped the tears from his eyes.
Even if she did run away with him, he knew that he would

never truly be normal. He was beyond any kind of redemption, whether he wanted it or not. He couldn't change his fate any more than he could stop the world from turning or make the sun grow cold. His thirst for suffering would always be too strong.

As he continued to watch her, he thought about all the paths that would never be open to him and of all the wonderful things that he would never experience. Such thoughts filled him with fury. The red shroud of rage fell over him, and the woman in the window ceased to epitomize all the good that could have been. Instead, she represented all that had been stolen from him and all that he would never know.

He hated her beyond reason. He hated them all, and he would take from them what had been taken from him long ago. He would take their lives.

# FOURTEEN

MARCUS FELT LIKE he had wandered a thousand miles. He was dead tired, and he cursed his insomnia. Murderous officers of the law hunted him. He knew that they couldn't allow him to live and that they wouldn't stop until they found him.

He pressed on down the deserted highway. The night consumed everything around him, and the lonely stretch of road seemed to continue on forever, trailing off into oblivion. He felt like the lone survivor of the apocalypse, navigating his way to a destination that no longer existed in a futile attempt to find a lost loved one who had died in the cleansing fires that had marked the end of all things.

By the light of the moon, it seemed as if he had stepped into a different dimension. The very terrain seemed to have taken on a life of its own, and in his eyes, it appeared to hold dark and menacing intent. The darkness seemed to swirl and undulate like a ravenous animal waiting to devour his soul. The darkness was everywhere, surrounding him, creeping inside his heart, beckoning him to abandon hope and sleep forever.

He didn't know where he was going, or what he would do when he got there. All he knew was that he needed to get as far away from Asherton as possible.

His first thought was to walk to the next town, hiding every time a car approached. He felt that not being able to see who was approaching in the oncoming vehicles would put him in a vulnerable position and make hitchhiking a dangerous proposition. Hiding wasn't a viable option, how-ever, since the sporadic patches of vegetation checkered along the roadside didn't provide enough cover.

He didn't relish the prospect of hitchhiking, but other than grand theft auto, it was his quickest option. Plus, he hadn't taken the first road that he came to. In fact, he hadn't taken the second. He had decided on the third road, in hopes of throwing off his pursuers. As such, he concluded that he would be better off to take his chances with whatever vehicle came along.

He pressed on, trying to plan out his next move. It was his nature to deal with a situation using instinctual reactions rather than planned movements. This time, however, was a different situation. He needed a well-laid plan if he was going to get out of this alive.

Cold, gray clouds loomed overhead like the petty demi-gods of some ancient civilization, looking down on the toils and triumphs of mortal men. He could almost feel their gaze upon him, allies of the darkness attempting to wear down his resolve. The dark clouds drifted and flowed in the sea of space. From time to time, they eclipsed the moon and extinguished the last surviving light.

Then, a light born not of nature lit the landscape and stung his eyes as they hurried to adjust. A vehicle approached, a car from the look of it.

He had hoped that the first vehicle he saw would be a semi-truck. He knew the Sheriff wouldn't be coming after him in a semi, and he guessed that his chances of being picked up by a burly truck driver far outweighed the prospects of being aided by a single mom in a station wagon.

The car stopped about twenty to twenty-five feet from where he stood. He felt his heart sink and his adrenaline level rise as he noticed the red and blue lights mounted on the cop car's roof.

# FIFTEEN

ALICE RICHARDS PLACED the last of the plates in the dish drainer. Her feet throbbed and ached, and a possible muscle tear in her lower back forced pain up and down her spine if she turned the wrong way. She had put in another double shift at work. Her glamorous job consisted of folding a box, filling it with nail plates, and sending it down the line to the next cog in the industrial machine, who would label and ship it. After sixteen hours straight, she felt as if she had run two triathlons and given birth all in the same day. Mind, body, and soul ached, and she longed for sleep like a junky yearning for his next fix. Despite her exhaustion, she had decided to do the dishes before going to bed.

Sometimes, she wanted to run away from her troubles and never look back. She imagined that her whole life was a dream and that one day she would awaken from her world of unpaid bills and second mortgages. She hoped to find that all her problems originated from a realm of pure imagination that held no more truth in the world of concrete reality than flying elephants or talking mice.

She had two beautiful children, Lucas and Casey, and a not-so-beautiful husband, Dwight. She and Dwight were high school sweethearts and had gotten married following their senior year. She had just turned eighteen, old enough that her parents couldn't do anything to stop them. Her parents hated Dwight, and looking back, she felt that they were probably right about him. He was lazy and not all that bright or well-mannered, but he was the cutest boy she had ever seen.

It didn't take long for her girlish dreams to fade away. Although she loved her children always and her husband some of the time, she couldn't help but wonder what might have been if she would have taken some different turns on the road of life.

Out of necessity, she worked as many hours as possible, a situation that often left her in a zombie-like state. Over the past year, their financial situation hadn't allowed her much time with the children, and she felt guilty that she didn't get to see them at all on many nights.

She had just finished putting away the last of the dishes when she heard a noise from the kids' room. It was way past their bedtime, and they would be in big trouble if she walked in and caught them awake and playing.

A couple of nights before, she and Dwight had fallen asleep in the living room watching a movie. She had awakened at five in the morning and found Casey, still wide-awake, having a tea party with her dollies. She scolded the girl and sent her to bed, but she couldn't be too mad at her. The whole scene had been so cute.

She peered into the living room and saw Dwight passed out in his recliner. He sat limp and quiet in the chair, which was unusual for Dwight, since he snored like a hibernating grizzly. She didn't give much thought to the abnormality and decided not to wake him.

She continued down the hallway to check on the children. The carpet in the hall was bright green shag, spotted with elongated pools of white. The children often imagined the white spots were alligator heads, and they were adventurers who had to traverse a swamp in order to find a lost treasure of immeasurable bounty. She loved the games her children played and sometimes felt glad that she couldn't afford fancy toys for them. Unlike most of America's youth, her children used their imaginations, instead of having the games and stories laid out before them on computers and PlayStations.

She arrived at the entryway to the children's room and peeked inside, half expecting to see Lucas with the bed sheets tied around his neck in a makeshift cape and Casey serving tea to stuffed animals. Instead, she saw two beautiful children nestled snugly into their beds. She watched them in awe for a moment, amazed at the two wonderful children that she and her husband had created. She considered that, even though she would never have money, at least she would always have her kids.

The wind whispered in its cryptic and indecipherable language outside the children's window. The trees swayed back and forth in the darkness as the breeze caressed them like invisible waves crashing against a shoreline.

She had turned to go and wake Dwight for bed when a tiny, frightened voice called out from the darkened room behind her.

"Mommy," the voice said, "there's a bad man in my closet."

# SIXTEEN

Marcus stared at the cop car in disbelief. They had found him. *Wrong place, wrong time. Story of my life.*

He tried to determine whether he had any moves left, or if he was best to concede defeat. *Concede defeat?* The words sounded sacrilegious to him, as if stubbornness was an existential philosophy.

He saw a figure open the door and exit the vehicle, but he couldn't see more than the person's outline with the cruiser's headlights shining in his face.

"Don't move. Keep your hands where I can see them. Lie down on the ground with your hands behind your back. Palms facing up."

He complied and lay down on the highway's cool asphalt. An officer stepped out from behind the light, a member of the Texas Highway Patrol.

He smiled. *Whoever said, "Where's a cop when you need one?"*

Short blonde hair topped the officer's five-foot-nine frame. There was nothing exceptional about him. He wasn't big, but he wasn't small. He wasn't attractive, but he wasn't grotesque. He wasn't thin, but he wasn't overweight either. He was ordinary in every way that Marcus could see.

"Don't move," the officer said, as he approached with his weapon drawn and his muscles tensed like a coiled cobra.

The cop wasn't taking any chances, and Marcus began

to wonder why finding a man, who might only be a hitch-hiker or drifter, would make a state police officer so apprehensive. The officer cuffed his hands behind his back and ushered him to the rear seat of the police cruiser. He considered asking what he was charged with and wondered why the officer had been so quick to assume that he posed an imminent danger. But he really didn't have any other options, and he knew that finding an ally in this officer would be a step toward a resolution.

He had decided when the officer first told him to kiss the asphalt that he would wait until the man had him secure before unleashing the details of his story. That way, the patrolman would feel safe and possibly be more receptive. He knew how jumpy a cop, especially a rookie, could get when he or she felt threatened. He didn't want to start out on the wrong foot with his potential savior.

He didn't resist at all as the officer placed him in the backseat of the cruiser. The cop didn't even bother to place a seatbelt around him, as if he was going to bite the man in the jugular when he leaned over to latch the belt.

With that thought, he realized why the officer had treated him like a fugitive. Because the man thought he was a fugitive. After all, there was a serial killer presumed to be in the area.

The officer got into the front seat, put the car in gear, and drove. He didn't say a word.

A hollow feeling expanded in Marcus's stomach. "Listen, my name is Marcus Will—"

"I know what your name is."

Silence.

"Where are you taking me?"

Silence.

Marcus took a deep breath. "Am I being charged with something here?"

"I was told not to talk to you."

"By who?"

"You're wanted, and I've been told not to talk to you."

He ran all the possibilities through his mind. The officer hadn't even advised him of his Miranda rights. *Is this guy working for the Sheriff?* He didn't think so. The orders would most likely be to shoot on sight if that were the case.

"Listen, buddy, I don't know who you think I am or what you think I've done, but my name is Marcus Williams. I'm not Francis Ackerman. You can use your computer there to pull up his picture and—"

"Like I told you before," the officer said, tapping the computer terminal mounted on his console. "I know who you are. Marcus Williams. Suspect in the homicide of Maureen Hill. And I've been given strict instructions not to talk to you and to deliver you straight to the Dimmit County Sheriff's office. So sit back and enjoy the ride."

*Suspect in the homicide of Maureen Hill?*

The words shocked him at first, but after a moment, he realized that he should have thought of this possibility. It made sense. The Sheriff needed to discredit him and make sure that he couldn't find anyone sympathetic to his cause. The cop in the front seat didn't work for the Sheriff, but he might as well have been on the payroll. After all, the man was chauffeuring him to his death.

The Sheriff would take custody of him, and then it would be easy. *Hire a prisoner to take me out, or just kill me during a faked escape attempt.*

"I'm not a killer."

"That's exactly what a killer would say."

"Just listen for a minute. The reason that the Sheriff doesn't want you to talk to me is because he's the killer. He's trying to kill me because I found out about him."

"Uh-huh."

"I stumbled onto Maureen Hill's body because I'm her new neighbor. I went to introduce myself. But something didn't add up at the crime scene, so I called the Sheriff back there. I discovered that the thing that didn't fit was that the Sheriff had already captured the real killer…Ackerman. You heard of him, right?"

The officer didn't offer a reply, but he couldn't decide whether the lack of a sarcastic response meant that he was convincing him or just that the man didn't have anything else to say.

"The Sheriff's got some plan for Ackerman that doesn't involve a trial and prison. It involves murder. I stumbled onto the whole mess, so now he wants me dead too. If you deliver me to his office, then you're an accessory to murder."

"Why would the Sheriff do something like that?"

"I don't know. Maybe for some feeling of power? Maybe he got burned by the system one too many times? Shoelaces tied too tight? One too many swirlies in high school? It doesn't take much nowadays. I don't know why he's doing it, but I know that a police officer is supposed to enforce and uphold the law. Not make up the law as he goes along. Not bend the law when it suits him to do so. And the Sheriff's broken the law; he's taken it upon himself to be judge, jury, and executioner. The question really isn't whether Ackerman deserves to live or die because the bottom line is that it's not the Sheriff's job to decide. He's playing God."

The officer nodded in agreement, and then he glanced back at Marcus and said, "You're right. A policeman's not supposed to play God. But a wise man once told me that a cop is like a shepherd, and sometimes in order to protect the flock, you have to keep the wolves away."

# SEVENTEEN

*MOMMY, THERE'S A bad man in my closet.*

The quiet and meek-sounding voice was uncharacteristic for the boy who had called to her. He sounded terrified.

Lucas was a typical six-and-a-half-year-old boy. He possessed an excellent quality for mischief and had two favorite pastimes: playing with his action figures and teasing his little sister. Although his parents didn't really have enough money to buy them for him, Lucas had an army of action figures drawn from the ranks of *Star Wars* and *G.I. Joe*. He was rambunctious, full of energy, and always getting into trouble. He was everything you expected a boy of his age to be, but seldom had his mother ever heard him sound timid. Although she dismissed his claims as being the product of an overactive imagination, there was something in the tone of his voice that disturbed her.

"Honey, there's no one in your closet. You're safe here. Daddy and I are here to protect you. Now go back to bed. You're going to wake your sister."

"Mommy, there really is someone in my closet," he said. "I saw him standing in my doorway, and then I hid under the covers. But I heard him open my closet doors, and when I looked again, he was gone. So he must be hiding in my closet, waiting for me to go to sleep. I was too scared to scream even." The boy spoke at a machine gun's pace. Real or imagined, he had been rattled by something.

"Okay," she said, playing along, "we'll check the closet."

She tried to be confident and not let her own imagination run away with her. She considered waking Dwight so that he could check the closet and the rest of the room using the .38 Special revolver that he kept hidden and loaded in their bedroom.

*No, you're being silly. You're an adult, and you can't let yourself get scared over nothing.*

She walked to the closet doors but hesitated for a second. Her heart raced, and her palms were sweaty. *Don't be ridiculous.* She was the parent here. She was supposed to be the protector, the one who watched over the children. How could she fortify them against the likes of trolls that live under bridges, monsters that live under beds, or the dreaded bogeyman if she couldn't even take care of one little closet monster?

*No guts, no glory.* She grabbed the closet door's handle and threw it open.

At the same time, Lucas threw the covers over his head.

She half expected a wild-eyed madman to come bursting out of the closet, but its only inhabitants were clothes. Everything was as it should be, and nothing seemed to be out of place. She went on with the show and poked around on all of the clothes, in order to show Lucas that everything was okay.

She felt relieved but angered at how childish she had been. *Next thing you know, I'll be sleeping with the lights on.* She had never been given a reason to fear the darkness.

"See, I told you there was nothing to worry about."

The boy didn't seem convinced. "There really was a man, Mommy. Could you check under my bed?"

She walked to her son's bedside and leaned down, causing a pain to rip through her back. It started at the base of the spinal cord and worked its way up between her shoulder blades. She flinched but pressed on. The idea of a good night's sleep drove her forward. She pulled back the bed skirt with a jerk. Once again, Lucas threw the covers over his head.

She had always wondered what protection a child thought a cover would provide. She never remembered doing it herself, but it seemed that a lot of kids felt that a cover over the head was a monster-proof shield.

"Nothing under the bed, either. Nothing to worry about."

"What about under Casey's bed?"

Her patience wore thin, but seeing an end in sight, she checked under Casey's bed as well. "No monsters. No bad men."

"But, Mommy, he's here somewhere I know it. He—"

She cut him off with a raised hand.

She sat down beside him on the edge of the bed. "Listen to me. You're safe here. There are no bad men in this house. Daddy and I are here to protect you, and we would never let anything happen to you. You probably just had a bad dream or thought that you saw something that really wasn't there. It happens all the time, even to grown-ups, but the key is to not let your imagination get the better of you."

"But—"

"There's nothing to worry about." She wondered if something had jumpstarted her son's imagination tonight. "What did you and Daddy watch on TV while I was at work?"

"Nothing," he said a bit too quickly.

"Nothing, huh? Of course, you know that little boys who lie get grounded."

"Okay, we watched *Ghostbusters 2*. But I wasn't scared, and I'm not imagining the man I saw."

*Bingo*. Sometimes, she could kill Dwight. "So did the man you saw look anything like Vigo, the Carpathian?" Vigo was the bad guy in the movie.

Lucas's face scrunched up, and he gave her a dirty look. "No, Mom, he didn't look anything like Vigo. I watched *SpongeBob SquarePants* too, but he didn't look anything like Squidward either. He was real."

She fought back a chuckle and suppressed the urge to smile. She knew that either gesture would draw more harsh looks from her imaginative, young son. "Okay, well, if there was anyone here, they're gone now. So let's try to get some—"

A creaking noise filled the room.

At first, she didn't realize what it was, but then it came to her. It was the door to the bedroom, moving. *Did I check behind the door?*

Her heart stopped dead and then pounded with such volume that she thought her eardrums might shatter. She didn't want to see what was behind her, but she saw the fear on the face of her son as his eyes widened and his mouth hung open in a silent scream.

She rotated and saw a dark figure standing in the corner of the room.

# EIGHTEEN

*A COP IS LIKE a shepherd.*

Those were the exact words that the Sheriff had used. *Now, this officer makes the same analogy.* It could have been a coincidence, but Marcus didn't believe in coincidences. They didn't exist, as far as he was concerned. Everything happened for a reason. Everything was connected—even though, most of the time, that connection and the reasoning behind it was far beyond human comprehension.

He glanced around and took in every detail of the cop car. The seats weren't like regular car seats. They were plastic, in order to allow the officer to easily clean up whatever surprise might have been left for him. At one time or another, puke, piss, and every other manner of bodily secretion had been found in the backseat of a squad car. Plus, a plastic seat lacked the crevices where a suspect could hide incriminating evidence.

A metal grill and a piece of Lexan plastic a quarter inch in thickness formed the barrier between the front and back seats. He checked the barrier's frame for any possible flaws but found none—at least none that could be exploited. There were sections of the frame where the foam covering had worn down and cracked or was nonexistent. Some of the screws showed through, but he neither had the time nor the tools to unscrew any of them.

It took him only a few seconds to realize his options and formulate a plan. Whether he liked it or not, he was in his element. Under different circumstances, he could have been an impeccable criminal.

He had a plan, as well as the determination and ability to carry it out, but that didn't make him feel any better about what he was about to do. *A plan?* Could what he was about to do even be considered a plan? He felt like a football coach whose entire strategy consisted of the *plan* to score more points than the other team. It seemed to lack the subtle strategic nuances of which an actual *plan* would consist, but it was the only option that seemed feasible. If he would have thought about it much longer, he may have talked himself out of the idea. There was a real risk of getting himself killed if he carried out his *plan*, but there was an even greater possibility of getting killed if he waited.

*Don't think, react. Adapt. Improvise. Overcome.*

The officer had cuffed his hands behind his back but hadn't strapped him down with the vehicle's seatbelt, which made all the difference now. He pulled his hands under himself while bringing his legs up high enough to allow his cuffed hands to slip to the front of his body. All the while, he kept a sharp eye on the man in the front seat, to ensure that the cop wasn't aware of the maneuver.

He took in one last determined breath to stiffen his resolve, and then he threw himself down in the seat and kicked his feet against the rear driver's side window.

He knew that although a quarter inch of reinforced plastic composed the partition between the front and back seats, the side windows in many patrol cars were the same windows you would find in an average civilian vehicle and could be broken out. He continued kicking over the screams of the officer in the front seat, until the window shattered and the glass exploded onto the highway.

He leaned out of the car and smashed his cuffed fists against the driver's window.

The officer rolled down the window, took out his gun, and screamed at Marcus to get back in the car. He fired a warning shot to emphasize his point.

This, combined with the strong winds cutting deep into his skin and the asphalt rushing by at high speed, made Marcus wonder what he was thinking when he decided to kick out a window and hang out of a moving car.

Another shot sailed off into the night. He lunged forward and grabbed hold of the officer's wrist as a third shot traveled into the darkness. He threw his weight into a hard yank and pulled the officer partially out of the vehicle. The cop's gun fell to the pavement.

It was as much of an opportunity as he could have hoped for, and he took advantage of it. He wrestled his left arm around the officer's neck and squeezed. With his right fist, he pounded the man while trying to maintain enough balance to keep from falling out the window.

The vehicle swerved from one set of ditches to the other. He looked up and saw a slight jog in the road ahead. He knew that they wouldn't make the curve.

He shoved the officer back into the car and then pulled himself inside. The officer's foot must have pushed down the accelerator because he could feel the car gaining momentum.

He braced himself for impact.

The patrol car struck the ditch at high speed, smashing the right front wheel upward and compacting the front end as if it were made of aluminum foil. The car ramped the ditch and twisted in midair.

He was thrown around like a garment in a clothes dryer. Despite his earlier attempts to brace himself, he smashed into every hard surface. His head struck the rear passenger window, and a deep gash sliced into his forehead just above the right temple.

When the vehicle touched the earth again, it landed on its roof and skidded another fifty feet, tearing a large groove that resembled the path of a tornado.

As he lay bleeding, a looming sense of dread hovered within his mind like storm clouds rolling over a peaceful valley or an ominous fog blanketing a tranquil sea. To him, the darkness outside seemed to move with a purpose. He felt its weight pressing down against him. He thought for a moment that he was under attack from some dark and ancient entity that had stumbled upon them on its quest to rid the world of all light. Then, he realized that the growing darkness was only in his mind. Although he struggled to keep it from overtaking him, he lost his grip on consciousness and succumbed to the encroaching night.

# NINETEEN

ALICE RICHARDS HAD staked a small place in the world that she could call her own. It wasn't much, at least not nearly what she had hoped for when she was a young girl, but the cramped little house was still home. And now, her home would no longer be a source of security and fond memories. All of those happy times had been washed away in the blink of an eye.

The sanctity of their home had been violated and forever desecrated by a madman waiting in the shadows.

She stared in disbelief at the very real man that had invaded their home. She didn't know what to do. *Should I run? But what about the kids? Where the hell is Dwight? What does this psycho want?* A multitude of questions that she didn't have time to think flew through her mind.

She had to do something, and she had to do it fast. She knew full well that the man who stood before her had come with far darker intentions than to frighten them.

The man's eyes burned with an intensity that she had never before seen in her lifetime. She knew that there would be no bargaining or reasoning with the man from the shadows. Evil dwelled behind his eyes.

She clenched her teeth so hard that they began to ache, and her hands trembled with a fear that she could have never imagined before now.

Only one rational thought could penetrate the wall of fear that had been bricked up within her mind: *Dwight's gun…the pistol that he keeps loaded under our bed.*

She and Dwight had argued numerous times over the handgun. She had felt that it would be more of a danger to the family than a means of protection. Guns appalled her, and she felt that nothing good ever came from owning or using one. But now in the grip of fear and face to face with evil, Dwight's gun was the only thought that consumed her.

*If I run for it, I'll be leaving the kids alone. But if I don't go, we're all dead anyway.*

She took a deep breath and made a dash for the doorway.

The man reached out and grabbed her by the back of her shirt as she ran past. With a strong push, he sent her flying into the hall.

Her face smashed into a large picture frame across the hall from the doorway. She felt glass razor into her skin. She fell to her knees, and the picture frame and a shelf of knickknacks below it fell from the wall and onto her back. A few tiny figurines shattered against her neck and shoulders.

Before she could regain her bearings, the man was upon her.

She tried to crawl down the hallway, but he grabbed her belt with his right hand and a fistful of her hair with his left. He lifted her from the floor and slammed her underside into the wall, smashing in the drywall and sending dust into the air. He reared back and tossed her down the hallway like a garbage man tosses a bag into the truck.

She struck the floor with a thump that shook the house and caused more pictures and decorations to fall from the walls. She tasted something metallic in her mouth and realized it was her own blood. Her pain was great, but she had to be strong. More than her life was at stake.

*Where's Dwight?*

She was halfway into the kitchen and could see through

the entryway into the living room. She could see Dwight asleep in his chair. She called to him in a frail, battered voice, but he showed no sign of movement. *Can't he hear me?* She cursed him for not coming to their rescue.

She got to her feet and stumbled into the living room. The space once held such fond memories of Christmas time and presents under the tree, birthday parties, and her children's first steps. As she stared at her husband, all of those happy memories instantly faded away.

Dwight sat lifeless, soaked in his own blood. His throat had been slashed from ear to ear. His eyes still showed his last moments of terror, and his mouth hung open in a soundless scream.

She felt weak in the knees and almost collapsed from the shock. A sense of utter hopelessness washed over her. She wanted to give up, accept the inevitable, and invite the killer to get it over with. But the thought of her children kept her going. She would stop him. She would kill him. *I have to.*

Her husband's killer took his time making his way down the hall. He strolled in much the same way a man without a care in the world would stroll through a park on a summer day. It was as if he wanted to savor every moment of the chase.

She ran to the kitchen and straight to the knife block that rested on the countertop. From it, she pulled the largest knife, the one she never used because she was too afraid that she'd manage to cut off a finger or stab it into her leg. In the current situation, however, it was just right.

She flipped back around to face her attacker.

"Stay back," she said. She held the knife out toward him and readied herself, but he didn't even glance at the weapon. The confident look in his eyes added to her dread. He didn't seem human.

"What's your name?" he said. She hesitated.

"Name!" he said with bite.

"Alice."

"Ah…well, welcome to Wonderland, Alice." He glanced around the tiny kitchen, nodding his head like an old friend. "You have a lovely place here. Quaint, but quite lovely, nonetheless. It has a very homey feel to it." He spoke to her as if they were preparing to sit down and have coffee.

He looked deep into her eyes and continued in a serious yet soothing tone. "The concept of home is one that has been pondered and sought after from the time of man's earliest existence, a place that we can call our own, a place where we belong. It's more of a state of mind than a place, even though most merely associate home with a tangible location rather than an abstract concept. Home is somewhere that we all search for and many will never truly find. I envy the fact that you've made a home for yourself. That's something that I've never had, and I suppose that I never will."

"Who are you? What do you want?" Her voice trembled, but she forced out the words.

He seemed to consider her questions carefully. "Pardon my manners. My name is Francis Ackerman. And I want the world to make sense. I've always believed that there are no answers. No meaning. No point to our existence. But I'm not so sure anymore. I sometimes wonder if we are all just wandering through the darkness alone. But other times, I think that maybe I'm the only one in the dark."

He paused a moment and then continued. "Though I am certain about what I am going to do. I'm going to release you from the pain of living in mediocrity and obscurity. I'm going to set you free."

She sobbed. "Oh, God, please—"

"God?" he said. "There is no God. I'm your god now. I giveth…and I taketh away."

Her eyes hardened with anger, and her hands ceased their trembling. It was gut-check time. "There is a God," she said, "and I'm going to prove it to you."

On the final word, she thrust the knife at him, hoping to ram it deep into his belly.

He dodged her advance, seized her outstretched arm, and backhanded her across the face.

She dropped the knife and fell into the wall. But she did not go down. She regained her faculties and made a dash from the kitchen and back down the hall. Her only hope of salvation rested in the master bedroom, hidden under the mattress.

She moved faster than she thought possible. She turned the corner into her bedroom, slid to the ground, and stuck her hand under the mattress to retrieve the revolver.

She groped blindly, found the gun, and pulled it from its resting place. It was kill or be killed now, and she harbored no reservations concerning what she was about to do.

She whirled around, gun in hand.

He was almost on top of her.

She aimed the weapon at his chest, closed her eyes, and pulled the trigger.

She expected to hear a loud bang echo through the house as she ended the life of her attacker and saved her own. She expected to hear a deafening pop and crackle like on television. But she heard nothing—only silence.

She opened her tightly clenched eyes and looked up at the killer's smiling face. Astonished, she glanced at her own hand and saw that he had grabbed the gun as she fired and blocked the hammer from contacting the bullet.

"I told you there was no God," he said. "Sweet dreams… little lamb."

He ripped the gun from her hand and struck her across the face with it. The blow was too much for her to withstand, and she succumbed to darkness.

# TWENTY

HE WAS BACK in the Big Apple. He was a cop again. The time that had lapsed between past and present seemed to have sifted away like sands in an hourglass. The events between his last night as a cop and the present day seemed to be a fleeting memory of another life that he had lived in a dream.

Marcus had been a young homicide detective investigating a bizarre string of murders. Evidence had come up missing, and his superiors had told him to drop the investigation. But he was never one to let things go. He discovered a pattern among the killer's madness and followed his lead to that street on that night.

A scream shattered the air.

His heart froze in his chest for a moment and then erupted with blood pumping fire, as if it were a snowball thrown into the fires of Hell. Everything seemed so real. And yet, it wasn't. The street transformed before his eyes. The buildings bent and distorted into wild, incongruent shapes. The walls mutated into what looked like black tar—except that they possessed sharp edges like a billion tiny razor blades. The street became a river of blood, and the sidewalk fissured and cracked, as if an earthquake had struck but forgot to quake. It seemed like the entire landscape was alive and wished to devour him. Again, the scream beckoned him to an alley that looked like a gateway into some dark and ominous new dimension.

He had been here before. He remembered now. None

of this was real. It wasn't live. It was like a rerun of the past. Only in this rerun, the scenery in which the events had taken place assumed the dark characteristics of the events themselves.

Still trapped within the dream, he summoned all of his inner strength and let out a scream that was silent to the world of the waking but loud enough to break the trance of his sleep.

He awoke to a pounding in his brain that felt like a thousand tiny workers laying railroad tracks inside his head. For a moment, he forgot where he was and what had happened. He gained a moment's worth of comfort in blissful ignorance. Then, it all came rushing back.

He was bruised and battered, running from a conspiracy that possessed a depth he could not fathom and incorporated players reaching far and wide. He had no way to know who he could trust or what he was going to do next. The only thing that he knew for certain was that he had to keep moving. He had to find somewhere safe, and he had to do it fast.

Bringing himself up on unsteady knees, he retrieved the handcuff keys from the slumbering officer. He uncuffed himself before smashing the cruiser's radio. He searched the cop and found a cell phone in his pocket. He checked it, but the battery was dead. He smashed it as well. Leaving the crash behind, he walked toward a farmhouse that rested on a hill about a mile down the road.

He couldn't make out the exact details of the house, except for the pole light that shone like a beacon in the night and the outline of some structures. He hoped to find a vehicle on the property that he could *borrow* and commence with the only plan he had: to get as far away from Asherton as possible.

As MARCUS BLENDED into the darkness, the officer watched his former prisoner move away from the scene of the crash. He retrieved another cell phone strapped under the driver's seat in the ruined cruiser. He put a hand to his throbbing forehead and dialed. "Mr. Director? This is Michaels. I'm not going to make it to the rendezvous. He kicked out the back window and crashed the car. I'm sorry."

"That's fine, Michaels. Are you all right? Do you still have the package?"

"Negative, sir. The package is on the move. I'm not sure what direction he's heading in. I'm…I'm a little turned around, so I'm not sure of our exact location."

"Don't worry, Michaels. I know exactly where he is. We've had to improvise a bit, but everything is still going according to plan. We'll be in position."

# TWENTY-ONE

As ALICE SLUMBERED, Ackerman saw to the children and then picked up the phone that rested beside Alice's bed. He dialed a number that he knew by heart.

"Hello, Father Joseph speaking."

"Forgive me, Father, for I have sinned."

"What have you done, Francis?"

He sat down on the edge of the bed. "I dreamed of the dark man again last night. I—"

"Please, turn yourself in. This has to end."

He was silent for a moment, but then said, "As I said, before you rudely interrupted, the dark man visited me again last night. I'm sure you think of Lucifer when I describe him—a man of seeming beauty but with a face that the shadows seem to follow. A man who walks amongst the light, although the light never seems to touch him. There was a time when I might have agreed with you. I thought it was Satan himself, but then I wondered if maybe the dark man was my father. Now I'm beginning to feel that the dark man is what I'm becoming. I think he's me."

"What have you done, Francis?"

He spun the chamber of the revolver that he had commandeered from Alice. "I've taken a family. We're going to play."

"No, please. Lord, grant me strength. Why?"

He could hear in the priest's voice that the man was crying. Oddly, it gave him no satisfaction.

"Why do you have to kill? And don't feed me any of

the fairy tales that you tell your victims. I want to know why. I want to understand."

He hesitated a moment and then gazed at his own reflection in the mirror above Alice's dresser. He realized that tears had formed in his eyes as well. "Because it's the only time I really feel alive. The only time I don't feel hollow... and I can forget the pain. To know that I hold someone's existence in my hands... It's euphoric. It's transcendent. The greatest feeling you can imagine. I can't stop."

"I want to help you. The doctors can help you. They said you were responding to treatment...that you were making progress."

He dried his tears and sat up straighter. A scowl formed on his face. "The doctors didn't really want to help me. They just wanted to study me. To learn what makes me tick. I'm tired of being a lab rat."

"Your father was sick. You know why he did all that to you. The doctors aren't like that. They want to help you, but first, they need to understand you. I'll be with you every step of the way."

"I know what my father did and why. And that makes it even worse. I could maybe accept what he did if I thought that he was evil or disturbed, but he wasn't. Not really. He experimented on me for his own pride. A damn psychology study. An experiment. That's what they called me, *The Experiment*. I was nothing but a guinea pig...nothin' but a rat in a maze. It was all just a game. Life is just a game." He scratched at his scars until crimson stained his fingernails.

"You're wrong, Francis."

"Oh, really. About what?"

"Your father. There's nothing I can say that will erase the past, but if in some twisted way it gives you comfort, I do know one thing for sure..."

"I'm listening."

"Your father didn't hurt you for his work. He did it because he was a sick man…and evil in every sense of the word. We all have evil inside us, and we can't fight it alone."

"You really believe in good and evil?"

"Of course I do. There's always balance. Heaven and Hell. Angels and Demons. Darkness and Light. Good and Evil. Heroes and Villains. But things usually don't seem that clear-cut on the surface. Bad things happen to good people, but there is a reason for everything. The Bible says, 'And we know that all things work together for good to them that love God, to them who are the called according to his purpose.' God has a plan for us all, but we have to choose to walk the path. If we could step outside time and space, maybe we could understand the reasons, but we can't. We have to live by faith that we—"

He hung up the phone and reflected on Joseph's words. He walked to the kitchen and sat down at the table across from Alice. *Everything has an opposite.*

He reveled in her simple beauty and wondered what ugliness existed in the world to counterbalance such radiance. She looked at peace as she slumbered across from him. But she would awaken soon, and her peace would fade like a dream cleansed from her memory in the ether between worlds.

*Then, it'll be time to play.*

# TWENTY-TWO

When Alice Richards awoke, she found that her entire world had become a violent, malformed distortion of the reality to which she had become accustomed. The day-in-day-out monotony of her life looked like paradise now. Even if she survived the terrible ordeal which she now faced, the world through her eyes would never look quite the same. She would never be able to gaze into the darkness without fear. She would never feel safe.

Her eyes had been opened to the truth. She now knew that her safe, little world was an illusion and that she would always be at the mercy of the wolves. They would always be waiting just beyond the threshold of her happy home. If she allowed them any opportunity to penetrate the sanctity of her sanctuary, then she would be powerless to stop them from stealing away everything that she held dear.

Her head throbbed from the killer's blow, and it took a moment for the haze to clear from her eyes. When it did, the sight before her filled her heart with despair.

She sat at her kitchen table with her children in their own spots around her. Ackerman had gagged and bound them to their chairs.

The madman—who had stolen any dream of safety and security she once held, killed her husband, and now more than likely planned to kill her and her two innocent children—sat across from her.

"Hello, Alice," Ackerman said, as if he were a loving member of the family. "You look truly beautiful while you sleep. I bet your husband never took the time to notice. I bet there were a lot of other things he never appreciated about you."

She wanted to dive across the table and strangle him until his evil spirit fell to the hellish eternity that he deserved. She had never in her life felt such murderous anger. She made no attempt to quell her rage. Instead, she nurtured it at the sight of her children and the audacity of her husband's killer. He acted as if he was a friend and confidant rather than the invader and destroyer of her life and home.

She wasn't bound to the chair like her children, but she knew that she was no match for her attacker. Also, the fact remained that he had let them live when at any moment he could have extinguished their lives. She had yet to decide whether she should be fearful or hopeful regarding the reasons for his mercy.

"The world is a strange place, isn't it? It is a place of great cruelty and great compassion, a place of great tragedy and great joy, great corruption and great beauty. While I sat here and watched you, as I basked in the light of your beauty, I had an epiphany. Everything in this world has an opposite. For every light, there is a darkness. After every day, the night must inevitably come.

"This simple realization has sparked a sudden insight in me and allowed me to understand certain truths…truths concerning my place in this world and my inevitable purpose. You see, Alice, I've always felt that the world was meaningless. But maybe not? Maybe my purpose is to balance the equation? What if I was always meant to be a dark stain upon the world? I've never really thought of myself as evil. I never believed in good and evil. I just knew that something was broken in me…something that made me feed on the suffering of others. But maybe I'm not broken? Maybe I'm just the dark side of the equation? But I don't want to bore you with my own personal intro- spection and thoughts of my destiny, especially when your own destiny is at hand."

He rubbed at his palms, and she noticed for the first time that scar tissue covered his hands. "Since I am in such a benevolent and philosophical mood, I've decided to give you an opportunity to save your lives. Normally, I only play games with my victims when I am sure of an inevitable and satisfactory outcome. But with you, I have decided to offer a genuine chance to save yourselves. I toyed with the notion of just letting you go, but that kind of mercy isn't in my nature. In the end, we must be true to who we are. Don't you agree?"

Her eyes widened with fear at the thought of what ter- rible fate the deranged killer had dreamed up. Despite the man's calm and intelligent exterior, she had seen the pri- mal rage that lurked within his soul.

Under different circumstances, she would have found him attractive, both for his charismatic manner and good looks. But she had seen the man's true nature, and when she looked at him, she saw past the charming facade and straight to the monster within.

"I'm rambling again, aren't I? I have a tendency to do that. So, getting to the point, we're going to play a little game…"

# TWENTY-THREE

THE FARMHOUSE STOOD out like an oasis in the desert. It was a beautiful, two-story home with a wraparound porch and a tower of sorts jutting up like the conical spire of a medieval castle.

Marcus thought the house looked out of place, resting in the south Texas countryside. However, the details of the home's architecture were unimportant to him. The only issue of importance was the assistance that he might receive from the home's owners. He had considered simply stealing a vehicle from the property, but then he concluded that he wouldn't make it far without any allies. The home's owners were his best options, and he had nothing to lose.

He approached with caution since a guard dog might have been on duty. He made his way to the front door and rang the bell. From within the confines of the home, he heard a rustling as the inhabitants prepared to investigate their new and unexpected visitor.

A large man in his fifties or sixties answered the door. He had gray-white hair, a closely trimmed beard, and wore a pair of glasses that rested low on his nose. Despite his size, he looked intelligent, the kind of man who would be seen reading a book by the fire in an antique armchair. All of this seemed to fit with the home's architecture.

The man bathed him in the glow of the front porch light and said, "Can I help you, son?"

Marcus could tell by the look in the man's eyes that he was cautious, but receptive. "I think maybe you can," he said. "I hate to wander up here in the middle of the night and ask for help, but I'm all out of options."

The man seemed to notice the bloody gash on his forehead, a wound that he had suffered during the crash. "My God, boy, has there been some kind of accident? Are you hurt? Do you need me to call an ambulance?"

"No, sir. Thank you, though. I really don't know how to explain all this. It's kind of a long story."

A fatherly expression came over the man's face, and he said, "Why don't you start at the beginning, end with how you found yourself on my doorstep, and be as honest as possible."

Marcus wanted to share everything he had learned with someone, anyone. He wanted to relinquish some of the burden to someone else, but he knew that by doing so he would put that person in the same kind of jeopardy that he now faced.

"I'm sorry. I don't have much time, and the less you know the better."

The man seemed offended by his reply. "Nonsense, son, ignorance is never to be preferred over knowledge. No matter what knowing may cost you. Apathy and blindness to the truth are the chains that hold us down and make us prisoners within our own minds. The truth shall set you free. If we—"

From within the house, a female voice said, "Are you preaching a sermon, old man, or are you actually trying to help in your own twisted way?"

"I'm handling this," the man said in a defensive tone. He turned his attention back to Marcus. "There's something about you, kid. Something in your eyes, I suppose. I'm usually a pretty good judge of character, and I can tell that you're a good person."

The man's right hand had been concealed since the

beginning of the exchange in the pocket of his hooded sweatshirt. But now, the man removed his hand to show that he had been clutching a menacing black pistol from the first moment he had opened the door. Marcus recognized the weapon as the FNP-9 and knew that it held sixteen 9mm rounds per magazine. "I'm going to let you in, but I'm also going to hold onto this. And if you so much as get a funny look in your eye, we'll both find out if I know how to use this thing."

He liked this guy already. "Fair enough," he said.

Once inside, the man ushered him to the kitchen table, where the man's wife brought him a glass of water. He drank it down in large gulps. He hadn't realized how thirsty he was. Then, he recounted his story as best he could, and like the man said, he tried to be as honest as possible. The simple act of sharing his burden made him feel rejuvenated.

The man, who he learned was a retired English teacher named Allen Brubaker, and his wife, Loren, sat with rapt attention. Although there were a few skeptical glances exchanged between the two of them, he felt that they believed his story.

After he finished, Allen leaned back in his chair. "That's quite a story, Mr. Williams. But I believe you. I've heard rumors and had my own suspicions. To be honest, most of us around here know that something's been going on. And it goes far beyond the Sheriff killing off a few criminals. It's bigger than that. We look the other way out of fear, I suppose."

Allen shook his head. "Maybe we've all been blind for so long that we've stopped trying to see? Maybe we see what we want to see? I don't know. I've heard claims that the Sheriff and his men have permanently silenced people like us to hide their secrets. Maybe you were right when you said we were better off not knowing? Maybe we've eaten from the tree of knowledge and will now be cast out of paradise? But then again, as Edmund Burke said, 'All that is necessary for the triumph of evil is that good men do nothing.' And I'm not one to stand by and do nothing."

Allen turned to his wife and said, "Loren, wake the kids. We're going for a little drive."

# TWENTY-FOUR

ACKERMAN LAID THE revolver on the table.

Alice Richards exchanged looks of terror with her two frightened children but tried to express to them without words that everything would be okay. Her own fear, however, was impossible to mask.

The weapon that she had once thought would be their savior now appeared to be the instrument of their destruction. She wasn't sure what scared her the most: the thought of being shot with the revolver, or the unknown game of which she was now an unwilling participant. Fighting back tears, she said, "What do you want from us?"

"I told you," Ackerman said. "I want to play a game. If you follow all of my rules and don't try to cheat, I'll let you and your children live to see the light of another sunrise. But if you break any of my rules…" Ackerman brought his other hand up to reveal a large knife. He placed the knife on the table next to the revolver. "Do you agree to my terms?"

"What choice do I have?" She wanted to spit in his face, but she knew that wouldn't be good enough. She would have rather thrown scalding water in his face or maybe light him on fire and hit him with a truck. But she would play his game. She would do whatever she had to do to save her children.

Ackerman nodded. "You always have a choice, but I don't think that you would find any of the alternatives satisfactory. The game is my version of Russian Roulette.

I'm sure you've heard of it. The rules are as follows. The gun will have one bullet in it. I will place the bullet in the chamber and spin it. We will then each take a turn pulling the trigger with the gun pointed at our heads. You'll point the gun and pull the trigger on the children's turns. We will continue to do this until one of us is dead. The three remaining players get to live. If you or one of the children is the unfortunate loser, I will leave the other two unharmed. Either way, if you follow the rules, a minimum of two of you survive beyond this evening. Plus, you've got a one-in-four chance that I eat the bullet."

She heard the words come from the man's mouth, but she was in shock at what they meant. He didn't intend to kill her or the children. He intended for them to kill themselves.

"You're insane, and one day you're going to get what's coming to you! You're going to burn." This time she did spit on him, and although it was an impotent gesture, it made her feel better.

Ackerman wiped the spit from his face and said, "You're probably right. And maybe I'll find out soon. Either way, you are going to play my game. Do you agree to the rules?"

"Yes."

"Very well. Let's play." He picked up the gun, and although he moved it below the rim of the table where she couldn't see it, she saw Ackerman remove one of the bullets from his pocket and bring it down to the weapon.

The eerie sound of the spinning chamber made her wonder if she had actually died in the hallway and was now a contestant on the most popular game show in hell. Maybe Lucas was right when he thought that the bogeyman had crept into his room? Maybe Ackerman was more than just insane? Maybe he was evil incarnate, a real-life creature of the night?

He slid the gun across the table, and it came to a perfect stop in front of her. "You go first," he said.

She trembled all over. Now was her chance, and she knew that there would not be another. She had to act. She reached out to pick up the gun. She stared at it for a moment before grasping it. It had taken on an eerie luminescence that must have been a symptom of her head trauma.

*Do it. Do it now.* And she did.

She seized the gun and brought it to bear not against her own head, but at the man who had invaded her home, the man who had murdered her husband and intended to force her into an act of filicide, the man who had destroyed the sanctity of her sanctuary.

She squeezed the trigger.

She squeezed, again, and again.

She repeated the motion in rapid succession and felt a wave of hopelessness wash over her as she realized that the gun wasn't loaded. He had known what she would do. And now, she had broken the rules.

He stood up from the table and leisurely strolled around to the other side, where she sat in shock and despair. He reached out, took the gun from her grasp, and backhanded her across the face. The blow knocked the shock out of her and replaced it with an even greater sense of fear.

*What have I done? I've blown our one chance for survival. If I had played the game, I would have had at least a one-in-four chance of Ackerman taking the bullet. Now, that hope is gone.*

He walked back to his seat at the other end of the table. He sighed, reached out, and picked up the knife.

# TWENTY-FIVE

THE SHERIFF'S HEAD rested against the passenger window of the cruiser. He looked over at Lewis Foster, who sat behind the wheel with a blank stare and a rigid posture. *Always the good soldier.* As he turned back to the window and watched the scenery rocket past, his uncertainties and fears swelled inside him.

He wanted to punch something and then burst into tears, but he had to carry himself with calm and confidence at all times when in the company of the men. He couldn't let them see his doubt. He supposed that was an essential trait of a good commander, but it didn't make him feel any less cold and robotic.

Ackerman had escaped. Marcus was on the run. He worried that events may soon escalate beyond hope of containment—*but the train hasn't left the tracks just yet. I can still set things right and accomplish my mission.*

He wondered what his wife, Kathleen, would think of the man he had become. He supposed that it didn't really matter. She was gone. She could no longer feel shame or disappointment anymore than she could feel pride or joy—at least not in the terms by which he understood the emotions. He was certain there was an afterlife, and he hoped to see her again. But he prayed that she wasn't able to look down upon all that he had done and planned to do.

He didn't kill in her name, but it was the pain of her death that gave him the strength to do what was necessary.

Every time he doubted himself, he thought of her desecrated body and the look of terror in her cold, dead eyes.

His mind turned to the monster that had destroyed his
world all those years ago. The police had eventually captured his wife's murderer, but the man's family hired a
top-notch defense attorney. The slick lawyer tore the case
apart and had the most damning evidence thrown out due
to improper search and seizure.

*Not guilty.*

The investigators had still hoped to nail the killer on
some of the other murders. But that wasn't good enough
for him.

He could still see the dingy hotel in vivid detail. The
hall was dark and cool, the walls water-stained. The faint
scent of mold and rot masked by cleaning fluid filled the
space. Finally, he found room two-zero-eight. Time and
lack of upkeep had tarnished the gold letters on the door.
The zero had fallen away, but he could still see its outline.

He hadn't bothered to knock. Instead, he picked the
lock and let himself in. He found his wife's killer sleeping in the bed. Torturing the man had been a consideration and fantasy, but he knew the desire stemmed from
a longing for vengeance. And he didn't want the act to
be one of vengeance. He wanted justice. Most of all, he
wanted to make sure that this man never harmed another
living soul.

As the killer slept, he double-tapped two unsilenced
shots into the back of the man's skull. Then, he sat down
in one of the room's chairs and awaited the police. He had
considered running or trying to cover up his crime, but in
the end, he felt that he should be judged as well.

The image of the cell door slamming still resonated with
him. He had been resigned to his fate and ready to serve

out his punishment. He had even decided to waive his right to an attorney and plead guilty for his crime.

Fate had different plans for him, however. Within forty-eight hours, he was back on the street with a job to do.

# TWENTY-SIX

MARCUS LEARNED THAT Allen and Loren had two children. Allen described Charlie as the typical rebellious seventeen-year-old and their daughter, Amy, as well on her way to becoming a fully-fledged drama queen.

Upon hearing the situation, Charlie shook his head in disgust. "What are you talking about, Dad? It's almost midnight and you wake us for some crazy conspiracy theory. You've been listening to that *Coast to Coast* show too much. You think everything's a conspiracy."

Allen seemed to regard his son with annoyance for his naivety and lack of imagination and said, "That's because everything is. No time to discuss this as a committee. I'm the dad, and if I say that we're all getting up in the middle of the night to go dig up Jimmy Hoffa, then by God that's what we're going to do. And as long as you live under my roof, you had damn well better be there next to me with a shovel and rubber boots."

"Fine," Charlie said as he stormed from the room, "We'll do whatever you want—no matter how stupid it is."

Allen rolled his eyes. "That's the spirit, son." Allen turned to Marcus and said, "He'll be a great man someday...if I don't kill him first."

Marcus smiled. He liked Allen more every minute he was around him. Allen didn't pull his punches, and he respected that.

"It's a tough age," he said. "Looking back, I caused my aunt a lot of unnecessary grief for no other reason than to prove that I was a man. Now, I realize that nothing I did was very manly. Worst of all, I don't think I ever really apologized for any of it."

Allen patted him on the arm. "Trust me, son, you didn't have to. She knew the man that you'd become, and it made it all worthwhile. I know the same thing with Charlie. It's all just part of growing up. I guess it just gets those primal instincts in me going, and I don't like anyone threatening my alpha dog status. Anyway, do we have any kind of plan here?"

"To be perfectly honest, all I've been doing is rolling with the punches. Beyond escaping with my life, I don't have much of a plan. For someone to operate like this without any repercussions for such a long period of time, it means that the Sheriff is well connected somewhere. And there's no telling how high this might go. I'm pretty confident that the President isn't involved, but I don't think he gives appointments to ex-cops and retired English teachers."

"You never know. Maybe he could squeeze us in for a luncheon between the Prime Minister of England and the Ambassador of Kazakhstan?"

Loren walked into the room, frowning. "You could be a little more respectful to your son, old man. After all, he only acts that way because he inherited your bad attitude."

Allen's mouth hung open in shock. "He started it… old woman. But don't worry about that, he'll get over it. We've got more important things to discuss, and you're interrupting. Marcus and I were just trying to determine what we're going to do…"

"Why don't we just go to the FBI office in San Antonio and get their help?" Loren said.

Marcus nodded. "I've been thinking the same thing. Actually, I've been thinking that I go to the FBI, and you guys check into a hotel and wait for a call from me that everything's okay. If you don't hear from me after a certain amount of time, then you go to the papers or the TV news—or both. But if I go into the FBI building in broad daylight and make sure that I'm seen and as many people as possible hear my story, it's going to make it hard for anybody to cover it up—even if there are people there playing for the other team."

Allen took a deep breath. "That's about the only choice that we have, but never underestimate people's capacity to look the other way. We live in a society governed by the Church of the Almighty Dollar, built upon the foundations of man's greed and his never-ceasing bloodlust for power. It is a dark age in which we find ourselves; a time where doing what's popular has become what's right and doing what's right has become very unpopular. I sometimes envy the days of Genghis Khan and Napoleon. At least their wars for power were fought out in the open. Now, we face a quiet war, and as you said, Marcus, we 'roll with the punches.' That's all any of us seem to do these days."

Allen shook his head while wringing his hands together. "We destroy without remorse. We kill without mercy. And in this age of *progress*, the ideas of justice, compassion, and goodwill toward men have become outdated and forgotten concepts. Worst of all, fewer and fewer people are asking questions…about life, purpose, everything. We have become complacent and apathetic, and we all see the problems, but no one tries to do anything about them. We just keep our heads down and roll with the punches."

Marcus nodded, turned toward Loren, and said, "He's one of those glass-is-half-empty kind of guys, isn't he?"

She rolled her eyes. "Oh, you don't have to tell me. I've listened to this for the past thirty years. I keep telling him that, if things are so bad, he should run for President and do something about it. But does he do anything? No, he just sits on his fat ass, bitching."

"I would my horse had the speed of your tongue," Allen said.

"Quoting Shakespeare to me, huh. Couldn't even formulate an original comeback. And isn't it ironic that you would quote a line from a play entitled *Much Ado About Nothing*?"

"What, my dear Lady Disdainf! Are you yet living?" Allen said, quoting another line from Shakespeare.

"There you go again, letting someone else write your material."

Marcus just sat there and smiled at the exchange. Despite the hardships he had endured, there wasn't anything in the world that could keep him from smiling at Allen and Loren.

"Like usual, you're wasting time when there is no time to waste. We need to get in motion, and we can't afford to sit here and listen to you ramble on," Allen said.

Loren sat dumbfounded, speechless. "ME?" was the only response she could manage.

Before Loren could regain her composure and mount any retaliation, Charlie ran in from the living room. "Dad, two cars are coming up the lane. They're cop cars!"

# TWENTY-SEVEN

ALICE STARTED TO stand, but his words halted her.

"Don't you move," he said.

He stared off into the distance a moment, and then with a sudden jerk, he stabbed the knife into the tabletop. She couldn't decide whether the blade was left shaking from the impact, or if it only appeared that way because of her own trembling.

He thrummed his fingers on the table in rapid succession and then stopped with a final pop that made her jump. "Maybe I'm going soft…or maybe I just can't resist the chance to see you blow one of your own kids' brains out, but I'm going to give you a second chance. If you don't play nice this time, the strong sense of discipline that my father instilled in me is going to take over, and, as a matter of principle, I'll be required to slaughter all three of you like the stupid cattle you are. Are you ready to play by the rules like a big girl, Alice?"

"Yes."

"Good, then let's start over. Maybe I didn't adequately explain the rules of the game, so this time I'll go first just to show you how it's done." Once again, he brought a bullet to the gun and spun the chamber.

Although he must have only pretended to insert the bullet for the last round of play, this time she was sure that there would be a life-ending projectile in one of the revolver's six chambers.

He raised the gun to his head without any noticeable

hesitation. The action seemed to conjure the same feelings in him that would be summoned when a normal person brushed their teeth or combed their hair.

*He's completely insane*, she thought—not that this was the first time she noticed. It was merely a further affirmation.

As the gun clicked, her breath caught in her throat. There was no shot, no madman lying dead on the floor. Her odds of a good outcome to this game had just decreased by one sixth. Tears rolled down her face.

Ackerman slid the gun across the table to her. "See how it's done. Just think of it as flipping off a light switch, only instead of cutting the power to a bulb, you're extinguishing a person's life. Not a big deal, really. I read somewhere that roughly one-point-eight people die every second. That's over a hundred and fifty thousand people every day. If I kill all three of you right now, you just become another statistic, just another tally mark on the death list. You're insignificant, times three. What does it matter if I kill you today, or if you die a year from now in a car crash…or twenty years from now due to lung cancer? In the grand scheme of things, is anyone really going to miss any of you? I'll even let you choose who goes first. Sound fair? Just point and click. Like taking a picture, except someone dies."

She stared at the weapon in front of her. Earlier, she had risked everything to get to the revolver in hopes that it would be her deliverer, but now it was her condemner.

"Pick it up."

She knew the words came from right across the table, but they seemed muffled and far away. She felt dizzy. The world seemed to be growing and shrinking like there was a funhouse mirror on the back side of her eyes. Before she knew what she was really doing, she had reached out and picked the gun up from the table.

The choice was obvious.

*I'll go first.*

She placed the gun against her head. As more tears rolled down her cheeks, she faltered for a moment and brought the gun away, but then she stiffened herself again.

She knew what she had to do. She had lost all concern for her own life. The only thing that mattered now was saving her kids. For some strange reason, she believed that if she were the one killed by the bullet, Ackerman would let her children go unharmed. Maybe it was some kind of intuition, or maybe it was her mind trying to rationalize the irrational and give her enough strength to maintain her sanity in an insane situation. Either way, the choice was clear.

She pulled the trigger.

She felt lightheaded, and a terrible cold sensation swept through her whole body. *I'm dead. I have to be.* She opened her eyes and peered around the room. *Am I alive?* She still wasn't convinced either way. After all, she had never been dead before and had no idea what to expect.

Then, she realized that, from the moment she picked up the gun, she had been holding her breath. She released the held inhalation and gulped in a gasp of air. The lightheaded feeling faded, and she realized that the cold sensation must have been a sudden rush of adrenaline or some other bodily chemical associated with extreme instances of fear.

She was still alive. She felt a great sense of relief, but it only lasted for a brief second. When she looked around at the other chairs, she wished that she were dead.

Then, she glanced down at the opposite end of the table

and saw the smiling face of the madman. She knew that he was excited because the game was just now getting to the really interesting part.

# TWENTY-EIGHT

Marcus watched as the two cars sped down the lane, the outline of light racks visible on their roofs. *How did they find me?* He had disabled the radio at the crash scene and smashed the cop's cell phone. It didn't matter now, but it still gnawed at him. The cop finding him along the road had seemed like a coincidence, but he wondered if there was more to it. Coincidence or not, he had put innocent lives in danger.

Still, the Sheriff couldn't be sure that he was in that house. He could have just kept walking or abandoned the roads entirely. There would be no way for his hunters to track him to this point beyond a shadow of a doubt. If they played their cards right and put on a good show, they might convince the Sheriff. But that meant asking Allen to walk right into the Sheriff's sights.

How could he ask Allen Brubaker to walk out there, greet the Sheriff like an old friend, and convince the man that everything was business as usual? If the Sheriff held any suspicions and the rumors that Allen had heard were true, his new ally would be a sitting duck. *How can I ask a man I've just met to put his life on the line like that?*

He turned toward Allen, and their gazes locked. Allen nodded, and he knew that he didn't have to ask. Allen knew the score and would do what had to be done.

The older man reached into his pocket, removed the FNP-9, and handed it to Marcus. "Charlie, run up to my bedroom. The case for my gun is lying on the bed. Bring it down here, quickly." The boy bolted from the room. "There are two more loaded magazines in the case—sixteen shots per magazine. Hopefully, you won't need any of them, but…take care of my family…if…"

"Allen, I—"

"You just be the good man that your aunt knew you'd become. The rest'll work itself out."

The two cruisers came to a stop in front of the old Victorian home. The Sheriff, Lewis Foster, and three other deputies exited the vehicles.

Allen crossed the threshold of his front door, leaving the safety of his sanctuary and venturing into the cold unknown of the world beyond. He walked down the steps, smiling at the Sheriff and his men. "Good evening, Sheriff," he said. "Is there some kind of a problem, or something I can do for you?"

The Sheriff was calm and confident, and he spoke in a way that was friendly and yet demanded attention. The man was intelligent and collected in a way that made Marcus uneasy. "Good evening, Allen. We're just stopping by all the homes in this area to make sure that everything's okay. There's a dangerous fugitive on the run somewhere in this vicinity, and we just want to make sure that everyone is safe and secure. Have you seen or heard anything unusual tonight?"

Allen pursed his lips. "There was some strange, metallic disc hovering over the field, and I think I saw it beam one of the neighbor's cows up into its belly. But other than that, it's been a pretty quiet night."

The Sheriff laughed. "That problem falls beyond the realm of my jurisdiction. If you do see anything unusual that's a bit more my speed, be sure to let me know. In the meantime, lock yourself and the family up tight and don't open the door for any strangers. Do you have a weapon in the house?"

"No, I don't believe in guns," Allen said.

Marcus wondered if Allen's pistol was registered. He wasn't familiar with the way things worked in Texas, but he knew that the Sheriff could probably run Allen's name and discover that Allen did own a gun.

The Sheriff nodded. "If you do see anything, just barricade yourself in the house and contact us. Don't try to be a hero. I know that you've got more sense than that, but I'm telling everyone the same thing—just in case. There are a lot of people that think they're going to save the day like some scene from a movie, but what ends up happening is that they get themselves or others killed."

"All right, Sheriff. If we do see anything, trust me, you'll be the first to know. Good night and good luck catching your fugitive." Allen waved and walked back toward the porch.

"We'll need all the luck we can get. He's a slippery one. Good night, Allen." The Sheriff and his men began to pile back into their vehicles.

Marcus couldn't believe his eyes. They had actually pulled it off. If he had the power to give Allen an Oscar for his performance, he would have done so without hesitation. Since he had no Oscars to give, he would instead reward the burly, old English teacher with a big hug and kiss—whether he wanted them or not. *Finally, some good luck for a change.*

Just as the Sheriff was about to get back into his cruiser, he rested one hand on the open car door and said, "Allen, one more thing."

Allen turned back to the Sheriff.

"I'm truly sorry."

"For what?"

As soon as the words left Allen's mouth, the Sheriff raised his gun. Marcus counted seven pops. Seven bullets into Allen Brubaker's chest. Allen's lifeless husk fell to the steps of the porch with a dull thud.

His eyes widened with horror and anger. He wanted to run from the house like a madman and strangle the Sheriff with his bare hands, but he tried to keep his emotions in check. He had a responsibility to Allen's family.

Loren ran toward the door, but he blocked her.

He took aim at the Sheriff. He knew that he could end the man with a single pull of the trigger. The red shroud descended over his eyes.

A voice in his head urged him to squeeze, to kill. The man had just murdered Allen. He had every right to strike him down where he stood.

*The alleyway back in New York, the scream, the blood… No. I can be better than this. I'm better than him. I'm not a murderer.*

He had always been amazed at how books and movies sensationalized cops gunning down the bad guys without a second thought. Everyone thought that taking all that someone was and would ever be was an easy thing to do, if it was justified. Maybe it was for some, but not for him.

The Sheriff moved toward the house.

He lowered his aim and fired two shots in the dirt at the Sheriff's feet. He swung the gun toward the deputies and placed a bullet in close proximity to each, driving them back to cover and stopping any advancement.

Loren fell to the floor, screaming and crying. The children just stared out the window, probably trying to wrap their minds around the finality of what they had just witnessed.

Allen Brubaker's life had been cut short by the same type of injustice that he had spoken out against. A good man had been slain for no reason. In death, Allen had become a testimony to the injustice that he knew plagued the world.

Marcus knew that bad things sometimes happened to good people, but if it was the last thing that he ever did, he would make sure that bad things happened to the bad people as well. *Not vengeance—but justice.*

# TWENTY-NINE

ALICE WAS ONE step shy of insanity. *How can I choose?*

She could turn the gun on Ackerman, but what if he didn't load the gun this time either. They would all be dead for sure. Her mind was a hurricane of questions for which there were no answers, a maelstrom of confusion that thrashed with such violence that it threatened to rip her apart from the inside out.

"Excuse me, Alice," Ackerman said, as if he were asking her to pass the salt. "I don't mean to convey the impression that I'm not thoroughly enjoying our little game or watching you sit there trying to bring order to all this chaos, but can we please speed this up a bit? I do have a few other things I planned on accomplishing this evening." In the same calm, nonchalant manner, he added, "And if you don't hurry up, I may do something that you'll regret."

She dropped the gun and wept.

"Shut up!" Ackerman pounded his fist against the table.

She could see his anger rising, hellfire creeping into his eyes.

"You're going to pick up that gun and play the game. Do you want to know the true meaning of suffering, Alice? If you don't pick up that gun, I'm going to show you. Now pick it up."

Out of pure fear, she reached down and retrieved the gun.

"Good. Now I'll save you the trouble of your next decision. Your son goes next. Point the gun at him and pull the trigger."

She pointed the gun at her son. She put her finger on the trigger.

She tried to numb the horrible sensations that crept over her consciousness and convoluted her capacity for coherent thought. Once again, she tried to rationalize the situation and tell herself that the only hope of saving any of their lives was to do as she was told. But like almost every other difficult decision faced in life, there was no black-and-white, clear-cut answer.

"Pull the trigger. Death is not the execution. It's the pardon. Murder is an act of mercy. It's the amnesty granted to spare someone the burden of living a life of pain and anguish. The world is chaos. Life is pain. Release him, Alice. Pull the trigger."

She wouldn't do it. She couldn't do it. *There has to be a way out of this. There has to be.* Then, it came to her.

The devil that had violated her world required a sacrifice of blood and would not be appeased until the debt had been paid. *So, I'll sacrifice myself.*

Her only hope was that her death would not be in vain and that, by her actions, her children would be spared.

She pointed the gun at her own head and pulled the trigger.

# THIRTY

SURVEYING THE GRIEF-STRICKEN world that surrounded him, there was only one way Marcus could describe what he saw—*darkness*. In the absence of the light of Allen's life, darkness had descended upon the home of the Brubakers.

The children and Loren huddled together in the corner, swaying back and forth and sobbing. He wanted to comfort them in some way. He wanted to tell them that everything was going to be all right, but he couldn't. Number one, things would never be the same for them. Number two, they were all well on their way to joining Allen.

He looked back out the window and saw the Sheriff and his men appraising the situation from behind the cover of their vehicles. He had to keep them pinned down, so they couldn't circle around the house. So far, they hadn't tried to return fire, but that fact didn't fill him with any false hopes. He knew the Sheriff had a plan, and even as he formulated his own plan of attack, he had to assume that the Sheriff's plan was already in motion.

He should have shot the Sheriff dead where he stood, but he had vowed to never do such a thing again. If it came down to their survival, he hoped that he would be able to break his pledge. But in all honesty, he wasn't sure that he would ever be able to pull the trigger. He had to find a way to make sure that it didn't come to that.

A voice called out from behind the cover of one of the cruisers. "Come on out, kid. Let's not make this any more difficult or bloody than it has to be. You're the one we

want. If you come out peacefully and surrender, we'll let
Loren and the kids live. Nobody else has to die tonight."

"You're right, Sheriff. Nobody else has to die tonight.
All you have to do is turn yourself in, and I'll let you live.
I've got you surrounded, and I'm ready to accept the terms
of your surrender. Throw out your guns and come out with
your hands up."

"Don't play around now, kid. This is the only chance
you have, and it's the only time I'm going to offer it."

In response, Marcus took aim and fired. He placed two
rounds in the vehicle's hood, a foot in front of the Sheriff.
Then, he fired two rounds into each of the four tires visible from his position, crippling both cruisers.

An icy silence hung in the air. "If that's the way you
want to play it, kid. Then, that's the way we'll play it."

He ejected the spent magazine and slammed a fresh one
into the weapon. As he chambered a round, he said, "If
you or any of your men make a move toward this house,
you'll find out exactly how I'm going to play it."

The Sheriff didn't respond.

He hoped that his actions would make them hesitate for
a few minutes, but it wouldn't be long before they tried
something. The officers were too exposed, though. Their
vehicles were too far from any type of cover. They were
probably waiting for backup. Whatever he was going to
do, he needed to do it soon. The longer he hesitated, the
more their chances of survival decreased. He had to do
something that the Sheriff wouldn't expect. He always felt
that the best defense was a good offense, so that's what he
would do. He would go on the offensive.

"Loren, I know it's hard, but I need your help if we're
going to get through this."

She wiped the tears from her eyes and pulled herself up
from the floor. Her eyes were bloodshot, and she looked

like a strong gust of wind would blow her over. But he knew that she would do what needed to be done. She was tough. He had seen her in action earlier.

"Where's your car parked?"

"In the barn, right there behind that row of cop cars."

He looked out at the barn. There was no way they could make it, none he could think of anyway.

From across the room, Charlie said, "My car's parked around by the back door."

His wheels began to turn.

If they made it to the car, the Sheriff wouldn't be able to follow with flat tires. The Sheriff wasn't stupid, though, far from it. The elder cop could have had the entire perimeter covered in one way or another, even dark before approaching the house. *But maybe not?* Regardless, Marcus knew that he had to play it as if they had.

For some reason, the Sheriff seemed to want them alive. Otherwise, the vigilante could have just burned the house down with them in it. He tried to quell a lingering sensation in the back of his mind that the Sheriff was one step ahead of him and had been since the beginning.

*Adapt, improvise, and overcome.* "Do you have any other weapons in the house?"

Loren thought for a moment and then said, "My husband has an old double-barreled shotgun. He used to go hunting. He hasn't been in years, but I think he has a few shells left. Other than kitchen knives, those are the only real weapons we have."

He looked out the window and checked on the Sheriff. "It'll have to do. We need to hurry. I need the shotgun, an old T-shirt, a can of hairspray, a coffee can or a small trash can or something like that, a lighter, some matches, and all the bullets you can find."

# THIRTY-ONE

*CLICK.* THE FIRST squeeze of the trigger didn't end her life.

Alice hesitated before she pulled the trigger again. She didn't want to die, and she had always been taught that suicide was a one-way ticket to the fire. She hoped that God would grant her leniency due to the extenuating and coerced circumstances surrounding her demise.

She hesitated for a second longer, but this time, she pulled the trigger over and over in quick succession. *Click. Click. Click. Click. Click. Click.* She paused and then squeezed again. *Click. Click. Click.* She was still alive.

The gun wasn't loaded.

She dropped the impotent weapon to the floor. Her immediate reaction was great joy. After all, she was still alive. She had stared death in the face, and in the end, she had the guts to truly sacrifice herself to save her children.

The sense of joy lasted a split second before she realized that she had broken the rules once again.

She fixed her eyes upon Ackerman's face to gauge his reaction. His gaze was cold, but devoid of stronger emotions. She could detect no signs of the rage she had seen burning in his eyes earlier. Now, she saw the black eyes of a shark. She wondered if this was the same look that the spider gave the fly.

Then, the darkness faded from his visage, and he smiled a warm, loving smile. It was as if a different person sat across from her. The man she saw now was handsome with kind eyes. Ackerman had transformed.

This transformation should have filled her with some small sense of hope, but she dared not let herself be optimistic. She knew what lay beneath the surface of these calm waters. *Maybe this is only the eye of the storm?*

"You remind me of my mother, Alice." She thought of Norman Bates. He continued. "I believe it was Marion C. Garrety that said, 'Mother love is the fuel that enables a normal human being to do the impossible.' I also like a quote from some psychologist who said, 'Mother's love is peace. It need not be acquired, it need not be deserved.' It's a powerful thing, the love of a mother. I would guess that it's just some primal instinct that mankind has yet to exploit, corrupt, or filter out—but it's astounding, nonetheless.

"In a world where everything else will fail you, where everything else falls away and doesn't begin to live up to our expectations, a mother's love remains true. I can think of no other bond or loyalty that is harder to break. I sometimes wonder how different my life may have been if my mother hadn't passed away when I was young. I don't remember much of her. She died along with my unborn baby brother due to a complication during her pregnancy. I don't even remember her funeral or visiting her grave. But I remember her love."

He took a deep breath before his gaze went distant. "I sometimes think that my whole life has been just one long nightmare, and at any moment, she'll wake me up and tell me that it was all just a bad dream." Ackerman stood up from the table, and she noticed the beginnings of tears in his eyes. "Take care of your children, Alice. Don't take them for granted. Go put them back in their beds, and when you wake up in the morning, convince them and yourself that this has been nothing but a bad dream." He turned and walked toward the door.

She was still in shock at the sudden change in his mood. Joy overwhelmed a part of her, but another part wondered if he was merely toying with them. Before she even realized the words had come from her mouth, she said, "I told you there was a God."

Ackerman stopped dead.

*Idiot.* Dwight had always said that she never knew when to keep her big mouth shut.

When the killer turned around, she saw no signs of animosity. He looked toward the floor for a moment and then back at her. "For my sake…I hope you're wrong."

"It's never too late," she said.

"What do you mean?"

"To turn things around. To choose a different path. It's never too late."

He grinned. "I have a friend that tells me the same thing. Time will tell, I suppose." He stared deep into her eyes. "Good night, Alice."

With those words, he turned and left as silently as he had entered their lives.

She untied her children and held them tighter than she ever had before. From that moment on, she vowed to never take her simple life for granted. Every day was a blessing, each moment a gift. As she rocked back and forth and squeezed her children, she wondered if she would ever be able to let them go.

# THIRTY-TWO

CHARLIE SAT MOTIONLESS on the hardwood floor of the old Victorian home's parlor, his knees curled up to his chest. Marcus knew exactly what the teenager was thinking. He knew the symptoms of a guilty conscience all too well.

As he stared out the window, keeping a vigilante eye on the aggressors just beyond the porch, he said, "What's on your mind, kid?"

"What's it to you? You don't even know me. If you hadn't come here, my dad…"

"You're right. Your dad's dead because of me. But that's not what you were thinking. You were sitting there replaying every hurtful thing you ever said to your father—every argument, every hateful look, every time that you cursed him under your breath. And you're thinking how you'd give anything to take it all back and have one last chance to say that you're sorry and that you love him. But you're not going to get that chance this side of heaven, kid. So get over it. He knew."

"Knew what?"

"How much you loved him. And he loved you more than anything. That's why he rode you so hard. He wanted to help you become the good man that he knew you'd be someday."

He glanced over and noticed for the first time that Loren stood in the doorway between the kitchen and the parlor listening to their conversation. "Your dad died protecting his family. He wouldn't have wanted it any other way. He wouldn't want you to be sad or guilty. He would want you to live a good life and be the best man that you can be, and I know that you're going to make your father proud. Your family needs you to be that good man now more than ever."

Charlie said nothing, but he could see a gradual softening in the boy's eyes. Loren waited a moment and then entered the room. "We've gathered everything you asked for," she said. "I'm not sure what you're going to do with it, but you've got it."

"Good. Well, what'd one shepherd say to the other shepherd?" They stared at him a moment. He grinned. "Let's get the flock out of here."

*I HOLD THEIR lives in my hands.*

It was a duty Marcus didn't relish, but one from which he could not escape. He had put this family in danger, and Allen had already become a casualty of his mistake. Now, he was their sole chance for survival. The thought made him feel like some kind of mythological figure charged with holding the strands of life together, only to find that no mere mortal could ever hope to do so.

"What exactly are we going to do with all this crap?" Loren said.

"We're going on the offensive. Basically, the plan is that we distract the group out front long enough for us to get to the car in the back. They'll probably have someone back there watching the car, but maybe not. We'll just have to deal with that when the time comes."

She stared at him a moment. "Okay. So what exactly are we going to do with all this crap?"

He was glad to see that her fire had not been completely blown out. "It's all part of the distraction. Trust me."

She didn't look convinced. "But what are we going to do, even if we make it out of here in the car? They'll be right on our tails. They can radio ahead and set up road-blocks, APBs, air surveillance. Plus, you said the cop that found you along the road was a state officer, so this obvi-ously goes beyond the Sheriff. And we don't know how high. Which means, we don't know who to trust or where we'll be safe. What good does it do us to get to the car?"

He could see her anxiety growing as she rattled off the mountain of odds stacked against them. He felt her fear, not only for herself but also for the lives of her children. She looked like a different woman from the one he had met such a short time ago. She looked like a woman at her wits' end, and he didn't know what to say in order to make the situation seem any less bleak.

"Listen, Loren, I don't have all the answers. I'm just taking this one step at a time. Right now, the only thing that I know for sure is that if we stay here any longer, then we all die. So we're going to make it to that car, and we're going to get the hell out of here. Once we're out on the road, I've got a few tricks up my sleeve."

Loren was silent for a moment, and then she nodded her assent. "Okay. Let's do it."

She prepared the kids, and he surveyed the items he had requested while keeping a watchful eye on the men out-side. When he was content that everything he needed was present, he went to work. *Improvise, Adapt, Overcome.*

He loaded the double-barreled Remington that Loren had produced from the upstairs closet and handed the shot-gun and a few of the shells to Charlie. "You know how to use one of these?"

The boy nodded. "I used to shoot trap with my dad."

"Believe me, kid, it's a lot different when it's a living, breathing person you're pointing it at. If it comes to it, don't think, just point and squeeze. It's only a last resort, but if things go bad, it might save your life. A last resort. You understand?"

Charlie nodded.

He turned his attention back to the assembled items. He placed all the remaining bullets into the coffee can. He picked up the can of hairspray and sprayed some of its contents onto the bullets in the can. Then, he tore off a piece of the old shirt and wrapped it around the metal hairspray bottle, leaving a piece of the shirt hanging down like a tail.

A sound from out front drew his attention. They had started one of the cruisers. He looked out the window, and his heart sank.

Two of the men held their position while the Sheriff and the remaining deputies hid behind the other cruiser. They had started the vehicle, and one of them lay flat in the driver's seat. The car rolled forward, serving as mobile cover.

*A flanking maneuver.*

He snatched up the lighter and matches and stepped into position next to the door. He placed the coffee can in front of the opening. "Get to the back door," he called over his shoulder.

He held up the lighter, struck the flint, and lit the tail of the T-shirt tied to the hairspray. As soon as the fire began to consume the shirt, he flung open the front door and stepped onto the porch.

The world slowed.

He tossed the flaming can into the air over the officers. He raised the gun and sighted in on the fireball in its descent. He squeezed the trigger.

The bullet struck the can of hairspray dead on, and as the projectile penetrated its surface, the can's flammable contents spewed out onto the flames of the shirt. It burst into a brilliant explosion, and flaming liquid rained down upon the police cruisers and the men hiding behind them. The Sheriff and his deputies dove away from the falling debris of the makeshift Molotov.

He knew that the small explosion wouldn't kill or immobilize any of the officers, but it served as a great distraction. Now, it was time for phase two. He pushed the coffee can full of bullets onto the porch, and as he retreated into the house, he lit a match and threw it into the can.

He threw the front door shut behind him and ran toward the back.

The bullets in the can ignited like a pack of firecrackers. He could hear the uproar of gunfire and hoped it would force the officers to stay behind cover. His goal was to buy them enough time to get in the car and have a head start down the road. If he were lucky, the flames on the squad cars would prevent access to the vehicles. If that happened, they'd be home free.

The Brubakers waited at the back door. "Let me check it out first," he said as he reached them.

He stepped out onto the back steps and scanned the area. He could see no immediate threats, and they didn't have time to hesitate now. He called for them to come out as he continued to search for a sentry.

Loren and Amy were at his side—*but where's Charlie?*

He turned back to the house and saw Charlie standing in the doorway. His gut twisted as he saw the look in the young man's eyes, and he hoped that Charlie wasn't about to do something really stupid. "Come on, Charlie. Let's go."

"I'm staying. They're going to pay…and I'm going to make my dad proud."

"Please, kid, we're almost out of here."

"Protect my mom and my sister. I'll make sure that you're not followed."

He broke for the house, but Charlie slammed the door and locked it behind him.

He reached the door and wrenched on the handle. "Charlie! Open the door."

He glanced over his shoulder at Loren and Amy. They had wasted too much time already, but this was their one shot. They had to get moving fast, but he couldn't leave Charlie behind. *Stupid kid. What's he thinking?* There was only one thing he could do.

He turned back to the women. "Loren, take your daughter and go. I'll get Charlie, and we'll catch up."

Loren's eyes widened with shock and disbelief. "No, we go together or not at all."

"We don't have time for this. Go, now. We'll get out another way."

Tears cascaded down her face. "You save my boy, Marcus," she said. Then, she grabbed her daughter's arm and headed for the car.

He turned back to the door, and his heart wrenched when he heard a shotgun blast from inside the house. *Oh God, please don't let me be too late.*

He kicked the door. It flew inward on its hinges, splinters of wood shooting out like shrapnel from the doorframe. Throwing all caution to the wind, he sprinted into the house. The only thing he cared about was finding Charlie.

He ran through the kitchen and back toward the front door. He entered the living room, gun at the ready.

Charlie had a strong arm around his neck and a gun pressed to his temple. The Sheriff held the teenager as a human shield.

The Sheriff's mannerisms were a thousand times more

frightening than if he had worn a face of rage. The collectedness that he displayed showed that he was in complete
control and knew it. "Drop the gun, Marcus. It's over."

# THIRTY-THREE

THE DUSTY, GREEN El Camino pulled into the truck stop parking lot. Ackerman saw the lights of the interstate to his right and a sign next to the road on the left that read, *Asherton: 13 Miles.*

He had some decisions to make. Several possible paths stretched out before him, but he was uncertain of which road to take. His mind was a whirlwind of conflicting thoughts and emotions—rage, hope, pain, redemption. He needed to seek guidance, and only one person in the world could give it to him. He lifted the pay phone's receiver, inserted his money, and dialed.

"Hello," Father Joseph said.

"I let them go."

The man on the other end of the line was silent.

"Did you hear me, Father? I let them go. The family... the mother and the two kids. I spared them."

"That's...that's wonderful. It's incredible. You have no idea how proud I am of you. This could be the first step."

"Let's not get too carried away, but I have been thinking a lot about our last conversation."

"What about it?"

A trucker moved up behind him, apparently wanting to use the phone. The man hung back at a respectful distance and leaned against the hood of one of the cars. He gave the man a hateful look and then continued in a much lower voice. "About good and evil. About everything having an opposite and things happening for a reason. You see, I've come to realize that maybe I was born to be the villain."

"Francis, that's not—"

"Just let me finish. If things happen for a reason, then that would mean that everything I've endured was meant to serve a specific purpose. So I tried to think of what that purpose could be. I reasoned that if I'm the villain, then my purpose must involve a hero. That's when I realized that, on some level, I've been searching for my opposite for quite a while now. I thought that I was just looking for someone to make the game interesting, but now I believe that it was my soul searching out my other half. It was the natural order of the universe, trying to balance the equation."

"Can we hurry this up a bit, buddy?" the truck driver said.

Ackerman's hand shook, and his knuckles turned white around the phone's receiver. But he fought down the rage. "Wait your turn…buddy," he said through clenched teeth.

He turned his back on the man and continued. "Earlier this evening, I met a man named Marcus. There was something about him that I can't describe. A strange familiarity. Like being home. It was as if…I had known this man my whole life. But when I looked into his eyes, I felt overwhelmed with fear. It was like looking into the future and seeing my own death. His eyes reminded me of my father's eyes. I'm afraid, Padre. I think that if I continue down this path, he'll kill me. It's his destiny, and the truly strange part is that, for the first time in my life, I don't want to die. I've started to wonder what if. What if there is a hell? I hope for darkness in death, but maybe I'll find a punishment like nothing I can imagine."

"Hell isn't punishment, Francis. It's simply the alternative. God doesn't send people to hell to punish them for their sins. They go to hell because they've chosen to live their lives here on Earth apart from Him. By making that choice, they also choose to be apart from Him in the afterlife. That's why it's never too late. No matter what you've done, if you ask Him into your heart and home in this world, then He will bring you into His home in the next."

"I don't know what to believe. All I know is that my father's voice in my head has grown quieter lately. The hunger is still so strong, but for the first time, I wonder if maybe I can overcome it…"

"The first step toward redemption is seeing the need. The second is asking for it. You'll need help, Francis."

"I know." He stared in the direction of the interstate. "I've also considered what you said about me being even more of a legend if I was able to turn things around. I think you might be right. I'm thinking about turning myself in, but I would need you to be there with—"

"YOU HAVE GOT TO BE KIDDING ME!"

Ackerman's brow furrowed, and he turned back to the truck driver. "What exactly is your problem…buddy?" He over-accentuated the last word.

The truck driver shook his head and snorted. "This is really good. Really something. You're the one with the problem, freak."

The rage boiled inside him. He tried to beat down the hunger, but his thoughts kept moving to the gun in the back of his jeans and the knife resting on the passenger seat of the El Camino. He considered all the things he could do to this man.

*No. Not now.*

"Excuse me in my ignorance," he said, "but what the hell are you talking about?"

The truck driver reached past him and grabbed something on the side of the payphone. "I'm talking about this."

The man shook a bundle of wires at him. "I'm talking about me standing out here twiddlin' my thumbs, waiting to talk on a phone that's not connected. Not hooked to anything. You're out here talking to yourself, moron. Thanks for wasting my time." The truck driver shook his head and stormed off, mumbling something more under his breath.

Ackerman was dumbfounded. He grabbed the bundle of wires and examined them closely. He felt around the backside of the payphone. He checked for additional cables but found none. *There has to be some explanation…*

His breathing was short and erratic. His heart thundered.

He examined every inch of the payphone, and then he noticed a small slip of paper taped on top of the casing that must have been flipped up by the wind. With one finger, he flipped the little slip of paper down. It read, *Out of Order.*

*What the hell is going on here?*

He picked up the dangling receiver and placed it to his ear. "Hello," he said in a whisper.

"I'm here, Francis," the voice replied.

He dropped the receiver as if it was venomous and staggered backward away from the device. He almost fell as he tripped off the curb. Still walking backward and eyeing the receiver as if it would attack, he stumbled in front of a car pulling away from one of the pumps. The vehicle's horn blared at him, and he fell forward. He crawled back to the curb and sat up. He pressed his palms against his temples.

*This can't be happening.*

*Father Joseph is a real person.* He was certain of it. He searched his memories. The priest had been his only friend since he was a boy. The only friend he'd ever known. *He has to be real. He has to be.*

As his heart pounded against the walls of his chest and his breathing verged on hyperventilation, he rocked back

and forth. *No. No. No. This can't be happening.* The realization flooded over him. *I'm not getting better. There's
no hope for me. No redemption.*

He wept uncontrollably. His cries drew a few stares,
but most people that noticed him steered clear. After a few
moments, a voice echoed through his mind. His father's
voice, words spoken long ago.

*It's time to play a game, Francis… If you do as you're
told, the pain will stop… Kill… It's what you are… You're
a monster…*

He looked toward the road in front of the truck stop.
A car's headlights illuminated the road sign. *Asherton:
13 Miles.*

He dried the tears on his sleeve. "Okay, Father. Let's play."

# THIRTY-FOUR

HANDS ON HIS head, Marcus marched out of the house and past the body of Allen Brubaker, the man whom he had failed. It had cost Allen and his family so much by helping him. His mind ached and throbbed with an overwhelming sense of guilt and despair. He had done more than fail to protect them. He had been the source of their hardship. *They needed someone to protect them from me, not the other way around.*

A deputy told him to stop in front of one of the cruisers. He could still smell the burnt odor of his distraction, but the fire hadn't continued to burn in the way that he had hoped. The vehicle pointed toward the Brubakers' old barn, and its headlights bathed him in an eerie, artificial glow.

The Sheriff held Charlie close and kept a cautious distance between Marcus and himself. "Get down on your knees, put your hands behind your back, and put these on." The Sheriff tossed him a pair of handcuffs.

He felt helpless. He wanted to storm the Sheriff and his men and end the conflict one way or the other. If he hadn't had more lives to think of than his own, he might have done just that. The situation being what it was, however, he could see no alternative other than to comply with whatever he was told. With his arms behind his back, he placed the cuffs around his wrists and got down on his knees.

After he complied, the Sheriff moved in front of the cruiser. With a hard kick to the legs, he brought Charlie to his knees as well. Charlie stared at the ground, diverting his eyes away from Marcus.

He didn't blame the boy for any of this, but he knew that Charlie blamed himself. He hoped that they lived long enough for him to tell Charlie that it wasn't his fault. The only comfort he could find was that they had distracted the officers long enough for the women to escape.

But his heart sank when he saw a deputy lead two people around the corner of the house. The women hadn't gotten away. They had been captured. It was the final crushing blow to any feelings of hope that he still harbored.

His failure was complete.

He knew that he shouldn't blame himself. The Sheriff was the bad guy. He was the one who had killed Allen. It was the truth, but it didn't make Marcus feel any less guilty.

Loren and her daughter walked in front of an officer that he didn't recognize. He wondered how he could have missed a sentry in the backyard, and why the man hadn't opened fire and driven them back to the house the moment they stepped out. The officer brought the women to their knees beside Charlie.

Loren looked over at him. She looked haggard and beaten. "He was lying in the backseat of the car. We didn't have a chance. The Sheriff's thought of everything."

The Sheriff broke into their conversation and said, "Finally, someone with some sense. You're right, Loren. I have thought of nearly everything, but I didn't plan on our friend Marcus here. I never intended for any of you to get involved, but sometimes you just have to play the hand you're dealt. Unfortunately, Marcus, your little stunt in the shed allowed Ackerman to escape, and he was very important to our plans. Not to worry, though. I did a little checking on you, and I think that you may serve our purposes even better than Ackerman."

"Go to hell. I don't know what insanity you've got cooked up, but I won't be any part of it. You might as well just kill me now."

"Oh, all in due time, my friend. Besides, I don't need your cooperation or your permission. You'll play the part I've assigned to you, whether you like it or not. But I'm afraid I don't need any extra cast members, so these three are going to be cut from the production."

Loren's eyes widened with fear. She locked her gaze on his. Her eyes begged for help, but he was powerless to do anything. Besides, the Sheriff may have been warped and misguided, but he wasn't evil. Marcus couldn't imagine him actually murdering a defenseless mother and her children. Then again, the Sheriff had a cause of some kind, and throughout history, good men had committed the most unspeakable atrocities imaginable in the name of a cause.

"I guess we'll never know why you snapped and went on this killing spree, Marcus. First, Maureen. Now, the Brubakers. And tomorrow...who knows. Honestly, I wish you had never involved them in any of this. But what's done is done, and the task laid out before me is too important to jeopardize."

Tears formed in the Sheriff's eyes, and his voice cracked as he said, "I'm so sorry, but I have my orders."

The Sheriff shook his head in disgust, drew in a deep mouthful of air, and exhaled slowly. Then, he shot all three of the remaining Brubakers dead. Their lifeless bodies fell to the ground in grim succession.

His brain had barely registered the atrocity when Marcus found himself screaming and running at the Sheriff. He made it two steps before a hard blow from a nightstick into the common peroneal nerve at the back of his leg collapsed him to his knees. More blows followed the first and left him face down in the dirt. He looked up to see the face of Lewis Foster, enjoying his work.

"That's enough," the Sheriff said, though the voice seemed distant to Marcus.

He looked across at the lifeless bodies of the three Brubakers.

"I wish to God that their deaths weren't necessary, Marcus. But we're fighting a war here, and every war has casualties. Every war has collateral damage, and I'm afraid that they got caught in the crossfire. Evil is at the doorstep every day, and if good men like myself don't stand up to it, then countless innocents like them are going to continue to die for no reason. It's a quiet war, but it is perhaps the most important battle that anyone has ever fought. It's not a war against some foreign power beyond our borders and a world away. We're fighting against the darkness inside ourselves. We're fighting against injustice and corruption. We stand for everything that this country was founded upon, but we conveniently forget whenever it suits our needs."

The Sheriff circled Marcus as he spoke. "The fact of the matter is that we're fighting a losing battle. Evil, corruption, and injustice are winning because we refuse to fight them on their terms. Men like Ackerman are only the tip of the iceberg. There are others who are much more subtle, but a hundred times more dangerous."

The Sheriff reached down and pulled Marcus back to his knees. The older man leaned in close. "Events have already been set in motion that will protect the citizens of this nation from a threat far greater than any serial killer. I don't expect you to understand, but I cannot allow anything to jeopardize the events that will take place tomorrow. It's bigger than them." The Sheriff motioned at the three corpses. "It's bigger than you. It's bigger than me.

It's bigger than any one person. Sometimes, men like me have to make the tough choices and sacrifice the few for the good of the many. I know that doesn't make it any easier to accept, but it is an inevitable fact of life and someone has to do it."

He looked up at the Sheriff, cocked his head to the side, and cracked his neck. "Shut up and do whatever it is you're going to do to me. You're every bit as bad as Ackerman, maybe even worse. At least he doesn't think that he's a big hero for killing innocent people."

The Sheriff nodded. "Like I said, I don't expect you to understand." He turned to Foster. "Our guest looks tired, Lewis. Will you please put him to bed for me?"

Foster smiled down at him with a huge grin. "It would be my pleasure."

Marcus saw the nightstick descending toward his head before the darkness took him once again.

# THIRTY-FIVE

THE DUSTY, GREEN El Camino rocketed down the dark expanse of highway. Its new owner sat behind the wheel, the madness in his eyes shining out like two unholy torches and giving him a different perspective on his surroundings than anyone else who had ever traveled that particular road. His gray eyes shone with a newfound purpose and a frightening determination.

Ackerman had always felt that a strange causal and reactionary relationship bound all things together, but he had been sure that there was no real purpose or plan for any of the events. They were merely strings of random occurrences that perpetuated the day-to-day cycle of a world without meaning. He had never before seen any correlation or found any reason to believe that a grand design or higher power of the universe connected all the dots.

But now, he felt differently.

He had begun to see meaning, where previously there was only despair. He had begun to see design, where previously he had only seen chaos. He now believed that he had caught a glimpse of his own purpose and felt that his life held meaning. It was an exciting revelation. He felt like a speeding train traveling full blast into a head-on collision.

He knew what he had to do. Everything seemed so clear to him now.

He had tried to delude himself. He had tried to deny his true nature, but now he embraced the darkness within. He wasn't a broken man. He was a demon forged in pain and blood. He couldn't run from his true self.

Ahead lay the sleeping town of Asherton, the place where his story had been meant to go from the beginning. No doubt, the town was going about its business as usual, unsuspecting and unprepared. He intended to set the peaceful town on fire—literally.

So many things awaited him in Asherton.

He would exact his revenge upon the Sheriff. He would find a way to hurt the man who had intended to use him and then murder him. He would discover whatever he cared about most and destroy it. When he had drained the man of all hope and broken him completely, he would grant him the gift of death.

*So much to do, so little time.*

But there was more than just revenge awaiting him. There was purpose. He knew that the collision course he had been upon his whole life rocketed toward its preordained conclusion. He knew that this path would bring him to his other half. Even now, he could feel him. He wouldn't even have to seek him out; the other would find him.

His revenge and his destiny lay ahead, and he couldn't wait to see them both to their conclusions.

He felt as if he had become the living personification of evil. He was the dark man now. He was the night, and it was time for night to fall upon the unsuspecting town of Asherton.

# Part Three:

*The Rod and the Staff*

# THIRTY-SIX

THE CITIZENS OF Asherton had deserted the streets, but it was easy for him to imagine them teeming with life and activity. *Busy little bees going about their daily routines. Working, going home, sleeping, and doing it all over again the next day. Perpetuating the cycle, never breaking the routine. Apathetic, mindless, and unaware of anything being wrong.*

Ackerman could picture them now: walking their dogs, getting groceries, visiting the doctor, enjoying a meal at the local diner. He could picture the children on the playgrounds and see them ordering sweet confections from the back of an ice-cream truck. It was easy to see that when sunlight shone on Asherton, it became the epitome of the white-picket fence, all-American dream.

Just thinking about it made him sick. He had to put a stop to it.

*But where to begin?*

He needed information, but at such a late hour, only the local watering hole, the Asherton Tap, would be open for business. He had to park a block down since cars filled the parking lot and surrounding areas. It was the weekend and a small town; the bar would be filled well beyond capacity.

The crowd had spilled out onto the sidewalk, and people laughed and talked out in the fresh air. The establishment's sign hung askew, and he noted the absence of a few letters from the word *Asherton.* Neon beer signs lit the windows. He had to shove his way into the squat, brick building. The bar patrons were packed in like cattle, and he had to wind his way through the crowd just to reach the bar.

He straddled a bar stool made from an old saddle. A beautiful, young woman with tight jeans and a white cowboy hat had just vacated the seat. Her long black hair flowed down her back like a waterfall in moonlight. He could still feel the residual warmth left by her body, and a sudden desire crept over him. He imagined her body pressed close to his own. He entertained the fantasy of a normal life. He contemplated what it would feel like to be loved.

But he knew there wasn't a woman in the world who could accept him for the monster he truly was. Plus, perpetuating the Ackerman lineage was the last thing he wanted to do. He would be the last, and he could feel his long sleep close at hand.

A short woman behind the bar walked over. She couldn't have been more than four foot ten and had short, red hair. "What's your poison?" He noticed the name *Big Phil* stenciled over a pocket on her bright *Asherton Tap* T-shirt. "Big Phil, huh?"

"Philomena. What do you want?"

"I'll take a beer."

"What kind?"

"Surprise me."

The diminutive woman rolled her eyes, filled a glass with an expensive imported brand, and placed it in front of him. "Surprise," she said.

He smiled his best smile and poured on the charm until an aura of likeability seemed to permeate the air around him. "Excuse me, my wife and I are thinking of moving to this area, and I'm currently working as a deputy sheriff up in Oklahoma. I had thought of trying to get a job as a deputy for your fine county here, but I'm not sure yet.

I was just wondering if you knew the local Sheriff at all? I wanted to get a feel for him before I put myself out on a limb."

"The Sheriff? Sure, I know him. I know him pretty well, actually. He's in here a lot, on account of his daughter working for me."

His face brightened. *A daughter?*

"He's a great guy. I'm sure you'd enjoy working for him, but I know that he's extremely selective on who he hires as a deputy. They're a pretty tight-knit group."

"I'm qualified, so I'm sure that I could get the job, if I put my mind to it. You said that he has a daughter that works for you? Maybe I could pass along my number to her, and then he could get back in touch with me and set up some kind of interview. Is she here tonight?"

"No, I gave her the night off. After what happened last night, I figured she could use a breather."

"Why? What happened last night?"

"A group of guys tried to jump her and this new guy that was walking her home. Luckily, this guy she was with must have known karate or something 'cause he kicked all their asses and saved hers."

A voice from a couple of stools down interrupted them. "Hey, can I get a beer? Or are you going to gossip like old women all night?"

With a quick snap of her neck and fire burning in her eyes, the little redhead turned her attention to the man. "Hey, shut up! This is my bar, and I'll do whatever the hell I want. You don't like it, then get out." She turned her attention back to Ackerman with a shake of her head. "Some people. Anyway, I heard there were like seven or eight guys that jumped them."

His grip tightened around the beer. "Wow, the guy she was with must have been something. What did he look like? What was he, seven feet tall and three hundred and fifty pounds?"

He thought that he already knew the answer, but he couldn't quite wrap his mind around the possibility of such a clear intersection to all the paths.

"Nah, he was pretty normal. I didn't get a real good look at him. His name was something that started with an M. Matthew. Michael."

"Marcus," he said.

She snapped her fingers. "Yeah, that's it. You know him or something?"

"Lucky guess." He laid payment for his drink, plus a hefty tip, down on the bar. "Keep the change, and thanks for all the info. I'll let you get back to work."

"Thanks. Good talking to you. I hope you get that deputy job." She turned back to the man that had interrupted their conversation. "All right, pansy, what kind of fu-fu, girly drink did you want?"

He turned away from the bar and took a long, hard swig of his beer. He considered the implications of what he had just learned. He could kill two birds with one stone. Marcus was involved with the Sheriff's daughter. It was perfect. Any doubts regarding his destiny faded away. He was meant to be here. His life had meaning. He had been traveling the path to this day his whole life, and now the time was at hand. The world was not chaos. The world was an intricate tapestry of synchronicity and interrelated events that combined to form the grand plan, a plan in which he played a part.

For the first time since he was a boy, Francis Ackerman Jr. experienced hope.

And now, the path was clear. He had to find the girl. She was the key to everything.

He looked around the bar at all of the people gathered

there. He looked at them with different eyes. The band on stage played another droning top-forty hit performed for the sole purpose of getting people on the dance floor. It seemed to be working.

As he looked around the room, he no longer felt the same hatred and rage that he normally felt toward pretty much all other members of his species. The grand realizations and epiphanies that he had experienced over the previous twenty-four hours had bestowed upon him a different outlook on life.

He no longer hated them. *Unfortunately, they all still have to die…*

# THIRTY-SEVEN

MARCUS WAS IN and out of consciousness during the entire drive. Scattered, incoherent images passed before his eyes. He floated back and forth between the world of a horrible nightmare and the real world, but he was unable to distinguish which perception was real and which one was the bad dream. He had just enough comprehension of what was happening to realize that he had been moved into some kind of a cellar, but he didn't know much more than that. As he phased in and out of cognizance, he tried to bring himself out of the haze, but he kept sliding back down the slippery slope into the dream.

It wasn't the same dream that had been plaguing him, but it was one that stirred just as much guilt. He was in a great ocean surrounded by nothing but dark-blue water and gray skies. He wasn't alone in the water, though. The four Brubakers, his aunt, and Maggie were all in the water with him. They floated in tranquility for just a moment before the seas stirred and dark clouds spewed forth a torrential downpour. The currents ripped against them, and the rain stung their faces like a million tiny needles. But he held them all together.

He was strong. He could save them.

But Poseidon's rage continued to bombard the group. His grip loosened, and no matter how hard he tried, he couldn't hold them. His aunt was the first to slip his grasp. The waves took her, and he watched as the distance grew between them. She screamed his name, but her shouts became weaker and weaker.

He squeezed the others even tighter, but he couldn't hold them. One by one, they all slipped away. Each one screamed his name and pleaded with him to save their lives, but all he could do was watch.

Maggie was the last to go. After she was gone, he howled into the raging wind with a sound of utter helplessness and despair. Then, he stopped kicking and let himself descend into the murky depths.

As he slipped farther into the infinite blackness, he felt himself shaking. He concluded that this was the first sign of his encroaching death. But as the shaking continued, he thought he heard a faint voice in the darkness, not much more than a whisper. It told him to wake up.

But he didn't want to wake up. He wanted to slip into the darkness until there was nothing left of himself and only the darkness remained. He had failed everyone. He didn't deserve to live after the others had perished. He just wanted to sleep the long sleep and see if forgiveness lay beyond the borders of infinity.

But the shaking...

"Marcus! Marcus! Wake up. Damn it, we don't have time for this. Wake up." The man shook him and spoke in a soft but insistent tone.

Finally, he blinked back the last of the haze and sat up. His head throbbed, but he shook off the pain and looked at the man who had awakened him.

The black garments of a covert operation covered the man. Good shape, but average build. Sandy blonde hair, cropped short. The man couldn't have been more than a few years older than him, but soft wrinkles formed around his eyes that showed a level of hardness.

"I know you," Marcus said.

"We've met."

"You're the real-estate guy…Andrew Garrison." Garrison had offered to sell his property for him when they had first met. Looking back, he wished that he had sold the damn thing and kept moving down the road.

"I'm not sellin' real estate today," Garrison said. "You're on the Sheriff's ranch. I was monitoring the place when I saw them drag you out of a squad car and into the cellar. I'm risking a lot by helping you, but I'm hoping that you've got some information that I need. I don't have time to explain now. We need to get out of here, so stay quiet and follow me."

Marcus looked down and realized that he had been tied up, but Garrison must have removed his restraints. He couldn't determine where the Realtor possibly fit into the puzzle. There was something about the man that suggested there was a lot more to his involvement than a sense of civic duty. There was a collectedness in Garrison's eyes that wouldn't be present in the eyes of an average person placed anywhere near the current situation.

Garrison helped him to his feet and said, "Come on. We gotta go." He shook his head in an attempt to dust the remaining cobwebs from his brain and said, "Hey…I'm glad you're here. I've been seriously considering your offer to sell my house, and I think I'm going to go for it. This place just doesn't seem to agree with me."

Garrison smiled, and some of the intensity left his eyes. "Really? After you've made so many new friends."

"If these are my new friends, I don't want to stick around long enough to make any enemies."

Garrison nodded. "Can you walk?"

He still wasn't sure how Garrison came into play, but at the moment, he didn't care. "I'll make it. Lead the way."

He glanced around in an attempt to get a bearing on his

surroundings. Shelves containing canned goods, tools, and an assortment of junk sat on an old concrete floor. Cobwebs hung from the joists above his head. The whole area smelled damp and musty.

He noticed stairs leading into the main part of the house. There was, however, another smaller set of stairs that appeared to ascend up to an old-time cellar door and then, presumably, outside. He experienced a flash of a memory in which he was being dragged down those same stairs. He felt the bruises on his arms and back to confirm that it was more than just a memory.

Garrison moved like a cat as he led Marcus toward the cellar door. "I had to cut three heavy-duty locks to get through this access door, while avoiding the Sheriff's security patrols. There are always four to five sentries patrolling the outer perimeter." Garrison looked down at his watch and appeared to do a quick mental calculation. "In about one minute, we should have our best opportunity to slip past the patrols. Just stay close and keep your head down."

*Sentries patrolling the outer perimeter? That's not typical Realtor lingo. Plus, he's cased the joint to the extent of being able to predict holes in the security. Who is this guy?*

Garrison moved up the stairs, and Marcus followed his enigmatic new friend. Garrison turned back and said, "Here we go. Stay close."

They emerged from the cellar and ran across the open space between the house and a machine shed. They made it across the yard, and Marcus realized that he had been holding his breath. As they ran, he had noticed one man walking in the opposite direction, facing away from them. They had slipped by him, but Garrison had said that there would be at least three more.

He glanced back at the Sheriff's home. The massive

gray, white house consisted of two stories. Gables filled with intricately carved pediments adorned even the home's rear. The elaborate landscaping looked to be under the constant scrutiny of a professional. It was the dwelling of an oil tycoon, not a county sheriff.

They continued to the corner of the shed. Garrison peered around the edge and turned back to him. "There's a guard around the corner smoking a cigarette. We're going to have to go right past him and over that hill. I'll take care of the guard. Wait here until I give you the signal." He nodded and gave a thumbs up. He watched as Garrison glided around the corner and headed for the guard. The man stood about fifteen feet from the building, looking toward the perimeter. The sentinel clearly didn't expect opposition to come from within.

As he watched Garrison move toward the guard, his companion reminded him of an Indian brave floating across dry leaves. He had been told that the Indian warriors could do so without crunching the leaves and alerting their enemies. Although there were no dead leaves to be trampled, judging by the way that Garrison moved, he wondered whether or not the ground being covered by autumn's offerings would have made any difference.

Garrison crept up to the guard's back. With unsettling precision, the so-called Realtor disarmed the sentry while grabbing him around the neck and squeezing until the man passed out. Garrison accomplished this making little to no sound.

*Who is this guy?*

They crossed over the hill and made their way to Garrison's vehicle. The Realtor's large, black SUV sat hidden behind a few American sycamore trees alongside a dirt road. He recognized it as a Cadillac Escalade, just another vehicle that was way out of his price range and beyond his social class.

They jumped into the vehicle and sped down the dirt road. He didn't know where the road led, but at this point, he really didn't care. The only thing he knew for sure was that he left behind certain death and the role of a pawn in some sick game cooked up by a backwater sheriff with delusions of grandeur. The question remained, however, whom the mysterious man sitting next to him really was and what part he played.

It occurred to him that Garrison's participation could have been a trick and part of the Sheriff's plan. He would keep that in the back of his mind. At that moment, he trusted no one.

GARRISON BROKE THE silence first. "I know that you found Maureen Hill's body, so I'm guessing you saw something at the crime scene that the Sheriff didn't want anyone knowing about."

Marcus recounted his story. Afterward, Garrison said, "Did the Sheriff mention anything about his big plans for tomorrow?"

"Not really. He said that Ackerman was important and that I messed things up by letting him escape. But he said that he could use me instead. For what…I have no idea. The only thing about a plan that he mentioned was that he had someone he wanted to kill."

"Think, Marcus. You didn't overhear anything about a location or a target, a time? Anything?"

"No. I'm sorry."

Garrison punched the steering wheel. "So am I. I risked everything to break you out of there because I thought you might be able to fill in the blanks. But you know less than I do."

His eyes narrowed at Garrison. He hesitated a moment but then said, "Who are you?"

"Who do you think I am?"

"For starters, you're a guy who answers a question with another question—which pisses me off. Reminds me of a damn shrink. Beyond that, if I was going to play Sherlock Holmes, I'd start by deciding on what you're not. You're not a Realtor; that's obvious. And you're not a killer. Otherwise, you would have ended that guard back there instead of incapacitating him—which rules out Mafia, contract killer, and mercenary. Not that any of those crossed my mind anyway, but I like to be thorough. You're not a cop, state or otherwise. Anything that's happened tonight is a domestic matter, ruling out CIA and NSA. And you're not just some hometown hero or Good Samaritan. If you were, you wouldn't have that look in your eyes. So, my dear Watson, my money's on FBI."

Garrison's eyes left the road for a second as Marcus peered over at him. "Seems like you've got it all figured out, but if I was FBI, why would I go in alone and risk my life to save you? Why wouldn't I call in the troops and end this once and for all?"

"Elementary, my dear Watson. You don't know who to trust either. You're in the same position as me. All dressed up, but no one to take you to the ball. You've got at least some evidence, but no idea where to go with it. No idea of who to trust. Am I close?"

Garrison hesitated but, after releasing a long sigh, acknowledged the question. "Unfortunately, yes. The bureau has suspected some of the Sheriff's activities for quite some time now, but never had any hard evidence to prove it. They've sent in several agents to investigate, but all of them have been mysteriously taken off the case just when they began to make headway."

"Someone in the bureau must be involved. Someone with enough influence to force re-assignments."

"That's why my presence here isn't official. It's as much a mole hunt as it is an investigation into the Sheriff's activities, but I think this goes way beyond the bureau."

"What do you mean?"

The dark highway whipped past at a blur outside the window. Garrison reached down and turned up the air. "I have my suspicions that the Sheriff is doing a lot more than ridding the world of serial killers. You remember that congressman who was killed in a bad car crash in Washington about six months ago?"

He searched his memory for a moment and said, "Vaguely. Hit by a drunk driver. But the guy who hit him fled the scene, and they never caught him."

"Right. That's the official line anyway. Most people don't know this part of the story, but before his death, he was under scrutiny for having ties to the Mafia. The investigators linked him to several shady deals that made a lot of people a lot of money. But if you want to play the game, you have to get your hands dirty. Somewhere along the way, you're going to make some enemies. So, it wasn't much surprise to the investigators that the circumstances surrounding his death might seem a little suspicious. After all, there could be some pissed-off Italian out there who didn't get the construction project he was promised.

"But here's the kicker. Our friend the Sheriff and his number-one goon, Lewis Foster, were in Washington at the time of the accident. They arrived the day of the crash and flew out the next morning. I can find no reason for the trip."

"You think they were responsible? But he's a local sheriff…why use him and not some professional killer?"

"He used to be with the bureau until a killer he was

tracking murdered the Sheriff's wife. They caught the guy, but he got off on some technicality. The Sheriff tracked him down and put two in the back of his head while he slept. From what I heard, he didn't even try to run or cover it up or anything. But after a couple of days, the police dropped the charges, and the Sheriff walked out a free man. He moved down here and set up shop with a big, fat wallet. Now how exactly does that happen?"

"You think that someone high up in the government is using the Sheriff and his lackeys as some kind of avenging angels? Someone who can take out the dirty laundry that nobody else can legally touch? That's why they're being protected and allowed to wage their own private war…because the orders come down from somewhere up the food chain." Garrison nodded his assent. "That's why we can't call for backup or go for help. Even if we told the right people, somewhere along the way the information would work its way to the wrong ones. We're all alone in this. The Sheriff has been given some big mission that—according to my source on the inside—is supposed to be going down tomorrow."

Marcus drummed his fingers on the dash in a rapid staccato. "Do you know who's pulling the strings?"

Silence.

"You have some idea. I can tell."

Garrison rubbed his right temple. "I spent two years quietly tracing some money that found its way to the Sheriff, keeping the investigation under the radar. The trail is real thin, and I made some assumptions and inferences along the way. But, as best I can figure, that money came from a company that has some very…influential people on its board."

"So who's pulling the strings?"

"The info I found doesn't prove anything. Besides, it's crazy. It's—"

"I'm not the grand jury. Who?"

Garrison exhaled. "The man on the company's board is named Matthew Jameson. He's the brother of—"

Marcus interrupted and finished the sentence. He spoke with reverence. "Adam Jameson." He swallowed hard and clenched his eyes shut.

*This couldn't possibly get any worse.*

# THIRTY-EIGHT

THE SHERIFF SAT behind the antique walnut desk and stared into the darkness toward Asherton. The desk dated back to the seventeen hundreds, a gift from his late wife. He liked to imagine the founding fathers sitting at similar desks, drafting the words that made America free. He closed his eyes. *What would they think of us now?*

Everything was falling into place, more or less. He had been forced to make a few improvisations along the way, but his men were the best. They could adapt to any situation. Besides, he was confident that—despite anything Marcus might do—the end result would be the same. *The only wild card left in the deck is Ackerman.*

He turned to Lewis Foster, who sat a few feet in front of the desk in a chair of equal value. Foster awaited his instructions, the epitome of the obedient soldier. "Lewis," he said, "I have a bad feeling that I can't seem to shake. I don't think we've heard the last of Francis Ackerman."

"Sir, we're so close to the border that someone in Ackerman's position would have to be completely insane not to just jump over to Mexico."

He wanted to laugh, but Foster was serious. The young man didn't see the irony in his choice of words when he said that Ackerman would have to be insane not to run. After all, Ackerman *was* insane, so the rules and logic of the sane world would never apply to him.

"When dealing with a lot of men, I would say that you're right, but Ackerman is a beast the likes of which few have ever seen. He has no fear, and when he sets his sights on you, you either end up dead or wishing you were. And now, he has motive against us. I need you to go to Asherton and get Maggie out of there. I'd go myself, but I have to prepare for the final act of our little drama."

Foster nodded in assent. He was a good soldier and would do as ordered. "I understand, sir. Don't worry. I'll bring her back."

He smiled at Lewis with a wide, fatherly grin and tender eyes. Lewis had become like a son to him. Foster's family had been brutally murdered when he was only a teenager. Afterward, the Sheriff had taken him in. In the moment when Lewis needed someone to take his hand and help lift the crushing weight of the world, he had been there.

Now, the roles had been reversed, and the Sheriff was the one feeling the crushing weight pressing down on him. He had just learned of a game Ackerman had played at a local farmhouse and couldn't help feeling responsible for what had transpired. And this was only the first report. He knew that more would follow, and he felt helpless to stop it.

"Please, promise me that you'll be careful. I don't think that I can stand any more death this evening." The Sheriff shook his head and continued in a low tone. "Damn it, Lewis, I'm beginning to wonder whether any of this is truly worth it. I should have known better than to allow a monster like Ackerman out of my sight in the first place. How many more people are going to die before this ends? What price must we pay? It wasn't supposed to happen this way. No innocent people were supposed to get hurt."

"Sir, things may not have gone down exactly the way that we planned, but we'll find Ackerman. We'll stop him. We'll set things right. But we have to stick to the plan. You said it best yourself when you told me, 'Sometimes, the only way to get a person to open their eyes is to slap them in the face.' You were right, sir. And we will succeed in opening someone's eyes tomorrow. I guarantee you that. There's no way you could have known that any of this would happen the way that it did. What's done is done, but are we going to let all who have fallen along the way die in vain, or are their deaths going to mean something?"

The Sheriff nodded and said, "I think my good sense must be rubbing off on you. What's done is done. Right now, we have to stay focused. We have to stay the course. Tomorrow's going to be a long day."

A humming filled the air, and the cell phone resting on the desk lit up. He reached out and picked up the phone. He checked the number and recognized it as coming from South Africa. At least, that's where it appeared to originate. In actuality, the call had been bounced around the world to obscure its true origin—Washington D.C.

An image from long ago flashed in his mind as he took a second to ready himself for the call. He remembered sitting in his cell when the guards came and escorted him to an interrogation room. Then, a man entered and gave him a choice. Looking back, he supposed it wasn't much of a decision. Go to prison for the rest of his life or accept the man's offer. The path was clear. Whenever he thought back on it, though, he knew that he still would have chosen this path—even if a multitude of other options had been available to him.

The Sheriff flipped open the phone and pressed it to his ear. "Hello… Yes, sir. Everything is proceeding according to schedule."

# THIRTY-NINE

*ADAM JAMESON...PRESIDENT of the United States, the most powerful man in the world.* "You're tellin' me that we're up against the leader of the free world...and his death squad?" Marcus said.

Garrison shrugged. "It fits, but come on. It's just crazy speculation. I have no proof that the President's involved. The connection's weak, at best."

"But it's possible, and until we know differently, we have to operate under the assumption that he is involved."

They were silent for a long while. He felt the weight of an entire country's worth of resources pressing down. Nothing seemed real anymore. The dark landscape rushed by, and his world spun. He felt like he was underwater.

"One thing I can't figure," Garrison said.

"One thing?"

"Well, a lot of things, but one thing about your story. I can't figure out how the Sheriff and his men kept finding you everywhere you went."

He had wondered the same thing but had dismissed it as paranoia.

"I get that he could have found you on the highway. After all, you didn't know the resources he would put into your search, but he could have canvassed every road. So, I get that. But you said that you smashed the cop's radio and cell phone before leaving him at the crash site, and the cop hadn't called in his position. Granted, he probably had low-jack in the cruiser, and they could have traced that.

But from the sound of it, they didn't even know that there was a problem. So, number one, how did he find you so quickly? And number two, how was he so sure that you were in that house? Sure enough that he gunned down Allen Brubaker on his front lawn?"

He mulled over what Garrison had said. It made sense, but what was the answer? He searched his memory banks, and his eyes went wide. "My shoes. The Sheriff took my shoes at the Hill crime scene to make castings."

Garrison slammed on the brakes and whipped the big SUV to the side of the road. Marcus heard unknown items shift, fall, and clang in the back of the vehicle. "Take them off," Garrison said.

He complied, and Garrison examined them. "Look at this."

He looked closer and noticed a small spot of new glue showing on the back of the shoe. Garrison removed a pocket knife and used it to pull back the heel. A tiny, hollowed-out area contained a small electronic device.

"Son of a...I shoulda thought of this earlier," Marcus said.

Garrison shook his head. "How were you supposed to know that a local sheriff had access to this kind of technology?"

"What are we going to do with it now? Attach it to some rabbit and let the Sheriff chase Bugs all the way to New Mexico?"

Garrison snickered. "No. That might work in the movies, but the Sheriff would track us down before we could ever hope to catch some animal." Garrison stepped from the vehicle, removed the small tracking device, and threw it into a clump of bushes alongside the road.

They rode in silence for a few minutes longer before

he realized that they were not just driving in a direction, but toward something. "So, Garrison, do we have a plan?"

"Andrew."

"What?"

"My name. Call me Andrew. And the first thing we need to do is get my source within the organization to safety."

"Who's your source?"

"I guess at this point it doesn't hurt to tell you. You know her...the Sheriff's daughter, Maggie. She works for me at the real-estate office, which is all just a cover."

Marcus reached up and massaged the bridge of his nose. He had been afraid of that answer. In many ways, he was ecstatic at the thought of seeing her again. In many other ways, however, he wished that he could keep her as far away from himself as possible. The dream kept returning to him with increasing intensity. In the dream, he had failed her just like everyone else.

A sign read, *Asherton: 13 Miles.*

He had often heard that animals could sense when a bad storm or other natural disaster like an earthquake or tornado was about to hit. That was the way he felt at that moment. It was like he could sense that a storm was on the horizon and that everything he had experienced so far was a prelude of what was to come. The kiss before turning out the lights.

He glanced over at the speedometer. An unexplainable sense of urgency had overtaken him. He didn't know why, but he had a feeling that they were already too late.

# FORTY

MAGGIE WALKED ACROSS the cold tile floor of her apartment's tiny kitchen. The coolness below her feet saturated her body and crept up her legs. She had hated the tile floor when she first came to the small apartment, but she had grown accustomed to it. In all honesty, she liked the cool, calming embrace that greeted her when she stepped out onto the kitchen floor. It made her feel alive and allowed her to forget everything else in the world beyond the sensation.

On that night, however, the chilled kiss of the tile wasn't nearly potent enough to steal her thoughts from the events taking place around her. All of her preparations and work approached fruition. The die had been cast, and there was no turning back.

The moonlight shimmered in through the window over the kitchen sink. It cast a dim glow over the counter and the kitchen table but failed to penetrate the deeper shadows of the room's corners. She crossed the kitchen and opened the door to the refrigerator. With the moonlight backdrop, the light from the fridge sent out a striking luminescence that lit her face with an angelic aura. Her smooth skin glowed, as if touched by a divine light, and her eyes shimmered like diamonds. Her loose-fitting T-shirt and baggy sweatpants hid her trim form. A pair of bobby pins held her hair, still damp from the shower, back in a ponytail. A few loose strands hung around her face.

From the fridge, she retrieved the supplies needed to

accomplish her goal of the perfect sandwich. She always strove for perfection in every undertaking, and sandwich making was no exception. She always made her sandwiches the same way. She ran through the process in her mind, further adding to her hunger. She would begin with the mesquite, thinly sliced turkey breast, followed by two slices of provolone cheese and one piece of lettuce, for good measure—all enclosed by the coup de grâce, the homemade Italian herb and cheese bread. There were no condiments placed on top, as they would only serve to offend the palate and convolute the flavor.

But it was the quantity of the ingredients that made Maggie's techniques distinctive. She always made the sandwich the same way with the same precise amounts of turkey, cheese, lettuce, and bread. The Sheriff—or the Director, as some knew him—had taught her a great deal, but the thing that he stressed most to all of those around him was an acute attention to detail. "The devil is in the details," he always said.

She retrieved a plate from the cabinet and organized the ingredients in front of her. She unsealed the loaf of bread and took in its aroma. It smelled wonderful. It was the best bread that she had ever had, and it came from right below her feet at The Magnolia Bakery.

Alexei, the baker, would often make extra portions solely for delivery to her doorstep. She had only lived there for a short time, but in that span, she had often joined him in the bakery and watched as he prepared a barrage of culinary delights for the early morning coffee and pastry crowd.

Beyond the list of products to appease those with a sweet tooth, Alexei also had an extensive catalog of gourmet bread that he prepared fresh every day in the early morning hours. He would arrive around ten o'clock and work until the shop opened at five-thirty. His son would then take over for him mid-morning. She knew that he was hard at work downstairs even as she prepared her own plat du jour.

She laid the loaf on the counter. Without looking, she reached to the knife block. She felt around for the bread knife, but she noticed an anomaly. The carving knife was missing.

And she never forgot to put things back in their places.

She checked the counter and surrounding area but to no avail. She looked in the sink and dishwasher, but it wasn't there either.

She let the sensation of fear wash over her. It had been in the back of her mind since she noticed the knife's absence, but now, it was in the forefront, undeniable. Someone else could have the knife. Someone waiting in the shadows with a dark, malicious purpose.

Her breathing became shallow and erratic. Her mind spun with different possibilities and scenarios.

A thump resonated from the vicinity of her bedroom.

*Is there someone in the apartment?*

She pushed the fear aside. She wasn't about to let herself be frightened by a misplaced knife and a noise that occurred often enough due to everyday occurrences like the creaking of the building or Alexei banging around downstairs.

She reached behind her back and retrieved a compact Glock 19 pistol from the waistband of her sweatpants. The Sheriff had insisted on her being armed, and under the circumstances, she had elected to keep the weapon close.

Another thump, but she couldn't be sure from where it originated.

Something had caused the noise, and it wasn't an overactive imagination. She needed help. If Ackerman was the source of the noise, she would not be able to stand against

him alone. She had heard the horror stories. They said that
he was a ghost and couldn't be killed. They said that he
had made a deal with the devil. They were just tall tales.
But no one had been able to stop him yet, so there must
have been some truth to the killer's abilities.

She thought about Alexei working downstairs. They
would fare better together, strength in numbers. She
needed to get to him and then hold out until Andrew and
Marcus arrived. They couldn't have been too far away.

Keeping a close eye on the bedroom, she darted across
the kitchen and the living room, muscles tightened. She
saw no movement, but she felt a presence.

She moved to the front door of her apartment. In fear of
awaking any sleeping giants, she tried to make no sound.
Yet, the quieter she tried to be, the more every sound
seemed amplified. Her footsteps sounded like the crashing of thunder to her heightened perception.

She opened the door and glanced around the hall. *All
clear.* She looked back to the bedroom. Still no movement.
She stepped into the hallway and shut the door behind her.

Maybe it was all just her imagination. Either way, it
was better to be safe than sorry.

A foreboding darkness seemed to occupy the hallway,
but she tried to shut out such irrationalities. The hallway
hadn't changed. The situation had merely altered her perception of it. It was the same poorly lit corridor that she
always walked.

She headed for the stairs, sticking close to the wall. She
held her gun with a two-handed grip and carried herself
with a steady professionalism. She kept an eye on the path
behind her to guard against a sneak attack, but she pressed
forward and down the stairs to the landing at the bottom.

The door in front of her led outside, and the door to
her right led into the bakery. She watched the stairs for a

moment. She saw no pursuers and entered the door lead-ing into the bakery.

The main lights of the dining area were dark as they al-ways were at that time of night, but in the part of the bak-ery where the magic happened, the lights burned brightly. The light filled her with as much warmth as the sun on a summer day. She would feel much safer by simply not being alone.

Remembering her training, she kept the gun ready, ever vigilant. She walked across the dim customer area and headed for the back.

When she entered and looked around, she saw no sign of the baker. It appeared that he had left treats baking in the oven, and a thick dusting of flour covered the table.

*But where's Alexei?*

She spotted something strange and walked closer. What she saw made her heart skip a beat.

There were droplets of blood spattered across the flour-covered table.

*Human blood? Alexei's blood?*

She continued around the table with the pistol stretched out in front of her. Her finger rested on the trigger, ready to bring a quick end to any possible confrontation. As she moved forward, she noticed a stream of red flowing from behind a neighboring table.

She rounded the second table and saw the body of her friend laid out on the floor. Deep gashes covered his body, and chunks of flesh had been torn away, exposing bone and internal organs. Torn from his abdomen, his intestines lay strung across his right shoulder.

The bile rose, and she threw up. She wanted to run, but she couldn't tear her eyes away from him. She stared at his lifeless body—transfixed, mesmerized, in shock. She had seen dead bodies before, but nothing like this.

A voice from behind snapped her out of the stupor.

"Admiring my work?" the voice said.

She spun around and pointed her gun at the man behind her. He stood on the opposite side of the flour-covered table.

"Don't move!" she said.

She wondered how had he gotten so close without alerting her. *Where did he even come from?*

"I was paying homage to one of history's most notorious murderers, Jack the Ripper. I took a bit of creative license in the moment, but it's meant to be a tribute not a true recreation. My father forced me to study all the gruesome details of every known killer's work. I've always found the method behind Jack's madness to be fascinating."

She stood ready to blow his head off if he moved a muscle. She knew that he must have been able to see that, but he didn't seem concerned. In fact, he looked calm and collected—a man without a care in the world.

He held a towel and appeared to have just finished washing his hands. She could see that he had cleaned a great deal of blood from his face, but a few rogue streaks of red remained.

He continued to dry his hands and ran his eyes up and down her form. She could almost feel his gaze as it crawled over her body. "You're quite beautiful, and there's a certain…fire in your eyes. I like that. Not much family resemblance, but I can see why Marcus is interested in you. And that's why I'm here. You're the intersection. The connection that binds all the threads together. You're the key to unlocking my destiny."

He looked deep into her eyes. She felt him knocking on the door to her soul. "I want to play a game, my dear…a game called *Cat and Mouse*."

She had never killed anyone before, but there was a first

time for everything. She increased pressure on the trigger and considered squeezing.

"Let me guess," she said. Her voice shook, but she tried to mask her terror. "You're the cat, and I'm the mouse?"

He shook his head. "Oh no, sweetheart. I'm afraid that you're merely the cheese for the mousetrap."

Without warning, Ackerman dropped the towel and swept his hand across the flour-covered table. The movement stirred up a white cloud that made her lose sight of him for a split second.

She fired into the cloud only a second after his movement, but it was too late. He was too fast. Her shot sailed wide. She fired blindly in the area she had last seen him. Flour filled the air and obstructed her visibility.

Before she could react, he had rounded the table and was upon her. He wrenched the gun from her hand and struck her across the face. She hurtled through the air and pounded against the linoleum. Blood flowed from her mouth and nose, and tears welled in her eyes.

She considered running, but she knew there was nowhere to go. She pulled herself up on her hands and knees and spat blood on the floor. A small portion of her fear had evolved into rage. She wanted to kill the man who had struck her, not only for herself, but for all of those who had suffered at his hands.

She turned back to her attacker and said, "You can't kill me. You need me as your bait, and I won't be very good bait if I'm already dead."

He placed her gun in the back of his pants and picked up a carving knife that lay next to Alexei's body. He twisted the knife, appearing to admire the blade. "You're partly right, my dear. But what you've overlooked is the fact that they only have to *think* that you're alive. Plus, I truly hate to admit this, but sometimes…I simply can't control myself."

# FORTY-ONE

"SOMETHING'S WRONG," ANDREW said as he placed the cell phone back in his pocket. "She knew we were coming. She wouldn't have just left." He had already attempted to reach her twice, once on the road and once in front of her building.

After a cursory scan of the area, they decided to investigate. Marcus went upstairs to her apartment while Andrew went to ask Alexei if he had seen or heard anything. They met back on the landing that led up the stairs.

"She's not in her apartment. No signs of a struggle," Marcus said as he came down the stairs. "Did the baker know any…" His words trailed off when he saw the look on Andrew's face. *She's dead. I've failed everyone. None of this would have happened if it wasn't for me.*

His knees felt weak. His heart pounded, and the air in his lungs grew heavy. The act of breathing became a chore instead of a reflex.

"What's wrong?" he said and tried to steel himself for the response.

Andrew wouldn't meet his eyes. After what seemed like an eternity, Andrew said, "Ackerman's been here."

He didn't wait for another syllable to be uttered. He pushed past Andrew and ran into the bakery. Visions of Maureen Hill flashed into his mind, only now he saw Maggie in her place. He couldn't shake the thought of Maggie nailed to the wall and tortured—her lifeless husk trapped in an eternal scream, torment forever carved onto her face.

It was no way to die. He held to the belief of what a warrior from the past would have called "dying a good death." His father said it was "dying with your boots on." He simply thought of it as a death with meaning. It was almost as important as a life with meaning. But the atrocities left in the wake of Ackerman's rage were senseless and pointless tragedies that only served the purpose of quenching a madman's thirst for blood.

He pushed his way into the bakery's back room. From somewhere far away, he heard Andrew asking him to wait, but he pressed forward anyway. He had to see for himself.

It only took a moment for him to find the mutilated body of the baker, Alexei. He searched the rest of the kitchen but saw no sign of Maggie.

"She's gone," Andrew said from the doorway.

A wave of relief passed over Marcus, but he felt guilty for the emotion. He hadn't found Maggie lying there in a pool of blood, but there was still an innocent man dead on the floor whose only crime was being in Ackerman's way. *And it was my fault.* He had allowed Ackerman to escape in the first place. He cursed himself for feeling relief in the wake of such tragedy. Plus, there was still no sign of Maggie, and if Ackerman had taken her, the chances of a happy ending would be about the same as winning the lottery without buying a ticket.

He leaned over one of the tables to keep from falling to his knees. He wanted to drop to the ground and weep, but he didn't have time to cry. Now was a time for action. He turned to Andrew and said, "I'm going to get her back."

The words gave him strength. He stood straight again, and a look of determination filled his eyes. "I'm going to save her…and put an end to this."

Just then, what sounded like an explosion pierced the night. It came from somewhere close, no more than a couple of blocks away. He and Andrew glanced at each other and didn't have to say a word. Within seconds, they were both out of Maggie's building in pursuit of whatever had caused the sound.

His determination grew with every step. He wasn't sure how he knew, but he was certain that Ackerman had caused the noise. They were on a collision course. All of his inhibitions and reservations were gone. He would save Maggie, no matter what the cost.

# FORTY-TWO

IF MARCUS WAS his other half, then he would come and put an end to this. If Ackerman's suspicions proved to be true and there was meaning to the universe, Marcus would save these people.

Ackerman raised Maggie's gun and took aim at the propane tank that he had placed by the back door. He had draped a flaming towel over the tank, in order to ensure that the escaping gas found a spark.

He stood at the back corner of the Asherton Tap and prepared to run—not only to get out of the path of the explosion, but also so he could get to the front of the bar before the people began to pile out.

He squeezed the trigger and rounded the corner. He wished he could have seen the explosion, but that wasn't part of the plan. He had to settle for auditory gratification in the form of the shocked screams emitted by the bar patrons.

He reached the front of the building and took aim. *Here they come. Like lambs to the slaughter.*

The first person out was a young, blonde woman, who couldn't have been more than twenty-one or twenty-two. He squeezed the trigger, and the woman's head snapped back.

The next victim was a thirty-something man with wavy black hair, who had apparently never heard of "women and children first." A squeeze and a pop, and the man joined the blonde on the pavement.

Apparently still in shock from the explosion and not comprehending what awaited them, the people kept coming.

He aimed and squeezed with cold, mechanical movements. *Pop*, *pop*, *pop*. A couple members of the group escaped and ran down the street, but he expected some stragglers. They weren't important. He had plenty of playmates still within his grasp.

Finally, the herd seemed to realize that the act of stampeding carried them into the jaws of a predator, and they retreated away from the doorway. So far, everything had gone as anticipated. By now, he surmised that the fire from the explosion should have eaten its way through the back portion of the building. It wouldn't be long before it reached the main part of the bar, but that was far from the only concern with which the establishment's patrons would have to contend.

They also had to worry about the madman blocking any escape from the front. Unfortunately for those trapped inside, there were only two ways out. One was into the jaws of the fire, and the other was into the jaws of a wolf.

But he wasn't satisfied with waiting for them to come to him or burn inside. That was just the beginning.

While keeping a watchful eye out for anyone trying to escape or be a hero, he walked over to where he had left the can of gasoline. He reached down to pick up the can but caught movement in the bar's doorway.

A pale, young man with red hair tried to make a break for it. He raised the gun. *A squeeze and a pop*.

The terrified screams and shocked gasps were music to his ears. He wouldn't have to worry about anyone else trying that again, at least not until they saw what he was about to do. By that time, they would be past the point of no return.

He retrieved the gas can, walked to the front door, and doused the front of the bar with gasoline. He almost emptied the large can but left just enough in reserve to run a trail of liquid to act as a fuse.

He tried to stay in the moment, but his true thoughts wandered away from the events taking place around him. His inner ponderings remained fixed upon the young man he had met earlier that night.

He wondered whether Marcus would show. Maybe his epiphanies of meaning and preordained purpose were only delusions conjured by a warped mind and a twisted perception? Maybe the grand ideas of meaning and destiny were only what he wanted to believe?

He reached into his pocket and retrieved a lighter. He fired a few shots into the building, just to let them know that he was still there, and flipped open the top of the Zippo held in his left hand.

He struck the flint and lowered the beautiful flame toward the trail of gasoline.

Then, he paused. The flame hovered less than a foot from the gas. A sound had come from behind him, and with it, all of his prior doubts faded away.

"Don't you move," the voice behind him repeated.

He had heard that voice earlier in the evening.

*Marcus.*

*Maybe there is such a thing as destiny after all?*

He turned to see two men standing about twenty feet from him. One of the men, the one with the sandy blonde hair, pointed an H&K 9mm pistol at his head. The other man wielded only a fierce look of determination. Given the choice between them, he would have rather gone up against the man with the gun.

He had outrun bullets and beaten armed gunmen in the past, but he had never faced someone that filled him with a sense of dread the way that Marcus did. He wondered if this was the same sensation that his victims felt when they met his gaze. He couldn't explain from where the feeling stemmed, but when he looked into Marcus's eyes, he saw death.

MARCUS STARED INTO Ackerman's eyes and tried to anticipate the killer's next move.

"Slowly close the lighter and drop the gun." He saw the gas can and knew what Ackerman had been about to do. He also knew that, if Andrew fired, the lighter's flame would fall into the stream of gasoline and burn everyone in the bar alive. Unfortunately, he didn't know if Andrew had seen and realized all that he had.

"I knew you would come," Ackerman said. "You were meant to come. Both of our lives up to this point have been leading to an inevitable confrontation. You're one side of the coin, and I'm the other. It's who we are, who we're meant to be."

He and Andrew moved closer and tried to slowly circle Ackerman. But he didn't want to get too close. As long as Ackerman held the flame, they were at the killer's mercy. "Just close the lighter, and then you can tell me all about our destinies and how we're connected."

"How about I keep the gun and the lighter, and I tell you about your friend, Maggie."

Marcus shivered at the mention of her name.

"She's a real sweet person, Marcus. Beautiful, of course, but she also possesses a certain undeniable charisma. Quite a catch. I'm sorry I had to take her from you. After you're finished here, why don't you come by the abandoned school down on the edge of town and see if you can stop me from turning her insides outside. Come alone…those are the rules. Just you and me. Dark and Light. Yin and

Yang. If you break the rules, then she'll die. I promise you that. And you had better hurry. Patience is not one of my virtues."

On the last word, Ackerman dropped the lighter.

# FORTY-THREE

Within the blink of an eye, the flames quested along the line of liquid to the gasoline-soaked building. The sudden wave of heat nearly pushed Marcus and Andrew off of their feet.

As soon as the lighter left his hand, Ackerman dove toward the alley.

Andrew fired, but the wave of heat and a split second's hesitation made all the difference. Ackerman was gone.

Marcus watched helplessly as the front of the bar transformed into a churning wall of fire.

The wailing from inside had become a deafening barrage of sound. He imagined that this was what hell would sound like. Two walls of flame ensnared the bar's patrons and crept closer to their prey like a pair of hungry predators. The people trapped inside could do nothing more than wait to burn and pray for a quick death.

He thought about Ackerman, but at the moment, he had more pressing concerns. He stared into the blazing inferno, calculating. *React. Adapt, Improvise, Overcome*.

He glanced around, trying to find something that he could use to save them. He felt so helpless. He couldn't allow those people to die, even if it cost his life. He scanned the area, and then inspiration struck.

He noticed that a car had stopped about a block away and its driver sat enthralled by the carnage. He had an idea. He had no clue if it would work. In fact, he had serious doubts that it would work, but he couldn't sit by and watch as these people burned. *I have to do something. I have to try.*

He took off in a dead sprint toward the car. His footfalls on the pavement seemed to be coming not from his own feet but from somewhere far away. His heart raced, and his body ached from the abuse he had sustained over the course of the past few days. But his mind was clear. Instinct had taken over. There was a time to think and a time to react, and the time for thinking was long past.

When he reached the vehicle, he threw open the door and dragged out the driver. He caught the vehicle's owner so off guard that the man didn't even utter a word. The driver just fell to the ground and stared in disbelief as Marcus drove off.

He floored it. He wanted to be sure that his blow would have the desired effect. He had noticed the fire hydrant close to the front of the building, and as soon as he saw it, he knew what he had to do.

When he was about six years old, he had desperately wanted to be a fireman and had dreamed about saving people from a burning building. He always romanticized the experience in his mind, imagining the thrill of running into the flames as everyone else ran out—being the big hero.

Now that the moment he had fantasized about had finally come, feeling like a hero was the furthest thing from his mind. A horrible fear that permeated his whole body and twisted his stomach into knots came much closer to describing the experience. It was screaming and crying and the thought that one mistake could cost someone his or her life.

He hit the hydrant, and the car jerked back. His head smacked into the windshield.

The car's owner wasn't going to be very happy, but at this point, the only thing that concerned him was that the collision had accomplished its task. The geyser of water, which shot into the air next to the car, told him that it had.

He shook the stars from his vision and backed the car around into the proper alignment. Then, he swung the car door into the stream of water that shot out from the hole where the fire hydrant had recently sat. The pressure from the water wasn't as great as the pressure from a fireman's hose—since it was the fire truck that amplified the flow into a high-pressure stream—but even the reduced pressure combined with the slick pavement made the task difficult.

Andrew ran up next to him and helped to hold the door and angle the water flow toward the building.

The spray of the water stung his skin and fell everywhere like a cold December rain. It was hard to hold the water at one constant angle, and the curvature of the car door made it impossible to aim the stream directly at the building's opening. But enough of the manmade rainstorm hit the door to quench the flames.

After a moment, the flames dissolved enough to afford those trapped inside a chance to escape.

The patrons fell over each other and knocked one another out of the way, clawing for a chance at freedom. Courtesy, consideration, and chivalry were long-forgotten concepts. People swarmed from the bar like a stampeding herd, resorting back to a primal state and acting on their most basic survival instincts.

When it appeared that everyone had been given the opportunity to escape, he and Andrew released the geyser they had been trying to wrangle and retreated into the street. Upon reaching a safe distance, Marcus turned back toward the carnage. He put his hands on his head and tried to slow his thundering heart.

Andrew hunched over next to him, hands on knees. "Where did you come up with that?"

He looked at Andrew and shrugged. "Haven't you ever put your finger over the end of a garden hose?"

Andrew looked around at the people that Marcus had saved and nodded. "Time to go after Ackerman."

"No. You're going to stay here and help these people. I'm going after Ackerman alone."

Andrew straightened. "Since when are you calling the shots? I'm the FBI agent, remember. You're just a civilian, and there's no way that I can let you face that psychopath without me. I would say the opposite and tell you to stay behind, but I'm not stupid enough to go after Ackerman alone."

His expression didn't waver. "Guess I am stupid enough, 'cause I am going alone. He said that if I don't come by myself, he'd kill her. I don't know much, but I know that he means to keep his promise if I break his rules. Besides, I can't tell you how I know it, but I know that I have to do this by myself. Ackerman said that our destinies are connected. I didn't realize it until now, but I've felt the same thing since the first moment I looked into his eyes. I have to face him. I'm meant to face him."

"I don't give a rat's ass about your destiny. There's no way—"

With a flash of movement, Marcus stripped the gun from Andrew's hand and aimed it at the agent's head. "This isn't up for discussion."

Andrew released a slow breath, narrowed his eyes, and gritted his teeth. "Fine."

Marcus stepped out of reach, lowered the pistol, and twirled it like a gunslinger from the Old West. He ejected the magazine and checked the number of rounds. He prayed that he wouldn't have to use any of them. Satisfied, he thrust the magazine back into the gun and pulled back the slide, jacking a shell into the chamber. "Which way to the school?"

Andrew's eyes still burned, but he pointed down the street. "Two blocks up. Take a right. Follow that all the way to the edge of town. You can't miss it."

He nodded. "I'll meet you back at Maggie's apartment. If I'm not there in an hour, don't worry about me…'cause I'm already dead."

With those words, he turned and ran in the direction of the old school building. As he moved away, he clicked on the gun's safety and placed it in the back of his pants.

He felt the rush of a thousand bad memories swirl around him. He hated guns, even though he had a certain talent for them. Once again, he wondered why all his talents involved violence and death. He wondered if he was really that different from Ackerman. Maybe Ackerman was merely farther along on the path to madness.

He wasn't sure whether life, death, or insanity awaited him, but he knew that there was no turning back.

# FORTY-FOUR

As Lewis Foster made his way to Maggie's apartment, he changed course when he heard what sounded like an explosion. As far as he could tell, the noise had come from the direction of the Asherton Tap. When he reached the bar, he parked down the street and crept close to the commotion on foot. He arrived at "The Tap," as the locals called it, just in time to see the confrontation between Marcus and Ackerman. He didn't stay to see what happened with the fire. When Ackerman fled the scene, Lewis followed.

Ackerman was fast, but he stayed close enough to see Ackerman enter the abandoned middle school on the edge of town. He didn't rush in behind the killer. He took his time and scouted the perimeter, analyzing all points of ingress and egress. When satisfied that he had the lay of the land and that Ackerman hadn't set any obvious traps, he snuck into the building from the opposite side that Ackerman had entered.

He scanned the interior with cautious eyes. He half-expected Ackerman to pop around the corner wearing a wig and his dead mother's dress. At that point, nothing would have surprised him regarding the depths of his adversary's insanity.

He took out his military-issue 9mm Beretta and a Surefire 6P flashlight. He utilized the Harries flashlight technique—the back of his support hand, which held the flashlight, pressing against the back of his shooting hand. His particular model of flashlight had the on/off switch conveniently located on the tail cap. This would allow him to keep the light off until he needed it.

He also wore a standard bulletproof vest, which didn't make him feel much safer when it came to Ackerman. The psychopath used firearms but could just as easily fillet him with a stabbing weapon or rip the life from him with bare hands. The vest provided little defense against these attacks, but it never hurt to be prepared.

He walked up the back stairs and into the main hallway. He paused to listen, but the only sounds were his own heartbeat and rhythmic breathing. The eerie calm made him feel uneasy. Ackerman could have been hiding anywhere. The killer could have been behind any door or lurking in any dark corner.

He walked down the corridor, stopping to look into each room. Ackerman couldn't have known that he was even here. He had kept his distance during the pursuit, and Ackerman would have expected Marcus and Andrew to have their hands full with the bar fire for at least a little while. Despite these facts, he couldn't help but feel that Ackerman was waiting for him and that he was playing right into the madman's hands.

Being a man that didn't scare easily, he hated himself for what he felt. He tried to push his emotions aside, but he couldn't deny his fear.

A voice came from behind him.

He tensed and whirled around. The school intercom announced, "Paging Mr. Foster. Paging Mr. Foster. Mr. Foster, please report to the principal's office. The last time I saw you, Lewis, I told you that I'd make you pay. Time to give the devil his due."

The voice echoed down the dark hallways of the forgotten school and compounded in on itself. It made Lewis feel surrounded.

He tried to keep his emotions under control, but as he continued to check the rooms, he kicked in the doors with more fervor than necessary. He wanted to put an end to Ackerman once and for all. He wanted him to pay for all of the horrible things that he had done. He wanted him to pay for all of the pain he had caused and the innocent lives that he had cut short.

Lewis never had the chance to confront the man that had murdered his family, and he never would. He would never avenge their deaths, but he could avenge the deaths of other innocents. Ackerman hadn't killed his family, but he would pay for it, nonetheless.

Over the intercom, Ackerman said, "I had hoped that your boss would come for Maggie, but I guess you'll have to do. The farther I go down this path, the less I'm concerned with revenge anyway. I've been in a sporting mood as of late, so keeping in the spirit, I want to play a game. The rules are simple, but I believe that honesty is the best policy. So I want you to know up front that I cheat and that you're probably going to die either way. At the end of this hallway, you'll find stairs that lead to the second story. Take the stairs up. Then, a quarter of the way down the upstairs hallway, you'll see two bathrooms on your left. One is a trap and leads to death. Maggie awaits rescue in the other. You have a fifty percent chance of being the hero and a fifty percent chance of dying. At the end of your miserable life, you'll beg for a showing of compassion and mercy…of which I am not capable. And just to mess with your mind even further, I'm going to admit to you that death awaits in the girls' bathroom."

Lewis continued to check each room as he moved down the hall toward the stairs.

"The problem is that now you'll have to ask yourself whether I'm lying and trying to make you think that I'm telling the truth, or telling the truth and trying to make you think that I'm lying. Should you even consider these possibilities, or leave the decision to chance? Lots to consider. One last thing…keep in mind that I wouldn't be playing this game if I thought for one second that it wouldn't end with your death. That being said and considering that dealing with you is taking away valuable preparation time for tonight's main event, I'm going to offer you a chance to walk away now. You wouldn't be any less of a man if you just left now and let Marcus save the girl. Go now and all is forgiven, or stay and dance with the devil. The choice is yours. I'll be waiting."

Lewis shook his head in frustration and clenched his teeth. Part of him wanted to run, but his ego and male bravado would never allow that. Marcus surely wouldn't fare any better against Ackerman than he would. He told himself that he was good at what he did. He could be the hero. *This maniac has to be stopped, and I'm going to be the one to stop him.*

He made his way up the stairs and onto the second floor. He paused in front of the doors leading into the bathrooms. *Door Number One, or Door Number Two?* Ackerman had said that the trap was in the girls' restroom, but after all the people Ackerman had murdered, he didn't expect him to have any qualms regarding the violation of other commandments. Then again, maybe the killer wanted to throw him off the trail by telling the truth? Either way, Ackerman had succeeded in his real goal of making him doubt and second-guess himself.

He made his decision, stepped forward, and pushed his way into the girl's bathroom.

Pistol at the ready, he scanned the room but didn't see anything other than dust and cobwebs. A row of five enclosed stalls sat to his left, and a group of sinks hung on the wall to his right.

The grade-school ambience made him picture young girls staring into the mirrors over the sinks saying "Bloody Mary" three times with the lights off. Although he had tried it himself and survived, his younger sister had always maintained that a cousin of a girl in her class had become one of Mary's victims after performing the ritual. He missed Caroline, his little sis.

The memories fueled his anger. He had his own monster to face, the kind of monster that sparked such urban legends.

As he stepped toward the first stall, his breathing was the only sound. His gun in hand, ready to face the demon, he kicked open the stall's door. Nothing but a sturdy American Standard toilet and an empty toilet paper dispenser. Four stalls remained.

He took three deep breaths and kicked open the second stall. *Nothing.* Another kick revealed the third. *Nothing.*

His blood pressure boiled as his chances of finding a trap grew with each kick. Ackerman obviously had some plan, and once again, he felt like he was playing right into the psychopath's hands.

*It's too late to turn back now.* He had to see what was behind the last two doors.

He kicked. The door swung inward but showed only the same toilet and dispenser that populated the other stalls— nothing more, nothing less. He wasn't sure if he wanted to see what was behind the final door.

*You can do this.* He grasped for some shred of reassurance.

He was about to kick open the last of the stalls, when he heard a loud bang come from the hallway. He jumped and almost pulled the trigger. Forgetting about the final stall, he headed back toward the dark corridor.

Swinging his flashlight and gun in a sweeping motion, he caught sight of Ackerman standing in the middle of the hall. The killer had his hands raised, but the look of fire in Ackerman's eyes said that this wasn't an act of surrender. Lewis knew that Ackerman still had something diabolical up his sleeve, and this was all part of the game.

# FORTY-FIVE

MARCUS MOVED TOWARD his destiny. He wondered if everything really did happen for a reason. He wondered if everything in his life up to this point had been preparation for the situation in which he now found himself. If that were so, then maybe some of his gifts—although violent in nature—could serve a purpose.

Maybe his abilities held a similarity to the concept of a gun. A gun wasn't inherently evil. It was merely a tool. The soul of the person who wielded it determined the nature of the tool's use. If that was true, then maybe Ackerman was right, and they were truly reverse sides of the coin. Two men with similar gifts, but polar opposites. One man with righteousness at his core, the other harboring a darkness inside.

Then again, maybe he was just seeking justification for all that he had done and was about to do.

As he pressed forward, the school came into view. The building appeared to be in decent shape. It was apparent that someone had kept up moderate maintenance of the structure and grounds. Various shades of gray bricks with white bricks thrown in as accents covered the exterior. One end of the school was rounded and filled from top to bottom with translucent glass blocks. What appeared to be a gymnasium comprised the school's south side. A fire escape, which ran from the ground up the building's three stories to the roof, clung to the north edge.

He saw the playground in front. It wasn't hard to imagine

children laughing and running, playing four square, and swinging across the monkey bars. He felt glad that there were no children present now, considering the monster that had taken up residence within the halls that gossiping preteens and the clangs of closing lockers once filled.

As he moved toward the building, he heard thunder in the distance and felt the first few drops of rain. The wind increased in intensity. A storm was brewing.

# FORTY-SIX

PERHAPS IT WAS only a trick of the light or an overactive imagination, but Lewis could have sworn that he saw a flash of red in Ackerman's eyes. "Don't move, or I'll splatter your brains all over that wall. Where's Maggie?"

"Where's Maggie? That's an intriguing question, Lewis. Where are any of us really? Why are we here? What does it all mean? All very relevant questions, but I never took you for the philosophical type."

"Shut up, you sick freak! You know damn well what I mean. Where is she?" He considered shooting first and worrying about Maggie later, but the Director would never forgive him if she died.

"Sick freak? Splatter my brains all over the wall? You're starting to scare me, Lewis. Honestly, is that any way to speak to an old friend?"

"We are not friends. We are not acquaintances. Hell, I doubt we're even the same species, so just shut your mouth and tell me where she is."

"How am I supposed to shut my mouth *and* tell you where she is? If I shut my mouth, I won't be able to speak."

"Tell me what you've done with Maggie," Lewis said through gritted teeth. He shook with rage as he spoke.

Ackerman just grinned.

He had endured this long enough. If Ackerman wasn't going to tell him of his own free will, then he would beat it out of him. He moved toward Ackerman with his gun held at the ready.

Ackerman's demeanor abruptly changed. His smile faded. "Take another step forward, and she dies."

Lewis stopped dead in his tracks. As Ackerman's words sank in, he noticed for the first time that the killer held something in his right hand.

"Drop the gun and step away, or the beautiful Maggie won't be so beautiful anymore."

"Drop the gun? You must think that I'm a complete moron. I'm not dropping anything. Show me what you have in your hand."

"My hand? Oh, yes…this is the remote detonator to the bomb that I've strapped to your precious Maggie. If you don't drop your gun by the time I count to five, I will, as you so elegantly phrased it, splatter her brains all over the wall."

A frantic wave of defeat washed over him. Ackerman could have been bluffing, but he had already caused one explosion that night. He didn't have a clear view of what Ackerman held, but he could see enough of it to know that it could be some kind of detonator. He had a gut feeling that this was a trick—*but can I wager Maggie's life on a hunch?*

"I tell you what," Ackerman said. "I'll make you a deal. You drop your gun, then I'll drop the detonator. We can finish this like men. Mano-a-mano. No weapons."

Lewis considered this a moment and decided that he had no choice. He lowered his weapon and placed it on the ground. "Okay. Your turn. Drop the detonator."

"Detonator?" Ackerman said. "Oh…this?" Ackerman raised his hand to show the item contained in it. "It's just a garage door opener."

Ackerman let the false detonator slide from his hand. Before the opener hit the floor, the killer kicked Lewis in the stomach. As Lewis doubled over, Ackerman continued the assault with a punch to the face that knocked Lewis to the floor.

He pulled himself up and turned to confront his insane attacker. Ackerman seemed unbeatable, but he had a surprise of his own—a little treat to help even the odds.

He reached into his pocket and removed the ASP tactical baton. The device was basically a collapsible nightstick that could be compressed into the size of a flashlight. He flicked his wrist down and extended the weapon to its full length. Then, he swung on Ackerman before the madman could react to the new development.

Ackerman sustained a blow to the side and retreated back from the reach of the weapon. "Lewis, you continue to surprise me. I thought we agreed on no weapons."

Lewis rotated the baton. "What can I say? I cheat." Ackerman smiled. "I guess turnabout is fair pl—"

Lewis snatched at the opportunity when he saw it, and before Ackerman could finish speaking, he lunged out and landed a strategic blow to the killer's right kneecap. The madman fell, and Lewis continued the barrage with several more strikes to the back as he drove Ackerman to the floor.

The adrenaline flooded through him. He was doing it. He was defeating the man who only a moment ago had seemed invincible.

He raised his arm over his head to deal the hardest blow yet to the killer's most vulnerable area. If the madman died, then so be it, but at the very least, he would be incapacitated.

The baton sliced the air, flying toward Ackerman's skull. As Lewis brought down the deathblow, he released a guttural scream.

As the final strike traveled like a homing missile to its intended target, Ackerman reached out and caught the nightstick in mid swing. The rage in his eyes burned like the fires of a funeral pyre, ready to accept the sacrifice of flesh.

In one fluid and violent motion, Ackerman twisted the baton and Lewis's arm with it, regained his feet, and struck a quick succession of rabbit punches into Lewis's abdomen. Ackerman finished his attack with a powerful head butt that sent Lewis flailing backward. The baton slipped from his grasp.

Lewis wobbled and his knees felt insufficient to hold the weight of a two-year-old. Before he could fall, Ackerman grabbed a handful of his shirt and pounded fist to skull, over and over. The killer finished the barrage and shoved him into the railing that overlooked the stairwell.

Using the rail for stability, Lewis tried to steady himself, but he couldn't shake the starry sky that crept over his field of vision. He shook his head and looked up to see Ackerman reveal a concealed weapon of his own.

The blade of the knife shimmered in the light of the moon like an ancient weapon with mystical properties, a remnant from an age long forgotten when magic was still alive and flourishing. Ackerman's eyes seemed to shine as well. The killer slunk forward like a lion about to pounce. "It really has been fun, Lewis, but playtime's over."

Ackerman charged with the knife.

Lewis grabbed Ackerman's arm before the knife could be thrust into his abdomen. He held the arm in place while Ackerman tried to drive it home.

He knew now that his pride would cost his life. The truth was that, ever since Marcus had come into the picture, he had been jealous. The Director was his mentor, his friend, and more. He was like a father to him. Despite these facts, there was something in the way that the Director spoke about Marcus that made his blood boil. He sensed somewhere deep inside that his mentor respected

Marcus—even as an opponent—more than he would ever respect him. He had made the decision to prove himself, and now he would pay for that choice.

Ackerman pushed the blade closer as Lewis pressed desperately against the advance.

They fought a battle of strength, and he was faring no better than he did in their previous battle of wits. The killer had leverage on him and was using it.

Inch by inch, the blade drew closer.

His face turned red from the strain, and fear lived behind his eyes. He knew now that his life was over. Tears streamed down his face, and he whispered, "No."

He spoke more to some higher power or presence, praying for help, as opposed to seeking mercy from his adversary. He knew that any cry of mercy would fall on deaf ears.

Ackerman responded to his plea in much the same way a mother hushed her child to sleep. "Shhhhh," he whispered, and then he made the final push, running the blade through the ineffective protection of the bulletproof vest and into Lewis's abdomen.

A mask of death fell over his face. He went pale as the cold hands of the reaper crept over him. He thought back on his life and how everything had ended up. He thought of the long road that had brought him to this point. *It wasn't supposed to be this way.*

Ackerman jerked the knife up, slicing through his body and ending his life.

The cold night carried him away. He slipped into the darkness and through death's door, past the boundaries of this world into whatever lay beyond.

# FORTY-SEVEN

MARCUS COULDN'T PUT a name to the emotion that had over-taken him. The only other time he had felt the same way was his last night as a cop back in New York. It was like knowing that he was in the right place at the right time—not even the right place, but the only place...the only place that he could have possibly been at that moment. He knew that he could run away and never look back, but he also knew that for whatever reason, he would never choose that path. He would press forward into unknown and danger-ous waters and fight his way to the other side.

Maybe he would be the hero, or maybe just another ca-sualty. Either way, he would find out soon enough.

The rain poured out of the heavens as if all the angels wept in unison. He was soaking wet, but he didn't rush into the building to find shelter. He took his time and ex-amined the perimeter.

Satisfied, he slipped into the back door of the abandoned school. Cobwebs filled the corners, and eerie fingers of light lit the hallway when lightning struck and illuminated the world outside the windows. The flashes appeared to show dark figures around each corner. He knew that this was only a trick of the light, but he also knew that around one of the corners lurked a dark presence that could prove deadly.

Although he hadn't slept in what seemed like an eter-nity, his mind was sharp, and his senses were attuned to the slightest sound, the slightest movement.

At the end of the corridor, he reached a stairwell that led up to the second floor or down to the basement. He checked up and down with his gun at the ready. There was no sign of Ackerman, but he could feel the killer's presence close by. He decided to check upstairs and began to ascend. The stairs creaked beneath his weight.

He heard a slight noise from above and looked up just in time to see a shape hurtling toward him.

The stairs ascended to a landing before turning and leading up to the second level. He dove for the landing and narrowly missed being crushed by what he then recognized as a falling body.

He took cover in the only place he could, the spot where the railing of the stairwell curved upward. The area was just wide enough for him to hide behind.

He looked up to the place from which the body had fallen, but he didn't see anyone. He looked back down at the body and recognized Lewis Foster, the Sheriff's right-hand man.

Foster was bare-chested, his abdomen split open by a deep gash. The deputy looked like a surgery patient who had gotten up in the middle of an operation and walked off.

Marcus couldn't help but feel sorry for the man. No matter who he was or what he had done—enemy or not—no one deserved to die that way. Then again, he could think of one person who did.

Foster's dead eyes stared at him and burned into his soul. He had seen that look of death too many times. People died every day without the aid of a killer like Ackerman, but he couldn't do anything about those deaths. He could, however, make sure that no one ever died at Francis Ackerman's hands again.

An eerie voice echoed down the stairwell from somewhere above. "Marcus, come out and play."

He looked up but saw no signs of the killer. He ascended the stairs, staying low and keeping his weapon fixed on the next floor.

When he reached the top, he found the madman standing in the middle of the hallway with his arms stretched out at his sides. In his right hand, Ackerman held a small object, but from Marcus's vantage point, it wasn't clearly discernible.

Their eyes met. One set of eyes shined with madness while the other shined with determination.

"I've been waiting for you, Marcus. I've been waiting a long time."

# FORTY-EIGHT

"Don't move a muscle," Marcus said. His voice and mannerisms were calm and collected. His breathing was steady, his hand like a rock.

The storm raged outside, and the rain struck the roof above them like a billion tears falling at once. It created a constant roaring whisper, adding to the dread that permeated the moment. Lightning continued its periodic illuminations, accompanied by the roar of thunder.

In the past, Marcus had found the sound of falling rain to be soothing, even tranquil, but now it sounded like a thousand dark entities whispering with beastly intent. Judging by the day he was having, he wondered if this would be a storm that raged for forty days and forty nights, washing the world away.

He moved forward.

"Don't come any closer, or the girl dies."

Fear flashed in his eyes, his composure faltering. "Where is she?"

"She's safe for now. She's wired to an explosive device. In my right hand, I hold the detonator for that device. I quite literally hold her life in my hands, which is quite intriguing really. With a simple press of a button, I could end her life as easily as flipping a light switch. Such a fragile thread that holds us together, isn't it? Everyone scurrying around like cockroaches leading pointless, little lives, never taking the time to stop and consider why we're here or what it all means. Then, one day, someone like me comes along. Then and only then, at the end of life, do we realize how blindly we've wandered. Only then do we realize what we've lost. I almost provide a service. I speed along the process. I help people to realize what they have by taking it all away."

"Even though I find your philosophy totally fascinating, why don't you speed along the process for me and get to the part where you tell me what it is that you want. Then, you can write me a whole book about your worldviews and the meaning of life from prison."

"We both know that you'll never get me in a prison cell—not alive, anyway."

"The morgue it is. It makes no difference to me how, but one way or another, this ends tonight."

"You talk the talk, don't you? Your voice carries the proper cold determination, but your eyes tell me a different story altogether. Your eyes are telling me that you don't have the balls—not yet."

A righteous anger flowed through Marcus, but he kept his composure. He had wondered whether he would be able to pull the trigger when the moment came. He didn't want to find out. He didn't want to go down that path. It cost him too much. "You go ahead and test me if you really want to find out. But don't be disappointed if I blow a hole in your head without blinking an eye."

"Oooh, scary. We might as well get on with it then. We're going to play a little game. If you don't play by the rules, I'll push this button and blow your precious Maggie into oblivion. The rules are sim—"

"You want to play a game? That might be a problem."

With a tone of surprise and piqued interest, Ackerman said, "Why is that?"

"Because I don't play games."

With a swift and strong movement, he kicked Ackerman in the center of his chest, knocking him toward the floor.

The false detonator flew from Ackerman's grip. In mid-air, the killer's hand swung behind his back to produce Lewis Foster's gun.

Marcus already had his gun trained on his opponent. He should have been able to fill Ackerman with holes before the madman could have pulled his weapon, but he hesitated.

Ackerman sent a spray of bullets toward him.

He dove into the doorway of a nearby classroom, not even registering that one of the bullets had grazed his shoulder. He regained his composure and returned fire.

Ackerman rolled for cover and leapt into the women's bathroom.

FROM BEHIND COVER, Ackerman said, "How did you know I was bluffing?"

"It wasn't your style."

"But you couldn't know that for sure."

There was a long silence. "I just knew."

Ackerman smiled as he leaned against the cold bathroom wall just inside the doorway. Everything was coming together, the culmination of his entire life. And the farther he walked down this path, the more he knew that it was the right one. *Marcus knew…he knew.*

The man truly was his other half. But in that moment, he also realized that Marcus, although formidable, wasn't ready for the main event. He had hesitated. He had yet to embrace his true self.

Ackerman's wheels began to turn. *Time for Plan B.*

In order to keep Marcus pinned, he sent a string of shots in the direction of his adversary's hiding spot. Then, he moved to a small closet beyond the bathroom's last stall.

He threw open the door to reveal Maggie's lifeless form and retrieved a few items that he needed for the next little game.

With a couple of hard slaps, Maggie's eyes rolled open. "Wake up, sleeping beauty. Your prince has arrived."

# FORTY-NINE

MARCUS HEARD MOVEMENT in the hall. He was about to fire but stopped abruptly when he realized that Ackerman was not alone.

As he moved backward down the dark corridor, Ackerman held Maggie as a human shield.

*She's alive.* He felt a wave of relief rush over him. From the moment that Maggie had gone missing, he had felt like Atlas, condemned to hold all the sky upon his shoulders. Now, some of the weight lifted.

She was still in danger and in the clutches of a madman, but she was alive. He still had a chance to save her. "Let her go, Ackerman. This is between you and me."

Ackerman answered with bullets, driving him back into the classroom. "You're right," the killer said. "She is between you and me."

He could hear the killer's voice growing farther away as he spoke. It was just like in his dream when Maggie slipped away from him and into the dark waters. He knew that if he let Ackerman leave with her, she was dead for sure. He had to stop them here and now.

He swung into the hallway, gun at the ready.

They were gone.

He frantically scanned the hall as he moved forward.

*Where could they be? What if Ackerman had this all planned and has a secret escape route? What if I've lost them?*

He swung his weapon through the doorway of the first

classroom. Pale runs of illumination swept across the ceiling like bony fingers with each lightning strike. Empty desks lined the room, and the blackboard still showed signs of chalk dust.

He felt like he was in the schoolhouse of a ghost town and half-expected to see spectral children appear at the desks with each flash of lightning. But he didn't see any ghostly apparitions, nor did he see any sign of Ackerman or Maggie.

He moved toward the next room. With each second that passed, his despair and sense of urgency grew, but he couldn't just rush after them and into whatever trap Ackerman had planned. If he died, then Maggie died with him.

As he swung into the next classroom, a cool breeze stung his face. The gust he felt had carried across the room from an open window that led onto the fire escape.

The world beyond the window possessed an eerie luminescence and gave the impression that to walk through was to step into another dimension.

He didn't care if it was another world. He would follow her to the ends of the universe and back again, if that's what it took.

Outside the window, he heard Maggie scream.

# FIFTY

As MARCUS STOOD in the open window, the rain pelted him as if some unseen supernatural force willed him to turn back. He knew, however, that he could never run away. He didn't run. He didn't back down. He never had.

He didn't see anyone running from the building, and the ladder that allowed someone to reach the ground was still raised. The only direction they could have gone was up.

He inched forward onto the fire escape. The term *fire escape* seemed funny to him at that moment, considering that he was jumping into the fire rather than escaping from it.

He looked up and saw two shadowy forms on the fire escape's upper most platform. They weren't moving. They were waiting. A bottomless pit opened in his stomach. Ackerman had something up his sleeve.

He slowly moved up the metal-grated stairs toward whatever madness awaited him.

Ackerman stood against the back railing of the platform and held Maggie as a human shield. He couldn't get a clear shot. Even if he saw an opening, the killer would take Maggie over the edge with him when he fell.

Marcus was a few stairs shy of the platform when Ackerman said, "That's far enough."

He stopped and stood with his gun trained upon the killer.

His eyes locked with Maggie's. Fear had replaced the usual warmth he felt from her gaze. "Everything's going to be okay," he said to her.

"Do you believe in destiny, Marcus?"

He moved his eyes back to the killer and chose his words carefully. "I believe that we're here for a reason... that our lives mean something."

"Meaning. That sums it up, doesn't it? It's what everyone from a priest to a serial killer is searching for. Meaning. I never even knew I was truly looking for meaning until it found me...until the realization came."

"What realization?" he said, playing along, waiting for an opportunity.

"My meaning. The purpose of my existence. You see...I am the darkness."

He didn't know what Ackerman meant by that, and he didn't want to know. Trying to understand the philosophy of the insane sometimes meant sacrificing a piece of what made you sane in the first place. He knew from experience.

"I'm the villain, the dark half, or even more simply put...I'm the bad guy. I was meant to be who I am. Without evil, how do you define good? Without darkness, how do you know the light? Without a villain, there can be no hero. And when I met you, I knew. That is my purpose."

Ackerman's eyes gleamed with passion as he spoke. "It takes a fire or a disaster to create some heroes, but there are also myself and others like me who force ordinary people to realize that they are capable of extraordinary feats of bravery and courage. My purpose is to make *you* realize your own purpose. We're two sides of the same coin. So you see, Marcus, I am the darkness, but you... you are the light."

Marcus hated to admit to it, but at least a small portion of what Ackerman said had made sense. Without a villain, a hero was just an ordinary man or woman, no different from anyone else. The way that a person reacted to a villain was how he or she became a hero. He had always been afraid of his abilities, but maybe he possessed them for a reason? Maybe he was meant for something more?

"If you have everything all figured out, why don't you tell me how this ends?"

Ackerman chuckled. "You kill me, of course. You are the hero, after all."

"This is the real world, not the movies. Good doesn't triumph over evil. There is no riding off into the sunset, and happy endings are few and far between."

"Oh, ye of little faith. You can shine the light into the darkness, but you can't shine the darkness into the light. In the end, good triumphs."

"If that's true, then things aren't looking up for you. I hear hell is warm this time of year."

A moment of silence passed. "Do you believe that anyone can be forgiven?"

The question caught Marcus off guard. He had often wondered the same thing. After a moment, he said, "You'll find no forgiveness from me or from the people you've hurt. But...I like to think that God is wiser and more forgiving than any of us. So...maybe. I don't know."

Ackerman's face turned somber. "I have just one more question. Nothing really important in the grand scheme of things, but something I was curious about. I overheard the Sheriff say that you used to be a cop in New York. Why aren't you one anymore?"

Silence.

Ackerman grabbed Maggie's throat with his free hand and began to crush her larynx. She issued a sharp scream before the breath left her.

"I asked you a question!"

"Because I murdered someone!"

Ackerman released his grip and let Maggie breathe again.

She looked up at Marcus with shock born not from the attack, but from his response.

He wanted to explain, but he said nothing. He couldn't change the past. He could only ask forgiveness for it.

Ackerman didn't seem surprised by his declaration. Somehow, the killer had known his answer before asking. "One of the only lessons of value that my father taught me was that you always finish what you begin. I'm leaving now, but keep in mind that if you think like my father, then you'll know where to find me."

Marcus stepped forward. "You're not going anywhere."

Ackerman smiled and said, "You're going to have to do better the next time we meet. Playtime's over."

Without warning, Ackerman swung out a powerful arm and swept Maggie backward over the railing.

# FIFTY-ONE

MARCUS STARED IN shock and disbelief as Maggie tumbled over the edge. Her scream pierced his heart as she plummeted toward the ground.

Within a split second, Ackerman jerked the black nylon rope attached to Maggie's ankle. The killer used the railing as leverage as he held her in place. With his other hand, he raised the gun to Marcus and halted any advancement. Maggie dangled upside down a few feet below.

Marcus trained his gun on a spot between the killer's eyes, but he couldn't fire. If he did, the killer would release the rope and Maggie would fall to her death.

"Throw the gun over the railing," Ackerman said.

He hesitated as he searched for an alternative.

Ackerman let slack into the rope, and Maggie fell another few feet before the killer halted her descent.

"Wait!" With no other options, he tossed his gun into the night.

Ackerman nodded. "See you soon."

With those words, the killer released the rope and leapt from the top of the fire escape to the building's roof.

Maggie plummeted head first toward certain death.

He dove forward. The killer forgotten, saving Maggie was his only thought. He grabbed the end of the rope just as it slid over the railing's edge.

The sudden weight wrenched on his shoulders, and fibers from the rope dug into his skin as it slid between his palms.

But he held tight.

Maggie swung like a pendulum below.

Hand over hand, he arduously pulled her toward him until she was safely back on the platform.

He held her tighter than he had ever felt the need to hold anyone before. She returned his embrace. They melted into each other.

He considered pursuing Ackerman, but he knew that the killer was long gone. As he held Maggie, the rest of the world and the events of the past few days faded away. In that moment, they were the only two people on Earth.

But a part of him knew that Maggie hadn't forgotten the revelation into his past that Ackerman had forced into the light. *Because I murdered someone.*

He also knew that, even though they had survived this battle, the war was far from over.

# Part Four:

*The Wolf in Sheep's Clothing*

# FIFTY-TWO

"IF YOU THINK like my father? What is that supposed to mean?" Andrew said.

Marcus shook his head. *Finish what you begin… Some unfinished business? Something from his childhood?* His mind was overloaded. He couldn't concentrate. He needed to clear his thoughts. "I don't know yet, but I'm going to figure it out. And let's not forget that we have more than Ackerman to worry about. We need a place to think this thing through. Figure out our next move."

Andrew nodded in agreement. "I know a place. Hotel in the next town to the east. I know the owner real well. We can trust him. We can hide there, rest for a couple of hours, get patched up, and come at it again with fresh minds."

The idea seemed to be a consensus.

They decided Andrew's Escalade was too conspicuous, so they took Alexei's car and left Asherton behind. When they arrived at the hotel, Andrew went in and spoke with his friend. He returned in a few moments with three room keys and a first-aid kit. "We'll meet up in four hours and figure out where we go next."

Andrew entered his room and shut the door behind him.

Marcus put the key in his door, but Maggie halted him when she said, "Marcus, why don't you come to my room."

He looked deep into her eyes. He knew exactly what she wanted. She had questions that had to be answered before her mind could rest.

He stepped into her room and sat down on the bed. She

locked the door behind them. She hesitated a moment, as
if what she was going to ask would change everything between them. Her teeth found her lower lip. She seemed to
contemplate whether they could possibly move forward
without the words being spoken.

They couldn't.

He knew that as much as she did.

The fact that she had asked him to her room alone to
discuss the matter showed him that—even after hearing
and seeing what he was capable of—she wasn't afraid of
him. Maybe they could still find a way to be together? He
prayed that they could. He prayed she would understand.

After a long silence, she looked deep into his eyes, as
if to let him know that a smartass comment wasn't going
to deflect the question. "Why aren't you a cop anymore?"

# FIFTY-THREE

MARCUS HAD HOPED to never speak of that night again. He had hoped to begin anew with a clean slate. But he supposed that no matter how far he ran, he would never truly escape his past.

"I wasn't just a cop. I was a detective. Homicide. One of the youngest on the force. I was doing well for myself, making a name and all. A real up-and-comer. Cracked a few big cases. Got my name in the papers. Working hard enough to get noticed and earn some respect. But that all changed when I stumbled into this one case."

He told her about the pattern that he had seen emerging. How he had formulated a theory about the killings, and how no one else in the department would listen to him. He told her how he came to be on that street on that night.

"What happened there?"

"According to the pattern, it was the area where this possible serial killer would strike next. I wasn't completely sure of that, but I didn't have any other leads and couldn't stop thinking about the case. So, I just went on patrol. It seemed to be as good of an idea as any." He hesitated. "That's actually not true. It was more than just a hunch. Somehow, I knew that was where he would strike. I just... felt it."

He rubbed the cross that hung on a chain around his neck. "I was walking down that street when I heard a scream that I'll never forget..."

MARCUS GLANCED UP and down the deserted street. The emptiness echoed what he felt inside. He wondered how he could live in a city of over eight million people and still feel so alone. But when he delved deeper, he knew that it wasn't loneliness. It was more than that. He felt hollow, and the only time that he felt whole was when he cracked a case.

*The shrinks would have a field day with that one.*

He sipped his coffee and continued down the dark street. His eyes attempted to penetrate the shadows. "You're here somewhere. Aren't you?" he said under his breath.

Then, he heard the scream.

The sound defied reason. He had never heard such suffering, such anguish. It resonated in his soul.

The scream brought to memory the faces of the dead. He thought back on the victims of homicides he had investigated. But he had never been there at the time of death. Unlike the cops of books and television, his job didn't consist of gunfights and car chases. He had only drawn his gun a handful of times, and he had never had to use it. But if the moment came, he knew that he could wield the weapon with deadly and frightening precision.

The coffee cup fell from his hand, the liquid splashing across the pavement. He pulled the Sig Sauer P226 from his holster and sprinted down a nearby alleyway, following the scream to its origin.

The alley ended in a secluded parking lot. A dilapidated building sat on one side. Boards covered the windows, and graffiti covered most of the walls. The faded letters of a beat-up and spray-painted sign read, *the Blue Oyster Bar.*

As he scanned the area, he took in all the details. The most shocking of which was the white, stretch limousine in the center of the parking lot. In that neighborhood, he would have been less surprised to see a flying saucer.

From the opposite side of the limo, he heard a man's

voice. "Where do you think you're going? We're not finished yet."

A woman's voice said, "No! Please!"

He sprinted around the limo. A chain-link fence cordoned off the back of the parking lot, and the woman had her back pressed hard to the metal of the barrier. She was naked with numerous cuts running along her body.

He recognized the wounds. The killer liked to cut his victims while he raped them.

The man stood naked from the waist down a few feet from the woman, a bloody scalpel in his left hand.

A righteous rage overtook Marcus. A veil of red fell over his eyes. He didn't tell the man not to move. He didn't proceed like he had been taught at the academy. Instead, he rushed forward, kicked the scalpel from the killer's hand, and slammed the pistol into the back of the assailant's head.

Dazed, the killer stumbled forward. Before the man could react in any way, Marcus slammed him against the fence and twisted his right arm behind his back. With a flash of movement, the first cuff fell over the killer's wrist. He twisted the man's other arm back and did the same.

The killer said, "What the hell are you doing? Who do you think you are?"

He stepped away and trained his pistol on the back of the man's head. He then turned his eyes to the woman. "Are you okay?" he said and then chastised himself. *Stupid question.* "I mean, can you walk?"

Her voice cracked as she sobbed out the words. "Yes. Thank you. Thank God you were here."

"Everything's going to be okay. You're safe now. Get your clothes on and find a place to sit down. We'll get an ambulance. You're going to be fine."

"You're going to pay for this. Do you have any idea who I am?"

He turned his attention back to the killer. His heart pounded like a freight train inside his chest. Things were getting complicated.

The murderer didn't think that he had been recognized, but he had. His name was John Mavros—Senator John Mavros.

Marcus fully realized that he had just slapped the cuffs on a powerful senator from an even more powerful family. The Mavros name conjured allusions to the Kennedy and Rockefeller dynasties.

*What have I gotten myself into this time?*

"You have the right to remain silent. Anything you say can and will be used against you in a court of law."

"I'm a senator. Call your chief or the Commissioner. Better yet, let's call the Mayor. I'll give you the number."

"You have the right to an attorney present during questioning. If you cannot afford an attorney, one will be appointed for you."

"You're going to burn for this. You think that you're the big hero now, but when I'm done with you, you're going to be homeless, jobless, and penniless."

"Do you understand each of these rights I have explained to you? Having these rights in mind, do you wish to talk to me now?"

"Or even better, maybe we'll pin the murders on you, and you can rot in a jail cell for the rest of your miserable little life." Mavros slowly turned to face him.

"Don't you move," Marcus said. His finger twitched against the trigger.

"Listen, kid, you're in way over your pay grade here. I won't see the inside of a jail cell. I can guarantee you that. Call your chief. 555-2368. Save us all a lot of time and trouble."

The thoughts flew through his mind at gale-force speeds. He started second-guessing himself. He questioned every action. *Will slamming Mavros against the fence or twisting his arm be considered brutality?* He thought about horror stories where a person pulled someone out of their car just before it exploded and got sued because the rescued person fractured his or her collarbone in the process.

*No good deed goes unpunished.*

"Fine. Let's call the chief." He removed the cell phone from his pocket and dialed the number that Mavros had provided. The Chief of Police answered. Mavros had known the number by heart. He told the chief who he was and informed him of the situation.

After a moment of silence, the chief said, "So you haven't called this in yet?"

"No, sir…not yet."

"That's excellent. We've really dodged a bullet here. You did the right thing by calling me. You stay put. I'm going to come down there and straighten this out. You can keep your gun on him, if you want, but take the cuffs off. And be gentle."

"Be gentle? Sir, what are you saying? I don't care who this guy is. I only care about what he is. He's a serial rapist and murderer."

"I know damn well what he is…me and a lot of other people. And you're going to do exactly what all of us have done. If you don't, it's your funeral. Do you understand what I'm saying? You're going to take the money and look the other way. All the women he's killed were prostitutes. You going to throw your life away over some whore? If you pursue this, he'll walk away squeaky clean, and you'll wind up either disgraced or dead. Be smart, kid. It's all in how you look at it. This is a good thing for you. You just hit the lottery. You and me both."

"I don't want his money."

"Then don't take the money, but don't throw your life away either. He's above the law. If you—"

He closed the phone and killed the connection. He looked toward the limo. The victim sat on the ground next to one of the tires. With her legs curled to her chest, she rocked back and forth while whimpering like a frightened animal. Their eyes met. The look of terror was still present. Her eyes pleaded with him, begged him to make the world safe again. Visions of dead bodies and the eyes of other victims flooded his consciousness.

"Don't feel too bad, kid," Mavros said. "There's nothing you can do. I'm untouchable."

The killer's voice sounded surreal, like something from a dream. Marcus turned to face the monster. "Not tonight."

He raised the gun and shot Mavros between the eyes.

# FIFTY-FOUR

THE SILENCE IN the room was oppressive. It was so quiet that Marcus wondered if he had gone deaf. He didn't want to look at her. He didn't want to see her disgust or her fear.

He turned and saw sad but compassionate eyes. The look wasn't one of judgment or condemnation as he had expected.

She reached out and placed a hand on his back. "What happened next?"

"The senator's family didn't want his exploits and the inevitable scandal to tarnish the good family name, so they covered everything up. They bought off the girl. She was just a poor kid from the Bronx. They threw so much money at her that her grandchildren's grandchildren will never go hungry—and who could blame her?"

Maggie nodded in understanding.

"As for me, they gave me an opportunity to walk away without any criminal charges and with an 'early, honorable retirement,' as they called it. They also offered me a lot of money to ensure that I would keep my mouth shut. And…I took it. I kept some of it but gave most to charity. It didn't seem right, getting paid for my sins—even though that's the way a lot of people make their fortunes. That's the long and short of it. My sob story."

Another long silence descended upon them. He couldn't begin to fathom what thoughts might be racing through Maggie's mind.

"You did the right thing," she finally said.

The response sent a wave of shock over him. "I killed an unarmed man in cold blood. I'm a murderer." He spat the words from his mouth with finality, as if he could never be forgiven—or at least never forgive himself.

"You saved that girl and all the other girls who would have come after her. He was the cold-blooded killer, not you. He was a monster. He deserved a lot worse than what he got."

He shook his head in disbelief. His face flushed. "It's not like Mavros was getting ready to shoot her or running at her with a knife. He was standing there defenseless with his hands cuffed behind his back. I murdered him execution-style like some Mafia hit man. I should have arrested him and taken him in. But I didn't. I killed him. I should have gone to prison for what I did."

"You know he would have just walked away scot-free. You may have stopped him from killing that girl, but what about the next one and the next one after that? He would have gotten away with it, and he would have kept getting away with it until somebody like you stopped him."

"I could have gone to the press or maybe the FBI. I could have forced the department into action."

Maggie snorted derisively. "Number one, he probably owned the FBI and the press. Number two, if he was as powerful as you say he was, he could have made sure it was swept under the rug. Even if it did get out and hurt his reputation, probably the worst-case scenario for him would have been losing re-election. That's worst-case for him and best-case scenario for you. You being found dead one morning just like one of his other victims would have been more likely—the price for knowing too much. Or maybe you just disappear and nobody ever hears from you again? Sometimes, you have to do what you know is right, even when the rest of the world is all wrong."

He once again rubbed the cross that hung around his neck. This time, he noticed what he was doing. "The Bible says, 'Thou shalt not kill.' It doesn't say, 'Thou shalt not kill, unless the guy you want to kill really deserves it.' I don't know what to think. Nothing seems right anymore." His eyes took on the watery sheen present just before the dam bursts and the tears rain down.

Maggie didn't say another word. She just reached out and embraced him.

They curled up together on the bed. He still couldn't forgive himself for all that he had done, but Maggie's forgiveness was enough for now. They held each other until sleep finally came.

MARCUS DIDN'T DREAM about his last night as a cop.

Instead, he dreamed of Asherton. Only the Asherton in his dream was strange and distorted. The sky was bright orange, casting a strange glow upon the town. Desert surrounded him, and the buildings were misshapen and disturbing. He stood on the edge of town and gazed out over a great abyss.

The chasm was so wide that the other side couldn't be seen with human eyes. A mist covered the pit. Flashes of light and electricity showed through the clouds as they swirled over the gap, concealing its depths and its secrets. The swirling mists rose and fell like waves crashing over a vast ocean.

The more he stared at it, the less the mist resembled normal fog and the more it seemed like some ethereal specter that couldn't be properly comprehended on our plane of existence. It was an enormous swirling entity that moved with purpose and intent.

He looked back toward Asherton. From the center of town, the Sheriff and all his deputies moved toward him with a strange, shuffling gait like a horde of the undead. Ackerman and Mavros joined them. They came closer and closer. Their eyes burned red, as if they had come straight from the pit of hell and intended to drag him back with them.

He turned back to the abyss and noticed a staircase that descended into the unknown depths of the void. The world felt like it had turned itself upside down and inside out.

As the brood of demons closed in on him, he decided to descend the stairs into the unknown. He started down, and the world shook with a violent quake. The heavens thundered. He felt himself being pulled or phased into another world, somewhere far from all the pain, the sorrow, and the tears.

Then, he awoke.

The thundering he had heard within the dream was someone banging on the hotel room door. In a flash, he moved to the entrance and drew his gun. He didn't peer through the peephole. Instead, he knelt low and looked through the window. He let the shades fall back into place and opened the door.

Andrew had a foreboding look in his eyes. "It's time."

# FIFTY-FIVE

THE TRIO RECAPPED the events of the past few days and tried to find some clue that would elucidate the details of the Sheriff's plan. They discussed possibilities, none of which seemed viable. The only information they possessed was that the Sheriff had said it would be big and that it would be taking place that day. An infinite sea of possibilities still remained within their radar, and they failed to find any method to narrow the search.

Marcus felt like a fisherman who had decided to catch a great white shark by sailing into the middle of the ocean and dropping a line.

"I've got a thought," Andrew said. "It's simple. A direct approach. I just remembered an old, very politically incorrect saying. It goes something like, 'When in doubt, beat it out of them.'"

Marcus chuckled, but then his wheels began to turn. He raised his eyebrows and said, "They have to leave somebody behind at the station." Andrew nodded. "It would look pretty suspicious if they didn't. Plus, they have to have somebody around in case Ackerman is spotted. Whoever it is will definitely be on guard. How do we get in without a firefight?"

He turned his eyes toward Maggie, and Andrew followed suit. Maggie's eyes darted between them. "I don't know what you're thinking, but I can tell that I'm not going to like it."

Andrew smiled. "Have you ever used a blackjack?"

WITHIN MOMENTS, THEY were on the road.

Marcus pondered his recent dream of Asherton and the stairway descending into the depths of the unknown. He felt like he was descending those stairs now, only he wasn't walking. He was tumbling down them, out of control.

He'd always found it hard to tell whether he was moving quickly in the right direction, or tumbling down the wrong path at a speed so great that he would have no hope of catching himself before he hit the ground. Most of the time, all he could do was enjoy the fall and brace for the impact.

When he was younger, danger and velocity had been the catalysts to excitement and fun. But as he realized the consequences of jumping in head first, he became wary of velocity. The greatest velocity achieved was often the precursor to the impact. And the impact was never fun.

As he learned to question his own mortality, velocity ceased to induce excitement and began to induce fear.

They were moving at high velocity now. And he was definitely afraid.

WHEN THEY ARRIVED at the Sheriff's office, Maggie ran frantically inside.

The deputy on duty jumped up when he saw her burst through the door. "What's happening, Maggie? What's wrong?" he said with a deep Southern accent.

"He's after me. He's right behind me."

The deputy ran to her and pulled out his pistol. He moved her behind him for protection, went to the window, and peered out. "I don't see—"

The man fell to the ground, unconscious.

Maggie stood behind him with the blackjack, a small club designed for maximum damage.

## FIFTY-SIX

"WHO'S GOING TO be the good cop, and who's going to be the bad cop?" Andrew said.

Marcus grimaced. "Come on, we're not really going to use that old cliché, are we?"

"Why not?"

"It's the twenty-first century. We're two intelligent and creative guys. I think that we can come up with something better than good cop, bad cop...and something a hell of a lot faster."

"Trust the classics. It's an old cliché because it works."

Marcus shook his head. "I've got a better idea."

"It had better be good. We don't have time to waste. If we can't break this guy, we're all out of options."

He fixed Andrew with a look of cold confidence. "I only need ten seconds."

The deputy sat strapped to a chair in the middle of the interrogation room, his hands cuffed behind his back. The man was still unconscious, but it was time for him to wake up and smell the roses. Marcus recognized the deputy from the group that besieged the Brubaker farm. The recollection of that event helped to steel his resolve and make what was about to happen much easier.

He dumped a plastic trash can full of cold water over the deputy. The man jerked his head and opened his eyes. But the deputy still looked groggy, so Marcus decided to help wake him up. The hard punch across his face brought the deputy out of his stupor quicker than smelling salts. "What the hell!"

He circled the man like a shark before the first bite. He didn't waste any time. "We know the Sheriff has something big planned. You're going to tell us what that is."

The deputy remained silent with a defiant look contorting his countenance.

Marcus repeated the question but received no response.

He nodded. "I thought you might play it this way." Reaching behind his back, he retrieved a 9mm pistol, checked the clip, and chambered a round. He looked deep into the man's eyes with an icy determination. "I'm going to count down from ten. If you haven't told me what I want to know by the time I reach zero…I'm going to blow your head off."

The deputy tried to act tough but was visibly shaken. "You expect me to fall for this? You wouldn't just shoot me."

He leaned in close and spoke through clenched teeth. "Why not? That's what you and your friends did to the Brubakers."

The man's eyes went wide. The deputy looked toward the two-way mirror of the interrogation room, as if beseeching someone for help.

Standing up to full height again, he simply said, "Ten."

"Come on, man. You can't do this."

"Nine."

"Listen, I just work here."

"Eight."

"He's the boss. He's the one you want."

"Seven."

"He doesn't tell me everything. I—"

"Six."

"I don't have any information for you. I don't know anything."

"Five."

"You wouldn't just kill an unarmed man."

The image of Senator Mavros standing before him with that smug smile flashed before his eyes. He shivered, but he didn't think that the deputy noticed.

"Four."

"He'll kill me if I tell you."

"I'll kill you if you don't. Three."

"Please, don't do this."

"Two."

He fired the gun point-blank. The bullet whizzed by no more than two inches from the man's left temple.

"NO! Okay, okay, you win. I'll tell you whatever you want to know."

Marcus looked toward the observation room behind the two-way mirror. He gave Andrew and Maggie a wink. "I'm listening," he said, getting back into character.

"The target is Paul Phillips."

"The presidential candidate?" He wasn't expecting an assassination, but less and less surprised him nowadays.

"Phillips is an evil man. He's trying to get rid of the competition. That's the way he operates. He uncovered some evidence about what the Sheriff has been doing. It links the Sheriff and his activities to...some powerful people. He—"

"I know about President Jameson," Marcus said, fishing.

The deputy's eyes nearly bulged from his head. The man continued without responding to the statement, which was a definitive response in itself. "Phillips thinks he's going to profit from the information politically. What he doesn't understand is that no one is going to let him live that long. End of story."

Marcus nodded. Often the most powerful men were the most desperate. They had the farthest to fall. They would do anything or kill anyone to keep the power they had attained and gain more. "Where's it going down?"

"San Antonio. During the speech. They want it to be public and shocking. High-powered rifle to the head."

"Where's the shooter going to be?"

"I have no idea."

He fired another round past the man's head.

"I swear. I don't know. But I do know who's taking the shot."

He already knew that answer. "The Sheriff," he said, finishing the man's thought.

"Yeah. He'd never trust anyone else with something that important. Phillips might be acting like he's the angel trying to bring the evildoers to justice, but the truth is that he's worse than all of them. He's lied, cheated, and stolen his way to where he is today, and a lot of people have gotten hurt in the process. The Sheriff believes that Phillips is a murderer."

With raised eyebrows, he said, "What do you mean?"

"The Sheriff uncovered evidence that Phillips likes to frequent prostitutes. A couple of years ago when his career began heating up, one of them saw a golden opportunity. She tried to blackmail Phillips. Next time anybody saw her, she was a bloated corpse washed up along the banks of the Mississippi. It doesn't take a mathematician to put two and two together on that one. And the Sheriff has also linked him to some other deaths that occurred under mysterious circumstances. That could be the next President of the United States. The Sheriff won't let that happen. He sees this as an opportunity to rid the world of corruption at the highest levels. When Phillips's past comes into the light, it's going to make a lot of people look a lot closer at the kind of men that are running this country."

He nodded, amazed again at how nothing shocked him anymore. "What about our current President? What are people going to find if they start looking into his closet? The Sheriff can't assassinate the whole country."

The deputy's eyes filled with a passionate indignation. "President Jameson is a great American and a great man. Everything he's done has been on the side of justice and righteousness. He's trying to take this country back from those who would twist and corrupt the vision of our founding fathers. With our help, he's going to make this country great again."

He resisted the urge to spout off a smart-ass comment. There was no point in arguing with a zealot. "I'm sure. Anything else I should know?"

The deputy's face contorted into a vengeful grin. "Yeah," the man said. "They're going to pin the whole thing on you."

*THAT'S WHY THE Sheriff wanted me alive...I'm the fall guy.* The new development didn't surprise him. He no longer wondered why this was happening to him or felt sorry for himself. He was simply rolling with the punches, until he had the chance to punch back.

"The original plan," the deputy said, "was to pin it on Ackerman. That's why they were holding him. He happened to be in the area at the right time. Sheriff caught him. It would've worked out perfectly. The beauty of that plan was that it wouldn't take any explanation and no one would question it. After all, everyone knows how much of a psycho that guy is. It wouldn't be much of a stretch to think that he would kill a presidential candidate after all the other people he's butchered. But when you let Acker-man escape, plans changed. The Sheriff made some calls and did some digging. He learned about what you did in New York. Even though it's been all covered up, it doesn't take much to dig up old skeletons. Some of his associ-ates in that area have been gatherin' enough evidence to bring that sordid ordeal into the light and paint you as the avenging angel. A deluded young man bent on ridding the world of every dirty politician. Just like what you did to the senator in New York. The beauty is that he can bring out the evidence of illegal activities against Phillips and make it look like you just stumbled across it and decided to take justice into your own hands once again. Nice and tidy, just the way he likes it. You're the perfect fall guy—even better than Ackerman."

Marcus felt the righteous rage filling him again. He wasn't angry that the Sheriff planned to pin the crimes on him. He was furious, however, that people like the Sheriff always seemed to get away with it. *Not this time. Not on my watch.* He felt himself losing control.

He leaned in close to the half-smiling deputy and said, "And if I happen to be eating in a diner full of people that can verify that I was nowhere near the scene of the crime? Or if I go to the press? Well, I suppose those people just have to disappear too."

"That's the nature of the game."

He placed the barrel of the gun against the man's fore-head.

The deputy's eyes widened with terror.

He cocked his head to one side, cracking his neck. "I don't play games."

The deputy screamed.

*This one's for you, Allen.* He pulled the trigger.

The screaming abruptly stopped.

Andrew burst into the door and stared in disbelief.

Marcus secured the gun in his waistband.

The hammer had fallen, but there was no shot. He had only loaded two bullets in the weapon's fifteen-shot magazine. He noticed that the deputy had pissed his pants.

"Have a nice nap." He produced the blackjack, brought the weapon down against the back of the man's head, and returned the deputy to the world of dreams.

# FIFTY-SEVEN

THE DINGY MOTEL room made Maggie's skin crawl. It was the kind of place normally rented by the hour, not by the day. Ugly green wallpaper, greenish flower motif on the bedspread, television controlled by turning a knob, not with a remote or by pushing a button. The place hadn't been updated since the seventies. She wondered if it had been that long since the sheets had been washed as well. She could almost sense the thousands of tiny insects and vermin teeming through the bedclothes, under the mattress, and in every shadow and crevice of the room. She intended to sleep in her clothes and shoes, if she could bring herself to lie in the bed at all.

Marcus rested on the bed with his arm over his face, breathing deeply and rhythmically. Apparently, the thought of bedbugs, fleas, and lice didn't bother him. Maybe under the present circumstances, it shouldn't have bothered her either, but it did.

She sat and stared at him. She wondered what would happen between them once the current situation played out to its conclusion. She wondered if Marcus would ever be able to forgive himself. In her mind, he had done the right thing back in New York, but she knew that he wasn't convinced. He seemed to have a terrible compulsion to carry the troubles of the whole world on his back. Despite his calm, smart-ass exterior, she knew that he carried a deep well of pain inside.

Without lowering the arm from his eyes, Marcus said, "I can't sleep with you staring at me like that."

*How did he…* "Why don't we just go to the press?" she said.

"Number one, it's not like you can just walk in off the street and go on national television claiming that the President is going to have his competition assassinated. Number two, even if we did get on TV or to the right person, we don't have proof. Who'd believe us? They could discredit, debunk, and sweep us under the rug before the newspapers hit the stands in the morning. Number three…I don't want to put anyone else in danger."

"What about the Internet? We could at least get the word out."

He snickered. "Another conspiracy theory? Internet's full of stuff like that."

She hesitated. "We could run."

He sat up and looked at her.

She walked over and sat next to him on the bed. "We could get as far away from here as possible. We could jump the border and never look back. We could be in a non-extradition country within a couple of days. You don't have to do this."

He averted his eyes and stared at the wall. A moment passed in silence. "If I don't do this, who will? Before Allen Brubaker died, he told me, 'All that is necessary for the triumph of evil is that good men do nothing.'" He hesitated and then met her eyes. "I'm going to do something. Sometimes, it's not about succeeding or not. It's about standing up and being counted. It's about doing what's right. I'd rather die standing up for what I believe in than live by looking the other way."

Once again, silence descended upon them. Neither averted his or her gaze.

"You know, this could be considered our third date," she said. "You obviously kiss on the second date, so what do you do on the third?"

A smile spread across his face.

She didn't hesitate. She grabbed him by the shirt and pulled him close.

The kiss was like an explosion.

His hands caressed her shoulders and moved down her skin. His touch felt electrically charged.

She thrust closer to him. She could feel the firmness of his body.

Her heart pounded. She felt warm all over.

She slipped her hand inside his shirt. She—

In a flash of movement, he was gone.

She heard a noise from the other side of the motel room door. Someone had inserted a key in the lock.

She registered that Marcus was lying on the floor in front of the door. He was on his back, gun drawn. His calm and cool demeanor in a dangerous situation amazed her. She wondered what he was doing but then realized that a hostile visitor wouldn't be aiming at the floor when entering the room.

Marcus still had his gun at the ready when Andrew entered.

Andrew staggered back in surprise. Marcus jumped to his feet, moved to the door, and glanced up and down the row of rooms before shutting it. He concealed the gun in the back of his pants.

"Tell me that you have good news," Marcus said as he engaged the door's locks.

She watched in shock and horror as the blackjack appeared in Andrew's hand. Andrew thrust the weapon out and struck Marcus across the back of the head.

Marcus fell limply to the floor.

She jumped up and said, "What the hell are you doing?!"

Andrew turned a cold gaze upon her. "The game's over, Maggie. It's time to end this."

# FIFTY-EIGHT

MARCUS AWOKE IN a dark, confined place. He felt disoriented and only half coherent. His thoughts turned to coffins and horror stories of exhumations where medical examiners found scratches on the insides of caskets. He thought about being buried alive. His breathing grew labored. A wave of claustrophobia swept over him.

Then, he realized that he was not alone in the coffin. Another body shared the space with him. His head throbbed, and he felt nauseous. *This can't be real.*

"Marcus, it's okay. It's me. Maggie."

"Where are we?" His voice came in a ragged whisper.

"In the trunk of Alexei's car."

He shook off the disorientation and brought his mind into focus. Now, he could smell rubber and feel the vibration of the road. He tried to move, but he felt the bite of handcuffs around his wrists.

"What? What happened? I remember being at the hotel and…then, I woke up here. Wait…I remember opening the door for Andrew…and then the lights went out."

"Andrew betrayed us."

The revelation didn't surprise him. He had sensed that something was off with Andrew from the beginning. "Has he been playing us all along?"

"I don't think so. After he knocked you out, he told me that he had called my father and made a deal. Apparently, when we confirmed the President's involvement, he decided that we didn't stand a chance. So, he sold us out."

Now that his eyes had time to adjust, he could make out dim shapes within the trunk and discern the faint outline of Maggie's features.

"What are we going to do, Marcus? My father will kill you when he's done with you, and I don't know what he'll do to me."

"Don't worry. I won't let anything happen to you. Are your hands cuffed too?"

"Yes."

"Feel around as best you can and see if there's anything we could use."

"I already did. There's nothing on my side."

He groped blindly with his hands and feet, but he felt nothing. *Andrew must have cleaned everything out before he put us in. Smart.*

"There's nothing over here either. Give me a minute to think."

He closed his eyes. Ideas and scenarios flew through his mind. He played out several of the possible conclusions to their current predicament. All of them ended badly. The constraints of the trunk prevented him from bringing his hands around front. With his hands bound behind his back, he could do little to subdue an armed assailant.

He needed to determine what tools he had at his disposal. There was always something—some minuscule factor that turned the tide, some variable that the opposition had overlooked. The hard part was finding it.

Within the trunk, they only possessed the clothes on their backs. He decided to start there. Using his eidetic memory, he pictured every piece of clothing worn by himself and Maggie. He started with their feet. Within his mind, he broke the items down to their base components. He analyzed them. He combined them. How could they be used against their opponents?

His mind traveled up Maggie's legs to her waist. He opened his eyes. "I'm going to roll over to my back, so I can get my hands to your waist."

He struggled to turn within the cramped space but was finally able to move into position. His hands quested over Maggie's firm midsection to the top of her jeans. He began to undo her belt.

She cleared her throat and said, "Umm…I don't think now's the time."

"Trust me."

# FIFTY-NINE

Light flooded the trunk, and Marcus felt himself torn violently from the small space. His captors tossed him to the ground. His face smashed into the dirt. A puff of dry earth billowed into the air as he exhaled. Then, he felt hands slide under his arms as his adversaries jerked him to his feet.

"Sorry, Marcus," Andrew said. "Nothin' personal."

"You pretended to be my friend and then stabbed me in the back. Don't think it gets any more personal than that. If it helps to ease your conscience, I never trusted you anyway. I just didn't know for sure. Didn't have any other choice but to go along for the ride."

"I never meant for things to turn out like this, but you and I both know that there are just some battles you can't win. And if you can't beat them…"

"Yeah, I get the concept. You're a traitor. Can we just get this over with?"

"Fine by me."

Andrew and another man led them at gunpoint across a flat, desolate piece of land dotted sporadically with short, gnarled bushes. The Sheriff stood a couple hundred yards from the vehicles. His back turned to them, he stared out across the plain. He held a silenced 9mm in his right hand. A bird with dark brown plumage and auburn shoulders circled in the distance. An open grave sat to the Sheriff's right.

As they approached, the Sheriff turned to them. His

face was somber and mournful. "You know, kid, you never cease to amaze me. Most men would have given up by now, but not you. You've gone up against forces well beyond your control and have walked through the fire and come out the other side. You've fought an admirable battle, son, and it pains me for you to have come so far and ultimately fail."

Marcus fixed the Sheriff with a withering gaze. "I can't change the past and bring back all the innocent people that have gotten in your way, but I am going to make sure that you never hurt anyone again."

The Sheriff shook his head. "Confident to the end. I'm truly sorry for everything that's happened. But I'm a good soldier, and I have my orders. Sometimes, tough choices have to be made, and the few must be sacrificed for the good of the many. Like I told you, kid, I have someone that I need to kill. But I also need someone to go down for it. When Ackerman escaped, your neck went into that noose. So you and I are taking a trip to San Antonio."

As the Sheriff's words sunk in, a disturbing thought floated to the forefront of Marcus's mind. *If I'm going to San Antonio, then who's going in the grave?* His thoughts turned to Maggie.

Apparently coming to the same realization, Andrew spoke up. "San Antonio? Then why would you have me drive them out here?" Andrew looked toward the open grave and then back at the Sheriff. "And who are you putting in the ground?"

He tensed and readied himself to dive in front of Maggie, but then he realized that his concern for her safety had made him overlook another possibility.

Andrew swung the aim of his weapon away from Marcus and toward the Sheriff.

The Sheriff raised the silenced pistol and fired three shots into Andrew's abdomen.

Andrew staggered back and let out a sickening wheeze. He tried to speak, but the words were unintelligible. The Sheriff pumped three more rounds into his chest, and Andrew toppled backward.

Marcus closed his eyes and exhaled slowly. Fury. Pain. Sorrow. His stomach churned in knots. *So much death.*

The Sheriff looked down and spoke to the dead man. "Traitors never prosper."

The vigilante rolled Andrew's body into the open grave and said, "What am I going to do with you, Maggie? I knew that you didn't agree with what I was doing, but I never thought you'd betray me."

"You're a murderer," she said in a whisper.

The Sheriff's face remained stoic. "No, I'm a soldier. And believe me, we are at war. I hate that my life has come to this, but sometimes good men have to commit necessary evils. We all have to make sacrifices, myself included. I'm sorry that the two of you got involved."

The Sheriff turned from them and stared into the distance.

Marcus knew that the older man was weighing his options one last time. He also knew what conclusion the Sheriff would reach. Once Paul Phillips was dead, an investigation would be launched. Not only by agencies within the government that could be controlled, but also by outside forces. The Phillips family may hire investigators. An Independent Counsel may be assigned. They would backtrack the assassin's activities. Maggie would be questioned. Could she be trusted to remain silent? If the Sheriff hid her away, it may raise unwanted questions. It would be cleanest if she were one of the victims. Leaving her alive could be a costly mistake, but would the Sheriff really kill his own daughter?

Marcus realized that—as with the Brubakers—her association to him meant she had to die. *More blood on my hands.*

He knew what had to be done.

He had vowed to never kill again, but he had no other choice. *Am I just rationalizing?* He wondered if this was the way the Sheriff had begun his descent. It was a slippery slope. *The road to hell is paved with good intentions.*

Then, he thought of Ackerman and the killer's ramblings of destiny and purpose. Maybe God sometimes called the righteous to do the unspeakable? Maybe he was meant to kill in order to save?

He had no way of knowing for sure. The only certainty was that if he didn't act, more innocent people would die.

The deputy behind him repositioned the gun. He felt the cold kiss of the silenced barrel on his neck like the icy breath of the grim reaper.

*It's time.*

Placing the barrel against his skin was a mistake. His captor had just informed him of the exact position of the weapon.

Under most circumstances, that fact wouldn't have been a concern when the captive had his hands cuffed behind his back. In this situation, however, the captive had released himself by using the tongue of a belt buckle as a shim to slide between the pawl and ratchet of his cuffs. He had then re-cuffed his right hand on the loosest notch, so that he could slide it free at will.

The Sheriff looked down for a moment longer, as if contemplating his next words and actions carefully. Then, he said, "You know what your problem is, Marcus…you always hesitate. You know what must be done. You know in your heart which is the right path, but you always hesitate to walk down it."

Looking deep into the Sheriff's eyes, Marcus said, "I won't let it happen again."

He whirled on the deputy. In one fluid motion, he slammed an elbow into the man's temple and ripped his gun away. As the deputy fell, he took aim.

This time, he didn't hesitate.

He fired six silenced shots into the Sheriff's chest. Flowers of red blossomed outward.

The Sheriff's eyes went wide with shock, but then it seemed as if the eyes softened and the emotion changed. The Sheriff's eyes seemed to say, *I'm proud of you.*

The vigilante then stumbled backward and fell into the open grave.

# SIXTY

MARCUS SHIFTED HIS aim to the deputy, but the blow had rendered the man unconscious.

The sound of Maggie screaming was like a dagger of ice slicing deep into his core. He thought of the last thing she had said to him in the trunk. "If it comes down to it...I mean...with my father. He's chosen his path. I guess what I'm trying to say is...do whatever you have to do."

But he knew those were just words. The Sheriff was still her father, no matter what the man had done. She might understand. She might forgive him. But he knew deep down that whenever she looked at him from that day forward, she would see the man who had murdered her father.

Eventually, her wailing died down. With her cuffed hands pressed to her face, she sobbed quietly.

He sifted through the pouches on the unconscious deputy's belt and found a pair of handcuff keys. He hoped that the cuffs Andrew had used were taken from the Sheriff's office and that the deputy's keys would work in them as well. If not, he'd have to pick the cuff on his left hand and the cuffs on Maggie's wrists. That would require him to get close to her, and he wanted to give her some space.

With a twist of the key, he freed his left hand and placed his cuffs on the sleeping deputy. He threw the key into the dirt in front of Maggie. She didn't reach for it. She didn't acknowledge him.

He stared out across the desolate plain, and tears formed

in his eyes. He had killed again. The questions and doubts flooded over him. *Was there another way? Is this really who I am…a killer?* Then, he thought of the Brubakers. *If I had killed the Sheriff then, would the Brubaker family still be alive?*

He hated himself—for what he had done, and what he had failed to do.

He looked down at the gun in his hand. *Maybe I should finish it. Truly finish it. Maybe I should just… Finish it… Finish what you begin…Ackerman.*

His knuckles turned white as he squeezed the pistol in a crushing grip. He closed his eyes. *What does Ackerman have left unfinished?*

His mind sifted through all the tiny bits of information he knew about the killer. He wished that he had been able to study an actual case file, instead of just hearing second-hand information.

Then, he did something that he hated to do. He put himself inside Ackerman's mind. He became the killer.

He had always been able to think like a killer. It was another dark gift that made him question his own sanity. *What do I consider unfinished?*

He thought back to the first time he had seen Ackerman's face, and the realization washed over him like a tsunami claiming the shores of his mind.

He opened his eyes and looked back toward Maggie. He knew that she couldn't follow where he had to go. He considered telling her that he was going after Ackerman but decided against it. He turned and ran back up the path to Alexei's car.

Behind him, he heard Maggie screaming for him to stop, to wait. "You don't understand," she screamed.

But he understood all that he needed to. He now knew

where Ackerman had gone. He had let the killer escape. He had caused so much death. And now he would set things right.

# SIXTY-ONE

ACKERMAN WATCHED THE couple as they slept. *So peaceful. So serene.*

He reached out and brushed a strand of hair away from the woman's face. She stirred and made a quiet mewling sound, but she didn't wake. He felt like God as he watched them. He felt all-powerful. *I giveth, and I taketh away.*

He flipped on the bedroom lights and said, "Wake up."

The man sprung into action and dove for the gun on the nightstand. The cop's eyes filled with terror when he realized the weapon was missing.

Ackerman aimed the sawed-off shotgun at the man. "Do you know who I am?"

"You're a crazy son of a—"

"You know, Major Steinhoff, I considered playing a little game with the two of you, but I'm on a mission. I have more important things to do. So let's cut to the chase. If you know who I am, then you can guess why I'm here. Tell me where she is."

Major Steinhoff's eyes widened with understanding. "You can go to hell, you sick freak."

He sighed with disgust. "Probably will, but I think you should worry about your own soul at the moment." He shifted the shotgun's aim to Steinhoff's wife. "I won't blink an eye, and you know it."

"And what? I'm supposed to believe that you'll let us live if I tell you?"

"Listen, I'm a different person now. I really don't want

to kill you. That doesn't further my goals. Believe that or don't believe it, but you had better believe that you'll die screaming if you don't tell me."

Steinhoff's eyes hardened. "Fine. She's under guard at Penrose Hospital."

He smiled, but the expression didn't reach his eyes. "See, that wasn't so hard, was it? What room?"

"1408."

"Wonderful. Let's go."

"We're not going anywhere."

"Don't worry. It's just a little ride in the trunk. If you're telling the truth, then I'll have more important things to worry about than the two of you. But if you're lying to me, then I'll remove a piece of your wife's anatomy, and we'll start all over again." He let his words hang in the air a moment and then said, "Are you ready to go?"

Steinhoff hesitated and looked over at his wife. "Wait. She's in the new building at Memorial Hospital on the north side of town. It's still under construction, but we convinced them to open up a room for her on one of the partly finished floors. She's on the fifth floor. I don't know what room. Some of my best men are guarding her. They'll take you down. You won't even get close."

"I appreciate your honesty and your concern, but I'll take my chances. Let's go for a little ride."

# SIXTY-TWO

MARCUS PUSHED THE sedan beyond its capabilities. He hadn't encountered any police along the road, and he prayed that his luck would hold. He made a conscious effort to slow his speed, but he knew that within a few moments his velocity would increase again as urgency pressed upon him. He had followed a similar pattern for the past several hours. Colorado Springs wasn't far now. He hoped that he had gained ground on Ackerman, since the killer had most likely obeyed the posted speed limit.

Earlier, he had watched baby blue melt into shades of yellow and purple as the bringer of life conceded to the darkness. He had wondered if it would be his last sunset. He wondered if he would ever see Maggie again. He supposed not. After this was over, he would have to run. Not only had he just murdered an officer of the law, but he also knew too much. Powerful men would see to it that such knowledge died with him.

He supposed that for most men such realizations would have devastating implications, but it didn't matter much to him. He left no one behind. Maggie had been his last hope for a normal life. His dream of a future had melted into the ether and faded back into the place where all dreams were born. He hoped that another would live that life. He hoped that Maggie would find happiness, but he knew that he could never give it to her. He couldn't undo what he had done. He couldn't forgive himself, and she would never forget.

On the long drive, he had thought a great deal about destiny. He supposed Ackerman was right. They had been traveling on a collision course, and sooner or later, the tracks would converge.

In reality, he doubted that running from the Sheriff's superiors would be a concern. He doubted that he would live to see another day, but he would find a way to stop Ackerman.

It wasn't vengeance, and now he realized that it wasn't justice either. He merely wished to ensure that no other innocent person endured pain at the hands of Francis Ackerman. In his mind, reason had overshadowed emotion. As long as Ackerman lived, people would suffer. That was a fact that he couldn't deny.

For the first time in his life, he would embrace the monster within.

One question remained a thorn in his mind. Would he be the hero, as Ackerman claimed, or would he be too late?

# SIXTY-THREE

COLORADO STATE TROOPER Travis Depaolo's head lolled to one side, and his eyelids slid shut. The paperback novel fell from his hand. He felt a hard blow to his leg and came awake, his hand instinctively reaching for the 9mm.

"Keep it frosty there, sunshine," his superior, Nelson Girard, said.

"I don't know how much more of this I can take. This guy ain't comin' back here."

"You know what I would do if I were him, Travis? I would wait around until the cops started thinking like that. As long as we're told to be here, we're going to do our jobs. And we're going to operate under the assumption that this guy's right around the corner. Don't you forget who we're watching over."

"Yes, sir. You're right. I'm sorry."

"Ain't nothing to be sorry about, kid. Just keep your eyes open, okay?"

"Yes, sir."

After a moment, Travis heard footsteps echoing down the hallway of the half-finished hospital building. He pulled his gun but quickly placed it back in its holster when the man came into view. He checked his watch. He could set the thing by Dr. Callow's visits.

Girard nodded to the doctor, a rotund man with a thick gray beard, but Travis noted a strange look on Girard's face. "I've been wondering why you hadn't called for us to open the door. How the hell did you get in here, Doc?"

The older cop looked directly at Travis. "The place is supposed to be locked up tight."

Realizing the implications, Travis sat up straighter. "I checked everything, boss. I swear that—"

The doctor chuckled as he moved closer. A stubby finger reached up and pushed the glasses back onto the bridge of his nose. "Don't worry yourself, Travis. The work crew opened up the new access tunnel today."

"What tunnel?" Girard said.

"They didn't tell you? Since this new building is located a good distance from the others, they needed to come up with a way to transport patients back and forth. The board ended up deciding that a tunnel system connecting all the buildings would be more economical than some sort of enclosed skywalk. It'll be really useful, once it's finished. We'll be able to transport patients between all the different sections of the hospital as easily as just going down the hall."

Girard closed his eyes and released a slow breath. "Great. I wonder what genius on the work crew decided that tidbit of info wouldn't be useful to me?"

The doctor shrugged. "Sorry, not my area. How's our patient?"

"Trying to sleep, last I knew. Her kid just left a few minutes ago."

Girard opened the door for the doctor.

After a few moments with the patient, Dr. Callow exited the room and noiselessly slid the door shut. "Vitals are good. I gave her some medication to help with the pain and let her get some sleep. It won't be long until she's well enough to get out of here."

Girard nodded. "Thanks, Doc. Heading home? You look tired."

"Yeah, enough excitement for one day. See you boys tomorrow."

With those words, Travis watched the doctor's shoes clip-clop down the hallway. Work lights positioned at sparse intervals would illuminate Callow's path through the hall and down the stairs. The construction team foreman had promised that the overhead lights would be active within a couple of days, but Travis hoped to be gone by then.

With the departure of the day's only visitor, he returned to his book.

The scream echoed down the hallway like the characters in his crime novel had stepped from the page into the real world. For a split second, he thought the sound originated within his own imagination, but the idea faded when he saw Girard pull his gun. The other member of their group, a potbellied trooper named Dobbs, also came awake and went for a shotgun. The novel skidded across the floor as his trembling hand pulled the 9mm. He took cover next to an empty nurse's station.

No one spoke. The air felt thick. The silence pressed in on him as if he was underwater.

The last set of work lights at the end of the hall blinked out.

A tremor shot through his arm. He glanced at Girard. The man was rock-steady. His commander's strength gave Travis confidence.

He watched Girard retrieve his portable packset radio and bring the device to his lips. "We've got a Code 30. Send backup immediately."

Movement in the darkness. An impact. The sound of rolling wheels.

His finger shook on the trigger as the white object rolled into view.

The hospital gurney skidded down the hall toward their position. It gradually veered to the right until it came to rest against the wall, halfway between them and the darkness.

A large sheet covered the gurney on all sides, almost reaching the floor. Other than a flower of red on the very top, the sheet seemed ghostly white. The layer of white concealed an object shaped like a human body.

Girard caught his eye. "Wait here. Cover us."

He nodded in rapid fire as a response.

Girard and Dobbs moved toward the gurney in leapfrog formation, taking cover in the doorways. All the doors along the corridor were closed, but the doorjambs were deep enough to provide concealment. Within a few seconds, they arrived at the gurney. Girard shined his flashlight toward the end of the hall but illuminated no threats.

Travis kept his gun trained on the end of the corridor but watched as Girard motioned for Dobbs to cover the gurney. He saw Girard reach out with a steady hand and pull back just enough of the sheet to reveal the face of the body.

He couldn't see the face from his position. Dobbs swung the shotgun away from the gurney and toward the end of the hall, and Girard uttered something unintelligible under his breath.

He couldn't contain himself any longer. "What's happening?" he called to them.

Girard shook his head and looked toward Travis. His voice barely over a whisper, Girard said, "It's the Doc. He's dead."

The sound of a shotgun erupted through the confined space, and Girard flew into the wall. His ruined body fell to the floor.

Dobbs swung his shotgun back and forth with wild, jerky movements as he backpedaled rapidly down the hall.

Travis also searched for the source of the blast, but he

couldn't locate the assailant. Fear threatened to overwhelm his faculties.

He watched in horror as the sheet fell away to reveal a man with a sawed-off shotgun hiding on the gurney's lower platform. The man fired, and his fellow trooper's legs exploded in a spray of crimson.

Travis unleashed a barrage of panicked shots in the killer's direction, but the man dove toward the cover of a doorway.

Dobbs wailed as he crawled for cover and discharged the shotgun blindly into a wall near the killer's position.

Two more shotgun blasts exploded down the hall. The trooper's screaming ceased, and a set of the work lights exploded in a shower of sparks. Darkness consumed the bodies.

A shadow flitted through the black, and Travis fired in the direction of the apparition. Another set of work lights exploded. The darkness crept closer.

Travis trembled all over. His body felt cold, the world surreal. He couldn't breathe.

The fight or flight instinct took over, recommending flight. He kicked through a set of doors into another hallway near the nurse's station. This hall contained no lights, but he didn't care at the moment. Escape was his only thought. After a few feet, he tripped over something in the darkness and remembered his flashlight. He cursed his stupidity and retrieved it from his belt.

As he sprinted through the hall, the beam of illumination bounced up and down until he reached what would soon be a small waiting room. He slid within the doorway and wheeled back in the direction from which he had come. The flashlight's beam irradiated no pursuers.

He felt light-headed, and he couldn't catch his breath. For the first time, he remembered why he had been stationed in the hallway. His guts churned, and the bile began to rise. He bit down on his lower lip.

He had been there as protection, and he had just left Emily Morgan behind.

# SIXTY-FOUR

EMILY MORGAN SCANNED the hall from the doorway of her hospital room. She had been sleeping peacefully when the screaming began. When she had heard the shotgun blasts, she pulled the IVs from her arms. She steadied herself on the doorframe, but the world crested and fell like ocean waves. Her legs didn't feel like her own. She seemed to float instead of walk. She wondered if the disorientation stemmed from the trauma to her head or Dr. Callow's prescription. Either way, she was in no condition to fight or run—but she could hide.

Only the closest work light was in operation. Darkness suffocated the rest of the hallway. She stumbled from the room and headed away from the ruined lights. The corridor was also dark in that direction, but that was her plan. She could hide in the darkness just as easily as the killer.

She had only moved a short distance down the hall when the last of the work lights blinked out.

Her knees threatened to buckle, but she steadied herself against the wall and pressed forward. The darkness seemed fluid as if she were drowning in a sea of oil. Her plan was simple: move down the hall as far as she could, hide in a random room, and pray.

Her breathing and the noise made by her socks shuffling along the floor were the only sounds.

She stopped. There was another sound behind her.

The air was still. After a moment, she continued on.

She stopped again. *Nothing.*

She prayed that the noise existed only in her imagination, but she could have sworn that she had heard the rustle of fabric at her back. And the sound seemed to be keeping pace with her.

The world rolled, and she trembled all over. The shaking caused her head to throb.

When she advanced, she did so with as slow and calculated movements as she could manage. She moved to the opposite side of the hall and crept forward. *A little farther...just a little farther.*

She felt a warm wind against the back of her neck, but that wasn't possible. There was no wind here.

She imagined another possibility—*the killer's breath.*

She pushed the thought from her mind. He would have been just as blind as she was in this place. Unlike some, she didn't believe Ackerman to be the bogeyman. He was just a man whose mind had been twisted. He couldn't see in the dark.

She thought back to the night when Ackerman had forever changed their lives. It seemed long ago, but it had only been a matter of days. She remembered his eyes the most. At the time, she had mistaken the look in his eyes for only madness or rage, but looking back, she also saw pain and hopelessness within his gaze. After the incident, she had studied the man who had killed her husband. She had learned of his past. She had needed to understand.

She felt the wind on her neck again. Then, she felt something else, something of substance. A finger traced the line of her neck down her shoulder.

The terror crippled her. She stood petrified.

She gathered her resolve and thrust an arm back against the killer. Her forearm struck flesh, but she was weak and knew that she could do little damage.

She ran down the dark hallway, tripping, stumbling.

The swaying of her reality finally overwhelmed her, and she toppled forward. She crawled in desperation, questing for a place to hide.

She found what felt like a table. Something the workmen had used? No, not a table. A cabinet of some kind? She felt wheels under the object. Whatever it was, it was empty, large enough to hold her, and her only option. She crawled inside and quieted her breathing.

Her heart beat at such volume that she feared he would find her by it. She felt him drawing near. She imagined the hammering in her chest calling to him like a beacon.

She willed the pounding to stop. She had never thought of herself as a strong person, but Ackerman had made her realize that she could survive anything. Death would not claim her tonight. She would beat back the reaper.

She thought of her daughter. The loss of a parent and the trauma of the incident would affect the girl in profound ways. Ashley needed her mother by her side, and she vowed that nothing in this world or the next would take her away.

The voice froze her thundering heart.

"Emily. I see you."

# SIXTY-FIVE

TRAVIS DEPAOLO STARED into the darkness and reasoned that the killer must have extinguished the last of the work lights. He cursed himself again. He felt like a coward. He had to make it right.

He left his flashlight off and listened.

The absence of light made him feel as if he stood in the vacuum of space gazing into the belly of a black hole. He feared that to step forward was to give himself as offering into the arms of oblivion. He stepped forward anyway.

The approximate location of Emily Morgan's room from his former position next to the nurse's station was across the hall and back to the left. He wanted desperately to turn on the flashlight and illuminate his path, but he knew that the killer would find him by the light. It would draw death down upon him like a moth to a flame.

The doorway eluded him as he moved across the hall and groped blindly for the entrance. He found the opening and moved inside. Once through the entry, he pushed the door almost closed, in order to block the light from entering the hall, and then activated the beam.

His heart sank as the light shone upon the empty bed. The sheets had been thrown back. Tubes ending in needles lay strewn across the floor.

The killer had claimed his prize. He was too late.

He fought back the guilt and fear. *Maybe she made it out of the room?*

He extinguished the light and opened the door. He listened in the darkness again.

This time, he heard a faint whisper down the hall. The voice reverberated off the walls. By the time it reached his ears, it sounded as if a legion of the damned lived in the darkness. The voice repeated Emily Morgan's name.

He moved in the direction of the voice. He didn't turn on his light at first, but then he decided that he might bump into the killer or walk right past the man and not even know it.

He flipped on the flashlight. His eyes adjusted while his gun sighted along the beam. He mimicked his deceased commander and moved forward by taking cover within each of the doorways. He prayed for strength.

# SIXTY-SIX

ACKERMAN WATCHED EMILY Morgan tremble in the pale green light.

In the past, night-vision goggles had been expensive pieces of equipment purchased by mail order or at military surplus outlets. Now, however, the ability to see in the dark could be attained for less than a hundred dollars at a local toy store. The black goggles had been designed for children playing hide and seek, but the straps could be adjusted for more mature gamers as well. They weren't quite military grade and didn't have the range and capabilities of their more expensive brethren, but they served his purposes just fine.

The bandages that encompassed Emily Morgan's skull made him think of a little girl from long ago—the first person he ever killed.

He remembered the little girl's pale features. Although he reasoned that Emily came by her complexion naturally while the little girl's ghostly pallor was only temporary, caused by her heart drawing the blood away from her face.

*Set her free, Francis. Pull the trigger.*

His father would cut him if he refused, which was better than the burnings. He remembered raising the gun.

At the time, he didn't think that she would actually die. His father had played the same game before with another girl, a little blonde girl wearing a blindfold. In that instance, his father had cut him until he succumbed to the man's will. But when he pulled the trigger, the girl didn't die. The gun had been empty. His father had ended the game and claimed to have released the girl a few counties over.

He remembered thinking that the same thing would happen with the pale child.

In this case, Ackerman Sr. didn't have to persuade the boy with force. He didn't hesitate. He aimed the gun at her bandaged head.

Looking back, he wondered why his father had taken the time to bandage a wound when the girl was about to die. He never could understand his father's way of thinking.

He remembered the shot like an explosion in the small space—the ringing in his ears, the girl falling, the blood. He remembered his father crying and the feeling that he had done something wrong. He had done as he was told, but no matter what he did, his father never seemed pleased. The pain never stopped.

Frank Sr. had hugged the dead girl and sobbed, repeating, "I had to know. I had to know for sure." When the father turned to his son, he gave the boy a look of disdain and said, "You're a monster."

Ackerman remembered the tears flowing down his face as his father left the room, leaving him alone with the dead girl.

The memory seemed so real. He could almost still feel the warm liquid running down his cheeks. He reached up and realized that the tears weren't a memory. He pulled off the goggles and wiped them away.

From the corner of his eye, he saw the light of a flashlight and a man moving down the hall toward him. He replaced the goggles and looked back at Emily Morgan as she cowered within the empty tool cabinet. The doors were open. A stack of uninstalled slide-out shelf units sat next to the industrial cabinet. A white mark on top showed where the price sticker had recently been peeled away.

He swung the cabinet doors shut on Morgan's trembling form. Moving to one end, he pushed the cabinet down the hall in the direction of the approaching light. As his legs pumped into a full sprint, the container gained momentum.

As he drew near to the trooper, he aimed the cabinet at the man and released his grip. The container rocketed forward on its own momentum. It slammed into the dumbfounded cop.

Following behind the cabinet, he launched himself upon his stunned opponent. He stripped away the trooper's pistol and pummeled his face. The man fell backward and lost his grip on the flashlight.

As the trooper crawled away, Ackerman retrieved the gun and flashlight from the ground.

The trooper reached one of the rooms and pulled himself up. The man opened the door and stumbled inside.

Ackerman wondered what protection the man hoped to find there. Watching in the pale green glow, he followed the cop into the room. He removed the goggles, lit the flashlight, and placed it on the floor. A dim glow filled the empty space.

The trooper crawled into a corner of the room like an injured animal hobbling away to die. Upon reaching the corner, he turned to face his pursuer and whimpered in short ragged breaths.

Ackerman placed the shotgun and the man's pistol on the floor and produced a knife from a sheath at his side. He twisted the blade, but the meager light wasn't adequate to illuminate the steel.

He moved toward the trooper. The man shook as if having a seizure. He noticed a pool of liquid spreading out from beneath the man. The trooper had pissed himself.

A wave of exhilaration washed over Ackerman. He imagined this was the way that eagles felt. He soared upon the winds of fear. "What's your name?" he said.

"Travis." The man stuttered as he spoke.

"Well, Travis, today's your lucky day. You're going to live beyond this evening. I need you to go back to your cop friends. Tell them that I have Emily Morgan and that I'm holding her hostage. Tell them that I loaded a car with cans of gasoline and stashed them away before we played our little game here. I'm going to douse this whole floor, and if any of them come into this building, I'll kill her and burn the place to the ground. I don't know if the sprinklers and fire systems are even completed, but I disabled them and shut off the water just to be sure. Tell the world what you've seen here, Travis. Make them believe. I'm waiting for a friend to arrive. If he's not here within twenty-four hours, I'll turn myself in without a fight. Everyone lives. Everyone goes home happy. But if anyone challenges me, we all die. Now go."

Travis scurried to his feet, stumbling over himself and slipping in the pool of urine.

As he moved past, Ackerman slammed him into the wall and pressed the knife against the artery in the trooper's neck.

"Please, no."

"Shhhh…" In a whisper, Ackerman said, "Travis, I want you to remember that, from this day forth, the only reason you are alive is because I allowed you to live. I'm your god now. I own you. I have given you the gift of life, and at any time, I may decide to reclaim that gift and take back what is mine. Just remember to cherish every second that you have, and realize that one day you may close your eyes and when you open them…I'll be there."

He shoved Travis toward the door, and the trooper darted away like a house pet with a wolf at its heels.

# SIXTY-SEVEN

MARCUS HAD NO trouble finding Ackerman. He just followed the sound of sirens and flashing lights.

He pulled Alexei's car into a parking lot a block from the scene. He looked over at the glove box. He had tried to ignore the weapon that he had used to murder the Sheriff, but he had to face it now.

He retrieved the gun and ejected the magazine. He stared down at it for a moment. Then, he reclined back against the headrest and released a long breath. He thought of the path that had brought him to this point. He tossed the useless weapon onto the floorboard of the passenger side. There were no life-ending projectiles in the magazine. He needed information and another weapon.

A cool breeze struck him as he exited the vehicle. Pandemonium reigned at the scene. Cop cars and other emergency vehicles surrounded the building. The police had placed barricades at a safe distance, and a multitude of onlookers gawked up at the glass and brick structure. He scanned the faces and saw a mixture of morbid curiosity and genuine excitement.

*We're so fascinated by what we fear.*

He glanced at the other buildings of the hospital. He could tell that the facility had been recently built. The architecture struck him as modern and yet somehow reminiscent of the nineteen fifties. Red brick and pillars of glass composed the buildings' faces. The building that had been surrounded shared the same look but was unfinished. The landscaping was nonexistent, and a walkway of plywood served as the sidewalk leading up to the new construction.

He watched the scene for a few moments and tried to calculate his next move. Then, he noticed one of the officers step around the barricade and move in the direction of a nearby parking lot. The lot was a maze of empty vehicles, many of them marked and unmarked squad cars.

He moved toward the parking lot and flitted among the maze. Keeping low and trying to remain unseen, he approached the officer. The man fumbled in his pocket, and a marked police SUV chirped as its alarm disengaged and the locks released.

As the man reached for the handle, Marcus slammed into the officer's back. The cop went for his gun but found the holster empty.

"Don't move, and keep quiet. No one will be able to hear over all this noise anyway."

"You're making a big mistake here, pal." The middle-aged cop's voice was deep and confident.

"You're probably right. What can I say? I have a self-destructive personality."

He spun the officer around and stepped back to a safe distance with the gun trained on his opponent. "I need information. What's the situation here?"

"Some whacko's got a hostage."

"Specifics."

The man remained silent, defiant.

"Listen, let's not make this any more difficult than it needs to be. I just need specific tactical information."

"Why does it matter?"

"Because he's my responsibility, and I'm going in there after him."

The officer's expression changed. "So you're the one he was talking about…"

"What does that mean?"

"He sent us a message. Said he was waiting for a friend to arrive. Said if this friend wasn't here in twenty-four hours, then he'd turn himself in."

"That won't happen. He'll kill the hostage and as many cops as he can before you take him down. I won't let it come to that. This is between him and me. Now give me the information I need."

The man rolled his tongue against the back of his teeth. "Suspect's name is Francis Ackerman, but you already know that. The hostage is Emily Morgan. He's on the fifth floor, last we knew. He claimed that he's going to douse the place with gasoline. We're holdin' back while we wait on some hotshot FBI negotiator and tactician on his way down from Denver."

"Have you drawn up any entry plans yet?"

The man shook his head. "Not my area, buddy. That's all I know."

"Thank you. Now turn around."

The man complied. He moved forward, retrieved the officer's cuffs, and placed them around the man's wrists. Then, he grabbed the flashlight from the cop's belt.

"Think this through. What are you going to—"

He slammed the butt of the pistol into the back of the man's skull, and the cop fell to the pavement. He retrieved the keys from the unconscious cop's pocket and stepped into the SUV. The steering wheel felt worn down against his palms. He could relate. He gazed toward the building and calculated the path of least resistance.

*Moment of truth.*

The SUV growled to life. He threw it into gear and sped from the parking lot.

He laid on the horn as he approached the barricades. The onlookers and cops scurried out of his way as he plowed through the barriers and sped toward a line of cruisers.

The SUV jerked as he slammed into the rear of one cruiser, sending it spinning. The big vehicle roared over the unfinished landscaping and across the wooden walkway.

He braced himself for impact.

The front entrance of the new structure was a giant pillar of glass that rose up the entire height of the building. He didn't slow as the vehicle broke through the transparent spire and rumbled into the building's interior.

Glass poured down like icy raindrops with teeth.

Once inside, he slammed on the brakes and cut the wheel. The SUV spun sideways through the spacious lobby and came to rest as it smashed into the newly constructed front desk.

He stumbled from the vehicle, heard the sound of approaching footsteps outside, and made his way into the belly of the beast.

# SIXTY-EIGHT

EMILY MORGAN TWISTED her wrists within the cuffs and tried to find a comfortable position on the floor. The smell of gasoline wafting from down the hall made her feel nauseous. Her head throbbed, and the world still rolled. A moment ago, they had heard a crash. Ackerman hadn't seemed surprised by the sound. Without a word, he had moved her farther down the hall near the back stairwell of the building.

"I feel sorry for you," she said.

He chuckled. "Oh, you do? Why is that?"

"And I forgive you."

His expression fell. "I don't need your forgiveness or your pity. Don't try to get in my head. You wouldn't like what you find there."

"I'm sure I wouldn't. It has to be hard. It's been difficult for me over the past few days carrying around the pain of one night. I can't imagine what it must have been like for a little boy living in a constant nightmare."

He didn't respond, but his nostrils flared with each deep inhalation.

When she looked at him, she tried to see beyond the man who had stolen her husband to the scared little boy inside. She had to release her hatred and move past it. His unshed tears glistened in the pale luminescence of the flashlight's beam. "You don't have to do this. You could—"

"You don't know anything about me. You're right. You can't imagine what it was like to live in my father's house.

But that doesn't matter. My father's actions might have been the fuel, but the flame was there from the beginning. I don't blame him. This is who I am. I'm not human. I'm a monster. I could never be like you. I could never be normal. Have the white-picket fence, two-point-five kids, and a mortgage. It doesn't matter what I want, or if I wish that things were different. You can't change the past, and when the darkness is in your soul, you can never tear it out. I can't just be washed clean and rehabilitated. There is no cure for what I have. This is who I'm meant to be. My destiny."

She was quiet for a moment. "When I was eleven, there was a little boy who used to tease me every day. He'd walk behind me and call me pale-face or slant-eye or gook and much worse. One day, he pushed me down, and when I stood back up, I had a rock in my hand. I hit him as hard as I could. He fell, and I thought that I had killed him. It ended up being nothing but a bump on the head, but for a moment I wasn't afraid or sorry for what I had done. I was glad. I was exhilarated. For a split second, I hoped that he was dead. It made me feel…powerful. The darkness is in us all. You just never learned how to contain it. Instead, your father forced you to embrace it."

He was still for a moment. Then, he smiled at her, but the expression seemed different somehow. She wondered if this was the only time in his life that he had ever truly smiled both on the inside and the outside.

"I'm glad that your husband beat me and saved you. It was a good feeling. It got me thinking about things. Got me thinking that maybe things really do happen for a reason. And maybe we all have a part to play. Maybe your purpose hadn't been fulfilled, so you couldn't die there that night? Your survival doesn't prove anything, of course, but it still made me wonder."

"Maybe God doesn't want to be proven to exist? Then… we wouldn't need faith."

He seemed to consider her words. "Thank you."

"For what?"

"For talking to me like I'm a real person. I think you're the only *real* person who has ever done that. I didn't come here to kill you, by the way."

"Then why did you come?"

"Faith."

"I don't understand."

"I don't think we're supposed to."

A flower of light bloomed at the opposite end of the hall. Ackerman retrieved a lighter from his pocket and picked up a bottle with a rag poking out of the top. He extinguished the flashlight.

As the darkness returned, the fear filled her, but she willed it away. *I won't die here tonight.* She had *faith* in that. "What are you doing?" she said.

The killer lifted her from the floor. "Fulfilling my purpose."

# SIXTY-NINE

MARCUS SHINED HIS light down the fifth-floor hallway and took cover in one of the rooms. He wished that he had the ability to see in the dark. He hated to move down the hall with his light on. It would give away his exact location, but he couldn't see any alternative. Ackerman might have set a trap. If that were the case and he moved forward in darkness, the hammer could fall before he even knew what had hit him.

He swung into the hall and directed the beam down the corridor. He continued forward, moving from room to room and performing a cursory check of each. The smell of gasoline grew in intensity.

"That's far enough," a familiar voice called out.

He could tell that the voice had originated from a good distance away. He shut off the flashlight and moved forward in darkness. Ackerman liked to talk, and he hoped to use that against the killer.

"This isn't the right setting for what I had in mind," Ackerman said. "Too dark, too constricted. Turn around and go back down the hall to the stairwell where you came up. It'll take you to the roof. Emily and I will meet you there, and we'll finish this."

Not wanting to give away his position, he didn't respond.

The floor felt slick under his feet. The smell of gasoline was overwhelming now. He stopped. His heart sank as he realized that he had just stepped into Ackerman's trap. He began to quietly backpedal away from the killer's position.

A light blazed into view at the end of the hall. He saw Ackerman's outline, the light burning in the figure's right hand. Then, the light seemed to jump forward.

Time slowed, and within a split second, he realized that Ackerman had just tossed a flaming object into a gasoline-soaked hallway.

# SEVENTY

MARCUS SPRINTED AWAY from Ackerman and toward the stairwell. At his back, he heard the voice of the fire call out to him as the flaming object gave life to its brethren. The legion of flames hurtled toward him, consuming everything in its path.

He felt the heat at his back and dove forward.

The initial blast lost momentum as he made it into one of the open doorways.

But the heat remained. He felt pain on his shoulders and realized that he was on fire.

The flames sought to consume him as he rolled around the floor. The fire fought with ferocity, but he ground it out and stripped off his smoldering shirt. His shoes still burned where he had stepped in the gasoline. He kicked them off and backed into the corner.

His lungs searched for air. He felt disoriented. Looking over his shoulder, he saw that the burns weren't as bad as they felt.

He steeled himself and ran back into the hall. Luckily, the flames' concentration centered upon the area where Ackerman had splashed the gasoline, but he knew that it wouldn't take long for the fire to blossom out onto the entire floor and the rest of the building.

He reached the stairwell and ascended the short distance to the roof. He kicked through the doorway. Leading with the pistol, he scanned the immediate vicinity.

The wind howled like the shriek of a banshee whose

song could only be heard by those who had stood in the presence of death. He took in a deep breath of the fresh air. The cool breeze felt soothing against his back.

Several vents and pipes dotted the rooftop. Some were large, and some were small. As he rounded one large mound of vents, he saw Ackerman and Emily Morgan standing at the roof's edge.

Ackerman held Emily as a human shield.

A feeling of déjà vu hammered against his heartstrings. He thought of his last encounter with the madman. He glanced down at Emily's foot as he approached but saw no rope.

Ackerman pressed the gun against her right temple.

His eyes met the killer's.

"Marcus, I want to play a game. Let's call this one... *Last Man Standing.*"

# SEVENTY-ONE

"THE RULES ARE simple. You throw down your gun. I do the same and release Emily. Then…we try to kill each other. The winner lives, the loser dies. Now's our chance to prove once and for all whether everything that is good in a man's soul is stronger than all that is evil. I've come to believe that through all the trials and tribulations and winding paths and roads less traveled of my life—that through it all—I am who I was always meant to be. And now, it's time for you to embrace your destiny as well."

A part of Marcus had known from the first moment that he saw Ackerman on the TV that this was where the road would lead. Ackerman wasn't the only one who felt that they were somehow connected.

He tossed the gun off to his right. But he didn't throw it too far, in case he needed to get to it again in a hurry. His head cocked to the side, and his neck cracked. He wasn't afraid that Ackerman would double-cross him. He knew that the killer believed this confrontation was a part of both their destinies.

Ackerman followed suit and threw his gun to the opposite side of the roof. Then, he shoved Emily away and bowed, as if they were engaging in some type of old-world duel.

Marcus didn't bow, and he didn't show any hesitation either.

He ran full-bore at Ackerman like a linebacker cutting through the offensive line and zeroing in on the quarterback. They collided with such force that he felt the impact deep in his bones. He hit Ackerman low. He had spent enough time on the varsity football team to know that the lowest man won. Using his advantage and lower center of gravity, he uprooted Ackerman and slammed him back down to the roof.

The blow knocked the wind out of the killer, but it didn't immobilize him. He regained his composure and head-butted Marcus above the eye, breaking the skin and allowing blood to flow free.

Marcus retaliated with a quick series of punches.

Ackerman countered and returned the attacks blow for blow. The pair rolled around the rooftop like wild dogs fighting for the last scrap of food in a barren winter.

Marcus glanced in Emily Morgan's direction and saw her watching the scene half dazed, half terrified. She held one of the discarded pistols in a shaking hand and looked as if she could barely stand. He knew that, even if she had full command of her faculties, a shot now would have as much chance of hitting him as it would Ackerman.

Both sustaining a lot of damage but neither gaining any ground on their opponent, he decided to change tactics. He pushed away and rolled to his feet.

Ackerman did the same. They circled each other, breathing hard. He searched the killer's eyes and waited for his opportunity.

But Ackerman struck first.

The killer came at him hard and swift. He landed a kick to the side of Marcus's leg, which buckled his knees. Then, the killer grabbed him by the neck and pounded fist to face.

After sustaining a few blows that would have knocked some men unconscious, Marcus countered. He caught Ackerman's arm with his left hand and dealt his own series of blows with the right.

THE SHEPHERD

They were a flurry of limbs, each blocking and countering with blinding fast movements.

As they traded blow for blow and circled each other, he realized how evenly matched they were. In some strange way, this gave further credence to Ackerman's claims of connection, destiny, and being two halves of the whole. But he still didn't consider himself to be a *good* man by any means, and despite the evil that fueled his opponent, he suspected there could be a small flicker of goodness buried deep within Ackerman.

He supposed that was the way of the world. Nothing was ever black and white. Both darkness and light dwelled within the inner depths of every soul. The choices a person made called him or her to one side or the other. Despite his many failures, he had always tried to do the right thing while Ackerman had always walked a path littered with dark and malicious deeds.

They fought like two immortal titans cursed to battle for the remainder of eternity. Each would offer a blow, and the other would block or retaliate—neither gaining nor losing ground. This continued until Marcus sustained a vicious blow and stumbled near the edge of the building. Ackerman charged full force and landed a swift strike to the abdomen.

The killer followed with a hard shove.

Surprised by a shove and not a punch or kick, Marcus tumbled backward, off balance. Only a short step from the edge, he didn't have time to regain his footing. His legs caught the raised rim of the roof, and he tumbled off the building and toward the ground.

# SEVENTY-TWO

*FALLING...*

His heart seemed to stop in his chest. Time seemed to slow. What was he falling toward? Death? Heaven? Hell? In the span of a second, the tide had turned.

He tumbled downward toward certain death and an uncertain afterlife.

Although his mind was close to abandoning hope, his highly tuned instincts and reactions were not. His right hand grasped for the roof's edge and caught hold. He screamed in pain as his body slammed against the building and his shoulder strained under the sudden twist and snap of his weight.

His muscles trembled. He knew that he couldn't hold on for long and that a small part of him would welcome the arms of death. He wondered if police snipers had noticed movement on the roof. They wouldn't have fired during his confrontation with Ackerman, but maybe they would take Ackerman down if the killer won the battle?

*Maybe I should just let go?*

But he couldn't know for sure that snipers were watching. He was rationalizing, conceding defeat. He cursed himself. His anger gave him strength.

He brought his left hand up. He held on, not only for his life but also for Emily Morgan's and the lives of all of Francis Ackerman's past and future victims. *I can't fail. I won't fail.*

He looked up to see the face of his adversary staring

down at him. But Ackerman wasn't smiling with triumph. His expression was somber with defeat. The killer leaned closer. "Maybe there is no meaning?" he said. "Maybe I've been a deluded fool? No balance to the universe. No darkness and light. Only men…and the lies we tell ourselves to justify all that we've done."

"Don't move, or I'll shoot!" Emily said from behind Ackerman.

Looking oblivious and unafraid, the madman did little more than glance in her direction. Turning back, Ackerman said, "Maybe you're not the hero I thought you were?"

Marcus looked up at Ackerman with fire in his eyes. "I'd hate to disappoint you."

With a rapid movement of his hand, he grabbed Ackerman by the shirt and pulled the killer down to the roof's edge while pulling himself up. His head slammed into his opponent's skull, sending the madman flying away from the edge.

As he tried to pull himself back onto the roof, he heard Emily say, "Don't move, or I will shoot you!"

He watched helplessly as the killer moved toward her.

"Give me the gun," Ackerman said.

Emily didn't fire. Instead, she backed away. "Don't come any closer."

His feet touched the rooftop, and he ran at the killer. Their bodies collided, and they struck the roof near Emily.

A strange crack and pop drew his attention. Emily screamed.

He looked up as she fell through a spot in the roof weakened by Ackerman's fire.

He rolled away from the killer and leapt toward the hole. The heat washed over him. He moved forward to the edge on his stomach and found Emily hanging onto a crumbling section of rooftop.

He grabbed her hand and began to pull her up. The sound of a pop and snap tore away all his hope. Their eyes met.

He felt the section of roof under his stomach give way, and they fell into the snarling maw of the inferno.

# SEVENTY-THREE

THE PAIN STABBED at Marcus's legs and chest. The pressure made it hard to breathe. He struggled to move but found himself pinned to the ground. His eyes fluttered open. He felt as if he had just stumbled through a doorway into hell.

A haze of smoke hung in the air. The room was like a furnace. Emily Morgan sat on the floor in front of him and clutched a wounded leg. Her breathing was ragged, and she shook all over.

Flames danced around the edges of the room, but it seemed as if the falling debris might have smothered some of the fire.

He tried to free himself from the pile of debris on his back. He pressed with all his strength.

The pile inched upward but then fell back against him. The sudden return of the weight expelled the breath from his lungs.

He glanced around the hospital room. A large section of collapsed roof buried the main entrance. He knew that each room shared a bathroom. But a quick look in that direction showed that a smaller pile of debris blocked the bottom of the bathroom door as well. He knew that he could lift the crumbled section of rooftop out of the way, if he were free. "Can you help me lift this?" he said.

Emily Morgan shuffled to him, and they pushed together. He pressed with every ounce of passion left in him, but it was no use. He couldn't lift it by himself, and

Emily was in no condition to help. She had no strength left to offer him.

"Okay. Okay," he said in a choked whisper as the pressure returned to his chest.

*This can't be the end. Not like this. Please God, not like this.*

His mind raced for a solution. He scanned the room, calculating, analyzing. He couldn't concentrate. The answer wouldn't come. He couldn't breathe. His vision blurred.

*There's no way out.* Hope abandoned him. He prayed that they would die from smoke inhalation before the fire took them.

"I'm sorry," he said in a breathless whisper.

"For what?"

"I can't save you. I failed. I failed everyone."

She smiled down at him and chuckled. "You remind me of my husband. He always had to be the hero, and he never understood either. Winning doesn't matter. It's not whether you win or lose. It's how you play the game."

He considered her words for a moment. He sensed profound truth beneath their surface. "You're one tough lady, you know that. I'm Marcus, by the way."

"Emily. Pleasure to make your acquaintance." She spoke in a hoarse whisper followed by a deep cough. "We're going to die here, aren't we?"

He didn't answer.

A strange whoosh and whir originated from the other side of the bathroom door.

*What now?* At first, he couldn't identify the noise, but then he realized. *A fire extinguisher?*

The bathroom door shook as someone tried to push through it.

*Oh, thank God. Firemen.* A wave of hope flooded the

shores of his despair, and tears of joy cascaded down his cheeks.

"We're in here."

"Please, help us."

An axe blade thrust through the door—then another strike, and another.

He laughed with delirium. "We're going to make it."

Within a matter of seconds, the axe had torn through the barrier, and a shadowy form stepped into the room. Marcus and Emily Morgan gazed up through the smoke at the man who had just entered. Light from the flames danced across his face.

Francis Ackerman stood over them, an axe dangling from his right hand.

# SEVENTY-FOUR

MARCUS SEARCHED FOR some type of weapon. His hand stretched out for a nearby piece of debris, but it was just out of reach. His fingers curled into a fist, and his teeth clenched. *At least we won't have to burn.*

The floor creaked and popped beneath them. He knew that it was only a matter of time before it buckled as well.

"Come on. I'm getting you out of here," Ackerman said to Emily Morgan as a strong arm flew underneath her body and lifted her from the floor. Then the killer carried her through the opening into the adjoining room.

Marcus heard the distinctive whooshing sound of the fire extinguisher, and then the only sounds were the exhilarated moans of the fire and the protestations of the dying building. Refusing to surrender, he pressed up on the debris one last time. A guttural scream emanated from somewhere deep in his soul.

He pushed with the ferocity of a caged tiger sensing freedom. His muscles quivered. He felt the debris shift.

The floor issued a disapproving pop, and he began to feel as if the fire and the building had amalgamated into some ravenous entity that sought to consume him.

He moved forward slightly. The burning in his arms made him wonder if the fire had already taken him.

He couldn't breathe. His strength failed. The weight gradually pinned him to the floor, and he felt as if the finger of God himself pressed upon his back. His vision darkened. He closed his eyes. A rolling fear tumbled through his guts as he wondered what the next world held for him.

He felt a shaking and supposed that he was breaking through the barrier between worlds.

"Help me," a voice said.

With great effort, he forced open his eyes and stared up with incomprehension at Ackerman's face.

"Help me," the killer repeated as he pulled up on the pile of debris.

Marcus searched deep inside, found a small reserve of strength, and pressed in unison with the killer. Working in tandem, Ackerman held the debris with one hand and tugged on Marcus's shoulder with the other while Marcus pressed up with his back and crawled forward.

With one last push, he tore his legs free from the debris and coughed on the smoke as his lungs sought fresh air. His body floated, and unconsciousness pressed in on his mind.

He flew from the floor and then through the bathroom and into the hall. When he reached the stairwell, he realized that Ackerman had just carried him away from the fire and out of the jaws of death.

The killer deposited him on the landing. The smoke crept through the space, but it traveled up toward the roof. Fresh air still flowed from the floors below, and he drank in greedy mouthfuls of oxygen. Emily Morgan sat next to him, doing the same.

"Can you walk?" Ackerman said.

He nodded. "I'll find a way." His voice came as a harsh rasp.

"Then get out of here before the place falls down around us."

He looked up at the killer. Ackerman still stood partly in the hallway. The fire danced and rolled in the background. Soot and blood covered the madman's face, but the flames at his back made his body seem luminescent.

"What about you?"

Ackerman looked back into the flames. "I think I'll stick around for a while."

A part of him wanted to shove Ackerman into the fire, and another part wanted to save him. But the killer had made his choice. In his condition, Marcus couldn't have forced the man to do anything. Besides, the police had the building completely surrounded. There was no escape for Ackerman, and he wouldn't deny the man a death under his own terms.

Marcus stood up onto trembling legs and willed strength into them. His arm slid beneath Emily, and he helped her to gain her feet. He braced his arm beneath hers and around her back, and they descended the stairs.

When they reached the next landing, he turned back to Ackerman. Reflections of the flames danced in the man's eyes.

"I've been thinking about your question," Marcus said.

"What question?"

"You asked me if I believed that anyone could be forgiven. I've thought about that a lot. And yeah, I think that no matter what you've done, no matter how far you've fallen, you can be forgiven…if you really want to be."

Ackerman smiled, and Marcus felt warmth behind it.

"Good-bye, Marcus." With those words, the killer walked back toward the fire.

Marcus turned away and descended to an uncertain future. He only glanced back once. A part of him hoped that even a man like Ackerman would find peace in the next world.

# SEVENTY-FIVE

Marcus had sat in the interrogation room at the Denver FBI field office for nearly two hours. He expected that at any moment some smug agent would enter and begin what was sure to be a long and excruciating process. He knew what they were doing. They were sweating him, but he had no sweat left to give. After going up against the likes of the Sheriff and Ackerman, the FBI didn't intimidate him.

*Bring it on. After the week I've had, this'll be like a vacation.*

He just wanted to sleep. He felt as if he hadn't slept in a week, which wasn't too far from being accurate. He wanted to fall into a bed and awaken two days later, refreshed and rejuvenated. But he didn't want to dream. He wondered if the dreams would get better or worse after this. Only time would tell.

His wrists ached from the cuffs. An overzealous agent had clasped them too tightly. He supposed that he should have been in cuffs a long time ago, so he couldn't complain.

He had accepted whatever fate awaited him. He had succeeded in what he had set out to do, and nothing else mattered anymore. He wished that he could put it all behind him. He wished that he could hold Maggie again. But he knew that wishes didn't come true.

He could see no way out of what had happened. He had no evidence, just a string of bodies. But he had nothing left to lose either.

He wondered whether his parents would be proud of him. He wondered about the life he would have led if he had never stumbled onto the Mavros case. Would he still be a detective? Would he be married with kids by now? His mind swirled with a series of what ifs and whys. In the end, he concluded that it was all meant to be.

Maybe Ackerman had been right. Maybe his whole life had been building toward something, some realization or purpose. Had he now fulfilled that purpose? Was he meant to stop Ackerman, and now that his task had been completed, the universe would allow him some measure of peace? Or had he only just begun to walk the path? So many questions with no real answers.

He supposed that was the essence of life. People quested for answers that they were never meant to know. Maybe no one was ever meant to see the big picture or know the meaning. Maybe people weren't prepared for the answers. Perhaps when a person finally comes to the grand real- ization and learns "the meaning", death comes for them. Maybe the asking and not the knowing was the impor- tant thing.

His head ached from the flood of thoughts that flowed through him. He knew that he couldn't save everyone, but he had played the game to the best of his abilities. If all that was necessary for evil to triumph was for good men to do nothing, then evil had not triumphed. He was a good man, and he had stood up against the darkness and refused to do nothing.

He tried to be resigned to his fate, but many questions nagged at him.

He didn't want to think about the events of the past few days, but he couldn't help it. There were too many things that still bothered him, pieces to the puzzle that didn't fit together.

Using his vivid photographic memory, he relived every event, every detail. With his eyes closed, he journeyed into the past. He walked through his memories.

Then, his eyes opened.

THE DOOR TO the interrogation room swung open, and a dark-skinned man in a black suit entered. The agent sat down across from him and laid a group of files on the metal table that separated them. The man smiled, obviously trying to gain his trust.

*All part of the process.*

"Hello, I'm Agent Monroe. Anything I can get you before we begin?"

He decided to play along. "Yeah, these cuffs are hurting my wrists. Would there be any way that you could take them off, or at least loosen them up?"

Monroe held the smile and nodded. "Sure."

The agent stood up and opened the door. "Could you please unshackle the prisoner for me?" Another man entered the room and removed the restraints.

He rubbed his wrists. "Thank you."

Agent Monroe walked back to the table but didn't sit. The man removed the dark jacket and rolled up his sleeves. Something seemed strange, but it took Marcus a few seconds to put a finger on it. Then, he realized. The agent still had his gun holstered at his side.

He wasn't certain, but he didn't think that regulations allowed agents to bring firearms into the interrogation room. He also noticed that the door stood open.

Agent Monroe, seeming to notice his eyes on the door, gestured toward the opening. "My partner is going to be joining us in a moment." Monroe shuffled through the stack of papers, his attention centering upon the documents and not his prisoner.

The agent had his gun in plain sight, and the door to the interrogation room stood open. *Is the plan for me to be killed during an escape attempt, or is this just another game?*

He let out a long breath. "Why don't we cut the crap? Tell him to come in here and talk to me himself."

The agent seemed perplexed. "I don't—"

"You know damn well who I mean."

"I'm afraid that I—"

He slammed his fist on the metal table. "Just tell the Sheriff, or whoever he is, to get in here. I'm tired of playing his games."

The sound of a familiar voice came from just outside the door. "But you're so good at them." The Sheriff strolled into the room with a look of triumph.

Marcus cocked his head to the side and cracked his neck. "You look pretty good…for a dead man."

## SEVENTY-SIX

MOVING WITH THE reflexes of a cat, Marcus jumped from his chair and tossed the empty seat in the Sheriff's direction. He spun toward the dumbfounded Agent Monroe. He grabbed the holstered weapon from the agent's side and wrapped his left arm around the man's neck. The gun's barrel bore into Monroe's temple.

With a calm, modulated voice, he said, "Why don't you tell me what's really going on here."

The Sheriff chuckled and then proceeded in a reverent clapping of his hands. "Bravo," the Sheriff remarked as he sat in the chair vacated by Agent Monroe. "You've never disappointed me, kid. You are all I knew you would be and more. But now is not the time to fight. This is the part when we pull back the curtain and look into the face of the real Wizard of Oz. Put the gun down, and we'll sit and talk for a while."

"Think I'll hang onto the gun…for old times' sake."

"Suit yourself, but you should know that there aren't any bullets in that gun."

"Really. Then, you won't mind this." He aimed the gun directly between the Sheriff's eyes and squeezed the trigger in rapid succession.

The weapon issued a benign clicking sound. *Empty.*

He shoved Monroe away and dropped the gun to the floor. Then, in a nonchalant manner, he walked over to where he had thrown his chair, placed it back in its original position, and sat down across from the Sheriff. "I'm listening."

"I'll answer all your questions, but I'm curious. How did you know that I was alive?"

"It's hard to kill a man with a gun that doesn't have any real bullets in it. They weren't blanks, though, at least not like any I've ever seen."

"We've got a great special-effects team. They were blanks, but they had been specially modified. We were betting that you'd aim for the chest, so we had the blood packs ready to go. If you would have aimed at my head, I would've made sure that I fell backward in a way that you couldn't see the wounds."

"And if I would have decided to fire another through your skull at point blank for good measure?"

"Then, we would have started this conversation at that time."

He shook his head in disdain. "I knew there was something more going on from the moment I found Maureen Hill."

"What do you mean?"

"I mean that someone staged the crime scene."

The Sheriff's lips curled up at the corners. "Explain."

"She had all the signs that she had been dead for a while, and yet the blood in the room was fairly fresh. It had been planted. And her hands had been nailed in place with some big spikes. Blood would have leaked out and streaked down the wall, but there was no blood behind the body. No splatter from the cuts. She had either been nailed or re-nailed to that wall after she was dead. There was also no blood pooled on the floor, as there should have been. Plus, she didn't look right. I'm no expert, but she looked like a body from the morgue…like she had been in a freezer and then unthawed. I assume her murder took place in Colorado at her real home, and then you moved her to that house."

The Sheriff raised his eyebrows and leaned forward. "Why Colorado? And how do you know that it wasn't her house?"

He felt that he was being tested, but that was fine. He'd play along—for now. "I found an envelope on the table that had her name and a Colorado address. I had other things to think about at the time, and I thought that maybe she had two homes or stayed with her kids part of the time. But it fits with the crime scene being staged. Plus, as I sat here, I remembered a vague feeling of familiarity when I first saw Maureen's house. When I ran my mind through everything that had happened over the past few days, I remembered where I had seen it before. You had an auction flyer on your desk. The picture on the front was the house where Maureen supposedly died. But she didn't die in that house, which means that Ackerman didn't kill her in that house. He was staged too. I started wondering why anyone would do something like that…and I still don't have an answer. So…what the hell is going on here?"

"Do you believe in destiny?"

He thought of Ackerman. "I'm not too sure of anything these days."

"I'm a firm believer in destiny, and I am certain that you are the man that is meant to be sitting in that chair. You've been traveling toward this day since your parents' murder, and now, you've reached the end of that road and the beginning of another. I suppose that I should begin by saying that a lot of things you believe to be true are not so, and I regret that this deception was necessary. First of all, your aunt never owned any ranch. Therefore, she could never will one to you. That was merely your invitation to the party. Second, well…maybe it would be better if I showed you." The Sheriff stood. "Let's take a walk."

Marcus rose from his seat. He felt like he was trapped in a dream.

The Sheriff exited the interrogation room and continued down a long stretch of hallway. He followed. He couldn't comprehend why the Sheriff would set all this up.

*Why bring me to Asherton in the first place?*

They passed several open doorways that showed the interiors of offices. Some contained men in suits sitting at desks. The unlikely duo continued down the hall until they reached a closed door marked *Briefing Room*.

The Sheriff stopped in front of the entrance. "You'll find some answers beyond this door but mainly more questions. When you're ready…"

Marcus turned the handle and experienced the sensation that he was about to fall down the rabbit hole. He had no idea what to expect on the other side of that door.

# SEVENTY-SEVEN

BEYOND THE THRESHOLD, Marcus found a room filled with a group of people. Members of the group talked amongst themselves, but it seemed as if they all awaited the arrival of one more party guest. When he entered, they turned toward him and ceased their conversations.

The room spun, and he felt weak in the knees. It seemed as if the world had been turned upside down and inside out. He wondered if he'd lost his mind somewhere along the way.

The world had become a place so alien to him. Everything that he knew to be true now appeared to be false. And everything that he felt was solid and tangible proved to be an illusion.

As he scanned the faces of the individuals gathered in the room, he felt such a wide range of emotions that he found it impossible to pick one and stick with it. He was on the verge of tears and the cusp of laughter, all at the same time.

He recognized some of the Sheriff's men, but it was no surprise to see them. It did come as a surprise, however, to see Maggie and the spectral figure next to her. Andrew wore a huge grin and held a green can of soda in one hand.

*Ghosts are not supposed to smile and drink Mountain Dew.* His breathing verged on hyperventilation.

Andrew's resurrection wasn't the only surprise, however. The ghost of an English teacher sitting in one of the briefing room chairs was even more shocking. The man's wife, Loren—if she was really his wife at all—sat next to him.

Allen Brubaker had apparently not died at the farmhouse that night, and neither had his wife. Their children, Charlie and Amy, weren't present in the room, but he supposed that their deaths had been falsified as well.

When he first laid eyes upon the group, he felt so overwhelmed with relief and joy that he fought the urge to embrace them all. The feeling of joy soon turned to anger when he thought of the pain and guilt he had felt at having failed them. The truth was that they had been aligned against him from the beginning.

The ghosts of Andrew Garrison and Allen Brubaker stepped forward to greet him. He noticed that Maggie shied back. She looked ashamed. *Good, run with that.*

Andrew gave him a wide grin as he approached. "Hey, buddy. Sorry we had to lie to you about all this."

Allen Brubaker stuck out his hand. With a playful smile, he said, "No hard feelings, right?"

Marcus looked down at the proffered hand with a blank expression. "Of course not." With a snap of movement, he reached out, grabbed a handful of Andrew's shirt, and slammed his forehead into the man's skull.

Andrew fell backward to the floor.

But before Andrew had even hit the ground, he threw a right hook into Allen Brubaker's jaw. Allen fell back, joining Andrew.

The pair sat on the briefing room floor, expressions of shock on their faces.

The Sheriff chuckled beside him. "Attaboy…let it all out."

He rounded on the Sheriff and landed a fast and vicious punch to the man's face. The Sheriff also fell to the ground, but he didn't seem shocked at all. He sat on the tile floor and laughed while he rubbed the side of his head.

Marcus turned back to Allen and Andrew, who had yet to make any attempt to stand. "What is wrong with you people? You think this is some kinda game? You let me think you were dead and made me feel responsible. You're all nuts. You stay away from me."

When he raised his eyes from the men on the floor, he saw Maggie. He pointed a finger at her and said, "You're lucky you're a woman, or you'd be on the floor with them."

He stalked past all of them and sat down in one of the briefing room chairs on the far side of the room. After a few moments, the Sheriff walked over and pulled up a chair across from him. "That went better than I expected."

"It's a good thing I don't have a gun."

"Oh now, you don't mean that. You don't even like guns, remember?"

"I'm starting to revise my policies." His voice trembled. He kept his gaze focused somewhere far away, not wanting to look the Sheriff in the eye. He would have walked out the door if he didn't want answers—or if he thought they'd allow him to leave that easily.

"As I look back, I'm certain that I made the right choice in bringing you here," the Sheriff said.

He brought his eyes up to the Sheriff and fixed him with a piercing gaze. "Why did you bring me here, and what exactly is going on? Up until a few minutes ago, I thought that most of the people in this room were dead. I saw them die, but here they are. How?"

"Those are very good questions, kid. The answer regarding the people in this room is simple. It's amazing what they can do with special effects these days."

He shook his head in disbelief. "Half the time, I was

running around with a gun. What if I would have shot you or one of them?"

"We controlled the environment as much as we could and wore protective gear. But to be perfectly honest, Marcus, I knew that you would never intentionally kill anyone unless you had absolutely no other choice. We've put together extensive psychiatric profiles on you. Although, the thing with the can of whatever it was that you used as a makeshift grenade at the Brubakers' house—which was classic, by the way—well, that made me question my assumptions a little, but not much. Besides, everyone here knew the risk. My people are the best, but a lot of planning went into this operation…a lot of work. I even made everyone go through an acting boot camp to make sure that they could be convincing. I did, however, leave some clues for you. I wanted to test your attention to detail. We improvised a lot, but things seemed to work out."

The Sheriff chuckled. "You really threw us some curves. Like with the Brubakers. The officer that had captured you was supposed to fake car trouble next to the Brubakers' house. Then, Allen would see something was wrong and rescue you, etcetera etcetera. But you run the car off the road and escape. You were almost where you were supposed to be and injured, so it makes sense that you would approach the house. But it was strange the way that things seemed to come together…definitely destiny at work. Maggie's another example. She's one of Allen's team and not my daughter, by the way. Her job was merely to observe you in the bar and then play a small role later on with you and Andrew. Fate had other plans. Regardless, after you took interest in her, she had to play things out."

The Sheriff looked over at Maggie and leaned in close. "Go easy on her, by the way. Some of the things she told you were lies, but I don't think that her feelings toward you are. Just keep that in mind. She—"

"I don't even know who she is."

"Now you can take the time for that, but it's really none of my business."

The Sheriff sat back and drew in a deep breath. "In regards to your other question of why you're here…that's a little more complicated. It all began with a list. This list contained the names of thousands of prospective candidates, people who for one reason or another had been flagged as having the right potential. You were one of the names on that list. Initially because of what happened to your parents, and later for the potential abilities that you possessed. As time progressed, we crossed off many of the names on that list for one reason or another, until only a select few remained."

The Sheriff paused as if choosing his next words with care. "After what happened with Senator Mavros, I knew that you were the one."

"Because you're looking to recruit a killer?"

The Sheriff sat up straighter. "Absolutely not. It's because I was searching for someone who would do what they knew was right—regardless of whether or not it was popular. Some people have unexplainable gifts. They are skilled in mathematics, or musical theory, or possess natural athletic abilities. Some people have…other gifts. Science cannot adequately explain it. I'm not sure whether heroes are born or made. I don't know if the special gifts that they possess are elements ingrained into the person's genetic structure, part of the soul, or whether the events of their lives shape them into extraordinary individuals with the power to do great things. What I do know is that you are one of those people. And that is who I've been searching for. I've been looking for a hero."

A moment of silence passed. "You got the wrong guy. I'm no hero."

"Which is exactly what a hero would say."

"You still haven't answered my question. What do you want from me? Why bring me here?"

The Sheriff scratched at his goatee and leaned closer. "I'm the head of a group within our government known as the *Shepherd Organization*. We are charged with doing whatever is necessary to protect the citizens of this country."

"Whatever is necessary? So you're above the law?"

"The short answer is yes. We're the good guys that do the necessary evil. I've brought you here because you possess abilities specifically suited to hunt down and eliminate serial killers."

"And by eliminate, you mean murder. Don't the cops and the FBI do a pretty good job of catching killers?"

"The groups you mentioned stop criminals. The majority of the people we hunt are not mere criminals. We don't often deal with people who kill for money, love, revenge, or any other rational motive. The individuals we hunt are monsters. They slaughter innocent people for no reason and feel no remorse. The FBI's Behavioral Analysis Unit released a study a while back that estimated there are twenty to fifty unidentified active serial killers in the United States. In my experience, that number is highly optimistic. Someone has to do whatever is necessary to protect the citizens of this country from these monsters. We're called the Shepherd Organization because we're charged with keeping the wolves away."

Marcus shook his head in contempt. "You bypass the justice system. You act as judge, jury, and executioner."

"We do what needs to be done. Some of our actions might bypass the justice system, but we don't bypass justice. We enforce justice, and all of our activities are sanctioned by the United States government and the President himself."

Marcus laughed. "Right. The President himself. For all I know, you're the Unabomber, and this is all just part of your manifesto."

"Sure, 'cause a man like the Unabomber wouldn't have any problems acquiring a Briefing Room at an FBI field office. Take a look over there at that man talking with Allen. I asked him to hang back when you came in, but he's very excited to meet you."

He swiveled around and saw a man that he definitely recognized. "That's…umm…"

"Thomas Caldwell, Attorney General of the United States of America."

The Attorney General noticed their attention and gave a two-fingered salute.

His throat went dry. He swallowed hard and said, "That's an impersonator. You set that up to trick me."

The Sheriff laughed. "You're getting paranoid, but after the week you've had, I don't blame you. I'll introduce you to him later. You can decide his authenticity for yourself. If you're not convinced at that point, then we'll set you up for a personal tour of the White House."

He opened his mouth to issue a smartass comment, but the words stuck in his throat. Being a smartass was his defense mechanism. He was beginning to understand that. It was just one of the walls he had erected to ensure many good acquaintances, but no close friends.

The Sheriff continued. "One of our former presidents issued an executive order that founded the Shepherd Organization. He felt that extreme circumstances sometimes presented themselves where the law failed, and in the end, some laws that were meant to protect allowed evil men to go unpunished. He envisioned a group that could cut through the red tape and bureaucracy and get the job done. Our founders designed the Shepherd Organization to operate under the direction of the President, Vice President, and the Attorney General. They also designed the group to be disbanded at any time if the current president felt that the organization was no longer necessary or had lost sight of its purpose. Despite that fact, the organization has never failed to have the complete and unwavering support of our commander in chief. We're a very small, elite group. No big, bloated budget like Homeland or the FBI. We take our recruitment and selection process very seriously. There aren't many Shepherds. That's why the Attorney General wanted to meet you. You see, we operate in cell groups—"

"Like terrorists."

Unfazed by the comment, the Sheriff said, "Exactly. This is to help ensure the safety of the group and their families. As you can imagine, we do make enemies from time to time. One Shepherd and his support team comprise these cell groups. That's where you come in. Allen's been a Shepherd for many years now. It's time for him to pass the torch. He's going to settle down and annoy his wife and kids for a while. You're here to take over his team."

"I'm surprised you're allowed to have a family."

"Actually, it's encouraged. Having the support of a family helps us to remember why we do what we do. Keeps us sane."

Marcus shook his head and asked, "Why me? Why not Andrew or Lewis Foster or anyone else but me?"

The Sheriff cast a deep, penetrating gaze. "Because it's your destiny. It's who you are. It's who you were born to be. As for the others you mentioned, Andrew is Allen's right-hand man, and quite frankly, he knows his destiny and his place. He's happy where he is. As for Lewis…"

The Sheriff hesitated, and tears formed. "Lewis was like a son to me, and he desperately wanted to be a Shepherd. I never had the heart to tell him why, but he wasn't the right kind of man. Lewis loved this work. He loved nothing more than to take down the bad guys and help people, and there is absolutely nothing wrong with that. He took great joy in the removal of every evil person that we hunted. But, to be perfectly honest, that's not the kind of man who makes a Shepherd."

"What do you mean?"

"I'm not looking for someone to take joy in this job. I'm looking for someone who is going to be haunted by what we do. I'm looking for a man who will agonize and question and see the faces of every person he has killed every time he closes his eyes. I'm looking for someone who is going to wonder whether what he is doing is right and whether his creator condones his actions. But the man I'm looking for presses forward and still does the job. Because deep in his heart, he knows what he's doing is right and just. That's who I've been searching for. When that man pulls the trigger, he'll be sure. And that's why I chose you, Marcus. Not because you killed Mavros, but because of the way taking his life changed you. The way the act haunted you."

Marcus raised two fingers to the bridge of his nose and squeezed. His headache was getting worse. A few moments of silence passed. "What about Ackerman? Why bring him into this?"

A look of sorrow fell upon the Sheriff, and he averted his gaze. "Ackerman was definitely not supposed to get free, but…I was sloppy and made a mistake. I'm just going to have to live with that. Allen warned me, but I felt that

Ackerman was a necessary part of your recruitment. We caught him in Colorado. He killed a couple of cops there and then shot up a diner. Allen, Andrew, and Lewis tracked him to Maureen Hill's home. They shot him with a tranquilizer gun from a distance. Looking back, we should have killed him on the spot. The plan was always to stage a murder scene using a cadaver and then have you stumble upon the killer. Ackerman provided those elements with Maureen Hill's murder. We had been tracking him for a long time. The timing actually forced us to escalate things. That's why Maggie took you to see Maureen on your first date. We—"

"But why did you need a *real* killer in the first place? Wouldn't it have been much safer to just have someone play a part?"

The Sheriff shook his head. "You would've known. It wouldn't have served our purpose. You can't just fake being a man like Ackerman. The plan was to capture you when you stumbled onto the murder scene and tie both of you up in the same room. You needed to be confronted with the face of evil. You needed to stare into the darkness of his soul and see the kind of man that we hunt. A man like Ackerman can't be rehabilitated or reasoned with. He was an animal. It might not have been his fault and a part of me feels for the man, but ultimately, he was a killer and would have continued to hurt innocent people until someone stopped him. Letting him roam free or even putting him in prison, is like…throwing a great white into a pool full of kids."

"Ackerman saved us. He actually seemed to be repentant. When we were at the school in Asherton, he asked me about forgiveness. If he really was redeemed at the very end of his life, killing him before would have denied him that and condemned his soul. We don't have the right."

"And how many people had to die for him to find his way? What about their souls? Does he have the right?"

"He could have been captured and locked away in a cell where he couldn't hurt anyone. Then, he would have had his whole life to think about all that he'd done."

"I used to have a friend who worked at this maximum security prison. He told me a story about this man who had killed multiple people. One day, they were serving eggs, and this killer complained that his eggs were runny. The server, of course, asked him who he thought he was and basically told him to sit down and shut up. The killer sat his tray to the side and then kicked the server in the throat. The man died almost instantly—all over some runny eggs. Killer didn't care. He was already serving multiple life sentences. And our tax dollars clothe, shelter, and feed that monster."

The Sheriff leaned back in his chair and steepled his fingers. "I understand where you're coming from, but we play a simple game of mathematics, kid. We bring one death to a murderer in order to save the lives of the killer's many potential victims. It's not perfect, but it's the only way to truly protect the innocent."

Marcus sighed. "Why play this game in the first place? Why not just have the conversation we're havin' now?"

"This has been no game, kid. You could think of it more as an entrance exam, but honestly, I've known all along that you were the man that I was looking for. All of this has been more for you to discover that for yourself. We've tried and failed in the past doing as you said. The men we recruited weren't prepared for the demons they would face—inside and outside. They would hesitate. People died. And there was no amount of simulation that could prepare them. That's when we devised this method of recruitment.

We threw you into a situation that forced you to confront your abilities and your destiny.

"That's why I chose an assassination plot. I wanted to put you in a position where you had to face saving the life of another person in power that was potentially a murderer. I felt that wrestling with those implications would force you to deal with your feelings about killing Mavros—bring it right to the forefront of your mind. We had a whole intricate plan worked out where you would try to stop me in San Antonio, but with Ackerman on the loose and people dying, I had Andrew cut our little drama short. We were going to bring you in after we completed the final act and then go after Ackerman together, but you bolted from the gravesite and went after him on your own. Which I suppose proves that you're ready, but you wouldn't have been before confronting who you are. Before you can move forward and discover what lies ahead, you have to come to terms with the road behind you."

"Come to terms with the road behind me? I've killed in cold blood. How am I supposed to come to terms with that? How can you expect me to work for you doing more of the same? Is that really my destiny…to be a killer?"

The Sheriff shrugged. "I'm sorry, kid. Nothing is black and white. If you're looking for a perfect world, you got off on the wrong exit. This world is filled with shades of gray, and every decision is a double-edged sword for which both sides can be argued. More often than not, there is no right choice, just the lesser of two evils. I don't have all the answers. I wish I did. I wish that I could quote some scripture or words of wisdom that would help you reconcile all this, but I can't. All I can say is that, in the end, you have to look deep inside yourself. Deep down in your soul, you know whether the things you've done are right or wrong."

"Let me ask you this," the Sheriff said softly as he

leaned in close. "Do you really feel guilty for killing Ma-vros? Is that what haunts you? Or is it the fact that you took another human being's life but didn't feel guilty at all?"

Marcus held the Sheriff's gaze for a few seconds but then looked away. His eyes stung with tears.

"It scared you, didn't it? It scared you because it made you wonder what separated a man like you from a man like Ackerman. It made you question what you were truly capable of. That's the real secret from your past that's been haunting you, isn't it?"

Marcus lowered his head and closed his eyes, trying to hold the tears inside. "I should have felt something. I should have felt guilt and remorse and a thousand other emotions that a normal person would feel after killing someone, but I didn't. I didn't feel anything. Ackerman commented that he could kill Maggie as easily as flip-ping a light switch. Those words stuck with me. Because that's as easy as it was. I just raised the gun and turned out his light." The tears broke free and rolled down his face. "You're right. Ever since that night in New York, I've been wondering how thin the line is between me and someone like Ackerman. When he said those words, I found out ex-actly how thin that line is. And yes…it scares me."

The Sheriff's eyes shone with warmth and understand-ing. "I may not have all the answers, kid, but I know one thing for certain. You are nothing like Ackerman. The two of you are at completely opposite ends of the spectrum. Maybe the reason that you didn't feel guilty about Mav-ros is because you knew in your heart that it was the right thing to do? You protected more than just the girl in the car that night. You protected every victim that would have come after her. Evil will flourish if there are no good men to stand against it, and that's what would have happened with Mavros. He would have continued to prey on the innocent until someone had the courage to do what was right and stand against him—even if that meant standing alone."

The Sheriff stood and placed a hand on Marcus's shoulder. "You've got all the time you need to think about my offer. But in my opinion, people can be categorized into three groups. You are either a shepherd, a wolf, or one of the flock. I can say with absolute certainty that you are not one of the wolves. Now, you have to decide whether you are a protector and a shepherd…or are you just one of the flock?"

THE DIRECTOR LEFT Marcus to his thoughts and joined the others. Allen walked up and said, "How's he taking it?"

"Pretty well, considering the situation."

"Do you think he'll accept?"

"It's too early to say for sure, but I believe that he will."

"Good. I'm getting too old for this." Allen hesitated, thrummed his fingers against his glass, and ran a hand through his gray-white hair. "Are you going to tell Marcus about…the connection between himself and Ackerman?"

"No."

"You don't think he needs to know the truth?"

"Ackerman's dead. Marcus never needs to know."

# SEVENTY-EIGHT

THE DEMPSEY BROTHERS had not been mistreated as children. They didn't have a father who molested them or a mother who didn't love them. On the contrary, their parents were loving, caring providers. Their father had been a carpenter and their mother a housewife. The boys went to parks and played Frisbee with their dog, Bobby. They went on family vacations with destinations comprised of national landmarks and roadside tourist traps. They were normal. They were just like everyone else.

Andy Dempsey, the younger of the two boys, imagined that was why it was such a shock to everyone when he and his big brother, Michael, murdered their parents and burned down their ancestral home. He liked to shock people. And people always seemed to be so astonished right before they died, as if they thought they would live forever.

He reached out and pulled a Baby Ruth from the shelf. He tore open the wrapper and bit off a large chunk. He didn't look up to see if the convenience store attendant had given him a dirty look or called the cops. He didn't have to. The attendant and the only other patron were tied up on the floor in the back room. He knew that fact because he and his brother had put them there.

He watched Michael empty the contents of the cash register into a paper sack. It wasn't much money, but that's not why they did this. They did it for the thrill. It was fun being the bad guys.

"We're done here," Michael said. "Let's clean up."

Andy smiled. *Time to have some fun.*

The two brothers entered the back room through a door marked, *Employees Only.* Inside the room, two people knelt with their hands behind their backs.

"Is there more money hidden around here somewhere?" Michael said to the attendant.

"No," the man said with a sob. "You've got everything. You don't have to hurt anyone."

Andy smiled at the man's comments, but Michael was expressionless. "That poses a problem, friend," Michael said. "You've seen our faces, and that's just unacceptable."

"I guess we should have worn those masks," Andy said.

The brothers chuckled together.

Michael's face turned back to stone as he peered down at the helpless attendant. "Guess we'll just have to kill them."

The attendant started to speak, but Michael silenced him. The man fell dead to the tile floor, a pool of crimson spreading around him and a smoking hole in his forehead.

The woman, a beautiful blonde in a red T-shirt and jeans, remained on her knees with her eyes clenched together. She had apparently decided that she would face her inevitable death where she was.

Michael pointed the gun at her face.

"Wait," Andy said just before Michael pulled the trigger.

"What is it, little brother?"

"I want to keep her," he said. "We can have some fun with her later when we've got time to do it right."

Michael shook his head and sighed. "Alright, little brother, but if you're going to have a pet, then she's your responsibility. I don't want to hear a peep out of her."

He smiled like a little boy on Christmas morning. "I promise. I'll take care of her. She won't be a problem."

"She had better not be. If at any point I decide that she

is, then I'm going to splatter her brains along the side of the road and let the buzzards give her a proper burial."

He just smiled and threw the sobbing woman over his shoulder. Then, the brothers walked out to their car, and he threw her in the trunk. He was already fantasizing about what he would do to her later.

The brothers climbed into the Buick Skylark and peeled out of the parking lot, still stinking from the death that they had left in their wake.

A FEW HOURS and a few hundred miles later, the Dempsey brothers pulled into the parking lot of a small diner. It was getting late and almost time to stop for the night. Andy couldn't wait. His heart was ready to burst from the anticipation. The woman in the trunk hadn't even made a sound, and back at the convenience store, she hadn't tried to crawl away or shown fear like the others. She was tough. He couldn't wait to make her scream.

"Why don't we just forget about this meeting?" he said.

Michael jutted out his lower jaw and stared into the distance, as if trying to center himself. "We can't keep doing this forever. They're going to catch us. We'll either end up dead or locked in a cage. Is that what you want?"

"Cops ain't smart enough or fast enough to catch us."

Michael shook his head. "It's only a matter of time. We've tried not to leave a trail, but somebody will eventually get lucky or smart. We will go down, but not if we get out of the country now. Jamie can help us with that."

"Do you really trust this guy?"

"I don't trust anybody, but Jamie's about as close as it gets. We go way back. Besides, it would take somebody scarier than us to make him turn."

Andy grinned. "And there ain't nobody scarier than us."

Michael placed a hand on Andy's shoulder and squeezed.

"That's right, little brother. So just stay cool. We'll meet up with Jamie, take care of business, and then you can spend some time with your little playmate."

The door swung open with a familiar ding that signified the entrance of new patrons. The place looked like one of the typical greasy-spoon restaurants found in abundance along lonely stretches of highway. At this hour, it was nearly abandoned. Other than he and Michael, there were only three people in the whole place.

The first was the cook, a man with short blonde hair. Judging by his athletic physique, he didn't partake in any of the food that he prepared.

The second person was the waitress, a strikingly beautiful young blonde. She had shoulder-length hair pulled back in a ponytail, but some of the strands were loose and hung onto her face. Her skin was a dark tan that made her hair seem lighter than it actually was.

The third person was the only other customer. He wore a dark jacket and a New York Yankees baseball cap. He sat at the counter on a red and chrome swivel stool, sipping a cup of coffee and reading a hardback novel. A plate flooded with leftover syrup sat in front of him.

The brothers elected for a booth.

"What can I get you to drink?" the waitress said as she offered the menus.

Andy looked up at her with a toothy smile. "I'll have some coffee—" He looked to her nametag in order to make his response more personal. "—Maggie."

"Make that two," Michael replied, eyeing his brother.

"Comin' right up. I'll be back in a minute to take your order."

Michael leaned in close, a look of disdain on his face. "You've already got a plaything in the trunk. You stay cool, alright? Jamie's going to be here soon. And I'm starving."

The waitress returned with their coffees, and the brothers drank in greedy sips of the dark liquid. Andy stared at the waitress as she walked around the diner, cleaning off tables. "I'm thinking of trading up. The one in the trunk's okay. She'll be fun for a while, but there's an intensity in that waitress's eyes that makes my blood boil."

Michael whispered in a harsh voice that left no room for discussion. "You listen good, little brother. You want her? Fine, we'll take her. You want to kill them all? Fine. But you're going to behave yourself until after we've taken care of business and I've enjoyed my meal. You always—"

"You boys just passing through…or are you visiting friends?" the man at the counter said, putting his book down but still looking forward.

The Dempsey brothers turned to the man. There was something strange about his behavior. Something wasn't right.

"What difference does it make to you, mister?" Michael said with a hard edge to his voice. "Why don't you just drink your coffee and mind your own business?"

"What if I'm prepared to make it my business?" the man at the counter said, still not turning to face them.

Michael gave Andy a look, and the younger brother lowered his hand to the gun tucked into his waistband. He felt dizzy and somewhat light-headed. He shook off the sensation and looked around the parking lot. *Only a couple of cars. No cops. No S.W.A.T. team. Nothing.* Still, he knew something wasn't right. The guy at the counter was eerily calm, and he obviously wanted something. He felt like he was in a showdown in the middle of an Old West saloon. He turned his full attention back to the man at the bar. "You some kinda cop, or just the welcoming committee?"

The man at the counter chuckled. "No," he said. "Actually, I like to think of myself as more of a shepherd."

The brothers exchanged confused looks.

"What the hell is that supposed to mean?" Michael said.

The man casually turned to the two murderers. There was fire in his eyes. "I keep the wolves away."

# SEVENTY-NINE

Francis Ackerman Jr. stared out across the dark waters of Lake Michigan. The lights of Chicago's Navy Pier burned brightly at his back. He glanced in the direction of the Grand Ballroom and noticed a couple in their late twenties as they strolled past him. The woman gave him a strange look, as if she had seen him before but couldn't quite make the connection.

Had she recognized him? He considered slitting their throats and tossing them into the water.

The familiar voice echoed in his mind. *We're going to play a game, Francis… You're a monster… Kill her, and the pain will stop…*

He clenched his fists with such force that his nails penetrated the skin. He concentrated on the pain. He lost himself within the sensation. *No. Focus. You're just being paranoid.* He felt the rage begin to lose its color. *She couldn't have recognized me.*

He changed his appearance on a regular basis. He had become a real master of disguise, but he hated living incognito. A part of him missed the old days, when he had killed whoever he wanted, whenever he wanted. But back then, he didn't care about being caught. He didn't care about dying. He liked the challenge of the cops being on his heels and being forced to tear through them in order to escape.

But things had changed now. He had discovered his place in the grand tapestry of the universe. He had found his purpose, and his journey was far from over. He was in for the long haul. His excitement swelled as he contemplated his plans for the future and all the games yet to be played.

He had been lying low for some time now. He had learned that he could suppress his hunger through meditation techniques and by cutting himself. Although he had experienced the occasional lapse, he felt that he was doing quite well, making real progress.

He needed to maintain discretion. He had to be cautious. He had to be selective. He couldn't leave a trail for Marcus to follow. That would ruin all his plans.

He watched the reflections of the city shimmer across the water for a few moments, and then a man with glasses and spiked hair joined him at the railing.

"Do you have the information?" Ackerman said.

The man's voice trembled. "Yes."

"Everything I requested?"

"Yes."

"Will they know that the files were accessed?"

"I covered my tracks. They won't be able to trace anything back or even know that I was there. What is this Shepherd Organization anyway?"

"I don't really know. That's why I need the files. That's why I needed you to track them down."

"Because they're after you, aren't they?"

Ackerman chuckled. "Maybe, but I prefer the role of hunter, not hunted. I overheard a couple of old friends mention the Shepherd Organization and that they were in the process of recruiting someone very close to my heart. I was bleeding and strapped to a chair at the time. I didn't enjoy the experience. Reminded me too much of my childhood. I don't intend to find myself in that situation again, so I need to know my enemy."

"Well, their security's right up there with the Pentagon's. I'd say they're some pretty serious government hombres. If I were you, I'd head for the hills."

"Your concern for my well-being is touching, but I don't plan on getting caught. That's why I recruited the best hacker I could find."

"Recruited?!" The man's voice cracked. "You—"

"Where are the files?"

The man fumbled in his jacket and held out a portable hard drive.

Ackerman took the drive and admired it. The wonderful device contained all the knowledge he required. He unconsciously reached behind his back and wrapped his fingers around the hilt of his knife. The act would complete such a glorious moment, but he had to resist the urge to kill his little hacker friend. He still needed the man, and he was better than that now. He was more than just a killer.

Before he had met Marcus, killing had been his only reason to live, his only purpose in life. Now, he had found his true calling, and his mission eclipsed his dark desires.

"You'll need a password to open the files, and I'm not going to give you that until you release my sister. When she's safe, I'll e-mail you the password."

His gaze burned through the whiny, little man. "Are you dictating the terms of the game to *me*?"

"I read the files on you. I know how you work. You had no intention of holding up your end of the deal. If I give you that password, my sister and I are both dead."

"You should keep in mind that there are worse things than death, my friend. If you've read the files, then you know that I could make you give me that password. But, well played. Besides, there's more to me than just a series of reports and tapes. I'll let you and your sister live as long as you keep your mouth shut about the job you've done for me. I'll release her this evening, but I expect to receive a prompt reply. Also, I'll be calling on you from time to time. If you run, I will find you. From now on, I won't bother your sister. As long as you do a good job, you won't have anything to fear from me. Is that acceptable to you?"

The man nodded like a bobblehead doll on a bumpy road.

"Do you have the phone number I requested?"

The man fumbled in his jacket again and removed a small piece of paper.

He snatched the paper from the hacker's hand and verified that he could read the man's chicken scratches. He waved his hand. "You're dismissed."

"What about—".

"Go. Before I change my mind."

The man scurried away.

Ackerman removed the cell phone from his pocket and dialed the number from the small sheet of paper.

"Hello?" the voice on the end of the line said.

His heart raced. The hairs on the back of his neck stood on end at the sound of that voice.

"Who is this?"

"Hello, Marcus. Have you missed me?"

Silence.

"I wish that I could have seen your face when they told you that they couldn't find my remains among the ashes. In the future, you'll need to realize that I always have a backup plan. The service tunnel that connected the new building to the old section of the hospital allowed my disappearing act to seem quite convincing, didn't it?"

"I'm going to find you."

"I love a challenge."

"How did you get this number?"

"I have my ways, but that's not important. I won't take

up too much of your time. I know you're busy with the new job and all, but I just wanted to say hello. Let you know that I miss you and that I'm thinking of you. I'm so happy for both of us. We've realized our destinies. Most people search their whole lives and never know what we know. We know the meaning of our existence. You have become the hero that you were always meant to be. But during our last confrontation, I realized that you still need me. You haven't reached your full potential just yet. You will need to be tested and tried. And that's where I come in. I've got such big plans for us. After all, every hero needs a villain."

He closed the phone, pulled the battery, and tossed both halves of the device into the water. Then, the corners of Francis Ackerman's mouth slowly turned up into a wide grin.

*Let the games begin.*

\* \* \* \* \*

# REQUEST YOUR FREE BOOKS!

## 2 FREE NOVELS
## PLUS 2 FREE GIFTS!

### WORLDWIDE LIBRARY®
MYSTERY™
#### Your Partner in Crime

---

**YES!** Please send me 2 FREE novels from the Worldwide Library® series and my 2 FREE gifts (gifts are worth about $10). After receiving them, if I don't wish to receive any more books, I can return the shipping statement marked "cancel." If I don't cancel, I will receive 4 brand-new novels every month and be billed just $5.49 per book in the U.S. or $6.24 per book in Canada. That's a savings of at least 31% off the cover price. It's quite a bargain! Shipping and handling is just 50¢ per book in the U.S. and 75¢ per book in Canada.* I understand that accepting the 2 free books and gifts places me under no obligation to buy anything. I can always return a shipment and cancel at any time. Even if I never buy another book, the two free books and gifts are mine to keep forever.

414/424 WDN F4WY

| | | |
|---|---|---|
| Name | (PLEASE PRINT) | |
| Address | | Apt. # |
| City | State/Prov. | Zip/Postal Code |

Signature (if under 18, a parent or guardian must sign)

#### Mail to the **Harlequin®** Reader Service:
**IN U.S.A.:** P.O. Box 1867, Buffalo, NY 14240-1867
**IN CANADA:** P.O. Box 609, Fort Erie, Ontario L2A 5X3

#### Want to try two free books from another line?
#### Call 1-800-873-8635 or visit www.ReaderService.com.

* Terms and prices subject to change without notice. Prices do not include applicable taxes. Sales tax applicable in N.Y. Canadian residents will be charged applicable taxes. Offer not valid in Quebec. This offer is limited to one order per household. Not valid for current subscribers to the Worldwide Library series. All orders subject to credit approval. Credit or debit balances in a customer's account(s) may be offset by any other outstanding balance owed by or to the customer. Please allow 4 to 6 weeks for delivery. Offer available while quantities last.

**Your Privacy**—The Harlequin® Reader Service is committed to protecting your privacy. Our Privacy Policy is available online at www.ReaderService.com or upon request from the Harlequin Reader Service.

We make a portion of our mailing list available to reputable third parties that offer products we believe may interest you. If you prefer that we not exchange your name with third parties, or if you wish to clarify or modify your communication preferences, please visit us at www.ReaderService.com/consumerschoice or write to us at Harlequin Reader Service Preference Service, P.O. Box 9062, Buffalo, NY 14269. Include your complete name and address.

WWL13R

# *ReaderService*.com

## Manage your account online!

- Review your order history
- Manage your payments
- Update your address

*We've designed
the Harlequin® Reader Service
website just for you.*

## Enjoy all the features!

- Reader excerpts from any series
- Respond to mailings and
  special monthly offers
- Discover new series available to you
- Browse the Bonus Bucks catalog
- Share your feedback

*Visit us at:*
## ReaderService.com

RS13